THE PRICE OF PASSION

by

EVELYN PALFREY

MOON CHILD BOOKS
Austin, Texas

OCT 2 5 1999

THE PRICE OF PASSION

This is a work of fiction. Names, characters, places and
incidents are either products of the author's imagination or are
used fictitiously. Any resemblance to actual events, locales, or
persons, living or dead, is entirely coincidental.

Copyright © 1997 by Evelyn Palfrey
Second Printing-1998

Printed in the United States.
This book may not be reproduced in whole
or in part, without permission, except in the case of brief
quotations embodied in critical articles or reviews.

For information address:

Moon Child Books
P O Box 142495
Austin, Texas 78714-2495

ISBN: 0-9654190-1-0
Library of Congress Catalogue Card Number 97-93486

Cover art and design by Evelyn Palfrey and Dale Wilkins Art,
Austin, Texas

SPECIAL THANKS

To Emma Rogers, for everything you've done for me.

To Lois Palfrey, my mother, for giving me a love of reading, and for being the kind of woman I want to be when I grow up.

To my sister, Vanessa, who has amazing x-ray eyes that see straight through BS.

To my children, John and Meredith, for making me a stronger and better person than I would have been, had I not been blessed with them.

To Darwin, my husband, for supporting me, and indulging me in yet another dream.

MANY THANKS

To my editor, Delma Lopez—the lady who makes sure I don't lie when I should lay—and who could not be convinced to have any empathy for Walter.

To my romance editors, Jeannye Polk and Tina Allen. Without you, there would be more heat than warmth.

To Nigel Gusdorf, my internet wizard.

To Paul Williams who's still trying to make me understand the difference between a bit and a byte.

To Detective Phil Bailey, Sue Coburn, Mosell Cofer, Donna Bavaro, Peggy Evans, Beth Fagin, Myra Green, Sylvia Kenig, Judge Brenda Kennedy, Irma Lopcz, Yvonne Matthews, Dr. Bill Mebane, Georgia Odom, Almaree Owens, Tony Owens, Nina Red, Christina Sanchez, Bill Stanley, Nina Stanley, Dawn Tisdale, Cindy Trautmann, Judge Ken Vitucci, and Nancy Walls for all of your advice, and for keeping me on the right track.

To Ginny Agnew, Bess Cofer, Roxanne Evans, Beverly Jacobs, Jeannette Kinard, Teresa Nichols Tate, and Ginger Whitaker, for all you did to make *Three Perfect Men* a success.

Long live the Beacho's. You know who you are.

To all of the booksellers who work tirelessly, against great odds, to bring all of us the pleasure of reading, especially *The Learning Tree*, Arlington; *BookPeople, Foktales, Just For Us, Mitchie's Fine Black Art*, all of Austin; *Nu-World of Books*, Beaumont; *Black Images*, Dallas; *Nia*, Houston; *Pickwick Books*, Pine Bluff; *Under One Roof*, Killeen; and *Eso Wan* of Los Angeles.

To the Delta Blues Museum, Clarksdale, Mississippi, for working so hard to preserve the legacy. See you at the Sunflower River Blues and Gospel Festival—1st weekend in August—this year and every year.

To the wonderful folk at the Austin Writers League, who do so much to assist writers.

To my readers. You encouraged me tremendously by telling me you enjoyed *Three Perfect Men* and by telling your friends about it. Thank you.

THE SEDUCTION

Valentine's Day fell on a Saturday that year. The massive hotel ballroom was humming with excitement. Huge elegant chandeliers were dimmed to barely on, except the one spotlighting the couples on the gleaming wood dance floor. Flickering light from candles adorning every table reflected in the mirrored walls, multiplying their effect to a thousand points of light. At every table, red heart-shaped glitter was strewn onto bright white tablecloths. The combo had a wide-ranging repertoire, from jazz to Oldies to the Top 40 R&B tunes. The musicians, including the female vocalist, wore black tuxedos. At the bottom of the invitation, 'Tuxedo required' was imprinted, and nearly all the men wore them. None of the other women did. They'd read 'male' into the statement—and apparently 'beaded dresses' as well.

The annual gala had an official name, but everybody just called it the Buppie Party. It was hosted by The Top Twenty, a loosely knit, fluid group of mostly men and a couple of women. Most brought the prestige of family or professional status to the table— a few brought only the desire to acquire it by association. Everybody who was anybody in Black Austin was there. Stylin' and profiling. And, of course, all the wannabes. She thought of herself as a gonnabe.

She was what she thought of as fashionably late. Hers was not the grand entrance she'd imagined when she bought the dress. Those whose presence made this the party of the season—those who could afford to pay—had received their gratis invitations in the mail. She'd had to buy her 'invitation' from one of the hosts who really couldn't afford to be one. She really couldn't afford to be a guest. Or the dress. She'd tucked the price tag inside and intended to return it on Thursday, citing fitting problems. The store would be more likely to waive its 'no return on holiday dresses' policy on Thursday than Monday.

She knew she looked stunning in the short sequined dress. It hung heavy and molded to every curve on her body. She admired her legs and the way the dress accentuated them, especially the length of her thighs that showed. Red was the color of the season so it was perfect, she had thought while surveying herself in the three-way mirror at the exclusive dress shop. Now she had second thoughts, seeing that most of the women had on long gowns. The appreciative glances she drew from the men lounging in the foyer as she passed told her that the miscalculation wasn't all that bad. But, she'd know better next time.

She'd declined to ride with her only girlfriend that could afford an 'invitation' because she'd planned for him to take her home. She loved riding in his Mercedes and imagined having one like it one day soon. She couldn't decide between red or burgundy. He'd told her he was coming to the party just to put in the expected appearance, and would leave just after the introduction of the hosts and hostesses, that he'd call her as soon as he got a chance. She eagerly anticipated his surprised smile when he saw her.

Searching the crowd for him, she recognized most of the luminaries. When she saw the city councilman, she knew she had found the right area and started walking that way. All of the politicians would be hanging together. Sure enough, he was among them, laughing and shaking hands. He looked gorgeous in the tuxedo. He turned and walked in her direction, a broad smile breaking out on his face. Her heart raced, and she controlled her steps so as not to seem too eager. The smile fell from her face, when he stopped two tables before her and put his arm around the woman's waist, then led her back to the group.

She recognized the woman from the gold-framed picture on his desk. He hadn't said he *wasn't* bringing his wife, she'd just assumed. She sank into the nearest chair. The two women at the table eyed her disapprovingly, then looked at their men to make sure they weren't looking at her. She ignored them all. She couldn't will her legs to walk at that moment, so she sat and watched him, disbelieving. He didn't look nearly as unhappy being with the wife as he had told her. He didn't look like a man on the verge of starting a new life. And the wife certainly didn't have the look of a woman whose husband had just asked her for a divorce. She noticed how he affectionately put his arm around the wife's waist, how poised the wife was as she stood by their table, talking and laughing with the others. She'd bet a week's pay there was no price tag tucked inside the plain, but elegant, royal blue dress that was cut to the waist in back. One day *she* would be the wife. *She* would be in that inner circle, up front among the reserved tables.

But tonight, she felt shabby in the short red dress. Too done up, like a blinking neon sign, the sequins catching every shard of light. She found her footing and slinked to the back of the room where the lights were dimmer, and where the bar was.

No free drink tickets came with her 'invitation'—she bet the 'host' kept them. She quickly calculated, the ten dollar bill in her purse would buy three drinks—no tips—and a dollar's worth of gas. That was all she needed to get home. She tossed back the first two standing at the bar among the men who were getting drinks for their wives or dates. Each of them stole glances at her bare legs, then their eyes traveled north until they reached the hateful stony stare in her eyes. How dare they look at her that way! And how dare he treat her that way! She'd fix him good for that—for making her feel lesser. And after she'd given him the best of herself.

She could see him on the dance floor, his arms around the handsome woman in the elegant dress, kissing her upturned forehead, whispering in her ear. She bought her last drink with no intention of drinking it. Just as the combo segued into another slow number, she started toward the dance floor. Liquor always made her feel a little woozy, and especially on an empty stomach, but her steps were determined. He'd ruined her night, and she would ruin his.

"Can I have this dance, sweetheart?" Without waiting for a reply, he took the glass from her hand and set it on the nearest table, then led her onto the dance floor. During the slow number, she surrendered to his strong, familiar arms. The effect of the liquor must have been more obvious than she realized because he said, "I'm gonna take you home. You shouldn't drive. The cops will be out all around this place, trying to catch some of these uppity Negroes. And they'll surely notice a beautiful woman like you."

He was correct, as usual, so she acquiesced.

* * * * *

At her apartment door, he took the keys from her and let her in. When he handed her the keys, she grabbed his hand and pulled him in.

"C'mon in. Have a little drink with me."

"I'd better not," he said, with a rueful smile. "I've got to be up early in the morning. Got a whole pile of legislation to review."

"Just one," she whined.

"No, I'd really better go," he said, turning to leave.

"Well, at least help me out of this dress," she purred, turning her back to him. "I can't reach the zipper."

She felt the uncertainty in his hands, as he slowly pulled the tab down, and heard the sharp intake of his breath as the dress fell to the floor. Before he could recover from the sight of her standing naked in the red sequined high heels, she stepped over the dress puddled on the floor, pushed him down on the couch and straddled him. She knew how to get the response she wanted. The look on his face told her that he recognized she had more power over his body than he did.

She loved having power. More than money, even. Money is just bits of paper and metal you have to give to other people to get something you want. Then it's gone. But power stays with you—and grows. Using it only gives you more of it. She intended to have both—money and power. And she had a plan.

ONE

Vivian couldn't think of the precise word for what she felt, as she stared at the small squirming mass of flesh. Disbelief? Shock? Dread? Detachment? Loathing? Disgust? Even nausea. None of them was strong enough alone, and there was no one word that encompassed everything she felt. Hatred? No. Any hatred she had was reserved for Walter. It had been that way for a while. She wasn't a hating kind of person, but he'd forced her, and she finally gave in. She sometimes wondered if her habit of keeping a good black suit ready, still in the thin plastic cleaner's bag, was wishful thinking. She couldn't remember the first time she'd thought, on hearing his car in the driveway, 'Why couldn't he have been killed in a car wreck?' There had been so many times. This night had been no different. The clock over the mantle said 10:45. Even for a Monday, he was early.

"Does it have a name?" she asked.

It was the only question she could think of. What *would* be the proper question to ask your husband of nearly twenty years, when he brings home his baby by another woman, and without a word, casually places the carrier on the table, as though it was a bag of groceries you'd asked him to pick up on the way? She stared at the little bundle swathed in soft yellow. It stared back at her, out of eyes just like his—same shade of brown, same shape.

Walter was at the bar pouring himself a drink—as if he hadn't had enough already.

"I don't remember what she said. You can name it whatever you want."

"What *I* want? I don't have anything to do with this." She heard her voice rising, despite her calm exterior. She had suffered the indignity of his affairs before—many times. Enough times that there was no indignation left. No hurt, either. She didn't care any more what he did in the streets, but her home was a cocoon of beauty she made for herself. She surrounded herself with contentment. Whenever he came home, no matter what time, she felt invaded. But bringing *this* home—this dirty linen, this evidence of his stupidity—was an extreme violation.

"What are you going to do?" she asked, as calmly as she could manage.

"Well, we'll just have to deal with it, Vivian," he said, his back to her. He turned the glass up and emptied it. "We have no choice."

"What do you mean, WE?"

"Just that, Vivian. What else is there for us to do?"

"US?! You must be out of your mind. What on earth makes you think I am going to accept this…this—"

"Cause you're that kind of woman, Viv." He poured another drink. "Besides, you've always wanted a baby. I thought you'd be happy."

"Happy?! Happy?! You…arrogant…son-of-a-bitch! How can

you fix your mouth to say you think I'd be happy about your child by one of your whores!"

She felt bubbling deep inside herself, hot lava bubbling. She took deep, measured breaths, to hold it down. She heard the baby's whimpering grow louder.

"You need to come see about your...this."

He turned to face her.

"You know I don't know anything about babies. You're a woman. *You* see about it."

The volcano erupted, spewing clouds of dry ash, pushed ahead by red hot lava. Vivian marched to him, and with a wide arc of her arm, slapped the glass out of his hand. Walter didn't react when it hit the hard ceramic tile and shattered.

"You low-life dog!" she screamed at him. "How dare you! How dare you!" The rage she felt was hotter than the lava, and it poured forth, heaping obscenities on him. The look on his face—the slight smile, the hint of smugness—infuriated her so, that she struck out at it. She tried to slap it off, claw it off, but he held her hands—and the smirk. She jerked her hands away and slashed wildly at him, but he caught them each time.

"Control yourself, Vivian. Calm down. Quit acting like a hysterical child. Try to act like an adult."

She didn't hear the words, but she heard the insult. The screaming she heard was her own—and the rage. She jerked her hands with her whole body, while he held them still. As the lava flow slowed to spurting, the release of emotion from her body left her limp on her knees amid the broken glass and wetness. He held her hands above her head. The screaming she heard in the distance was not hers. It came slowly into focus. It.

"Now, look what you've done," he accused. "I can't deal with this. I've got to chair the committee meeting in the morning. I'm going to bed." When he released her hands, she fell in a heap on the floor.

Walter was at the stairs before Vivian saw the piece of glass. It was large enough, and jagged. She picked it up and fingered it, rubbing the sharp edge against her thumb. She knew the perfect place to jab it into his soft flesh.

Angry, insistent screaming snatched her attention away from the thought. She sat up and stared at the carrier, across the room on the table. The screaming grew louder, echoing and reverberating in the cavernous living room. She stood up and slowly walked to the source. She stood over it, watching it. The yellow blanket had been pushed aside by its squirming, revealing tiny fists, balled up on each side of its face. The eyes were squeezed shut. No tears. Its face was red, its mouth tiny and O-shaped. With each angry scream, the little body shook violently. Vivian understood. She wished she could do that, too. Just lie on her back on the Persian rug, ball her fists, draw her knees up, close her eyes and scream until her whole body shook. But she couldn't. So why did *it* get the luxury?

"Hush!" she snapped at it.

It startled at the sound of her voice. The screaming stopped suddenly. The eyes opened and looked at her. A curious look, examining her. Just as suddenly, the screaming started again.

"Hush!" she tried again. The response this time was louder, more demanding.

Vivian was tempted to put her hand over its face and hold it there, until the screaming stopped—until the breathing stopped.

But she knew that wouldn't help—for the victims to be punished. They were both victims, she and it. And she couldn't harm the baby. Finally, she slipped her slender fingers around it and picked it up. It hushed immediately, drawing in two quick breaths, dregs of the screams, then let out a relieved sigh. She held it in front of her and it started squirming, jerking its little legs. It grew heavy in her hands. She walked to the sofa and sat down, setting it in her lap, its head flopping forward. It started waving its arms and screaming again. She stood up, still holding it around its torso. It stopped screaming. The arms and legs were moving, seeming to clutch for her. She put it against her shoulder and patted it. It quieted. She sat back down. It screamed again. She stood up. Maybe it was hungry.

Vivian walked to the table and picked up the baby bag that Walter had dropped in the chair. She set the bag on the table, and with one hand, rummaged through it, searching for a bottle. There was none, only three disposable diapers. Selfish, thoughtless jerk! He could at least have stopped and bought something for it to eat. It was probably wet, too.

She took one of the diapers, walked to the kitchen and wet a paper towel, before going back to the sofa. She lay it on its back, unsnapped the little yellow jumpsuit, and pulled its legs out. The diaper looked heavy, and the smell of urine offended her nostrils. It must not have been changed for hours. When she tore the tapes loose on both sides and pulled the diaper away from its chafed skin, she smiled. It was a girl. Goody for him! He always talked about having a boy. 'Real men produce boys,' he'd said.

As Vivian cleaned her up she noticed the place at the base of her buttock where the darker pigment looked like she'd been stamped with a little heart. She touched her forefinger to it, the size of half a joint. When she put on the dry diaper, the baby seemed to appreciate it, even stretching her little bowed legs, making it easier for Vivian to get them back in the jumpsuit.

Vivian sat back and closed her eyes, exhausted, but feeling a small sense of accomplishment. In a moment, she felt the little foot kicking at her. When she opened her eyes and looked at her, the baby was scrunching her face and squirming, working up to a wail. Vivian didn't know what to do. There was no milk in the house. There never was. He couldn't tolerate it, and she didn't like the taste. To quiet the wailing, she picked her up and put her on her shoulder. The tiny mouth latched on her shoulder and began sucking, then dissatisfied, screamed again. Vivian bounced her up and down, but it didn't help. This was *his* problem. He could deal with it. She carried the baby up the stairs.

Vivian flipped the light on in their bedroom. Walter was sprawled on his back across the bed, sleeping like a dead man, in only his suit pants. His chest and feet were bare. Drunk, she thought in disgust. She kicked his foot that was hanging off the bed, and called his name. He didn't move. She kicked his foot again, harder. He still didn't move. What help would he be, even if she was able to wake him?

Walter's head was turned sideways, and she saw the three long, thin welts across his cheek, that disappeared into his neatly trimmed beard. She'd seen welts on his back before. His newest lover must be kinky, she thought. Maybe the woman hadn't left the baby in his office as he'd said. He'd become a professional liar. Probably, she'd given him one last piece, then left him and the baby in a motel room. A gutter place, for a gutter man. Vivian thought about the piece of glass.

There was nothing else to do. Vivian lay the still-screaming baby on the bed, slipped into a pair of jeans and tucked her pajama top into the waistband. When she got to the car, she lay the baby on the seat and tried to fasten the seat belt around her, but it wouldn't work. She fastened her own and put the baby in her lap. The baby quieted some in the soothing ride of the Mercedes.

As soon as she parked in front of the 'Stop and Rob,' the baby started squalling again. Inside, she struggled with the baby and her purse, carrying items to the counter—a baby bottle, three cans of infant formula, and a bag of diapers. The baby's screams filled the store. The look of irritation on the clerk's face pissed her off, as she juggled the baby, the sack, and her purse back to the car. She was glad she'd left the motor running. She didn't know how she would have managed keys, too.

As she put the car in reverse, Vivian jumped at the knock on the window. Instinctively, she pressed the lock button, and turned to see the uniformed cop bent over, peering in the window. She breathed a sigh of relief, then rolled the window down.

"Evening, ma'am."

She nodded. The baby screamed and squirmed.

"Are you planning to drive off with that baby in your lap?"

"What?"

"State law requires you to have the baby in an approved child safety seat. Do you have one?"

"What?" she asked irritably. "No. Of course not."

"Then, I'm going to have to write you a citation. I need to see your license and proof of insurance."

"A ticket?! You can't be serious. This isn't even my baby.

Why would I have a car seat?"

"Your license and insurance?" he asked, more sternly this time.

Exasperated, she fumbled in her purse with one hand, holding the baby with the other to keep her from rolling off her lap.

"You say this isn't your baby?" he asked off-handedly, as he examined her documents.

"It's my husband's baby. He just brought it home a couple of hours ago. I don't even want this damn baby. Please don't give me a ticket. I've had enough shit for one night. He went to sleep, and left me with this screaming baby. It had to have some milk and so—"

The glimpse she caught of herself in the rearview mirror startled her. Her face was a mess, and her hair was all over her head. The way she looked, and was rambling, justified the suspicious look she saw on the cop's face.

"Are you having a problem, ma'am? Do you need someone to talk to?"

She understood what he was thinking.

"No. No. I'm sorry. I just made that up. I'm OK. Just give me the ticket, so I can get the baby to bed."

As he handed the ticket to her to sign, the suspicion melted into a chuckle. "I thought I'd heard them all, lady. But yours has been the best by far. I can't wait to tell my wife."

Again on the ride home, the baby quieted. Thank God. One more scream would have pushed her over the edge. She needed to hear herself think. She had it worked out for the night. But what about tomorrow? She had class tomorrow. What was she going to do? Why did *she* have to do anything? Why was this her problem? She'd take care of this tonight, but tomorrow it would be his problem.

As soon as she put the nipple in the baby's mouth, she sucked and slurped so hard, Vivian thought she would choke. As the liquid disappeared, the sucking became less frantic. Halfway through, the baby released the nipple, took a deep breath, and rested a minute before attacking it again. The baby fell asleep before the bottle was completely empty. Vivian didn't know whether burping her would wake her and start the noise again. She eased from the couch and carried the baby upstairs.

Walter hadn't moved, except that his mouth was slightly open, allowing a soft snore to escape. She lay the baby on her stomach next to him, thankful she didn't wake. Looking at him with disgust, Vivian was certain she would never share his bed again. She collected the few things she would need immediately—toothbrush, pajamas, underwear, makeup, a change of clothes—and carried them into the downstairs bedroom. She'd complete the move tomorrow after she finished studying at the law library.

Several hours later, the wailing woke Vivian just enough to be reminded of where she was. She punched the unfamiliar pillow into a shape to simulate the one she was accustomed to, and drifted almost back to sleep. Then she realized the noise was not in her head. She lay listening. There was no change in the pitch or level. She realized Walter was not going to respond. She looked at the clock on the dresser—4:54. She dragged herself out of bed.

"Hush, baby." The little girl opened her eyes when Vivian picked her up. She seems to recognize me, Vivian thought distastefully. She didn't want to be recognized. She was only doing what was necessary to get to tomorrow. She prepared another bottle, holding the baby on her shoulder. She took her to her room, lay on the bed with her, and gave her the bottle. Vivian realized the baby hadn't cried since she picked her up. There was a look of contentment on her face, as she sucked more leisurely than before. Even with her eyes closed, she looked like him.

Vivian wondered what the mother looked like. She ran through the pictures in her mind of the ones she suspected, the ones whose sly smiles she'd seen him return. But none of them had been noticeably pregnant in the last several months. Who could the mother be? She looked at the baby, trying to determine an age. He hadn't said. Four months? Six months? Karla's baby was six months old. This one was definitely younger. Two months? Maybe. Vivian couldn't tell. And what kind of mother would leave a baby this little? And why? Vivian couldn't imagine a circumstance that would force her to do it—if she'd been able to have a baby.

She looked around the room. This would have been the nursery, if things had gone as they had planned when they bought the house. The room had been bare the first years. As they became financially able to decorate it, the dream had faded. She'd finally chosen an Oriental motif—the furniture, the curtains, the wall decorations. Very adult. Very un-nursery. The baby, sleeping peacefully, even *looked* out of place, ensconced in the champagne-colored satin sheets and comforter. Vivian felt her own eyes being dragged closed, and surrendered to sleep. She dreamed of the baby she had wanted for so long, the one she'd prayed for.

She was awakened by the little foot kicking her in the stomach. She looked into the little eyes. His eyes. The baby didn't smile–exactly–but the kicking stopped momentarily. Vivian took a sharp breath, as she recognized the odd feeling as wetness and sprang out of the bed. She remembered she hadn't changed the diaper when she brought the baby downstairs. "Be right back, baby," she said, and headed for the kitchen.

"Ex-cuse me? Going somewhere?"

Walter stopped in his tracks, at the back door. By the steam rising from the cup of coffee on the kitchen counter, she judged he'd heard her coming, and thought he could beat her to the door.

"What about your baby? You know I have a class at nine. What are you going to do?" Vivian looked at the clock on the microwave—8:06. Even if she dressed as fast as she could, she'd be late.

When he turned to face her, she saw the desperate look in his eyes.

"Vivian, I'm going to work this out. I swear. I just need a little time. I've got that committee meeting this morning. At nine. You know what they'll say if I'm late—"

"Your baby, Walter?" she cut him off.

"I know, Viv. I'll figure something out. I'll take care of it. But I have to do this first. It's going to be televised. You can miss *one* class. I'll come back as soon as the meeting is over. We'll talk then. I promise, Viv." He was heading out the door.

"There's nothing to talk about, Walter. Walter! Walter!!"

The door closed behind him. The baby's cries stopped her from following him long enough for him to get the car started and roar down the driveway. Her mouth crimped tightly, Vivian picked up the cup of coffee, took a diaper, and the last can of formula with her.

The darkened wet spot on the satin sheet had spread.

"Hush, baby. It's me again. But not for long."

The baby quieted as soon as Vivian got close, and Vivian felt her eyes watching her intently and patiently. She moved the baby to a dry place on the bed, and changed her diaper. As she drained the last can of formula into the bottle, she told her, "This is the last of the milk. I wish I'd remembered to tell Walter to bring more on his way home."

He ought to be back before more was needed, she thought, as she lay on the bed and gave the baby the bottle. Ways and Means was an important committee, but it was early in the session, so the meeting shouldn't last that long. A couple of hours at the most. She'd just send him back to the store. She certainly wasn't going to risk another ticket. And, she wasn't going to pay for the one she got either. She was surprised that the cop hadn't noticed that the signature didn't match the one on her driver's license. She'd signed it 'Walter Carlson' in a perfect imitation of his writing. *He'd* have to take care of that, too. The baby's little hand touched hers, holding the bottle. A soft little touch. Tiny fingers, square-shaped on the ends, just like Walter's. She moved the baby's hand away from hers.

"Don't touch me, baby. I won't be in your life long. Walter's gonna take you back to your mama soon. Or maybe he'll keep you. I don't know. Don't care. Me? I'm going somewhere else. I just haven't figured out where yet."

When the bottle was finished, Vivian put the baby on her shoulder and burped her. Now what? 8:45. She needed to change the sheets. But what to do with the baby? She felt helpless and stymied. What on earth was she thinking! She wasn't helpless.

Stymied, maybe. Thrown for a loop, even. But not helpless. She lay the baby on a towel on the floor, replaced the sheets and comforter, and took the wet ones to the washer. As she walked out the bedroom door, the baby began to whimper.

"Don't even start with me, baby."

She could hear her crying from the laundry room. As soon as she came back to the bedroom, the baby quieted. She went in the bathroom to shower and change. When she walked out of view, the baby started. Vivian tried to ignore her while she undressed. The insistent cries brought her back to the bedroom.

"What do you want?!" she snapped.

The baby hushed immediately.

"Oh, I get it. You don't want to be alone. That's where you and me are different. I *want* to be alone. I'm *gonna* be alone. Soon. Right now, I've got to shower. You may as well come."

She picked the baby up, took her to the bathroom and lay her on the towel on the floor. The jumpsuit was wet and smelled of urine. It wasn't really fair to the baby for her to be stinky. It wasn't her fault that her daddy was a dog and her mama was a…who knows. Vivian took the little jumpsuit off, covered the baby with another towel, and rinsed it out under the faucet. As she left the room, she said, "Now you keep quiet, I'll be right back." The baby just looked at her and blinked her eyes. Vivian rushed across the house to the utility room, threw the jumpsuit in the dryer and rushed back. But there was no need. The baby was quiet. Vivian rushed through her shower, got dressed and put on enough make-up to pass. Now what? Nothing to do but wait. But she wasn't a woman to waste time. She lay the baby on the bed, went to the study and brought back her textbook. She would use the time to prepare for the next day's class. Administrative Law was the most boring class she'd had since she started law school. It wasn't long before she and the baby were asleep.

Vivian woke to the baby's whimpering and kicking. She looked at the clock—12:05. Where the hell was he? She called out to him. No response. She went to the garage. Only her car was there. She jerked the phone off the wall in the kitchen and dialed his office.

"Sherman, is Walt there?"

"No, Vivian, he left for lunch."

"Did he say he was on the way home?"

"No. He was with Representatives Bailey and Mitchum. I think they were going to Bailey's club for lunch and then to play golf. But he definitely said he was coming back later. Should I have him call you when he returns? Or page him now?"

Vivian had the urge to slam the phone down, but Sherman had done nothing to deserve such rudeness. He and Walter were cousins—sons of two sisters. She didn't know exactly what the trouble was that sent him to Austin from Philadelphia, but it didn't matter to her. He was an i-dotter like she was, and he looked out for Walter. That was enough for her. She and Sherman had a good understanding, and she trusted him. She often wished he could find a good woman who could help him keep his life on track.

On the other end of the line, Sherman frowned at the sound of Vivian's voice. He knew her well enough to know that she wasn't reacting well to this. In the office arena, they treated each other with respect. She treated him like the extremely competent aide that he was, and he treated her like the boss's wife who could fire him in a heartbeat. He knew what had happened to his immediate predecessor—the cute little mini-skirted, ambitious coed, who couldn't add. For her, the fact that Walter shared her bed fairly regularly added up to her having the license to disrespect Mrs. Carlson to her face. No matter that he thought Walter treated Vivian shabbily, he'd seen her put her foot down. When she did, Walter did what she wanted. Sherman wasn't about to lose another job—and he *was* good at math.

"No, that won't be necessary, Sherman. Just have him call me when he gets back."

"Is there anything I can do for you?" Sherman asked.

"No. That's alright. Just have him call me."

What Vivian really wanted to do, she thought as she eased the receiver back on the hook, was slam the phone up-side Walter's head. But Walter was unavailable and by now, the baby was in a full wail.

Vivian grabbed the jumpsuit out of the dryer, dressed the fretting baby, and carried her to the car. She spotted the box on the worktable. Just the right size. She took the plastic bottles of oil out and tried it. It fit perfectly on the floor in the front seat of her Camry. She went back in the house and grabbed two towels. She made a nest of one and laid the baby in the box. She'd use the other one to cover the box if she ran into Officer Friendly again. Not to take any chances, she passed by the 'Stop and Rob' and drove to the full-service grocery store.

The array of choices was amazing. Vivian hadn't stopped on the baby aisle in years—not since she'd given up hope of having a baby. She didn't remember whether there had been so many choices before, or maybe then she hadn't been looking for anything in particular. Then, her eye had been attracted to the cute things, the gadgets. This time she had a purpose. She picked the same formula she'd bought before, for no other reason than she recognized the can. A case this time. And another bottle. She wondered if the baby needed real food and picked a box of rice cereal and several jars of strained foods, just in case. The display caught her eye. Hair things. She looked at the baby's head. Lots of hair. She threw a package of barrettes in the basket. She took two pink jumpsuits down. A little girl should have pink. Yellow was motivated by uncertainty. Could fit either sex—didn't fit either. She looked at the rattles and toys, but decided she wouldn't be around long enough to bother. On the other hand, every girl needed a possession that was hers, and hers alone. She selected a soft, terry cloth covered ring with a clown head that made a muted rattling noise.

* * * * *

Vivian got the baby fed and dry and put her to bed before settling back to her studies. She kept her eye on the clock. At 6:30, she finally figured out, Walter wasn't coming home.

TWO

Even though Vivian had missed her classes, she kept up her reading assignments between caring for the baby. It was so constant she was worn out. She couldn't imagine how a woman who had suffered the physical rigors of childbirth would have the energy, or strength, to do it. She and Walt had barely spoken since he brought the baby home. Every time she tried to talk to him about it, he was late to some 'important' function, or staggering his way to bed—drunk. He wouldn't return her constant pages. He wouldn't take her calls. She could tell from Sherman's voice that he was being forced to lie and say that Walter wasn't in. One of the things she'd always liked about Sherman was that he protected Walter, but now it irritated her. Finally, on Thursday, she asked Sherman to remind Walter when he came in, about their appointment with Child Protective Services. Within minutes, the phone rang.

"What the hell is this about Child Protective Services?!" Walter demanded.

"I'm going to take this baby to them. You apparently don't want her."

"Don't you do that."

"Why not? They can find the mother. I can't miss any more classes."

At the tone of finality in her voice, Walter took a more persuasive tact.

"Vivian, please. Don't do that. You don't know those people. You can't just take the baby to them. They'll have a lot of questions. Want to know where you got the baby. They may even get the police involved. What could you tell them?"

"I'll just tell the truth."

"Don't be silly, Vivian. That would cause a big scandal. Ruin my career. Ruin everything we've worked for."

"Your getting some woman pregnant is the cause of the scandal, Walter. And with AIDS! I just can't believe you were that stupid. Even if you don't care anything about me, you should care about yourself more than that. Come get this baby right now, Walter. I'm not taking care of her any more. If you don't come right now, I'm taking her to those welfare people. I'm not joking." She slammed the phone down.

* * * * *

Vivian finally had to make a name for the baby. She couldn't keep calling her 'baby.' Everybody deserved a name—their own name. She remembered when she and Walter had talked about naming their little girl after their mothers. As she rocked the baby, she thought about his mother's name. She wasn't sure her mother-in-law would feel honored by that. Barbara Leah Carlson, a prim and proper Philadelphia lady, was going to be appalled at this news. And Vivian was not going to be the bearer. Besides, she didn't feel that 'Barbara' fit. It was of another generation, but not old enough yet to be quaint—like Victoria or Emily. Her own mother's name was out of the question. Maybe an African-sounding name—something like Imani. Or one of those new-fangled African-American names—Kenisha or Tarsha? Looking at the baby sucking leisurely on yet another bottle, Vivian thought none of them seemed right.

She looked so much like Walter—oval face, pointed chin, brown eyes, full lips with distinctive points. No question in Vivian's mind she was his child. She wondered if her own baby would have looked so much like him, taking none of her features. Maybe name her for him—Walterette. Vivian laughed. Just plain Walter. Walter, Jr. That would be a good slap in the face for 'Mr. Real Men Have Boys'. But *he* was a junior. Walt, the third? No. She wondered again who the mother was. What did she look like? Obviously, something like Walter, or had extremely recessive genes.

Walter had always been handsome, but in the early years of their marriage, he hadn't been concerned with his looks, or enticed by the come-on looks other women poured on him. He'd been a good husband. Attentive to her, doting even. Even when money was tight, he'd bring her little presents. He'd been a passionate lover. He had been full of passion—passion for life, passion for people. That passion was what had attracted her to him. Fueled by the passion of right, he'd take a case, even when he knew going in, there was no prospect of being paid. One of those cases had catapulted him into local fame.

It had started as a simple eviction. The public housing project was scheduled to be razed and new ones built on that site. The old lady had refused to move. She had lived there from the time the projects had been built right after the war, when she'd been a young woman. It was the only home she knew. She had raised children, grandchildren, and now great-grandchildren there. The lawyers at the government agency wouldn't help her—except to relocate. They didn't comprehend when she told them "Dat's my home. Where would I go?" When she found her way to Walter's office, he didn't hold out much hope to her, but said he would do what he could. The passion in him responded to the passion in her. Still, he was a realist. At every turn, he would tell her the same thing.

"Now Ms. Washington, I told you in the beginning I didn't think I could stop them from tearing it down, I can only buy you some time."

Each time, her response was the same.

"You can do it, Mr. Carlson. You the only one that can. You smart. Got all that education. It won't hurt you to use some of what you've been blessed with to help an old lady like me. I ain't gon' be round that much longer. You ain't gon' let them take the only home I got in this world. I have faith in you."

Somewhere along the way Walt began to believe her. And he didn't let them take it. He fought the bureaucracy all the way to Washington and back. Along the way, he learned the power of the press and the weakness of bureaucrats. In the end, the plan was revised. The projects were remodeled instead of torn down. Ms. Washington and her family were the only tenants during the two-year process. Every time Vivian drove by there, even now, Ms. Washington was sitting on the porch, surrounded by her plants and great-grandchildren.

It was during that fight, Vivian had seen an article in the newspaper about the maverick young lawyer who was taking on the government. In her senior year in college, with an acceptance letter to law school in hand, and a paper to write for one of her pre-law classes, she called him for an interview. She fell in love with the fire in his eyes as he talked about the case, and why he wouldn't give up. While they dated, she helped prepare documents for the case, and others. She worked as his secretary after her classes, taking her school work with her to his office. With an efficiency that came naturally to her, Vivian organized his office so that he could concentrate on the new cases that the notoriety brought. She never thought he would be a wealthy lawyer, and it didn't matter to her. They had a big wedding—at her mother's insistence—the summer after her graduation, in her home town.

Since he needed her in the office, she declined the acceptance to law school. She planned to wait until he was on his feet. That wait turned into ten years. She'd made a start at it the year she'd given up on the baby, but after a year she'd dropped out to manage his first campaign.

Vivian hadn't trusted the men who came to persuade him he would be the perfect Black candidate for the House of Representatives. She saw the slyness in their eyes as they lauded him for his history of community work, his education and background. She was puzzled why he didn't see it, why he didn't question what they wanted from the deal—since their good works in the community were noticeably absent. They persuaded him that he would be able to do even more for his community from a position of power. She took on the management of his campaign office to protect him from them, and from the thing that she could feel, but couldn't put her finger on—or a name to. She watched helplessly as the thing approached him, he being as attracted to it, as it was to him. It was soft and malleable—mercurial. Shiny and attractive like mercury—and just as poisonous. When she tried to push it away from him, it broke up and slipped from her touch. Ultimately, it enveloped him and won. The sly-eyed men won. It was a more bitter loss for her than never being able to have a baby.

She crossed all the t's she could, and dotted all the i's she could. She made sure all the right reports were filed with the right agencies by the right deadlines. At least he wouldn't be tripped up and disgraced on some bullshit. She learned election law inside and out. She kept his schedule and made sure he was in all the right places at the right times. She stood in for him at the functions he was stretched too thin to make. She was up late at night writing speeches for him, while he slept. There was never a lack of money for salaries, signs or the other requirements of a well-run campaign. The sly-eyed men made sure of that. Vivian fooled herself into thinking it came from people who believed in her man as much as she did.

It began during the second campaign, his taking her for granted. Little hints that he believed he was doing it all on his own. His suggestion that she turn over the office to 'the professionals,' and act like the other wives, hurt her. She *was* a professional, not a trinket. Other campaigns even called on her expertise. It hurt more to know that the sly-eyed men were behind it. She knew they would love to have her out of the way, not asking the pointed questions. Walt couldn't see it. He had become too full of himself, too mesmerized by the accolades heaped on him. Hypnotized.

The first time she smelled perfume on him, she knew. He lied. Denied. As though she was dumb. She had always worn perfume, but that was the last time. He didn't notice. She always knew. He always denied. When she tried to talk to him about divorce, he said it would ruin his career, destroy everything they'd worked for, keep him from accomplishing the things for the community he had planned. That he loved her. Had made a mistake. It wouldn't happen again. The next time she smelled perfume on him, she enrolled in law school.

She continued to attend the obligatory functions as his wife, but her mind and her heart were elsewhere. Since she had lost respect for him, she knew she wouldn't spend the rest of her life with him. But at that moment she didn't have a plan, nothing to go to, so she stayed. She made the house beautiful, and she studied. He blamed her for his indiscretions, saying she didn't show him any passion. As far as she was concerned, he'd lost the passion for the things she cared about. He obviously found his passion elsewhere. For money, for power, for other women. Then it came to her, this baby had been conceived of that passion. It would be appropriate, so that was the name Vivian chose for her. Passion.

* * * * *

The baby-sitter he'd promised didn't show up Friday either. Vivian thought about taking the baby with her to class. But she couldn't depend on her to be quiet. And babies always caused a big stir in places where they would be such an oddity. She didn't want to face the questions she was sure would be asked. She realized that she hadn't taken the baby anywhere but the grocery store—where a baby wouldn't be unusual. *She* hadn't been anywhere either. She hadn't had to explain it to anyone. And she didn't intend to, she fumed. Let him explain. She would get an apartment and leave his ass.

* * * * *

Saturday morning, her friend Cynthia called about shopping. Vivian made excuses, and didn't mention Passion. But that couldn't go on forever. Where was the mother? Vivian had thought sure she'd turn up by now, expecting Vivian to have fled, so she could take her place, with the leverage Vivian didn't have. This woman couldn't add any better than that silly aide. Walt hadn't shown the slightest interest in the baby. He *did* wince whenever she called Passion by her name. That made Vivian smile.

She had put Passion down for her nap, when Walter came downstairs in his robe.

"What are you going to do?" she asked.

"About what?" His groggy eyes becoming instantly alert.

Vivian just crimped her mouth and stared at him. He didn't look well. Dark circles under his eyes, the slackness in his jaw showing the weight he'd lost. But the welts had healed.

"Oh, yeah. Sherman found a housekeeper. A babysitter. A Salvadoran woman. Doesn't speak English, but that's fine. She'll come and keep it."

"Until when?"

"Until I figure something out."

"You've been figuring for a week and that's all you could come up with? Where's the mother, Walt? Who is she?"

"That's not important, Viv. Let's not get into all that. I told you she came to my office, left it. Said she was going to New York to become a star and I wouldn't see her again."

"Well, if you knew her well enough to get her pregnant, you should know where her family is. You could take the baby to them—"

"I didn't know her that well," he said, staring down into the cup of coffee he'd poured himself. "We didn't talk about anything like that,"

"I imagine not," she said, her voice dripping with sarcasm.

When he looked up at her, there was hope for forgiveness, or at least understanding, in his eyes, but he saw only disgust in hers.

Vivian snatched up her purse and keys and stormed out. She felt free, for the first time in a week. Only trouble was, she didn't have anywhere to go, no errands to run. She hadn't done any research on apartments, so that was out, for now. She dialed Cynthia's number on her car phone. Maybe she hadn't gone shopping yet. When she heard Cynthia's voice, she hung up. She knew she wouldn't be able to resist talking about it. Of course she would tell her—in time. But not now.

On impulse, she turned in at the sign that read BUTTONS AND BOWS. The pink jumpsuits from the grocery store had been too large. '9 months.' She hadn't even thought about size at the time— just baby. She held up one cute outfit. Looked like it would fit. She looked at the label—6 months. She picked up another just like it—3 months. Looked like it would fit. She bought them both. Then a couple of more outfits in the dual sizes. And the barrettes. And the elastic thing to go around her head. And the bottle that looked like a bear, with a hole in it. And the gift-boxed towel set. And the hand-made quilt. And the car seat. Walter would need that. When she couldn't answer the helpful clerk's questions, she explained it was for a baby shower. The clerk showed her the diapers just for girls. She charged it all on Walter's card.

On the advice of the divorce lawyer she'd consulted several years before, she'd separated her credit from his. She opened her own bank account for the money her father had left her. It hadn't been a lot, but enough for her to feel independent.

The clock in the car read 2:30. She knew Passion would be awake and clamoring for her bottle. She hoped Walter didn't have trouble finding the cans of formula. She heard the screams before she shut the motor off. Walter was passed out in the chair, the empty glass on the table.

"Poor little Passion," she cooed as she picked her up. "Don't cry." But she didn't have to say it. As soon as Passion saw her, she quieted. Vivian could tell she'd been crying a long time. Her face was red, and she was hiccing. Jerk! She changed her diaper, then gave her the bottle—the new one that looked like a bear.

* * * * *

Walter was up and gone early Sunday. Vivian was glad. She didn't even want to look at him. This would be their last day together, she and Passion. They stretched out on the floor on the luxurious Persian carpet and read the thick newspaper until they dozed off. When she woke to the baby kicking her, she thought she might actually miss the baby when she left. Vivian saw no reason to miss her usual leisurely Sunday bath. She put Passion in the tub with her. She didn't remember the little bumps all over the baby's chest being there before. She wondered if they meant she was sick, symptoms of some baby disease. Passion didn't seem sick, watching her as intently as she usually did. When they were dressed, she called Karla. She didn't have the answer, but she did have questions.

"Why on earth are you asking about babies? You and Walter haven't snuck something by me, have you?" she asked, laughing.

"No, of course not." Vivian heard the strain in her own voice. "Uh, I have a new housekeeper. From El Salvador. She wanted to know. By the way, who is your pediatrician?"

"I doubt your housekeeper could afford her."

"Never mind the bourgeois bullshit, Karla. Just give me the name, OK?"

"OK. OK. You don't have to get so huffy. Her name is Hastings. Jackie Hastings. In the Medical Arts Complex. She's very good, but I'm telling you she doesn't take that government aid stuff."

"Thanks, Karla." Vivian shook her head as she hung up, thinking how pretentious Karla was for someone who would have been on 'that government aid stuff' if she hadn't married the right man. Vivian was offended that she would disparage Walter's new housekeeper that neither of them had met.

* * * * *

On Monday morning, Vivian found the note in Walter's scrawling handwriting, by the coffee pot.

> "Meet me at the Capitol at noon. Important reception. Won't last long."

She called his office. "The babysitter isn't here. I'm missing another day of class." She hoped she sounded as pissed as she felt.

"I'm sorry, Viv. I'll have Sherman check into it. He'll find another one. I *need* you to come to this reception. You are coming, aren't you?"

"And just what am I supposed to do with this baby?"

"Bring it. One of the girls around here will keep it. It's just for a short time. I need you to do this, Viv."

Vivian slammed the phone down. She flopped on the bed, and fussed and fumed as Passion watched her. In the end, she managed to get them both dressed and to the Capitol minutes before noon. She went straight to his office, nodding to Sherman as though he couldn't see the baby carrier. Walter was waiting. To those who didn't know, he looked like the epitome of calm. But Vivian saw his nervousness, felt it.

"Who's going to keep the baby?" she asked.

"Uh, the girl left for lunch before I got a chance to talk to her about it. Just pick it up and bring it with you. I've got it all worked out. It's going to be OK. Come on. We'll be late." He was at the door holding it open for her. As she walked by, he said, "You look nice, Viv." She rolled her eyes at him as he took her elbow to guide her.

As they walked down the wide corridor, several strangers stopped and commented on how pretty the baby was. Vivian realized that the people at the reception who knew her would ask questions about the baby. She tried to formulate a response that wasn't a lie, but that wouldn't raise suspicion, or provoke further questions. Got stuck baby-sitting my sister's baby. Wouldn't work. She'd probably run into somebody who knew Adelma. She lived in Austin, too. Some distant relative's baby, in town on vacation. What would she say if someone commented on how much the baby looked like Walter? It was too obvious to miss. One of

Walter's relatives, in town on vacation.. That was the best she could do on short notice. She practiced it in her mind, until she thought she could say it without stumbling.

It took Vivian's eyes a moment to adjust to the bright light in the Speaker's Committee Room, where press conferences were usually held. She was certain he'd said reception. The room was full. He led her to the dais and pulled out a chair for her next to the speaker's podium. The public smile she wore hid her confusion and discomfort. Perhaps this was the prelude to the reception, she thought, remembering she hadn't even asked him who or what the reception was for—and he hadn't said. She watched him warily out of the corner of her eye as he took the mike and began.

"Thank you all for coming. I've asked you here today to bring attention to a big problem that is a shame and disgrace on the great state of Texas. We talk a lot about drugs, crime and taxes. But no one talks about the children. A wise man said 'Evil can only triumph when good people stand silent.' There is a crisis, my friends, and it's past time that good people do something about it.

"There are thousands of young Texans who are the victims of drug abuse, or victims of crime. They are homeless and helpless. They are wasting their lives away in foster care, longing for a family to call their own. I urge all of you who are able, to adopt one of these children—give them a home, a family, and a chance at a productive life. Like Vivian and I have done."

In the posture of a proud father, he placed his hand on her shoulder and smiled down at her, just as the flashbulb's popping blinded her.

Vivian felt like a lightning bolt had struck her. Although she recovered quickly, the smile froze on her face as her body went cold all over. What could she do? Cry? Fall out in a dead faint? She had the urge to throw the chair back, grab the mike and yell, 'He's a liar! This is his yard-baby!'

THREE

Marc Kline leaned against the mahogany-paneled back wall of the Speakers Committee Room, watching the proceedings. As he'd scanned the Schedule of Events at the Capitol on his computer the night before, his eye caught on the press conference on foster care scheduled by the Black representative. Adoption was the theme of his new book, and he noted the tangential relationship. Truth was, he didn't have anything planned for that day after his class, and the idea for the book had yet to come to fruition.

He'd come to realize that books came on their own time, not springing forth from genius, as he'd previously thought. The Pulitzer prize had proven that. It wasn't his scholarly work that won it, nor his favorite book, nor the one that he'd struggled so hard to bring forth. Rather, it was a story that just came to him. Although fiction was not his forte, it had been a novel. It was a little germ of an idea when he sat down at his computer. He'd started out to make a note of it among the many he had in his file titled 'Future Books,' that one day might evoke the many words required to become one. But as he typed, it took on a life of its own.

It was a strange phenomenon that he had not experienced before. The characters came to life on their own, and told their own story. He only reported it. When he tried to impose his will—his idea for the plot—they rebelled and went on with their story. So he went on reporting. When he stopped typing, three days later, exhausted from not having eaten or slept, the first draft was complete.

So this day he went to the Capitol out of boredom, more than anything, while he waited for the phenomenon to happen again, not knowing whether it would be another week or a decade.

The year after the prize was awarded had been a strange one for him. Initially, the swarm of activity and attention had nearly swamped him. He had been taken by surprise. But fame is fleeting, and he was glad. He couldn't have stood much more of it, by the time it died down, and they'd turned their eye to the next one roasting in the spotlight. The little jaunt he'd taken to Jamaica had helped it along. There, he'd blended in with the populace and enjoyed the peace that anonymity provided. His publisher had been totally pissed about him disappearing that way, but she got over it. He would have stayed longer, except he couldn't convince his ex-wife to let his boy join him. He'd even offered her money, the thing that seemed to motivate her most. She took it, and still wouldn't let him come. All that drivel about him not being able to miss school. What could a pre-schooler miss in two weeks that wouldn't be more than compensated for by an international experience? He couldn't figure why she had behaved that way. Since the divorce, he had scrupulously adhered to the visitation schedule, and she'd never denied him any other times he'd asked for Corey. He always called first, always treated her with respect, always paid the child support on time.

Corey was the only good thing that had come of his marriage to Allison. He would have stayed with her even so, but in the end decided that the years until the boy was old enough to come on his own would be better spent without the rancor and obvious lack of love between his parents. He didn't even get a lawyer for the divorce—he could read the visitation schedule. The rest was of no consequence to him. He wanted his son to grow up in a house with a yard, so he gave that to her. There wasn't enough money to argue over. Never had been, between his professor's salary and her insatiable desire to spend.

Allison had never understood him. She said he lacked ambition because he wouldn't fight for a department chairmanship. His only ambition was to write. He liked teaching, but he *loved* to write. She accused him of being withdrawn and anti-social. He supposed that may have been true, but he was comfortable with himself. He didn't believe he had changed, and in all fairness, neither had she. Perhaps, in the beginning, they had both looked beyond what was really there, to something they each wanted to see. It probably was his fault more than hers. He should have seen it—human behavior was his field. And he was unusually observant, as a good writer must be.

It was his powers of observation that drew his attention to the representative's wife now. The smile looked false to him, the kind he'd expect of a politician's wife. But more than false. Tense. Uncertain. Even fearful. Marc felt nothing but disdain for politicians, having seen the result of their 'work' in the educational system. So he'd only half-heartedly listened to the representative's spiel on foster care. The man's self-righteous posture offended him. But something about the woman held his eyes. He saw it. That fleeting moment, when the man put his hand on her shoulder, when she looked as though she'd taken a direct hit to the stomach. Then it was gone. Marc raised off the wall to watch more closely.

The man was helping her out of the chair, inviting her to speak. She held the baby awkwardly, as she stood before the mike. Before she could get a word out, as if on cue, maybe even pinched, the baby began to cry. Scream, really. The sound was so startling through the microphone that several of the cameramen reflexively clapped their hands over their ears. The sound covered whatever the woman mumbled into the mike through that tense smile, before she turned and walked past the row of chairs and out the door.

Hurriedly working his way past the reporters and the curious, Marc didn't really hear what the representative had to say when he took the mike again. Something about babies and new mothers that brought laughter from the crowd. When he walked through the tall etched glass door, she was not in the corridor. He hurried to the wall directory to find the representative's office number, but it wasn't there. He took the elevator to the ground floor and found it on the main directory. He went back to the elevator and impatiently punched the button over and over—as though that would summon the car faster. The door opened, and in his rush to get in, he collided into her rush to get out.

"Oh, sorry. Mrs. Carlson. I was looking for you. You got a minute?"

"No. Excuse me," she barked, walking around him.

He turned and followed her. "My name is Marc Kline. I'm a professor at the university. I'm writing a book on adoption. I'd like to interview you for it."

"I'm in a hurry. I don't have time."

"It won't take long. Just a few questions. It would help me a lot."

Her step was determined, even with the difficulty she had in the high heels, lugging the baby carrier.

"Here, let me help you with that," he said, taking the handle of the carrier. "Where are you parked?"

"I can manage. Thanks anyway," she said, trying to dislodge the carrier from his grasp.

"You can manage something else. Let me carry her for you. The walkway is very steep." His grasp was firm. His eyes were kind.

Vivian stopped and fixed him with an exasperated stare. She had the urge to jerk the carrier from him, but that would only upset Passion. And he wasn't really the object of her anger.

"Not nearly as steep as going up," she said, reluctantly relinquishing the handle to him. "OK. Thank you. C'mon. I'm in a hurry."

Marc fell in step beside her on the steeply sloping walkway down to Congress Avenue.

"She's a beautiful baby. A little princess. What's her name?"

"Passion," Vivian answered, not slowing her pace.

"Unusual. How long have you had her?"

"Not long," she answered curtly.

"Did you get her at birth?"

"This is my car. Thank you again," she said, reaching for the carrier.

"You don't have a car seat?" he asked.

"It's in the back seat."

"But it's not hooked up."

"I *know* that," she said looking at him with disdain. She had tried to hook it up before going to the Capitol, but it hadn't made any sense to her, and she didn't have time to read the instructions, so she had thrown it in the back seat and used the box.

Marc took the keys out of her hand and opened the door. In no time, he'd installed the car seat properly facing rear. He took the baby out of the carrier and strapped her in.

"How old is she? Don't you have the head thing?"

"Head thing?"

"Guess not," he said, smiling and shaking his head. "Doesn't look like you had much preparation for motherhood."

Vivian watched impatiently as he rolled the towel lengthwise and formed it in an inverted U around the baby's head.

"There. That ought to do—for now," he said, satisfied with his effort.

"You seem to know a lot about babies, Mr., uh, Professor Kline."

"Had one once."

"What happened to it?" she asked, looking concerned.

"He grew up. He's six now."

"Oh. Well, that's good. Listen, I gotta go. Thanks again for your help," she said, walking to the driver's side of the car.

"I'd really like to talk to you about your adoption experience. For my book. Don't you have time for just a cup of coffee?"

"No. I'm really in a rush. Talk to my husband. He's got the

whole story."

The phrase struck Marc as odd, but he didn't have time to dwell on it. She had started the motor. He knocked on the window.

"Here. Take my card. When you have some time, call me."

Vivian put the card in her purse and drove away.

* * * * *

Tuesday, Vivian was ready for class in plenty of time. As the clock inched past 8 a.m., she wondered if the woman was going to come. As usual, Walter had left early, while she was in the shower. She hadn't been upstairs since the day she'd moved the rest of her clothes and things out of his bedroom. If he thought he had trapped her in his little web of deceit, he was wrong. She planned to talk to her professors that day after class about the week she'd missed, to make sure it wouldn't affect her grades. After that, she would look for a place to stay until the semester was over, or maybe until she'd taken the bar exam. That was as far ahead as she needed to plan for the moment. When the doorbell rang, she dashed to the door.

The woman could have been old, she could have been middle-aged. She was nearly toothless.

"Good morning. I'm glad to see you. You're just in time. I'm Vivian Carlson," she said, offering her hand. The woman just stared at her, a shy and uncertain look on her face.

Finally, she said, "Buenos Dias."

"OK. Well, come on in. The baby's in the bedroom." Vivian started away from the door, and was in the middle of the room before she realized the woman hadn't followed her. She walked back to the door.

"Come in." The woman just stared at her, not comprehending. Vivian desperately searched her mind for the Spanish phrase, but that one wouldn't come. She spoke the only one that did.

"Como se llama?" she asked, taking the woman's hand and pulling her into the foyer, closing the door behind her.

The woman's eyes lit up. She began speaking rapidly in Spanish, but the only thing Vivian understood of it was 'Elena.'

"OK Elena, this is the baby—Passion."

"Passion," the woman repeated, with a soft accent.

"She needs the bottle at ten. And a bath. She's used to having it before the bottle. Then a nap. I'll try to be back about that time." Vivian searched the woman's eyes. She wasn't sure she had understood any of it, and she couldn't think of enough Spanish words to make her understand. Vivian tightened her lips as she looked at her watch. She handed Elena the notepad with Walter's number and her car phone number. The woman just nodded and took it.

* * * * *

Vivian worried all the way to school. And she couldn't concentrate in class, for worrying about Passion. She regretted not having poured the formula in the bottles. What if Elena mixed it with something? What if Passion was frightened when she woke to the unfamiliar face, and words? What if she had a screaming fit and the woman grew impatient? What if the woman was involved in a kidnapping ring? She'd read an article about that recently in the paper. Or what if she was a baby-killer! Vivian knew she was being ridiculous, allowing her mind to wander that way. She was out the door the minute class was dismissed, and ran all the way to her car.

When she hurried in the back door, she found the woman perched on her kitchen stool, watching television. The Spanish station. The TV was so loud, Vivian had heard it from the garage. So loud the woman hadn't heard her come in, nor had the man who was sitting at the table. The woman nearly jumped off the stool when Vivian touched her on the shoulder.

"Is the baby sleep?"

The woman said something in Spanish that Vivian didn't understand.

"Who is *he*? What is he doing here?"

Again, Vivian didn't understand the response. She wasn't sure Elena understood the question. She rushed to her bedroom. Passion was lying on her back awake, whimpering. The minute she saw Vivian, she began kicking her legs and her face became animated. Vivian rushed and picked her up, then carried her to the kitchen with her.

"You can leave now," she said. The woman looked at her and smiled. Vivian searched for the word.

"Vamanos."

They both looked at her curiously. Then the man put his hand out. It took Vivian a minute to understand. She took a twenty dollar bill out of her purse and handed it toward Elena. The man grabbed it from her, and continued to hold his hand out. Vivian found a ten and gave it to him.

"Es todo," she said firmly.

"Hasta manana," the man said at the door.

"No. No manana. Adios."

The man and the woman looked at each other and shrugged their shoulders, then walked to the old station wagon parked out front.

Vivian marched to the phone and dialed Walter's number.

"Sherman, this isn't going to work. Can't you find somebody who speaks English?"

"But Walter was very specific about that. Said he didn't want someone who would talk his business."

"Well, I'll speak to him about that. In the meantime, see what you can find."

Vivian hung up. She supposed Walter should have whatever kind of housekeeper he wanted. And, under the circumstances, privacy would be a big consideration. He would really have to explain about her leaving him with the baby. She wondered how he was going to work *that* into his little adoption scam. She knew it wouldn't take long for the word to get out that she'd left him. And she knew ugly words would be spoken about her for abandoning the young baby. That was really unfair. It wasn't her baby to abandon. The real mother deserved the rap for that.

Vivian took the newspaper and carried Passion to their spot on the Persian carpet. To her great dismay, the press conference had gotten coverage in the Metro section of the paper. As soon as she saw it, she set the answering machine to pick up at two rings. She listened to their voices—Karla, her sister, Cynthia. They all asked the same question—why didn't you tell us? There was silence from the one voice she was waiting to hear. She thought the picture of the three of them, Walter's hand on her shoulder, surely would bring the mother out of hiding immediately. Then she'd only have to tell one lie when she returned their calls. No matter what little ruse the woman had conjured up, Walter's very public lie had put that in check. She'd show up any minute now. Even that worried Vivian. She wondered what kind of life Passion would have with a mother who treated her with such callous disregard at a time when she was most vulnerable—and with Walter for a father.

"Poor little motherless child," she said to Passion as she took her to the tub for her bath. When she undressed her, she saw that the rashy place on her chest had grown worse, and had spread up to her neck. After the bath, while Passion was napping, she called the number Karla had given her for the doctor's office. The nurse wouldn't give her any information over the phone, but did give her an appointment for that afternoon.

* * * * *

The phone rang as Vivian was walking out the door. She was tempted to go on.

"Mrs. Carlson?" she heard on the answering machine.

She hesitated, then picked up the phone. "Yes?" she asked, her tone business-like, in response to the unfamiliar voice.

"Marc Kline."

"Who? Oh."

"I was wondering if you might have a few minutes this afternoon?"

"No. I was just leaving. Taking the baby to Dr. Hastings. So—"

"Is something wrong?" he asked, concern sounding in his voice.

"Well, of course, something's wrong. Why else would I take her to the doctor?" she asked impatiently.

"I'm sorry. It could have been for a check-up. I hope it's nothing serious."

"I'm not sure. I don't think so. I really don't know. Look, I've got to go. Did you talk to my husband? I'm sure he'll be happy to talk to you about all this."

"I'll do that. But I'd really like to get a woman's perspective. How about after the doctor's visit?"

"No. I plan to take the baby to the park. If she's well enough. Good-bye, Professor Kline."

Vivian didn't know why she'd said it. She had no such plan. And she wasn't prone to lying. Maybe Walter was rubbing off on her.

FOUR

All Vivian had wanted was for the doctor to look at the baby, tell her what was wrong, and how to fix it. She puzzled over the form the receptionist gave her to fill out. She didn't think all that was necessary, but the girl assured her that it was. So much information requested that she didn't know. Actually, about all she knew was her name—Passion Carlson. And address—12 Cedar Bend, Austin, Texas. So she filled that in. She thought of trying to make the answers up, just to move the ball forward, but rejected the idea. She wrote 'ADOPTED' in big letters diagonally across the form, then handed it to the receptionist. The young woman showed no emotion when she glanced at the clipboard.

Dr. Hastings was younger than Vivian expected, but had the mannerisms of a much older woman. She dressed dowdily and had a frank, no-nonsense style of speech. Vivian didn't like her. She had undressed Passion as instructed, and she lay squirming on the table. Dr. Hastings looked at the baby a minute, then at the clipboard.

"You didn't fill out any of the information," she said, looking at Vivian with disapproval.

"Well, uh, we adopted her. I wrote that on the form."

"If you weren't going to remember the information, why didn't you bring the Medical and Social History form they gave you at the adoption?"

"Uh, I, uh, I just forgot. I was so worried about the rash. Is it something serious?"

"Who is your regular pediatrician?"

"I don't have one. Look, can't you just tell me what's wrong with her?"

Owlish-looking through the thick glasses, Dr. Hastings stared at her long enough to make her feel uncomfortable, then pressed the button on the intercom and summoned the nurse.

"The nurse'll come in a minute. We'll run some tests. Next time bring the form."

She gave Vivian another long look of disapproval before walking out, her comfortable shoes making squishing sounds on the tile floor.

Passion screamed, when the nurse jabbed the needle into her. Vivian was on her feet in an instant, just in time to see her blood squirting into the vial. How could she hurt her like that! Before the nurse finished putting on the little round bandage, Vivian picked her up and petted her. She backed away from the nurse and rolled her eyes at her, while cooing softly to Passion.

"You can dress the baby, then take this form to the counter," the nurse instructed, before leaving with the vial of blood.

When Passion stopped crying, Vivian dressed her. At the counter, she expected to see Dr. Hastings, who would tell her how to cure the rash. Instead, it was the same girl she'd given the first form.

"That'll be $125.00 today, Mrs. Carlson. Did you want us to file on your insurance?" Now, she was smiling sweetly.

Vivian was dumbfounded. She didn't know any more than she knew before. And $125.00!

"But I don't know what's wrong with my baby!"

"Someone will call you in a couple of days," she said assuringly.

"Well, then I'll pay you in a couple of days. Send me a bill." She stormed out.

Vivian was so upset, she needed to sit down and collect herself. She remembered passing a coffee shop on the first floor on her way to the elevator. She realized she hadn't eaten. She'd just get a soft drink, maybe a sandwich. It was afternoon coffee-break time, so she stood in line among the uniforms—some white, some pink, some blue.

"The food's not the best here, but it'll pass—if you're really hungry."

Vivian turned around, then drew back when she recognized him.

"Are you following me?!"

"No. Of course not. The university is right there, you know," he said, pointing across the street. "This is the closest place to my office. That's how I know about the food. I eat here often. Get the roast beef sandwich. Or the avocado and bean spouts, if you're not into meat. The rest is kind of iffy." Vivian's anger melted at Marc's innocent smile.

"I'm sorry. I'm just upset. I shouldn't have taken it out on you. That—"

"Yeah, so what'd you want?" the man in the apron gruffly

interrupted.

"One roast beef sandwich and one avocado sandwich—cut 'em both in half. Two red sodas," Marc answered.

The line inched forward. By the time they got to the cashier, their order was waiting. He paid the cashier, then turned to Vivian.

"Let me carry the baby, you get the food. There's a nice little park a block from here. It's such a pretty day. And you were going to the park anyway." His brows were raised in a question mark.

Vivian remembered the lie she'd told. But if she actually went to the park, it wouldn't be a lie. And it *was* a pretty day. And having company wouldn't be bad. Somebody who already knew about Passion, so she wouldn't have to answer any questions...She snapped back to reality.

"This is just for your interview, isn't it?" she asked angrily.

"I won't ask you any questions," he said, holding both hands up in a gesture of surrender. "And if I do, it'll be off the record."

She believed his smile, and his eyes. She relinquished the carrier and picked up the white paper bag.

He was tall and had long legs, but walked at a pace that was comfortable for her. The trees were budding all along the walk. She brushed against the purple blossoms of a redbud tree, and then one covered with white blooms. She remembered spring, but it had been a long time since it had meant anything to her. How many seasons had she spent with her head in her books and her duty, never even noticing? For the last few years, the passing of the seasons had only meant a change of wardrobe for her.

"So, what did the doctor say?" he asked, as they turned onto the gravel path to the park.

"You weren't going to ask any questions," she said, reproachfully.

He laughed. "Off the record."

"Off the record? Nothing."

"Nothing?"

"Nothing. Except 'you owe me $125.00'," she said, with a pout on her lips.

He set the carrier on the picnic table so gently it didn't awaken Passion. Vivian opened the bag and handed him one of the soft drinks.

"Which sandwich do you want?" she asked.

"You pick. I'm easy."

"How 'bout half each?"

"That'll work. What's wrong with Passion?"

"Another question?"

"Off the record. Listen, let's get this straight. You know I really want to interview you for my book, but there *is* such a thing as journalistic ethics—even if it's hard to tell sometimes, these days. When you're ready, we'll do it in a formal way. In fact, I'll announce 'This is an interview,' probably into a tape recorder. OK?"

She eyed him warily.

"So what's wrong with your baby?"

She was reassured by the sincerity in his eyes.

"She has this rash on her chest. It's spreading."

"She doesn't look sick. What did the doctor say?"

"I told you. Nothing."

"Sounds like you need another doctor."

"Who do you use for your little boy?"

"Dr. Carrouthers. She's way south. She's good. What does it look like?"

"The rash? Bumps, you know. Red. I don't know. Here, look."

When Vivian unsnapped the jumpsuit, Passion jumped in her sleep, her arms clutching the air, but didn't wake. Marc looked at her, then ran his fingers across her chest. Vivian noticed he didn't wear a wedding ring.

"What formula are you giving her?" he asked.

"I don't know the name. The can has stripes on it."

"Why don't you change it? Corey had something like that. Some kind of allergy. We changed the formula to a soy-based one. It went away. How long have you been giving her this one?"

Vivian almost said, then became wary again. She didn't know what Walter had said about when they got the baby.

"Since we first got her." That was the truth.

"Did you get her at birth? What's she—two or three months old now?"

"Uh huh." Vivian grew uneasy. As she watched Marc eating the sandwich and washing it down with the soda, it appeared that he was only making conversation, not prying particularly. She supposed it was the kind of question anyone would ask under the circumstances. Still, she was leery.

"So where does your boy go to school?" she asked, changing the subject abruptly. "You said he was six?"

"Yeah. Six. First grade. My wife has him in a private school near where she works."

"You said that like you didn't have anything to do with it. Or that you disagree."

"Not really. He's real smart. And he can take advantage of

the academics that private school has to offer. But, I worry sometimes. You know, that he'll be the only one. Be different."

"You mean, because he's Black?"

"Well…yes. And that he'll get a false picture of the world.
That he won't learn how to get along with different kinds of
people. That he won't be tough enough."

"He'll do fine. I went to private schools. And I get along with
different kinds of people. And I'm pretty tough," she said with a
wink.

"But you were a girl. That's different. Anyway, she has the
right to choose. So that's that."

"Why? Because she's a woman? A mother? Isn't that a little
heavy? Don't you feel the father has some responsibility in those
kinds of decisions?"

"Of course I do, but the judge didn't. Well, I guess that's not
fair. It's in the decree, but I agreed to it. She loves him as much as
I do. And I know she's doing what she thinks is best for him. I
just worry, that's all."

She could see by the look on his face that he was indeed worried about it. She wondered if her father had worried that way
about sending her across town to the schools she'd attended. In
the sixties, she *was* literally the only one in her class—three in
the whole school. But she managed. Excelled, even. It hadn't
occurred to her that failing to meet her parents expectations was
an option. She could still hear her father saying, "I don't give a
damn whether those people like you or not. I'm not paying to
send you to a popularity contest."

When she had complained bitterly to him about one of the
teachers that she thought was prejudiced, his response had been

unsympathetic. "That's *her* problem. Now what's yours?" When she'd protested that it wasn't fair, he'd leaned over and in a sympathetic and conspiratorial tone said, "You think she's a racist, huh? You *really* want to gripe her ass? Keep her from sleeping at night?" Vivian had nodded eagerly. "Then make an A in her class!" he boomed.

That certainly wasn't the answer she'd expected. Her father had been right, as usual. Ms. Karchmier almost looked ill when she handed Vivian her report card at the end of the term with the A on it. Vivian could tell her ass was really griped, too. She never forgot that lesson. It stayed with her through many other Ms. Karchmiers—and some *Mr.* Karchmiers too, when she later learned that racism wasn't the only 'ism' she'd have to deal with.

"You could get him on one of the Greater East Austin football teams. For some balance. You know. Well, I guess it would be baseball this time of year."

"Where do they play?"

"How long have you lived here?" she asked, puzzled that he wasn't familiar.

"I moved here last summer."

"No wonder you don't know. I'll get a phone number for you. Where're you from?"

"I moved here from Atlanta. But I'm *from* a little town in central Georgia—Fort Valley."

"Why would you come *here*? Seems like all my friends are moving *to* Atlanta."

"My wife moved here right after the divorce. She got a job with one of those chip makers that Austin is becoming famous for. Accounting department. I was wearing myself out, and my wallet, flying and driving back and forth to keep up with my son. The university made me an offer I couldn't refuse," he said with a wry smile. "They were looking for 'minorities with credentials,' they said. I have a Ph.D. I'd been teaching at the university in Atlanta for about five years. And I'd written a couple of books. I fit the profile. So we're trying each other out for a year. After that, well…I don't know."

"What did you do before that?"

"I was a journalist. Worked for a newsmagazine for a while. Free-lanced for a while. Traveled the world. Covered the wars. That's what piqued my interest in adoption. International adoption. Our soldiers have made a lot of war, but they made a lot of love, too. The children who are the products of those liaisons have a really hard time of it. Now, there seems to be a growing movement in support of adoption. Bosnia's just the latest."

"Then there's no point in your interviewing me. My child is American." She was relieved to have an out.

"Well, that was just the catalyst. After I'd researched it for a while, I decided that the human interest aspect didn't dictate an international angle alone. There are lots of issues in domestic adoptions. Like the right of privacy for the birth parent, and how that, many times, conflicts with the adoptee's right, or I guess, desire, to know their history."

The shadow of a frown crossed Vivian's face as she thought of the implications of that in her situation, while Marc went on about developments on the Internet of web sites for the purpose of finding parents or children.

Passion stirred in the carrier. She opened her eyes and looked around. She whimpered until her eyes found Vivian. Satisfied, she closed her eyes and stretched her little body, yawning her mouth into an elongated O, eyes scrunched tight. When she opened her eyes again, she smiled.

"Look at that. She smiled! At you. I guess, you're really her mama."

Vivian smiled back at her, then picked her up.

"That's the first time she's done that." Vivian was a little amazed. At the same time, she wanted to say 'I'm not her mama.' She wondered if a real mama would feel all fuzzy inside like she did, looking at the baby smiling at her.

"Little girls are sweet," Marc said. "I always wanted one. But, I guess now it's too late."

"Why is it too late? You might have one, yet," Vivian answered, her eyes still focused on Passion.

"I'd sure have to get a move on. Most of my friends are grandfathers," he said, chuckling. "Can I hold her?"

"I guess," she said hesitantly.

"You're not going to be one of those over-protective mothers, are you?" he asked, teasing, as he took Passion from her.

Passion looked at him curiously, then gave him a smile, too. He held her up, then rocked her from side to side, cooing to her. Vivian was tempted to tell him to stop, but Passion was enjoying it. When he sat her in his lap, laying her in the crook of his arm, she put her fist in her mouth, and looked up at him, batting her eyes, almost flirting.

"She's gonna be a knock-out. Tell your husband he'd better start getting his shotgun ready now." He pushed his finger in Passion's stomach, and she giggled, still flirting.

Watching them play with each other, Vivian wondered again,

what kind of life Passion would have—after she left. A mother who'd abandoned her, and a father who ignored her. The thought made Vivian sad, but she couldn't get bogged down in that. Her plan for her own life was coming together. She supposed she had Passion to thank for that. There had been a vague plan in the back of her mind for a long time to leave Walter and get on with her life, but there never seemed to be a convenient time. Or comfortable. That was it, really. It had been more comfortable for her to stay. But now, it was different. Passion's coming into her life had given her a jump-start. She was mildly excited by the prospect of having her own place. A place Walter could never invade. She wouldn't take anything from the house. He could have it all. Just make a fresh start. Maybe she could find a furnished place.

"You live around here?" she asked.

"Not far. Why?"

"I just wondered if you knew what apartments were renting for in this area. And whether they come furnished." She looked at him expectantly.

"Well, I'd think one would be hard to come by until the end of the semester. Summer rates are better anyway. You looking for a place?"

She turned away from the probing in his eyes.

"No, a friend. I need to go. It's time for Passion's nap," she said, taking the baby from him and putting her in the carrier. "This was nice. I'm glad you suggested it." She hoped he didn't notice how flustered she was, and that she hadn't answered any of his questions.

"What's your rush? She just woke up. And she seems to be enjoying the sunshine—probably needs it." He looked at her quizzically, as she tucked the light blanket around the baby. Seeing her determination, he stood and picked the baby up.

"I'll bet she'd like to see something, other than the sky." He put her on his shoulder and carried her that way.

On the walk back to her car, seeing all the young people with backpacks reminded her that she still had to read the assignments for tomorrow's classes. But what would be the point? What if Sherman couldn't find a replacement for Elena on short notice? She really couldn't afford to miss any more classes. Maybe she should look herself. She'd call Karla when she got home. Then she remembered the lie she'd told her.

"You see your boy a lot?" she asked.

"As much as I can. I have a visitation schedule, but I get him other times too."

"What if you have something else to do when it's your time? Like a meeting or something?"

"That's only happened a few times. Mrs. Williams keeps him for me. I was really lucky. She was the first Black person I met here. The night after I moved here, they were having a retirement party for her. One of the professors I'd met invited me—so I could meet some people. She'd worked here at the university for 35 years. Everything from cook to dorm mother. At the end, they had given her some fancy title—probably in lieu of money. I liked her right off. She made me feel so welcome that I was sorry she was leaving. Not long after that, I was really in a jam, so I called her. She kept Corey for me that day—and several since. Corey loves her. She even cleans for me fairly regular, when I need it— and she has time. But she always has time for Corey. She's sort of adopted us both. She has me to dinner every Sunday."

"You think she'd keep Passion for me? Tomorrow? Just for a few hours."

"I could call her and see."

"Could I call her? It's kind of an emergency."

"Sure. I'll give you her number. Tell her you're my friend," he said, smiling down at her.

He strapped Passion into the car seat, then took out a card and wrote the number for her.

"You're going to call me with that other number, right?" he asked.

"Number?"

"About the baseball."

"Oh. Yes. I'll do that. Thanks for lunch. I owe you one."

"I'll look forward to it," he said softly.

As Marc watched her drive away, he realized he'd enjoyed the outing more than anything he'd done since he came to Austin. She was one of the few people he'd met outside the university circle. He thought maybe he should get out more. Maybe Allison had been right about him. Too bad Vivian was married, he thought. He would have asked her for a date. He hadn't had one since he moved. Not that he couldn't. He just hadn't wanted to. He'd had the usual come-ons from the single professors, but they were, to a one, White. Even if they hadn't been, he'd seen enough at the college in Atlanta to know that mixing one's love life with one's professional life—especially in the stewpot of campus politics—could be deadly. The week he moved to Austin, lawsuits against two of the professors for sexual harassment were front page news. He guessed those guys never learned 'you don't get your honey, where you get your money.' Or maybe they were the victims of unfair accusations by women without principles. Whatever. He'd kept a polite and professional distance. He had no trouble resisting the charms of the young coeds, batting their mascaraed eyelashes at him and stroking his ego. A woman twenty years his junior couldn't hold his interest beyond the physical release. Then what? Nothing but trouble.

He'd done some of the touristy things suggested by his colleagues, taking Corey to the LBJ Library and the ranch at Johnson City, and a quick tour one night down Sixth Street by himself. Outside of that, he'd kept himself absorbed in his research and writing.

Walking the manicured campus back to his office reminded him of what he liked about teaching. It was such a peaceful atmosphere. In the sixties, when he'd been a student, the campuses had been full of protests of one kind or another. And he'd participated in his share of them. The students of the nineties seemed complacent to him, cowed in a way. More interested in positioning themselves, than in issues. More attuned to the what and the how, than the why. He felt sorry for them. Didn't like them, really. Maybe it was his age. In any case, the environment suited him, for now.

* * * * *

On the drive home, Vivian felt buoyant. If Mrs. Williams would keep Passion tomorrow, maybe that would give Sherman time to come up with somebody for Walter, and give her time to go apartment hunting. She would *really* owe Professor Kline one. She wondered what had happened to his marriage. He was so unlike Walter. She couldn't imagine he and his wife would have had the kind of relationship she and Walter had. He seemed so concerned about his kid. What had he done that the woman left him? Must have been something, she mused. Maybe he'd gotten involved with a student. She could see how one would be attracted to him. His body, and the age of his son, made the gray streak on top of his head seem premature. She wondered how old he was. Thirty-five? Forty-five? Could have been either.

Vivian was relieved that Walter's car was not in the driveway. She hadn't expected it to be. She changed Passion. She was soaked, but uncomplaining—as though she was patient with Vivian's learning how to be a mother. Vivian gave her a bottle, and put her to bed. She called Sherman first. Nothing yet, but he was working on it. Then she took the card from her purse and dialed the number.

"Mrs. Williams?"

"Yes?"

"My name is Vivian Carlson. A mutual friend gave me your number. Professor Kline?"

"Yes?"

"I'm in a bit of a fix. I have a, ah, three-month old baby, and my sitter, ah, quit suddenly. Family emergency. I'm a student at the university. The Law School. I've already missed a week, and I can't miss any more classes. Professor Kline said you might be willing to help me out. By keeping her?"

"Aw, honey. I wish I could. But Wednesday is my grocery day."

"Please, Mrs. Williams. She's a good baby. She really is. She won't be any trouble. Just for, maybe four hours, in the morning. I'm really desperate, Mrs. Williams."

"Well, I suppose if you can't find *anybody* else…"

"No ma'am. I'm *really* at the end of my rope."

"I been there, honey," she said, chuckling. "If you're a friend of Marc's, you just bring that lil' baby by here around eight."

Vivian slumped on the stool, and exhaled. She could get through another day.

FIVE

Passion was kicking her before the alarm went off. It was almost as if she knew there would be an adventure this day, and she didn't want either of them to miss a minute of it. Vivian snapped to, pushed the button on the clock to keep it from sounding, and pulled playfully at Passion's little foot. She quickly showered and dressed. She bathed Passion, gave her a bottle, then dressed her in her cutest outfit. She hurriedly combed her own hair, pulling it into a bun at her nape—no time to fool with the curling wand. Then, she parted Passion's, and brushed as much of it as she could into a puff ball and tried to clip it in a barrette. Wouldn't work. The soft, curly hair kept crawling out on the sides, making her look like a clown. Finally, Vivian used the big comb to fluff it into a little Afro, then put the elastic headband on her.

"Don't you look cute?" Vivian smiled.

On the ride to the Eastside, Vivian talked to Passion. "Now you really need to act nice today. I think you'll like Mrs. Williams. She sounded nice over the phone. And it'll only be for a few hours."

Passion looked at her out of bright eyes. Eager eyes. Almost like she understood. She moved her mouth as though she was answering Vivian, but only 'ou-u-u's came out. Vivian drove slowly down the street until she came to the house.

The lawn was meticulously groomed. Yellow and purple irises bloomed in the flower beds, close to the white clapboard house. When Mrs. Williams opened the door, Vivian was surprised at the woman's stature. It didn't match her voice. She guessed she'd expected a short, fat woman because he'd said 'cook.'

Cora Williams was tall and dark—almost regal, in the flowing, African-print housedress. Her gray hair was cut in a medium length Afro. It had taken a lot to persuade her to the style. A dare, really. In response to his announcement that he was quitting school, she'd dared the young firebrand to tough it out, to stay and get his degree, despite the unwelcoming, even hostile, atmosphere on the campus. She knew he had what it took. In the fiery speech of his budding Black Nationalism, he returned her dare— 'Let go of that hot comb, sister.'

Sheepishly defiant, she was wearing the new style the next day when he came through the serving line in the dormitory cafeteria. She still wore it when she attended his graduation several years later—every bit as proud as his mama. She still wore it twenty-five years later because it was too easy, in a life full of hard, to do anything else.

"You must be Vivian," she said, reaching for the baby. "She's a pretty lil' thing. You are too. Come on in."

Vivian followed her into the impeccably neat living room. Didn't look like a baby kind of a place. Passion took to Mrs. Williams right off, doing her flirting thing.

"I'm glad Marc found a friend. It's 'bout time. He's sho' nuff a good-looking man. But he's a good man, too—and that's what counts," she said, smiling at Vivian and taking the bag from her. "You be good to him. Now what time are you gonna be back? Me and this baby got some running around to do."

Vivian wanted to correct her. To tell her that Marc wasn't the kind of friend she had in mind. But the important thing at that moment, was that she felt comfortable leaving Passion with her. So she left it like it was.

"Is noon OK?" Vivian asked, wondering if she would have time to scour the area for an apartment after her class.

"Did I say I have my church ladies meeting at noon? We meet at the cafeteria in the shopping center. They're gonna love this sweet thing. We'll be back around two. Anytime after that."

"Thank you, Mrs. Williams. I *really* appreciate it."

"Glad to do it, honey. I was a single mom, too."

* * * * *

Driving through the side streets of the Eastside, Vivian wondered why she hadn't told Mrs. Williams that she wasn't single— or a mom. Then she thought, she was one of those—maybe both. She realized that the night before, she hadn't had a thought of waiting up for Walter. She and Passion had gone about their routine as though he wasn't expected, wasn't even a part of their world.

* * * * *

The class was boring, as usual, the professor droning on and on. But she had read the assignment, and she followed along. When he abruptly turned to the sparsely attended class, and directed a question to Vivian, she stood and answered directly. He looked disappointed, although her answer was correct and on point. Another Karchmier, she thought ruefully. As he dismissed the class, he called her to the front.

"Ms. Carlson, you know I frown on students missing class. And you have missed more than a week."

Vivian thought about how more than half the students who were there the first day weren't there that day, or most days.

"I know, but I've kept up with the reading assignments. I had an emergency."

"I'm sorry to hear that. Nevertheless, the law is a jealous mistress, and the study of law must take precedence over everything. The trouble with you girls is, you think if a kid scrapes a knee, everything else has to wait. It's not like that in the real world. I don't tolerate 'no-shows' in my class. I turned in a withdrawal slip on you Monday. If you intend to remain in this class, you must go to the administration building and work it out—if it's not too late."

Although she was calm on the outside, Vivian was panicked inside. This was her last semester, and she didn't have time to repeat a class. Hadn't she answered the question correctly? Didn't that show she had kept up? What the hell did he want from her? This pasty-faced white-haired old man had no idea all the balls she was juggling. But if she had to walk all the way across the campus to the administration building, to hell with him. She'd do that, too.

* * * * *

It was a warm day, and she felt beads of perspiration forming on her forehead when she finally reached the infamous tower that housed the administrative offices. On the way, she'd geared way up for a big fight. All the work-study girl wanted to know was her intention. She had to put it on a form. Vivian rolled her eyes heavenward. 'Lord, give me a break.' She quietly explained that she'd had a family emergency, that she fully intended to complete the course. She watched as the girl checked some squares on the three-part form. She handed Vivian the pink copy and instructed her to give it to the professor.

As Vivian trudged back across the campus in the heat of the Texas spring, she looked at her watch and frowned. The extra time she thought she would have had evaporated. She picked up her pace, her walk determined.

"Looks like you're the one following *me*."

Vivian was startled to hear the familiar voice. She turned around and looked up at him.

"Hello to you, too. And I am *not* following you."

"Then what are you doing here? Looking for a lunch date?" Marc asked with an amused smile.

"Not hardly. It's a long story. And I don't have time to tell it," she said, in an exasperated tone, looking at her watch again.

"Well, why don't you treat me to lunch, and tell me about it. You owe me one, remember?"

Vivian took in a deep breath and let it go.

"I owe you more than that. Mrs. Williams is keeping Passion for me today. I like her. I really appreciate you giving me her number. I don't know what I would have done. I couldn't miss any more classes."

"Do you teach?"

"No. Student. At the Law School. Third year."

"Wow. I'm impressed. I hear it's really tough. But, why on earth would you pick this time to adopt a baby?"

"The time picked me," she said, shaking her head. When she saw the curious look in his eyes, she hurried on, "I mean, sometimes, well uh, you know, 'the best laid plans' and all that." She gave him a weak smile.

"Well, what about it?" he asked, his eyebrows raised.

"What about what?"

"Lunch."

"I, uh, don't have time. I've got to be at Mrs. Williams at two. Another time, maybe."

"But it's only 12:15. That's plenty of time. I heard about a place I want to try—Catfish Station. You heard of it?"

"Best catfish in town. You'll enjoy it."

"Good. Come on."

"But, really, I've got to—"

"Aw, come on," he insisted, taking her by the elbow. She relented, allowing him to lead her to his car.

The black Volvo station wagon didn't have a speck of dust on it. The front seats were clean, but the back seat had permanent-looking passengers—boxes and piles of books, folders and papers.

"My filing cabinet," he said laughing, when he noticed her looking askance at the mess. "I know where every piece of paper is. Really."

Vivian was unconvinced.

* * * * *

Marc had to circle the block several times before giving up and parking a couple of blocks away.

"You have to order at the window," she said leading him, once they were inside. "The two-piece dinner is enough for me.

No, wait, I'll have three pieces and take one home for my dinner." He ordered two of those.

"None for your husband?" he asked.

"Oh, he won't be there." She saw the one raised eyebrow. "I mean, he has a lot of late meetings. He's in the middle of a re-election campaign. He'll probably eat while he's out," she said, sitting in the chair he held out for her.

"No warm plate waiting on the back burner for a man after a long day's work?" He'd seen her stumble, then recover. His curiosity spiked.

Vivian's eyes glazed momentarily as she remembered when she used to do that, tolerating her own hunger to wait for him. She also remembered when she stopped.

"They have good jazz here. Live. At night," she said, changing the subject.

"I came down to this area once last Fall. It was run over with college kids and drunks. I didn't know about this place then. Maybe I'll come back."

The jazz playing over the speakers was interrupted as their number was called. They scooted their chairs back simultaneously.

"Let me get it," he said. "After all, I invited you."

"No. I owe you one."

"Now you owe me two," he said, walking away.

He'd taken off his sports coat and draped it around the back of the chair. She saw that it was dragging on the dusty concrete floor and picked it up. She folded it in half, and laid it across the other chair. From the feel of the jacket, she could tell he was a size or two larger than Walter. Watching him at the window, she noticed how broad his shoulders were. The white dress shirt fit close enough to show the outline of his muscles, and tapered to his waist. He had a dip at the back of his waist, like most Black men. She could tell he'd had the pants altered, by the absence of the tucks and bunches under the belt. When he started back toward her with the food, she saw just a hint of fullness around his middle, and decided 'forty-five.'

"I brought you a take-out container—for your dinner," he said, setting the dishes on the table and taking his seat. They ate for a while in silence.

"This *is* good. I'll definitely be back. So what made you go to Law School?"

"It's a long story. I'd always planned to do it. But first one thing, then another got in the way."

"Like what?"

"Well, for a long time, I wanted a baby. But that never happened," she said wistfully. "Then I gave up."

He recognized the pain in her eyes.

"Did you go through all the stuff? The temperature thing? The dye tests and all?"

She nodded.

"How do you know about all that?" she asked, surprised.

"Been there, done it. It was a real roller coaster ride too. You get your hopes all up, then nothing. Each test showed nothing. So you go after it again. More nothing. More insecurity about yourself. It causes a lot of strain. Then your friends all start having babies, and you have nothing to talk about with them."

She nodded as he spoke. The emotion on his face, more than the words, told her he'd walked through that valley.

"So did you adopt your little boy?"

"We talked about adoption, but didn't pursue it very far. We were so worn out from the trying. And the strain on my marriage was beginning to show. We started talking about divorce. The infertility didn't cause it, it only accentuated a lot of incompatibility. We just shut it down. Quit trying. Tried to forget the whole thing. Then she got pregnant."

"That's what people kept telling me. Just forget about it. Quit trying. Then it'll happen. But it didn't."

"So you decided to adopt?"

"Years ago. I wanted to. But my husband didn't."

"What changed his mind?"

Looking into his warm brown eyes, Vivian had the urge to tell him the truth, but thought better of it.

"Well, enough of this depressing stuff. What's Fort Valley like? Is that it, Fort Valley?"

"It's a small town. Has a state college. Fort Valley State University—second largest in the University of Georgia system. They make Bluebird busses there, too. It's mostly agricultural, though. The peach capital of the world. Lot of cotton and soybeans, too. I grew up on a farm. The middle of six kids. I couldn't wait to get off that farm. And I did, soon as I could. Funny though, I miss it now. Been thinking of retiring there. I don't know. Maybe nostalgia has replaced the memories of how much work it was. Anyway, my folks are getting on in years, and all my brothers and sisters are there, so I've been thinking about it. But enough about me. What about you? Where'd you grow up? Here?"

"Fort Worth. I came here for college and first one thing, then another. I'm still here," she said, shrugging her shoulders.

"'First one thing, then another' seems to rule your life."

It took her a minute to catch it. "Seems like it," she laughed.

"You should laugh more often." His fingers were laced together, thumbs under his chin, elbows on the table, his eyes fixed on her.

Vivian didn't know how to respond. It didn't really sound like a pass. And she couldn't believe he would make a pass at her. He didn't seem like the type. And he knew she was a married woman. Maybe she should be flattered. She hadn't thought of herself as a wanted woman in longer than she could remember. She'd been the wife for so long. The obliging wife. The taken-for-granted wife. She tried to remember what she'd been like before, when she had been young. And free. And her own person, with life gloriously unfolding before her. What had it felt like to be pursued? To have a man appreciate something about her, to touch her, exploring, for the first time? But it had been too long. She couldn't remember. She wouldn't look at him for fear he would read her thoughts in her eyes.

"We'd better go," she said, looking at her watch and reaching for her purse.

Marc smiled when he saw she was flustered. He hadn't meant it that way. Then he thought, maybe he did. She *was* good-looking. He wondered why she always looked so worried, and why she was always in such a hurry. She looked like she had reached the age she should be kicking back and enjoying life. The age where women became sure of themselves, of who they are, and where they are going. He stood and followed her to the door.

When they reached the corner, the signal light held them.

"I didn't mean to embarrass you," he said.

"Embarrass?" she asked, feeling heat on the tops of her ears.

"I'm not em—"

"Say lady, got some spare change?"

As Vivian turned her head in the opposite direction to the dirty, smelly man in the grungy blue coat standing by her side, too close, she heard Marc say gruffly, "You need to get a spare job, brother."

The man took off in a trot across the street, as she turned back to Marc, wide-eyed and frowning.

"I can't believe you said that! That poor man is probably a veteran. You know, not everybody is as fortunate as you and I have been."

The light changed and she started across the street in a huff. Marc was non-plussed by her reaction. He caught up with her as she reached the other curb.

"You don't even know him. He's just a lazy slob who won't get off his ass and work for what he wants."

She rolled her eyes at him and walked across the side street. He followed.

"How could you be so mean to another human being?! No one would live like that if they had a choice. And what's a couple of quarters to a college professor?! Nothing. It wouldn't have meant anything to you. That's less than the tip you left at the restaurant—where you had to serve yourself. There wasn't even a waiter to tip!"

"And so what are *you*?! His social worker?! He'd just go buy some wine. You know, you're pretty naive, for an aspiring lawyer. The sharks are gonna eat you alive, lady."

She stopped and glared at him. There were so many words in her mouth, they crowded each other and none could get out. She shook her head and started off again. They walked the next block in silence. Vivian wouldn't even look at him, as she marched toward the car. She thought of Walter. She could hear him saying the same things. Arrogant fool. Like he'd never needed any help. Had done it all by himself.

Vivian heard rapid footfalls and sensed the presence, just before she felt herself being jerked backwards by the shoulder strap of her purse. She reflexively pulled at the purse, then released it to break her fall. In that surreal moment, when she hit the pavement, she saw a flash of grungy blue. It was like watching a movie, running in slow motion. She heard the screams from the woman who had been walking toward them. She saw people coming out of the restaurants in response. In a daze, she watched Marc sprinting after the man. He leaped and tackled him, both of them falling to the ground. The man scrambled to his feet and started off, but Marc was up and after him in an instant. He grabbed him by the neck from behind, swung him around and slammed him against the building. She saw Marc's mouth moving, but couldn't hear what he said, as he twisted the man's arm up behind his back, pushing him against the wall. The woman was still screaming. A policeman skidded up on a bicycle, jumped off, and put handcuffs on the man as Marc stepped back. When Marc looked at her sprawled on the sidewalk, he hurried to her.

"Are you hurt?" he asked, pulling her to her feet.

"I'm OK. I'm fine. I think. I don't know," she said in a trembly voice, as she fell against his chest. She could feel herself shaking, but couldn't will her body to be still. She felt his strong arms surround her. Marc held her until the siren from the police car approaching made her draw back.

"Where's my purse?! That bastard took my purse!" she said pulling away from him and turning in the direction of the snatcher.

"The cop has it. Hold on," he said, pulling her back. "Where're you going?"

"I've got something to say to that...that—"

"Just wait a minute. They'll probably want to take your statement."

"I've got a statement alright!" She watched the policeman approaching, his muscular thighs well-defined in the black shorts. He pushed the helmet up slightly just as he reached her.

"You the victim, ma'am?"

"Yes. That's my purse."

"Fill out this form," he said, handing it to her, and a pen. "You'll need to go to the station first thing in the morning—theft detail—to get the purse."

"Can't I just kick him in the stomach, you give me my purse, and we call it even?" Vivian asked impatiently. "I need my purse."

He eyed her strangely, still holding out the paper and pen toward her. She heard Marc chuckling. When she cut her eyes at him, he instantly straightened his face.

"You have any identification?" the cop asked.

Vivian rolled her eyes and crimped her mouth. "Everything I have is in the purse." He pushed the helmet farther up, and scratched at his hairline with his thumb.

"Why don't you look in the purse for her driver's license," Marc suggested. "Compare the picture. Would that be enough?"

The cop thought about it a minute.

"It's in the side compartment." Vivian offered.

He found the driver's license, looked at her, then handed her the purse. When she finished the form, she handed it back to him.

"Theft detail," he reminded her. "First thing in the morning. Have a nice day."

Watching him ride off on the bike, Vivian remembered her mother saying 'you know you're getting old when the cops start looking like kids.' She was right.

When she turned back to Marc, she saw the chuckle tugging at the corners of his mouth.

"So you think this is funny?!" Vivian's entire posture shouted indignation.

"Who me? No-o-o. Not me," he said, with a look of feigned innocence, and clearly fighting back a laugh. "I just can't believe that you would kick a poor, unfortunate veteran in the stomach—and in front of a cop."

When she swung the purse and clunked him in the back with it, the dam broke. It started with a chuckle in his belly, then grew to heaving proportions. His laughter filled their corner of the street. She tried to suppress the smile, but couldn't. She started laughing, too. Before the moment spent itself, they were both holding their stomachs and wiping their eyes.

Marc noticed the passersby, who had missed the precipitating commotion, watching them curiously. "Whew! Come on. Let's go, before the cops come back and haul us both off to the funny farm."

* * * * *

When Marc turned east from the freeway that served as 'the tracks' dividing the city, she turned to look at him.

"Where're you going?"

"Didn't you say you had to be at Cora's at two?" he asked.

"Yes. But—"

"You don't want to be too late. That won't make a good impression," he said, pointing at the clock on the dash. 2:15. "And besides, I know you're anxious to see your baby."

Vivian hadn't thought about Passion most of the day. So much had happened to her that had no connection to Passion. She had been so comfortable with Mrs. Williams, that that particular worry had been pushed back in the line behind the others. She imagined that a *real* mother would have had her baby on her mind the entire time. As they walked up to the door, she *was* anxious to see Passion. To see her face light up in that way that said she was delighted to see her.

"I'll bet Cora'll keep her the rest of the week—if you ask her real nice," he said, as he rang the doorbell.

"That would be wonderful. Would give my husband's aide time to find a suitable sitter. That reminds me, I need to call Sherman and see if he's made any progress."

Marc eyed her curiously, but the sound of locks being turned kept him from asking his question. Cora pushed the screen door open to let them in.

"Lord ha' Mercy! What happened to you two? Come on in. And don't wake up the baby."

Marc and Vivian looked at each other, both noticing for the first time how rumpled and dirty the other was. They both suppressed giggles.

"Vivian tried to kick a poor old veteran in the stomach, but me and the cops stopped her," Marc said, matter-of-factly.

Cora looked at Vivian, as though she couldn't believe what she'd heard. When she turned back to Marc for confirmation, the crook of his smile told her he was teasing.

"That's not what happened at all!" Vivian said, indignantly. "A bum snatched my purse, and knocked me down!"

"Oh, he's a bum now?!" he said, laughing aloud.

"Shush, boy. Keep your voice down. You're gonna wake the baby. Ya'll come on out back. I was just having a glass of iced tea."

"Can I use your phone a minute?" Vivian asked.

"Sure, baby. Use the one in the front bedroom," she said, pointing. "We'll be out on the patio. When you finish come on out, through the kitchen."

Vivian heard Cora asking Marc about Corey, as she went to find the phone.

"Sherman, did you find somebody to keep the baby?" … "Not til Monday?!" … "Well, what's on Walter's calendar for the rest of the week?" … "Humph." … "No, I do *not* want to talk to him." … "Thanks, but I can't bring the baby up there. You'd be too busy to see about her. I'll call you tomorrow."

As Vivian hung the phone up, she caught a glimpse of her face in the dresser mirror, forehead in a knot, mouth in a grim set. She practiced her smile. When she started out of the room, she wondered where Passion was. She walked down the hallway, past the bathroom, and peeked into the other bedroom. Passion was sleeping peacefully, her fist at her mouth. Vivian smiled a real smile. She was tempted to walk over and touch her, but remembered Cora's warning. She turned and found the kitchen.

When she opened the back door, she caught her breath. A profusion of spring color burst before her eyes. There were flowers blooming everywhere. The yard looked like a tropical paradise. Two huge pecan trees served as a canopy, and palms and banana trees were strategically placed. On closer examination, Vivian saw that the riot of color was actually a well-planned series of beds, some raised, others bordered and flush with the ground. She walked down the brick walkway that led to the parquet patio where they sat, Marc in a swing and Cora in a glider chair, with her feet propped on a small stool. In the flowing housedress, Cora looked like a queen being entertained by her court.

"I love this!" Vivian said, sitting next to Marc. "I don't think I've ever seen anything this beautiful," Marc handed her a glass of tea, garnished with lemon and a sprig of mint.

"I do, too," Cora said. "I spend most of my time out here. Watching my birds," Cora said.

Vivian turned in the direction that Cora had nodded. A large masonry birdbath, surrounded by blooms at its base, sat in the center of a small lawn. A bevy of small birds were splashing around in it. A feeder hung from one of the pecan tree's low branches. Farther on at the back of the small yard, Vivian saw a row of raised beds that she assumed were used for vegetable gardening.

"I can see why. It's very peaceful. Did you do all this yourself?"

"Heavens, no," Cora said, laughing. "My two boys did all the heavy work. Put in the patio and the walkways, the raised beds. In their spare time. You should have seen all the dirt they hauled in here. Truckloads. They have a landscape service together, so it didn't cost them too much. I got the idea when I was in Jamaica. Marc, did I tell you they sent me to Jamaica for my retirement present?"

"Yes, you did, Cora. Showed me the pictures, too. More than once. Remember?"

"I'd never been out of Texas before that. I loved it. I wanted to stay there. But, of course, I couldn't. Even if I sold the house. I guess they got tired of me talking about it—and showing them my pictures," she said, cutting her eyes at Marc. "I do all the flowers though. I have something blooming nearly all year round. Most of what you see now are bulbs. But soon, they'll bring me trays and trays of different kinds of flowers. They're good boys. Really take care of their mama."

"You'll have to give me their number" Vivian said. "I'd like to talk to them about some work at my house." Then she remembered she wouldn't be there long enough for that. "How'd Passion do today? I hope she wasn't any trouble."

"Chile, that's the sweetest baby. We had a good time. I think I wore her out. And the ladies at lunch fell in love with her. They just kept passing her around, from lap to lap. Even ol' Mrs. Daniels insisted on her turn. She's in a wheelchair now. And what kind of food have you been giving that baby? She ate like a little pig! I hope she doesn't have a tummy ache."

"Food? What kind of food? Is she supposed to have food?" Vivian asked, alarmed. Not because Cora had given her food, but because she hadn't. She wondered if that was why Passion needed so many bottles.

"I'll bet you've been giving her that ol' jar food," Cora said laughing. "She's not going to want that stuff anymore."

Marc noticed the look on Vivian's face. "Your call? Did you find a sitter?"

"Uh, no. He can't, uh, send anybody before Monday."

"Cora, what are you doing the next couple of days? Could you keep Passion through Friday?"

"Sure. I can do that. If something comes up, I'll take her with me. She travels easy."

"You just don't know how much I would appreciate that, Mrs. Williams."

"Honey, call me Cora. Only thing is, why don't you pick her up later—around four or five. So she can get her nap out. And I'll bet you could use the time to study."

"That would be perfect." Vivian looked at her watch. "I think I'll go check on her."

When Vivian got to the bedroom, Passion was awake and looking around. When she saw Vivian, she broke into a big grin, and started kicking her legs, rubbing her feet together. Vivian was about as happy to see her. She changed her, then took her outside to join the others. When they sat in the swing next to Marc, Passion surveyed her surroundings, looking from Marc to Cora. When Marc poked her in the stomach, she grabbed his finger.

"Cora, we'd better be going. We've both got to prepare for classes tomorrow. Thanks for everything," Marc said, standing to leave.

"And we'll see you about eight-thirty. Is that OK?" Vivian asked.

"I'll be waiting," Cora said, giving Passion a kiss on the cheek, then showed them to the door.

When they reached her car on 26th Street near the campus, Marc took Passion and strapped her in the car seat. "So, how about lunch tomorrow? Since you'll be free."

"I'd better not. I need the time in the library. Thanks anyway."

"You'll have to eat lunch. It may as well be with me. I promise not to let anybody snatch your purse."

She returned his smile. "Thanks, but I won't forget that I owe you a lunch. Two," she said smiling, as she started the engine.

* * * * *

Later, when Passion began whimpering for her bottle, Vivian found the jars of baby food she'd bought. The teaspoon was too large, but Passion clearly wanted what was on it. Together, they made a big mess. Vivian carried her to the dining room, and held her on her hip while she searched through the china cabinet. She finally found the little spoons to the demitasse set. They went through one jar and were halfway through another before Passion lost interest. When Vivian changed her for bed, she noticed the rash was going away. She made a note to thank Marc for advising her to change the formula.

Vivian was studying in bed, Passion snuggled beside her asleep, when she heard Walter's car pull into the garage. She got up and closed the door to their room and turned off the light. She heard the whirring sound of the garage door lowering, the sound of the refrigerator opening, then closing, then footsteps coming down the tiled hallway. They stopped outside her room. Then silence. She held her breath until she heard the footsteps leaving. The next sound she heard was ice clinking in a glass.

SIX

Thursday morning, Passion seemed excited to see Cora, and Cora was happy to see her. Vivian was happy about it all because she could attend class and give it her full attention. She even had time, after class, to read her assignment for the next day. Then she scoured the university newspaper for rentals. Marc had been right, most of them were for summer. She wrote down numbers to the few that were available immediately. She drove by and wasn't impressed. Not that she needed anything fancy, just clean and quiet. If it was near campus she wouldn't have to fool with parking the car, she could take the shuttle bus and use the riding time to study. Then she thought, she'd need the car anyway to get Passion to Cora's house.

Vivian was startled, to have thought about having the baby with her. Walter's baby wasn't part of her plan. That thought seemed strange to her, too. She no longer thought of Passion as Walter's baby. She certainly didn't think of her as *her* baby. Or did she? No. She was just the caretaker until Walter worked something out. Then, she'd be free.

Now, Vivian thought of how accustomed she was to being

awakened by the little foot kicking her. She knew she would miss her little alarm clock—at first. That would pass. But, what would Passion think, if she wasn't there? Would she think she had abandoned her too? Would she miss her? Would she cry? Vivian shook her head, hard, to clear it. She didn't want to think about it. She felt the growling in her stomach and realized she hadn't eaten. She remembered Marc's lunch invitation. He was wrong. She didn't *have* to eat lunch. She had accomplished a lot, even if only by way of elimination. She'd have to broaden her search tomorrow. She no longer had to be concerned about the boundaries of Walter's district. She could live anywhere she wanted.

Vivian called Sherman from the phone in her car. "Any news?"

"Not yet. I haven't been able to find a soul. And Walter is adamant about non-English speaking. I'm afraid the only connection I had there was not appreciative about what happened before."

Vivian wasn't appreciative of the censure in his voice. It crossed her mind that Walter might be instructing Sherman to make this difficult for her. She wouldn't put it past him. He'd been decidedly unexcited about her returning to law school.

"Put Walter on the phone," she demanded. It was time for a show-down.

"I'm sorry, Vivian. He's gone for the day."

"Gone? Gone where?"

"He didn't say. The other line is ringing, and Carolyn left early. Gotta go."

Something in Sherman's tone put her off. She couldn't put her finger on it. It occurred to her that Sherman hadn't asked her one question about the baby. Hadn't even congratulated her. That didn't set right. Wasn't like him. Obviously he wasn't buying the adoption scam. Maybe he knew the truth.

When Cora opened the door, Passion on her hip, she said, "Girl, you look like you got the world on your shoulders. What's wrong?"

Vivian put on her practiced smile. "It's nothing."

"Nothing sure looks heavy. You want to talk about it? Sometimes it helps."

Looking into Cora's kind eyes, Vivian was tempted to spill the whole story. It *was* heavy. *Too* heavy. Too big a weight to carry inside herself, and she didn't feel she could carry it much longer without telling somebody. She had avoided her usual sources of strength—her sister, her mama, Cynthia. She didn't have answers for them. And with each day that passed, she had fewer answers.

"I appreciate your asking. It's just something I have to deal with. It'll work out," Vivian said, with a weak smile.

"Put your trust in the Lord, honey. He'll help you," Cora said softly. "He may not move your mountain, but He'll give you the strength to climb it. Just ask Him.

"I'll do that, Cora. Thanks," she said, taking the eager Passion and heading for the car.

* * * * *

On the ride home, Passion talked to her, making the 'ou-u-u' sounds. Vivian talked to her, too.

"What we gonna do, little girl? I can't take you with me. You're just gonna have to find another mama. Don't look at me like that. I told you in the beginning, I wouldn't be around long."

Cora's words came to mind. She remembered she had prayed

that God move a mountain for her once. The mountain didn't move. She supposed He *had* granted her the strength to climb it. She'd survived. Adelma had been her stalwart support, through the tests, through the let-downs, through it all. They were only two years apart, and were best friends, as well as sisters. They'd played dolls together, had planned to play babies together. Only, Vivian couldn't play. Adelma had done her part—three boys in close succession, then one trailing several years behind. Before she was conscious of what she was doing, Vivian was turning on Adelma's street. The big van was there, so she knew Del was home.

"Aunt Viv!" she heard as she put the brake on. Before she finished hugging Robby, he asked his perennial three-year old question, "You got some bubble gum?"

"I might have some in my purse. Go tell your mama I'm here, while I look for it." Off he ran.

By the time she got Passion out of the car seat, her sister was coming out of the front door, wiping her hands on a dish towel.

"I wondered how long it would take you. Oh, Viv. She's the prettiest little thing. Come to your auntie," she said, reaching for Passion.

Passion looked from Adelma to Vivian and back, then reached for the earrings that were identical to the ones Vivian wore. Their father had given them each a pair in gift-wrapped boxes with no names on them the Christmas before he died. As he did every Christmas, he'd made a game of having them choose which of the identical boxes they wanted. Both of them wore the earrings every day.

"And she looks just like Walter. Come on in and tell me all

about it. It must have been a long drawn-out process. The adoption and all. How could you keep this a secret? My feelings are hurt you didn't tell me about it first. Then, I figured you didn't want to get all our hopes up, in case it didn't work out. Seems like everybody I know who tried to adopt has a horror story—"

Vivian didn't hear much past the first sentence. She felt like she was going to burst while Del was going on and on, in the wrong direction. She didn't know how to tell her, what to say.

"You find my bubble gum, Aunt Viv?" Robby asked meeting them at the door.

"Sure, baby. Let me look in this ol' purse."

"Why are you crying, Aunt Viv? Bubble gum is happy. This your new baby, Aunt Viv?"

She heard Del's voice, "Go look in that drawer by my sewing machine, Robby. There's some gum in there. Then go watch TV for a while." She felt Del taking her hand, leading her to her bedroom. She heard the door close. She couldn't see through the tears, as Del, still holding Passion, gently pushed her on the bed and sat beside her. She felt Del's arm around her, and Passion's little hand touch her face.

"It's OK to cry, Viv. It's a little overwhelming at first. Having a new baby and all. It'll pass," she said soothingly, patting her shoulder. "They take so much from you. And I know you're not used to it. It'll get easier. Just let it go. Let it all out."

Vivian leaned against her sister and cried, and cried. It had been too long bottled up inside her. Del just patted her and let her cry. When there were no more tears, Vivian felt like she'd been crying for hours, for days. She hadn't cried like that since the day the doctor had told her that all the tests had been exhausted, that she might consider adoption. Adelma handed her the box of tissues off the night stand.

"That's not it," Vivian said, angrily wiping her face. "It's all a lie. There's no adoption. This is Walter's baby. He told me the mother brought her to his office, and left town. That was two weeks ago. It seems longer. He just dumped this baby on me and went on with his life, like nothing happened. Now he expects me to go along with this adoption scam, to save his public face—"

"You've had her two weeks?! That rat! Why didn't you tell me? What about school?"

"I missed a week. Then I had a sitter, but that didn't work out. Then I met a man...found a lady to keep her. But only through tomorrow."

"Then what?"

"Then I'm moving."

"Moving? Moving where?"

"I don't know yet."

"You *know* you can come here. We'll make room. We'll double the boys up, and ya'll can have that front bedroom. Til you and Walt—"

Vivian turned and looked at her. "Fuck Walter! I've had enough. I can't even stand to look at him. I just want him out of my life. Nineteen years is enough. I should have left him a long time ago. And I'm *not* taking this baby!" She couldn't look at Passion as she said it. "I'm going to finish this last semester, and take the Bar exam. Then I'll decide where to go from there."

Passion began to whimper. Instinctively, Vivian reached and took her from Adelma. "It's time for her bottle," she said, reaching into the bag. She felt her sister watching her, as she gave

Passion the bottle.

"You look like a natural mom, Viv."

"Well, I'm not. I'm just doing what I have to do. Til tomorrow."

"Then what? Is Walter going to take care of the baby?"

"Not if the past couple of weeks is any guide. He hasn't even touched Passion since he brought her home."

"Passion. Is that her name?"

"It's the name I gave her." Seeing Passion had lost interest in the bottle, she burped her, then laid her on her stomach on the bed on her little quilt. "I'm starved. I know you've got something going in the kitchen."

"Come on. I'll fix you a plate."

In the kitchen, Vivian sat at the table, while Adelma stirred in the bubbling pots, then put a plate of steaming spaghetti and meatballs in front of her.

"Have you told your mama?"

"No! Have you?" Vivian eyed her with alarm.

Adelma shook her head. "I figured you'd want to tell her yourself. I haven't talked to her this week. Has she called you?" Vivian shook her head, as she wolfed down a mouthful of spaghetti. "So I know the story didn't make it to the Fort Worth paper."

"I've been thinking. Maybe I'll go home for Spring Break. I'll tell her then. It'll all be over. I'll be settled in my new place."

"Are you really going to leave the baby? With Walter?"

Vivian gave her a hard stare.

"I mean, I don't blame you for leaving him. I'd kill Petey on the spot if he pulled something like that. Butcher knife right to the heart." Laughing, she demonstrated with a stabbing motion.

Vivian laughed too.

"I thought about it."

"You know, Viv, maybe your prayers have been answered."

"What are you talking about?"

"You remember how you prayed for a baby? We all prayed for you. You know God answers prayers. It may not be on our timetable, but He's always right on time. You want some more spaghetti?"

Vivian stared at her older sister. Just like her to drop a bombshell, then nonchalantly change the subject. Adelma had a way of accepting things, and always in a positive light. Vivian admired that about her, and wished she had more of that quality.

"Thanks, Del, but I'm full. We'd better get going. If I let Passion sleep much longer, she'll be up all night."

As Vivian strapped Passion in the car seat, she said, "Del, promise me you won't tell Mama."

"Aw Viv. You know I can't lie, if she asks me. But I promise I won't bring it up. Why don't you just call her and tell her?"

That was another thing about Del, she was just so insistently straight-forward. Vivian agreed with her, but sometimes things were just...complicated. Del didn't have any complications in her life, she had a way of not allowing them. She and Petey had been high school sweethearts. He was a particularly uncomplicated man. A hard-working, family man. Had a good job as personnel manager in a government agency. Del taught biology at the high school. Their lives were wrapped up in each other, their boys, their church, their jobs—in that order. Sometimes, Vivian wished her life was like that—orderly, secure, serene.

"I don't want to do it that way. I just don't think that's a good idea. You know how she is. Let me handle it, Del."

"OK. OK. Don't forget. You can come here, if you need to."

Vivian hugged her. "Thanks, Del. For everything."

* * * * *

Vivian and Passion played until bedtime. Since she'd done her studying earlier, she relaxed and enjoyed it. When Passion went to sleep, Vivian found the newspaper and looked through the classifieds for an apartment. She was surprised at the prices in the areas she considered, even for a one-bedroom. Her money would be seriously depleted that way by the time she took the Bar exam. Maybe she'd have to settle for an efficiency. She circled several, then put the paper in her purse.

* * * * *

The next morning, she felt overwhelmed by a sense of sadness as she dressed Passion. She knew if she found an apartment that she could afford that day, she would move the next. This might *really* be their last day together. To cheer herself, she reached into the back of the cabinet for the bottle, and put on a dash of her favorite cologne. As she breathed in the aroma, she regretted that she had given up another thing she enjoyed because of Walter. Well, all of that was about to come to an end. She was on the verge of a new life. Or was it her old life, reclaimed? Maybe she'd even get a kitten. *She* didn't have allergies.

Unaware, Passion was her usual happy self, kicking her legs and waving her arms. When Vivian came from the bathroom, she was surprised to find Passion on her back. She could have sworn she had left her on her stomach.

* * * * *

Cora and Passion greeted each other with an eagerness that

made Vivian sadder. This would be their last day together, too. Vivian could see in Cora's eyes that she was feeling it.

* * * * *

Vivian could hardly concentrate in class. She wasn't clear about what kind of law she wanted to practice, but she was certain it wouldn't be administrative law. Even if the money was good, it was too dry for her taste. She needed something she could sink her soul into. She eased the folded newspaper onto the desk atop her textbook. She surveyed the ads she'd circled and made a mental map of the order in which to view them. She would call the ones she wanted to see from her car phone. If she didn't waste any time, and everything worked out right, she could even sign a lease that day.

She'd never lived in an apartment. In college, her parents had insisted that she live in the dorm. And it was convenient, so there was no reason to fight with them about it. She'd shared a bedroom until Adelma left for Hampton University, so having a roommate had been no problem for her. Then she'd married Walter, and moved into the house he had. This would be the first place all her own. She was reveling in the excitement of it, as she walked down the wide steps outside the law school amid a knot of other students anxious to get out into the freedom of the day. Vivian nearly tripped on the last step when she saw Marc, leaning against the big oak tree. She walked over to him.

"Hi. What are you doing here?" she asked.

"I came over to meet with one of the profs. He wants me to give a talk to his upper class seminar on Journalism and the Law. Actually that was just an excuse to be here when you got out of class. I've grown unaccustomed to eating lunch alone and I don't like it anymore."

"Two lunches and it's a habit with you?" she asked in an amused tone.

"I'd like for it to be." Marc was surprised at his own words. He had thought about her in a way he knew he shouldn't think about a married woman, as he ate lunch alone in his office the day before, as he prepared for his class, as he went to bed, and when he woke up. He could tell she was surprised at his words, too, by the way she drew her neck back and tucked her chin, then looked away.

"I have some errands to run today," she said. "I'm going to skip lunch."

He raised off the tree and took the heavy backpack from her, easily slinging it over his shoulder. "I'll go with you, then. Are you driving, or am I?" he asked, walking away. She stared after him for a few steps, then caught up with him.

"Professor Kline, it's a private errand. I appreciate your offer, but you can't go with me," she said emphatically.

He didn't break his stride. "Does it have something to do with those classified ads in your hand? You job-hunting?"

"No. I mean, yes," she said, self-consciously folding the newspaper and stuffing it in her purse, as she trailed behind him. "Look, just give me my books, I'm late."

He stopped and turned to her. The look on his face made her regret the sharpness of her tone.

"You don't have time for just a bite?" he asked.

"We can have lunch another day. I'm sorry," she said in a softened voice. "Not today."

Marc reluctantly unshouldered the heavy bag and handed it

to her. "OK, another day then. Tomorrow, maybe?" He watched her walk away. "Nice cologne," he called after her.

Vivian almost stopped. She was glad he couldn't see the smile on her face.

* * * * *

None of the available apartments that were in her budget were suitable. The one with the most enticing ad and price turned out to be a courts-type motel. The only thing to commend it was its proximity to the school. The ad hadn't mentioned the disemboweled car, or the biker guys sitting around the courtyard. She pretended to be lost, then backed out onto Guadalupe Street. She thought about Del's offer, but decided it wouldn't be fair to her boys to uproot them for her convenience. Besides, Del wouldn't understand her leaving the baby. By the end of the day, the worst option seemed to be the best. She could just stay where she was, at least until school was over, then move back to her mother's. She could take the Bar exam in Fort Worth. Was it worth it to spend all her inheritance, just so she didn't have to look at Walter occasionally? She'd stood him 19 years, she could stand him a few more months.

* * * * *

As she parked in front of Cora's house, she put on her smile. She didn't want Cora to see how dejected she felt. But it was Cora who looked dejected serving iced tea on her patio as they waited for Passion to finish her nap.

"Is something wrong?" Vivian ventured. She wasn't one to pry into other people's business, but Cora had been so kind to her, she hated to see her looking so down.

"Oh, it's nothing. I was thinking about how much I've enjoyed that baby. We went up by the church this morning. I always go on Fridays and help tidy up." She saw the concerned look on Vivian's face. "She wasn't any trouble. She's like the grandbaby it doesn't look like I'm gonna have. Neither of my boys have married. Yet. She likes being out here, too. We sat out here this afternoon and talked to my birds. I didn't realize how lonesome I am, even with all my church work. I'm sure going to miss her."

"You just don't know how much I appreciate your keeping her. I don't know what I would have done without you. We never did talk about money. How much do I owe you for this time?"

"I suppose that means you found somebody else."

"Well, actually, no," Vivian sighed, remembering her conversation with Sherman on the drive over. "I was hoping to find someone who could come to the house and keep her 'til this semester is over, but no luck so far."

Cora brightened. "Then you'll bring her next week?"

Vivian knew if she didn't move to her own place, Passion was going to be her responsibility. But, with Cora's help, she could make it work. She could attend all her classes and study in the afternoon.

"You sure?" she asked. "Through May?"

"Of course, I'm sure. Do I look like a woman who doesn't say what she means?"

* * * * *

When she heard Walter's car in the garage, Vivian steeled herself for the show-down. She sat on the bar stool in the kitchen and waited for him. He looked shocked to see her, when he opened the door, but recovered quickly.

"Hi, Viv. I wasn't expecting to see you."

"I imagine not. You've done an excellent job of avoiding me."

"I haven't been avoiding you, sweetheart. I've just been so busy. How did your day go?" he asked, fumbling in the refrigerator.

"This was one of the better days I've had in a long time. I came to some decisions."

"That's good, Viv. What's this?" he asked, holding up a clear plastic container he'd retrieved from the refrigerator.

"Shrimp salad."

"Still good?"

"Probably."

Vivian patiently watched him place the container and a jar of mayonnaise on the counter, fumble in the drawer for a knife, then look around. There had been a time she would have been up in a flash to do it for him. When he looked at her in anticipation, she gave him a blank stare. He shrugged his shoulder slightly in recognition of her attitude.

"Where do we keep the bread?" he asked.

"Same place as always. In the breadbox by the microwave."

He hesitated a moment, to give her another chance to rescue him, then found the loaf.

"You want a sandwich?" he asked.

"No, thanks."

The silence and calm look on her face made him uncomfortable.

"Some people want me to get involved in an interesting project. They want to build a youth center. It's a grass-roots group from the neighborhood. The area is full of drugs and gangs. They think it's, maybe, a way to keep the younger ones out of trouble.

What they really need to do is form a non-profit corporation so they can qualify for grants. It seems like something right up your alley. Would you be interested in serving on their Board of Directors in my place? I really don't have time."

"Aren't you even going to ask about your daughter?"

"I know everything is fine. I appreciate the way you've handled this, Viv. I really do. And I'm sorry about school. But you can go back and finish next year. Everything will have settled down by then. Why don't you plan us a little vacation, say for June. You pick the place. We can go anywhere you want."

"I want a divorce, Walter."

He stopped chewing and looked at her. "You don't mean that. You're just tired. I know it must be hard, taking care of the baby and all. You need some help. I'll talk to Sherman first thing in the morning. Maybe we could go next month. Call a travel agent tomorrow. You'll feel better when you've had a little rest. And I'll start spending more time at home, as soon as the election is over. It's only a few more weeks. This turd that filed against me doesn't have a chance, but I have to campaign like—"

"I'm serious, I want a divorce. Get one of your lawyer friends to handle it, quietly. I don't want anything from you—but my freedom."

"No."

"No?!"

"No. You're my wife, Vivian, and it's about time you stopped this little childish game of yours and started acting like it. It's time for you to come back to our room."

"I'll get my own lawyer then."

Walter took another bite of his sandwich. He chewed slowly,

calculating.

"I'm going to a resort in the hill country tomorrow morning. Meeting with some of the contributors. Play a little golf. When I get back Sunday, we can talk about this."

"I've said all I have to say about it." Vivian climbed down off the bar stool and walked down the hallway to her room.

SEVEN

Sunday morning, Vivian and Passion were stretched out on the floor. Vivian made a pass at reading the paper, but she was really watching Passion practicing her roll-overs. Vivian would place her on her stomach on her quilt. Shortly, Passion would begin rocking and swaying until she got enough momentum to flip herself over. At first she would seem startled that she had done it again, then they would both get tickled at her accomplishment. When the phone rang, Vivian hesitated. She hoped it wasn't her mother. At the sound of Marc's voice, she breathed a sigh of relief.

"I'm calling to get that number," he said.

"Number?"

"Baseball? I have Corey with me this weekend. We talked about it and he wants to do it."

"Oh, yeah. Sure. Hang on a minute." She fingered through her address book. "Here it is, 555-1213. Ask for Howard Carter. Tell him I said 'Hello' and that I haven't forgotten about his fundraiser."

"I'll do that. What are you and Passion doing today?"

"Just chillin'."

"Corey and I are going to the park. Why don't you bring her? I'll pick up some munchies."

Vivian surprised herself when she asked, "What park?"

"The one by the school. Same one where we had lunch. There's a nice playground. Course, she's too young to play, but she'd enjoy the fresh air."

Vivian almost said yes, then realized that even though she had made up her mind about the divorce, she was still a married woman. It would have the appearance of something other than what it was.

"Besides, I thought maybe we could do the interview?"

"Oh, I'm sorry, but we've, uh, got other plans."

Marc forced himself to place the receiver gently in the cradle. He felt like slamming it down at his blunder. She'd made it clear from day one that she didn't want to be interviewed, so he should have left it alone. Why did he keep after her about it? There were lots of people, women, who had adopted children that he could interview. He had a list of names. He tried to convince himself that it was because the Carlsons were a high profile couple. But in reality he knew it was because something was gnawing at his gut about her. Something about her reluctance to talk about it. Almost like she was hiding something. He wanted to know what it was. It hadn't escaped his notice that she had not answered one question about the baby. In contrast, his other interviewees had been very open about the process, about how they felt when they'd first seen their child, how they'd felt about finally realizing their dream.

"C'mon Daddy. You *said* you were taking me to the park. Can't we go now?"

Vivian's brow was knitted when she hung up the phone. She thought he'd forgotten about the damn interview. Why couldn't he just leave her alone about that? She couldn't concentrate on the newspaper any more, so out of habit, she put all the sections in order and folded it just like Walter liked it. Realizing what she'd done, she opened it and deliberately mixed the sections up. She would have really enjoyed going to the park. She was surprised to find herself wondering what Marc would look like in casual clothes, a pair of cutoffs and a t-shirt. She hadn't had that kind of curiosity about another man in years. And she didn't need to have it now. Her life was already more complicated than she needed it to be. One day, she might actually be interested in another man, but not now. She had a mountain to climb first.

* * * * *

Vivian woke when she heard the knock on the door, but she didn't move. The fluorescent digital numbers on the clock shone 10:47. The door opened, and Walter was silhouetted by the light from the den. She pretended to be asleep, but could see him through her half-closed lids, approaching her bed. She felt him take her hand.

"Vivian?" he whispered.

She gave no response. He sat on the edge of the bed.

"Vivian. Wake up," he said, gently shaking her. "We need to talk."

"Go away. We don't have anything to talk about."

The light blinded her momentarily, when he turned on the lamp by the bed. She shielded her eyes with her forearm.

"Get up, Vivian. Come on upstairs," he said, his tone more stern. Passion began stirring next to her, from the light, her movement and the sound of their voices.

"Go away, Walter. Before you wake up my baby."

"OK. I've had about as much of this as I'm going to take. Get up." He pulled her by the arm into a sitting position. She jerked her arm from his grip. He grabbed her by both arms and pulled her to her feet. "You're my wife. And you're coming to bed. Now!"

"Stop it! Get your hands off me!" she said through gritted teeth, resisting so hard that he released his hold. She saw the rage building in his eyes, and his fists clenching with the urge to strike her. Maybe it was the defiance in her own eyes, or the set of her jaw that told him that if he gave in to it, he could never close his eyes around her again.

The sound of their angry voices jarred Passion fully awake. Her whimpering immediately gave way to crying, then screaming.

"See what you've done!" Vivian hissed. "Get out! This is *my* room! Get out!"

The baby's screams, more than her words, pushed him out the door. Vivian lay on her back, and pulled Passion on top of her.

"Hush, baby," she said, soothingly. "Everything's OK. Hush now."

* * * * *

The bell rang and Vivian stuffed her book and notepad into the backpack. She hauled the big bag onto her shoulder and walked at the back of the herd down the hallway toward the double doors. Outside, as she plodded toward the library, the herd thinned to the more serious students. She didn't notice when he fell in step beside her.

"I *brought* lunch this time. How about under that big tree across the street?"

"Professor Kline, I—"

"Marc. Call me Marc. Come on. I won't keep you long." He took the backpack from her and started off toward the LBJ Library. They crossed the inner campus drive together. When they reached the hillside spot, he said, "I didn't think to bring anything to sit on. Would you like to go up to that pavilion? There're tables up there."

She looked in the direction he was pointing. "In the broad open noonday sun? No thanks. Here," she said, pulling the backpack from his shoulder and letting it drop to the ground. She pulled out two of the thick textbooks.

"Voila! Chairs," she said, with a flourish.

She sat on one, and he followed suit. He opened the sack and handed her a sandwich, bag of chips and a soda.

"So why are you looking like the cat that ate the canary?" she asked.

"Well, I'll *tell* you," he said, finally giving in to the grin. "I assigned my class a project."

"Isn't that what the professor is supposed to do?"

"It wasn't on the syllabus so I'd expected a lot of resistance, especially right in the face of Spring Break. But they—well most of them—seem almost excited about it."

"What's it about?"

"I'm glad you asked," he said, handing her several sheets of typing paper neatly folded together, from his breast pocket.

When she unfolded it, she saw a masthead from the local newspaper dated Sunday and a small clipping, taped on it. The headline read 'Unidentified Body Found,' and in bold hand-written lettering above it, 'Who is Jamicka Doe?' She looked up at him, her eyebrows raised in a question.

"Jamicka?" she asked, perplexed.

"Read the article," he said.

> Late Friday, a couple walking their dog in the Lake Austin area, found a body floating in the lake. Fully clothed when found, the body was badly decomposed. Police sources say, that although the body has not been identified, they believe it to be that of a Black female. Police would not speculate as to the existence of foul play or give further details.

"I see. So what's your class got to do with this?"

"We're going to follow this case the rest of the semester. They can write articles on what they find—for extra credit. I've arranged it with a friend at the paper. Any that are good, I'll submit to him for publication with a 'Special to' byline."

"Sounds like it'll be interesting—and fun, if it wasn't so morbid."

"I hope so. They're gonna learn something about the real world now. Like where the police station is, for starters. And the medical examiner's office. You know, for you law students, it's 'where's the courthouse.' The second thing they should learn is that the

'official police spokesperson' is only the starting point. That sec-
retaries and clerks, even janitors, can be more reliable sources.
Of course, we'll get into ethical issues."

"You seem excited about it."

"I am. Here. Take a copy. I'll show you what they come up
with. For the extra credit, I suspect they'll turn up something."

She folded the paper and put it in her purse.

"Would you like for Corey to become a journalist? Or a professor?"

"I don't know. Everything is changing so much. I guess whatever he chooses, I'll have to like it. Right now, he's all excited
about baseball. I spoke with your friend this morning. We're going to meet with him next Wednesday."

"Good. I'd like to meet Corey sometime."

When they'd finished the sandwiches, he rolled up the papers and put them and the empty soda cans back in the bag.

"Thanks for lunch," he said, standing and shouldering the
heavy bag. "Now, you'd better hurry."

"Hurry?"

"You're always in a hurry. I don't want to hold you up."

* * * * *

Tuesday, he was waiting under the big oak tree. She smiled
and rolled her eyes, before joining him. He'd brought a quilt.

"I can't afford this," she said, as she walked up to him. "How
many lunches do I owe you now?"

"Two. The rest are a favor to me."

By Friday, she was looking forward to seeing him. He hadn't
missed a day. He was there in the shade of the big oak with a sack
in his hand and the quilt over his arm. Each day there'd been

something different. She enjoyed the different cuisines. French one day, Thai the next, Ethiopian the next. Each day he told her stories about the country where he'd been assigned. The terrain and the people came alive for her under the big tree as she ate dishes from that country. Each day, he had ended it by saying, "Thanks for lunch. Now, you'd better hurry." That day when he said it, there was no enthusiasm in his voice and she was tempted to say 'I'm not in a hurry.' Instead, she plodded toward the library.

* * * * *

On Monday, he was excited that he'd found the kolaches for dessert. He'd driven all the way to Round Rock before class to get them. She seemed distracted.

"Don't you like these?" he asked.

"Oh sure. They're delicious. Be better with nuts."

"You like nuts? Ever had boiled peanuts?"

"Boiled?" She wrinkled her nose. "Of course not!"

"They're good, especially warm. I can't keep them warm that long, but I'll bring you some back."

"Back? You going somewhere?" she asked.

"Spring Break's next week. I'm taking Corey home with me to visit my folks."

"That'll be nice. I'm sure you'll both enjoy it."

He wondered if the quietness in her voice meant that she was thinking the same thing he was, that she would miss their lunches.

"What are you doing for Spring Break?" he asked.

"I'm going home. To Fort Worth. I thought I'd spend the week with my mother."

"Family vacation?"

"No. Just me and Passion."

"I'll bet your mom will be glad to see her grandbaby. Are you flying?"

"No. I haven't really made a plan. I guess I'll drive."

"By yourself? With the baby? What's that, about a four-hour drive?"

She hadn't thought about it. Flying did sound like a better idea.

"Maybe we ought to fly. I won't need a car when I get there. I'll make reservations as soon as I get home."

"Are you kidding?! It's Spring Break. Fifty thousand students. I'll bet the flights have been booked for weeks. Why don't you ride with me and Corey? We're going right through Dallas, and coming back that way, but Fort Worth is only a few miles out of the way. I wouldn't mind at all."

"I'll think about that," she said.

* * * * *

On Tuesday, the first thing she noticed was that he didn't have a sack or the quilt. Then she saw the tension on his face.

"What's the matter? Your students have second thoughts about your project?" she asked in a teasing voice.

"No. That's not it. It's nothing. I just came to tell you...I don't know why I came. I didn't bring lunch."

"That's OK. I wasn't expecting—" She looked down. Lie. She *had* expected it. "I mean, aren't you hungry?"

He shook his head and stared into space.

"Let me treat you today. It's my turn. Come on. Have you ever been to Scholtz's?"

"No, but I've heard of it."

"It's a landmark. I think it's over a hundred years old. I heard they're closing it. Well, actually, that it's been sold or something. I used to go there a lot when I was in undergraduate school. We'd walk there from the dorm. We were so poor, even if we pooled our money, we could only afford a plate of French fries—if we wanted a pitcher of beer," she said laughing at the memory. "But it was fun. I hate to see it change. This may be my last chance to re-live my youth. Come on. "

The tenseness in his face eased a little.

"You really ought to go before it changes," she urged. "If nothing else, just to say you've been. It's not plush or anything, but it's the kind of place you might see anybody. Students, state workers, bums, politicians."

"Your husband?" he asked quietly.

She shrugged her shoulders diffidently. "Let's go in my car. It's close. I found a good parking place today for a change."

"OK," he said, reluctantly. "I guess I shouldn't miss out on you re-living your youth."

Marc was impressed that she parallel-parked the car in one pass. When he opened the old heavy door, the noise of the place whooshed out to greet them. He followed her across the scarred wooden floor, through the crowded bar area filled with raucous conversations mixed with the sounds of dishes banging together. Then, down the steps, past another dining area, and out the back door to the patio. She pointed at the only table that wasn't full, and he sat opposite her. The couple at the other end of the heavy wooden picnic table, acknowledged their presence with a nod, then went back to their lunch.

"You're awfully quiet," she said. "What's the matter?"

"It's nothing. Food must be good here," he said, clearly trying to change the subject.

"The food *is* good. I'll have the enchilada platter," she said to the waitress who appeared with a small tablet in her hand.

"Make that two," he said, and watched the waitress walk away.

"What's the matter?" she persisted.

The look on her face told him she wouldn't be put off. But how could he tell her he was having doubts about their relationship? They didn't even have a relationship. How could they? When he'd awakened from the dream the night before, it had seemed so simple. He would just meet her one last time to tell her there would be no more lunches, that they needed to put some distance between them, to stop this thing that was growing like Cora's bulbs. This thing that had him planning the next day's lunch no sooner than today's ended. This thing that had him daydreaming about her when he should have been preparing for his class, or writing his book. This thing that had him vividly imagining how it would feel to have her body pressed against his.

In the dream, he'd undressed her and gently laid her back on the quilt. In the bright noon-day sun, he'd savored the rich color of her body. He'd caressed her all over, then kissed her all over, then sucked her breasts until her nipples hardened into little knots and yielded sweet honey. He'd trailed kisses down her stomach, then pushed the curly hair aside with his thumbs and licked until he drew sweet honey there, too. When he joined her, dipping into her silky warmth, he was drawn farther and farther into the forbidden chamber. Their bodies were pressed so tightly together, her legs wrapped around his waist, not even air separated them.

He couldn't tell if the quaking came from the earth or from that place so deep inside. Then a dark shadow fell across them, blocking the sun. A cold wind extinguished its warmth. He looked up into the face of her husband, standing over them.

He'd awakened in a cold sweat. He sat on the edge of the bed, rubbing the heels of his hands against his eyelids. Had the dream been an omen? A warning? It had seemed so simple in his darkened bedroom. He'd just tell her 'no more.'

But now, looking at her, her head cocked to one side expectantly, the words wouldn't come. He looked up at the tree canopy and squinted his eyes, as though the words might be up there. When he looked back at her, she had the same insistently curious expression.

"It's my job," were the words that came out.

"What about it?" she asked.

"Well, my year is almost up. They haven't said anything."

"What do *you* want to do?"

"I want to be near my son, but there's nothing else here for me."

He saw a shadow cross her face, as the waitress sat two steaming plates in front of them and tucked the bill under his.

"Hot plate. Be careful."

They finished the meal in silence, avoiding each other's eyes.

* * * * *

When Vivian got Passion settled in bed that night, she picked up the phone and called her mother. She was tempted to tell her about Passion, but decided her original plan was better.

"Mama, if you're not doing anything next week, I thought I'd spend Spring Break with you."

"A whole week? That'll be great. It's been a long time since you've spent that much time with me. There's a new exhibit at the African-American Museum over in Dallas. Photographs by Earlie Hudnall, Jr. Let's go to that. Ms. Sykes said it's fabulous. And the Dallas Black Dance Theater is having something. I'll get tickets," she rushed on. "I'm so excited. You know I don't get to go as much since your father died, especially at night. Oh, and bring a swimsuit. I've been going to the pool at the Y for water exercises. You can go with me. You know, you're getting to the age—"

"I know, Mama. I know. I'll bring a suit."

"Let me holler at Walter."

"He's not here."

"Well, tell him I said 'hello'. I can't wait for ya'll to come. When will you get here? Friday night?"

"Probably in the afternoon. Maybe evening. See you then, Mama."

* * * * *

Vivian was curled up on the couch reading when she heard Walter come in.

"Hi, Viv. I'm glad I caught you home."

"Caught *me* home?"

"You know what I mean," he returned sharply. Then sensing her combative mood, added, "How's the baby?"

"Fine."

"I'm going to Washington Friday morning. There's a week-long conference for state legislators. The conference doesn't start 'til Monday, but I'm going up early and meet with some people. I thought you might like to go with me. We could do some things together."

"No, thank you. We're going to spend the week with mother," Vivian said, as she gathered her books.

"Is that a new cologne? Smells good."

"No," she answered flatly, from the hallway.

* * * * *

Wednesday, Marc brought a big duffel bag—and Corey. She could tell he would be a carbon copy of Marc when he grew up. He already had the height, the coloring, and the square forehead. When he said "I'm glad to meet you, Mrs. Carlson," Vivian knew Marc had been coaching him. Instead of their big tree, they walked to the park near campus where they'd had their first lunch. Marc took plastic containers out of the duffel bag.

"I hear that Wednesday is Mexican food day around here. Is that a Mexican tradition or what?" he asked.

"I think it's an Austin tradition. I imagine they have Mexican food in Mexico everyday," she said laughing.

"They ought to have it everyday here too," Corey said as he wolfed down his second taco. When he finished, he asked to go to the playground.

"Hold up, Corey," Vivian said. "I keep some bubble gum in my purse for my nephew. I bet he wouldn't mind if you had a piece. Would you like some?"

He nodded, and leaned up on his toes, peeking in her purse. When she handed it to him, he stuffed it in his mouth, saying, "This is the best kind. Thanks."

"Have you decided about riding with us?" Marc asked.

"You were certainly right about the airlines. Not a flight before Monday. Maybe I should take you up on your offer."

"That would be good. Wouldn't it, Corey?" he said as Corey ran over to him.

"What? Wouldn't what be good?"

"Could Mrs. Carlson and her baby ride with us as far as Fort Worth?"

"Sure. Daddy, can we hit the ball some more? Just a few more—plee-e-eze?"

"Sure. A few." Marc took the ball and bat from the duffel bag, and they walked off a piece.

Vivian turned around and leaned back against the table to watch them. She ended up playing backstop, since Corey missed nearly every easy lob Marc threw. Finally, Marc enlisted her to be pitcher. He positioned himself next to Corey and showed him how to hold and swing the bat again. Vivian imagined her father showing that same patience if he'd had a son. She couldn't imagine Walter taking the time. Together, they hit the first ball she threw. Corey got so excited, he said, "OK, Daddy. I can do it. I can do it by myself. You be the backstop."

"Get ready, Corey." She threw the ball. He missed. Marc caught it and threw it back to her. On the next pitch, Corey was surprised when the bat connected solidly with the ball. Vivian jumped as the ball sailed by, close to her head.

"Told you I could do it, Daddy!" Corey said beaming at Marc.

"I knew you could. Now, go get the ball. It's time for us to go."

"Aw, Daddy, let me show you. I can do it again."

"Just a couple more. We don't want to be late for our appointment."

On the walk back, Vivian saw Corey eyeing her purse.

"Want another piece of gum?"

He grinned and nodded his head.

* * * * *

That night, as she was dressing for bed, Vivian was surprised to hear Walter's car so early—before ten. He knocked on her door, then opened it.

"Viv?" he called out.

She stepped from the bathroom door. "Stop. Don't come in my room."

"Aw, Viv. Don't act like this. You look so pretty in that gown. And it smells so good in here. Can't I come in?"

"No."

"Well, why don't you come in the den and have a drink with me?"

She looked at him like she would rather walk through the fiery gates of hell.

"Have you thought about going to Washington with me?"

"No. Have you talked to a lawyer?"

He shook his head. "And I'm not going to."

"Then *I* will."

"No. No, you won't. We're not getting a divorce. Have you forgotten about the election? My only opponent is a White guy. If I lose, there will be no Black representation in this county. I know you're mad at me, and I can't say you don't have a right to be. But would you actually let your selfishness affect the entire community?" He knew it wasn't fair to accuse her of being selfish, but he knew it worked by the way her mouth was crimped.

"They'll just have to get over it," she said. "You should have thought about the community before you stuck your—You get a lawyer tomorrow. Else, I will."

For a long moment, he didn't say anything. Then his eyes narrowed.

"If you try to leave me, I'll take that baby from you."

He watched her head jerk toward Passion, asleep on the bed. When she turned back to him, the look in her eyes was one he'd never seen before. She put her hands on her hips.

"You just try it!"

"I mean it, Vivian."

"So do I, Walter. Now, close my door."

* * * * *

Thursday, Vivian smiled when she saw him, but Marc couldn't help but notice the wrinkle between her eyebrows.

"Remember my class project?" he asked.

She nodded.

"Well, it seems some of the class had a bit of a revelation. I didn't even get to give my lecture today. All they wanted to talk about was why the death was not being investigated." He laughed, then took another bite of the calzone he'd brought.

"They must have watched too much of the OJ trial. But at least they learned a little something about how police resources are deployed. They think just because *they're* interested in this case, the police ought to be. I was actually impressed that they're taking it seriously. One even went and got the autopsy report. There were pictures. He was shocked. Tickled me—these kids think they're so worldly. Ain't seen nothing," he said, chuckling. "Anyway, they found a gold chain in the woman's clothes. From the description he gave, the pendant on it sounded like the Alpha symbol." He stopped, cocking his head to the side. "Am I boring you? You don't seem like you're listening. Why don't you tell me about your daydream instead?"

"I was listening. You said an Alpha pendant. But that's a Black *fraternity*. Walter's an Alpha."

"Maybe I got it wrong. I was just going on what the kid told me," he said dismissively. "It could have been anything." He took another bite, looking off.

They finished their lunch in silence. The mention of her husband's name hung like an iron curtain between them. It disturbed him more than it should have. She realized she was on the verge of a precipice. She could still turn back. But back wasn't where she wanted to go.

The silence continued, unbroken, as they walked across the inner campus drive, up the hill, past the big oak tree. At the door of the law school, he handed her the backpack. Their eyes met, both filled with so many unspeakable thoughts.

"What time should we be ready tomorrow?" she asked.

EIGHT

"Detective Crane?"

When he heard his name, he looked up in irritation. The woman standing next to the partition that formed his 'office' had painted her face on—bright red lips, a splotch of loud rouge on each crepey cheek, blue eyeshadow under stark black eyebrows, penciled in a severe arc. She wore the most ridiculous hat he'd ever seen—a wide-brimmed straw number, covered with flowers and feathers. Matched her ridiculous dress. And that awful smell—gardenias. And white gloves, for God's sake. Now what, he thought, tearing himself away from the thick file he was poring over.

Crane spent every spare minute searching for some overlooked clue in a four-year old murder of three teen-aged girls in a record shop. It wasn't his case. It was his personal crusade. One of his daughters was the age of those girls. When the new Chief took over, he'd been shunted over to Auto Theft Division, instead of the promotion he'd expected to Homicide, where he could officially work on the case. He had looked forward to working again with his buddy, Gormann. Captain Gormann now. All that bull about his 'expertise' was just a cover. He knew it was punishment for his less than enthusiastic embrace of the new Chief's community policing initiative. But if he could crack this one, his career would be made. He'd get a 'real' office. Maybe even on a higher floor. Hell, with all the pressure the department was getting about the murders, they'd make him head of Homicide—when Gormann retired. Maybe even Deputy Chief.

"I called you yesterday," she said, hesitantly through very properly pursed lips.

His face registered no recognition. Twenty people had called him yesterday.

"About the tape," she prodded.

"Tape?" He frowned, trying to remember, but drawing a blank. "What's your name?"

"Well, I'm not involved in this or anything," she said, her eyes and feet shifting nervously. "I just think you ought to look at this tape."

"Oh, yeah. I remember now. The no-name lady. Have a seat." He reached for the tape. "Where'd you get this?"

"I told you. I bought a video camera from the pawn shop and the tape was in it. The one over there on Burnet Road. That was the first time I've been in one of those places. I mean, I don't want you to think I'm like that. But my friend told me I could get a good deal at a pawn shop. I'd never been in one before. I swear."

"What's on it?" he asked, brusquely. "And why do you think it's police business?"

"I don't know. It's just kind of…I just think you ought to look at it."

"OK. But, I've got to have your name. For my report, you

know," he said, trying to overcome her reticence with officialspeak.

She looked at him uncertainly. "Smith. Ms. Smith," she said, jutting her chin up.

A hint of a wry smile accompanied his disbelieving, "Humph."

Why did they have to route all the crackpots to him? Didn't they get it? He was in Auto Theft now, chasing gang-bangers and stripped cars. Sighing, he thought, may as well get this over with quick and get back to his case.

"Awright, come with me Ms....Smith."

He led her to a small room containing a metal desk and several mis-matched chairs. He put the tape in the VCR, and pointed to a chair for her, but she refused to sit.

The older model VCR emitted a whirring sound, then the picture appeared on the screen. He watched as the bride walked down the aisle alone. He could tell her hands were shaking, from the movement of the flowers in her bouquet. He felt sorry for her. Maybe that was why the fathers had to walk them, so they wouldn't shake that way. He wondered why this one's didn't. She joined the groom at the altar and the picture abruptly changed to scribble-scrabble. He turned and looked at the woman, his eyebrow raised, trying not to show his exasperation. She shifted on one foot and nodded her head toward the VCR. Rolling his eyes, he turned back to face it.

For three minutes, there was nothing but a bed. Flickering candles of various sizes on the bookcase headboard and the endtable, provided the only light. Then a woman, clad only in panties, backed into the frame, and laid on the bed, pulling a man on top of her. Her arms snaked around his neck and her legs wrapped around his waist, then rubbed up and down his thighs until he got with the program. In one fluid motion, she pushed him off of her and rolled him on his back, then straddled him. She faced the camera several times while she undressed him, but the man seemed oblivious to it. When she mounted him, moving up and down rhythmically, Crane fought to keep a straight face and folded his arms across his lap to hide his reaction.

When it was over, the man sat on the edge of the bed, his profile to the camera, wiping his hands across his face, then pulling on his shorts. When he'd put his pants and shirt on, he said, "I gotta go, Porsche." She crawled over to him and put her arms around his neck, pleading with him to stay. She tried to get him to turn to kiss her, but he was insistent, dragging her arms from around him and walking out of the room. She followed, buck-naked and still begging. Then, there was only the bed with the rumpled covers, and the muffled sound of angry voices. 'Bitch, I'll kill you.' Crane heard a door slam, then the sound of the door being kicked. Then 'Damn!' The bride and groom re-appeared, walking back down the aisle together, smiling. Then scribble-scrabble.

Crane pressed the stop button and turned around to face the woman, but he was alone in the room. What the hell! Maybe she thought it was pornography. No crime in taping yourself—even doing it. Just in case, he fast-forwarded the tape, then pressed 'play'. The same woman was seated on a picnic table, talking into the camera. Telling somebody off. Or maybe practicing for a drama class. If so, she wasn't very good. He pressed 'stop' again, and fast-forwarded a good piece. When he pressed 'play' the wedding party was arriving at the reception. He skipped through the rest of the tape, playing momentary pieces here and there, but it was all of the wedding reception. He re-wound the tape, thinking about the very brief report he would make of 'Ms. Smith's' visit, so that he could get back to his file.

* * * * *

The bags and the car seat were in the foyer. Vivian thought she had packed everything the night before, but kept remembering little odds and ends. She was amazed that Passion had more stuff than she did. Marc had said he'd be there at 1:00. She'd rushed by Cora's from class, then home. Passion was fretting, because Vivian wouldn't let her take her nap at the usual time. She thought it would work better if she slept in the car. Vivian needed her to be at her best when they got to her mother's. She wasn't sure how her mother was going to react to her decision, but Vivian was sure she would be supportive—once she got over the initial shock. She was reaching in the top of the closet for her camera when the doorbell rang.

"Where'd you get that?!" she asked, when she saw the big vehicle over his shoulder in the driveway.

"What?" he asked, a mischievous smile on his face.

"Don't even say 'what.' You know what I'm talking about! That."

"Oh, that. I thought you and Passion would be more comfortable in the motorhome, than the car. Besides, I didn't want to disturb my filing cabinet," he chuckled. "You ready? I'll take your bags out."

"OK. I'll get Passion."

She stepped up two steps into the motorhome. "I like it. Oh, look. A bed. This *is* going to be nicer than the car. Where's Corey?"

"He's not coming."

"Why not?"

"Allison wouldn't let him come. I just knew she was going to pull something like this," he said, through gritted teeth. "You can put Passion on the back bed. I'll put your stuff on the overhead bed. You come on and sit up front."

Vivian propped the pillows so there'd be no way for Passion to roll off the bed.

"And a bathroom. This is great. How long have you had this?" she asked, taking her seat.

"A couple of years," he said, as he started the motor.

"You take many trips?"

"Not as many as I'd like to."

"I've never been in an RV before. What got you interested in it?"

"I don't know. I'd wanted one for a long time. Thought it would be a great way to show Corey the country. So when I came into a little money a couple of years ago, I just did it."

"Speaking of Corey. What did she say? Why wouldn't she let him come?"

"She said her family's having a reunion."

"Oh." Vivian pursed her lips. "But didn't she know you had planned your own family reunion of sorts? And didn't you say it was your time under the decree?"

"Yes," he answered tightly.

"Then, you should have insisted."

"I don't want to talk about it anymore, if that's alright with you."

"Oh. Alright." She turned and looked out the window, but not before he saw the hurt look on her face. Several miles passed, with him stealing glances at her, trying to decide whether to tell her.

"Corey told her about our lunch."

"So?"

"I think the thought of me with another woman was... well...new."

"But I'm not another woman. I mean, we aren't...I'm sorry."

"It's not your fault."

When they got to Fort Worth, she directed him off the Interstate and through the tree-lined streets with large brick houses set back on expansive lawns.

Vivian rang the bell twice, but no answer. She frowned. It wasn't like her mother to not be there, since she was expecting her. She handed Passion to Marc and fished in her purse for the key. Opening the door, she expected to hear the buzz of the security system, and hoped she remembered the code to disarm it. She was relieved that she didn't have to.

"Mama? Mama?" she called, walking through the house.

The smell of a Sunday kind of dinner filled the air—greens, pot roast, and potatoes. Vivian knew without looking, there'd be a pot of carrots on the stove, too. Her mother loved carrots. From the patio door in the bedroom, she saw her mother in the back yard garden. She knocked on the glass to get her attention.

Gloria Johnson turned her head at the sound, then recognizing Vivian, rose from the low stool with a big smile. Vivian was always struck by how agile her mother was, even as she approached seventy. She hoped it was hereditary. She was annoyed that she couldn't open the patio door like she used to. It would open, but it was too much trouble to unlock the burglar bars that had been installed after her father died. The neighborhood was quiet and had a low crime rate. Probably because, like her mother, most of the owners of the large brick homes were retired. Her mother's growing obsession with security concerned her. She watched Gloria remove the gloves and the big straw hat on her way to the garage. Vivian hurried back to the other part of the house. She and her mother met in the kitchen and exchanged hugs.

"I'm so glad you're home, Babysis."

"Me too, Mama. You've picked up a little weight."

"Hush your mouth, girl. You hungry? I didn't know what time you'd get in. Dinner's not ready yet, but I could fix you a snack."

"No, not really. Mama? I've got something—"

Vivian stopped when she saw that look on her mother's face. She turned and looked over her shoulder, then back to Gloria.

"Oh. Mama, I want you to meet Marc Kline. He's a professor at the University in Austin."

"Pleased to meet you, Professor Kline," she said, extending her hand. "I'm Gloria Johnson. What a pretty little baby you have. What's her name?"

Marc turned and looked at Vivian, puzzled. She looked away.

"Uh, Passion," he answered.

"Passion. Huh. How unusual. Is she a 'daddy's girl'?" she asked, slipping her finger in Passion's fist.

"Well, uh…I mean…she's a friendly baby, if that's what you mean."

Gloria reached for Passion, and Passion reached for her.

"Ou-u, she *is* friendly. How old is she, Professor Kline? Six months?" she asked, taking Passion from him.

"Please, call me Marc."

"Alright. Marc. Please, have a seat. How old did you say she is?"

He looked at Vivian again. She looked away, then anxiously at Gloria.

"Isn't she pretty, Mama?"

"She sure is. Like a little doll," Gloria said. She removed the big shiny earbob Passion was pulling on, and handed it to her. "Where's Walter, Babysis?"

"He's in Washington."

"Oh, I see. And your wife, Professor Kline? Is she in the car? Bring her on in. Ya'll can join us for dinner. I have plenty, and it'll be ready in about thirty minutes."

"I don't have a wife, Mrs. Johnson. But I'd love to have a home-cooked meal before I head on to Georgia. It sure smells good. Tell you what though, I need to check one of the tires. We passed a station not far away. I think I'll just go do that now. It shouldn't take more than thirty minutes." Marc was talking all the way to the door. He'd read the look on Gloria's face, and knew he didn't want to be a part of the conversation that was coming.

No sooner than the door had closed behind him, Gloria turned to Vivian.

"What are you doing, Babysis?"

"Huh?"

"Just what on earth are you doing, traipsing around with some man, and while your husband—"

"Traipsing? Traipsing?! Mama, I'm not traipsing. We just rode up here with him. He's just a friend. You don't understand."

"You got *that* right. What are you trying—we? What did you say? We? We who?"

"Me and Passion. Passion's *my* baby, Mama."

Gloria's eyes bucked as wide as they could. She held Passion out and looked at her. Then her eyes bucked even wider.

"Yeah, that's right, Mama. She's Walter's baby. But, actually she's my baby now. That's what I came to tell you."

"What do you mean, 'your baby now'?"

"Walter brought her home a month ago. Said the woman didn't want her. And we haven't heard from her since. I was mad as hell about it at first. But now—"

"Wait a minute, let me get this straight. Ya'll are gonna keep his outside child?!"

"No, Mama. *I'm* keeping the baby. I'm divorcing Walter."

Gloria's mouth fell open. Then, her eyes narrowed and her lips pressed together rhythmically, as she digested what she'd heard. Vivian waited. She'd seen that look on her mother's face once before.

"Have—you—lost—your—mind!"

Gloria had enunciated each word sharply and separately that same way, when Vivian announced her plan to try her hand as a professional musician, instead of going to college. Vivian braced herself.

"What the hell are you thinking about?!" Gloria stormed.

"Now, Mama—"

"Don't you 'now mama' me. You listen. You've got a good life, Vivian. A beautiful home. A smart, handsome husband who loves you. Standing in the community. The freedom and money to do as you please. Don't you even think about giving all that up—just because Walter made a little mistake."

"A little mistake?! I can't believe you said that. Walter's made a lot of 'little mistakes,' but this baby is not one of them. In fact, I'm not sure she's a mistake at all. I've wanted a baby for a long time. Maybe this is the only way I can have one. And as for Walter, I should have left *him* a long time ago. Passion just gave me the courage, or whatever I needed, to do it. Besides, Del said this baby is God's answer to my prayers." Vivian finished with the confidence that her sister's pronouncement was the definitive statement on the situation, and Gloria would just *have* to respect that.

"Del? Del?! What the hell does Del know about anything?! Look at the mess she's made of her own life. She gave up her chance to go to medical school, just to marry that boy. And look at her now, saddled with four kids, barely making ends meet on a teacher's salary. And Petey—can't do no better than a government job—".

"Daddy had a government job," Vivian said quietly.

"Don't bring your sainted father into this," Gloria said indignantly. "If he wasn't dead already, it would kill him to hear you talking this foolishness. Besides, that's different. Times were different then. Now, a Black man can do whatever he's capable of, and willing to get off his butt and work for. That boy just doesn't have any ambition. Never did. Didn't come from nothing. I *told* Del she would never have anything with him."

"They're happy, Mama," Vivian said, straining to remain calm.

"Happy!" Gloria snorted. "What's 'happy' got to do with anything? Happy's just some fairy tale crap. Happy sure won't send those boys to college. Or pay off her mortgage."

"Money isn't everything, Mama."

"Oh, what's this? Words of wisdom from somebody who's never been without it? Now, *I* can tell *you* a thing or two about not having money. About doing without things so your children can have a better future. About wearing hose with runs in them, so your daughter can have a new dress and be the prettiest girl at the prom. About having your phone cut off, so your kids can have the kind of education they deserve—"

"Our phone was never cut off! You're being ridiculous!"

"Well, it *nearly* was," Gloria conceded. "Only wasn't, because your father always had a little hustle on the side. Like those rent houses. You know the nights he spent fixing up those rat-trap houses and making them decent places to live. He always did what he had to do to make sure you girls didn't have to do without. And now you're talking about throwing it all away."

"I'm not throwing away anything but Walter. Mama, you're talking like we were on the brink of poverty. You must be getting Alzheimer's!"

"Watch your mouth. I'm still your mother, Vivian." Gloria's squinted frown softened as she sighed. "Babysis, you know I wouldn't tell you anything wrong. I know this whole business hurts you. But, in time, you'll find a way to forgive Walter. Most men are just weak. You can't expect any better from them. And especially a man in Walter's position. Women are drawn to power. Some of them will do anything to trade places with you. That's no reason to ruin your life."

"I'm not ruining my life."

"Let me tell you something. A friend of mine told me that

when she was a young woman growing up in the country, a man got after her, wanted to marry her. He was ugly, and fat. But he was a doctor. She and her mama did washing for people in this little town in Alabama. Her mama told her if she didn't marry the man, one day his wife was going to pass her in her limousine, as she walked down the street with a washbasket on her head. So, she married him."

"That's the most horrible thing I've ever heard! And I suppose she lived happily ever after—married to a frog."

"There you go with 'happy' again. She was about as happy as anybody can expect to be in this life."

"Your little washbasket story doesn't have anything to do with me. Nobody in our family has done washing since slavery."

"Vivian, that's beside the point, and you know it," she said sternly. Then in a more conciliatory tone, "Honey, life is really hard on a woman by herself."

"But I won't be by myself."

"I can *see* that," Gloria said sarcastically.

"What does *that* mean?!"

"Does the good professor know you're a married woman? Or care?"

"Mother! This is between me and Walter. Don't try to castigate Marc's—"

"Oh, it's Marc now, is it?" She rolled her eyes. "Vivian, this just isn't like you. You always had a rebellious streak, but you made the right decision every time."

"I know, Mama. I've always been the obedient child. The good daughter. The good wife. I've always done what you wanted. Done what Walter wanted. But I'm forty years old now, Mama.

It's time for me to make my own decisions."

"Humph! Well, if this is any indication—"

"I don't know why I thought you would be supportive," Vivian said, pouting. "I guess it's only when I'm doing what *you* want."

"I've had about enough of your sass, little girl. You'd better—"

The chiming of the doorbell stopped Gloria, but Vivian was oblivious.

"Little girl?! Little girl?!"

"Get the door, Vivian," Gloria commanded. "It's your friend. Let's put dinner on the table. We'll talk about this later."

Vivian took a deep breath, to try to look as composed as her mother did.

"Hi. Come on in. Get the tire fixed, or whatever?"

"Yeah. It was OK. Are *you* OK?" Marc asked, concern showing on his face.

"Sure. Why?"

He shrugged his shoulders. "Just wondered."

"Is that Professor Kline?" Gloria called from the kitchen, in a sweet voice, that gave no hint of the argument. "Vivian, why don't you set the table. We're almost ready in here."

Vivian showed Marc to the bathroom, then obeyed her mother, taking her grandmother's plates and sterling silver from the china cabinet. She smoldered from the unfinished business, as she took the delicate serving bowls to the kitchen and dished up the food. She and Gloria didn't speak. No words could penetrate their mutual frowns of disapproval. Gloria carried Passion into the dining room when she heard Marc returning.

"This way, Professor Kline. Have a seat," Gloria said sweetly.

She walked to the high backed chair at the head of the table.

"Thank you. This is a beautiful room. I really appreciate your having me to dinner," he said, as he held the chair out for her.

"I'm glad you could stay," Gloria said, with her perfect hostess smile, as she sat. "Why don't you bless the table, Professor? You know, we raised Vivian in a Christian home."

Sitting across the table from Marc, Vivian cut her eyes toward her mother, just in time to hear Marc say, "I'd be honored, Mrs. Johnson."

He held a hand out to each of them. Vivian took his and her mother's, forming a circle. " Dear Lord…" Vivian bowed her head.

"We come this day, with humbled hearts, asking for guidance and strength to face the challenges in our lives. We ask for wisdom, understanding and grace. Help us love our children, as you love Your children. We thank You for the loving hands that prepared this food for the nourishment of our bodies. In the precious name of your son Jesus, Amen."

"Amen. That was very nice, Professor Kline. You were obviously raised a Christian, too. Help yourself. Where're you from?"

Vivian scowled at the feigned sweetness in her mother's voice.

"Where I come from, the cook is always served first. Let me," he said, taking her plate and serving it from each bowl. "I grew up in Georgia. I'm on my way there now. Spending the week with my parents. Can I serve your plate?" he asked Vivian.

"No, you go ahead." She watched him heaping food on his plate.

"Please take some carrots, Professor. They're my favorite."

Gloria mashed some of the carrots and potatoes on her plate, and began feeding Passion.

"Love 'em," he said. "Especially with that little touch of cinnamon. Just a pinch of ginger bolsters the flavor of the cinnamon."

"Ah, you know something about cooking too," she said to Marc.

"A little. Sort of a hobby for me."

"How interesting. Do you cook for Vivian?"

"Mama, that—"

"You ever been married, Professor?"

"Mo-ther," Vivian said, under her breath.

"Yes, I was," Marc answered directly.

"Did you know Vivian is married?"

"Mother! That's enough!"

"I just wondered if he knew what he was getting into, Vivian," Gloria said, innocently. Then added, "Even if you don't."

"That's it!" Vivian said, throwing her napkin on the table and rising. "Let's go, Marc."

"Go?" Marc asked, frowning from Vivian to the plate with the thick slab of pot roast and potatoes covered with gravy, and back. She was already walking away from the table. He looked at Mrs. Johnson, to see if this made sense to her. Only a benign smile was on her face. Passion was pulling at the other earbob. Vivian came back, her purse on her shoulder, and took Passion from her mother's arms.

"Thanks for dinner, Mama. Sorry we can't stay. Maybe when you're feeling better. Come on, Marc."

"Well, ah, Mrs. Johnson, it was a pleasure to meet you. Next time you come to Austin, I'd like to have you over to dinner."

NINE

"What are we doing here, Vivian?" Marc asked, hesitantly from the driver's seat.

"Just go, Marc!"

"OK, OK," he said, trying to placate her.

He started the motor and re-traced the route through the neighborhood, then eased the motorhome onto the freeway. Fort Worth was just a big yellow blob on the map for him, next to a bigger yellow blob that was Dallas. Texarkana was his next planned gas stop, so not knowing what else to do, he headed in that direction. He alternated between looking for a place to pull off where they could talk, and stealing glances at her to gauge her mood. He expected her, at any moment, to tell him to turn the RV around and take her back to her mother's. All he got was an angry pout.

At the big interchange in Dallas, he took Interstate 30. After a while, he began seeing signs for Lake Ray Hubbard. He was already 40 miles from the house and not only would the trip back and forth put him off his schedule, but at eight miles to a gallon it would be wasteful to go any farther. When they'd crossed the long bridge over the lake, he took the first exit, then drove toward the edge of the lake and stopped near a picnic table.

"Why're you stopping here?" she asked.

He got out, easing the door closed so as not to startle Passion. He walked around to her side and opened the door.

"Come on. Let's sit at that table. We gotta talk."

Vivian took his hand and jumped down, then followed him to the table. She climbed up and sat on top of it, with her feet on the seat. He stood facing her.

"You mind telling me what's going on?"

"Nothing," she answered, not looking at him.

"Nothing, huh? Let's see, you show up at your mother's with a baby she *obviously* didn't know anything about. Not to mention a man she doesn't even know. Then, you blow up when she calls you on it."

"She shouldn't have said that to you," she said, pouting.

"I'm a big boy, Vivian. I can take care of myself. But she's your mother. She has a right to be concerned."

"No, she doesn't. Well, maybe. But I'm a grown woman. I have a right to make my own decisions."

"Of course you do. But you'll always be her little girl. Just like Passion will always be your little girl—no matter how old she gets. And you'd be just as worried about her under the same circumstances."

"Humph."

For a while, there was only the sounds of an occasional motorboat in the distance, and birds chirping overhead. He began picking up flat pebbles at the base of the table and, with an underhanded pitch, sailing them toward the lake. Each one skipped across the surface, leaving concentric circles in its wake.

"So, what're you gonna do?" he asked.

"I don't know."

Vivian stared at the colorful sailboats on the lake, not seeing them.

"Well, I'm taking you back to your mom's. You have some making up to do."

"You will do no such thing. I'm *not* going back." She meant it. There was so much she would not go back to—even if she didn't know what lay ahead.

"Alright. But I can't take you to Austin. That would kill a whole day. It's a long drive to Georgia. I could take you to the airport in Dallas? You could get a flight to Austin."

Vivian thought about it. That would be going back, too. She didn't have a plan. She didn't know what she wanted to do, but she wasn't going back.

"I've never been to Georgia."

Marc's eyes widened momentarily. Then, a frown crossed his face.

"You know somebody in Georgia?" he asked.

"Only you."

"I see," he said, twisting his mouth to the side.

Although he would be glad to have the company, and especially her, he was pretty sure her husband wouldn't like it. Carlson was a powerful man in state government. It occurred to Marc for the first time that he might be putting his job at the state university in jeopardy. Not that he needed the job for the money. His books hadn't brought big advances, but the royalty checks coming in now were fat. For him, it was more the easy access to one of the finest libraries in the country, and the time and space to do his research, that the job provided.

What really bothered him was the prospect of being caught up in some mess. He'd had reservations about going to her house to pick them up. Despite his uneasiness, he preferred that to meeting her somewhere. That would have had an undertone of deceit and sneakiness, and he had nothing to hide. His intentions were honorable. Well, mostly. He had to admit he'd had some pretty dishonorable thoughts about her, but none he'd intended to act on. They were just thoughts. Now, he realized the seriousness of the situation. It had been foolish of him to allow his loneliness to override his common sense with the lunches. He'd been acting on impulse, like a teenager, and he'd have to stop it. But, he couldn't just leave her here. Maybe she'd grow weary of playing the 'run-away' soon. He looked at his watch—6:15. Texarkana—8:45. Maybe she'd be ready to go home by then. He doubted there was a flight to Fort Worth at that hour. Maybe there was a late bus.

"OK, then. Let's go," he said, holding out his hand.

Marc drove for a while, trying to think of something to say.

"You want something to drink? There's plenty in the refrigerator," he offered. "Ice in the freezer. Glasses over the sink. Be careful when you open the cabinet. Something might fall on your head. And check on Passion while you're back there."

It took a minute for Vivian to get her sealegs. She held onto the little table to steady herself in the swaying of the big vehicle. When she got to the back, she saw that Passion was entertaining herself with the clown rattler. She got two plastic tumblers down, then the ice. When she opened the fridge, she got out one soft drink, and feeling adventurous, a beer. She poured the soft drink and carried it to him.

"Got a koozie?" she asked.

He turned and quickly glanced at her. "Same cabinet as the glasses. Be careful."

She came back and buckled her seatbelt, then put her feet up on the big dashboard. Outside the windshield, the topography was slowly changing as the miles passed. She first noticed a few scattered pine trees 20 miles past the lake. By Sulphur Springs, they were predominant.

"So, you ready to talk about it?" he asked.

She took a slow sip of beer.

"Texas is amazing, isn't it? We've got everything, from desert to tropical beaches, mountains—everything," she mused.

He nodded, casting a sidelong glance at her.

"You seen much of it?" she asked.

"Only the part between Austin and Georgia. I guess that means 'no'?"

"Right."

She rummaged through the tapes in the console, selected one and put it in. The harmonious voices were young and the beat was new, but the song was from her youth—*Killing Me Softly*. She put her head back against the tall captain's chair, closed her eyes and snapped her fingers in time with the beat. She felt free. She didn't know what lay ahead, but for now, free was enough.

While Marc filled up in Texarkana at the brightly lit Flying J station, Vivian picked Passion up and brought her to the front.

"We're having us an adventure, little girl."

Passion responded with 'Ou-u-u,' as though she understood. Vivian spread her quilt on the floor in front of the couch and lay her on it. She filled a bottle and got out a jar of baby food, then sat on the floor, her back against the couch. She couldn't see Marc using the pay phone. Vivian put the spoon in Passion's mouth. Passion rolled the goop around, then spit it out. Vivian scraped it off her chin, and tried again. It came right back out. In again. Right back out.

"Cora's spoiled you. I guess you don't want this stuff." Passion accepted the bottle. When she was finished, Vivian burped her and lay her on the quilt. She put the clown rattler just out of her reach.

Marc handed her a sack, as he climbed in the cab. "Thought you might be hungry, since you didn't eat much dinner," he said, with a smile. "Hold on to this while I pull around to the side."

After he'd parked around back by the big 18-wheelers, he joined her at the table where she'd spread out the potato logs and fried chicken he'd bought. She brought him another soft drink and another beer for herself.

"So? You ready to go home?" he asked seriously.

She didn't answer.

"There're no flights out of here until tomorrow morning, but there's a bus to Fort Worth leaving at 10. Get you there at 1:30 in the morning."

She didn't respond. He picked Passion up and set her in his lap. He pushed the drumstick bone in her fist, and she took it straight toward her mouth. She jabbed it in her cheek a couple of times, before he took her hand and guided it for her.

"You could call your mother to pick you up at the bus station.

Or take a cab to her house."

"Does that mean you don't want me to go with you?" she asked, staring at him.

He sighed. Passion squirmed and kicked from having lost her grip on the bone. He guided it back to her mouth.

"It's not about whether I *want* you to go. There's nothing I'd like more than for you to go. But you know as well as I do—"

"Then it's settled. What's our next stop?" she asked, a determined smile on her face.

He stared at her a long time, while he ran through his options. He could go south eighty miles and pick up Interstate 20. Along that route, there were more, though smaller, airports—Shreveport, Louisiana, Jackson, Mississippi and Montgomery, Alabama. More opportunities to persuade her to go back. That was the more direct route to Fort Valley, but he'd planned to go by the blues festival. If he stayed on Interstate 30, he'd make Little Rock, Arkansas before midnight. That airport was large enough that there might even be a direct flight to Austin Saturday. Even if the flight was mid-afternoon, he could still make the festival in time for the Saturday night performances. He *could* be as bull-headed as she was. Just stay right where they were—amid the 18-wheelers, their diesel motors humming—until she changed her mind. Every scenario involved them spending the night together. That certainly lowered the level of plausible deniability. In the end, he decided there was no point in missing the blues festival.

"Little Rock. Three hours."

* * * * *

When they got back on the road, she turned on the map light and picked up the map from under his seat. She moved her finger around central Georgia until she found Fort Valley.

"Are you sure you know where you're going?" she asked, tracing their route.

"Why?"

"Seems Interstate 20 would be the right way."

"Ever heard of Clarksdale?"

She shook her head.

"A little town in northwest Mississippi. Famous for blues music. Delta Blues Museum does a great job of preserving the legacy. There's a festival there this weekend. It's a little out of the way, but from looking at the line-up, I know it'll be worth it."

"Sounds like fun. How long will it take us to get there?"

He knitted his brow, cutting his eyes at her.

The concrete slab of the interstate had been cut right through the thick of the forest. In places, the tall pines ominously crowded the edge of the road, as though they intended to reclaim the land that had been theirs. In other places, they'd been cleared way back from the road as though the conquerors had been onto their plan.

They passed a lighted billboard that said 'Welcome to Hope— Home of the President.'

"I met him once," she said. "A long time ago, before he was governor even. It was at a conference on education. I was impressed with him. If I'd had any idea he'd end up being president, I'd have at least gotten his phone number," she said, laughing. "He's a lot taller than he looks on TV."

Marc's brow was furrowed as he pondered the irony of his situation.

"When we get to Little Rock, I'll get you a motel room," Marc said.

"Why?" she asked.

"What do you mean 'why'?"

"Are you getting a room for yourself, too?"

"No. Of course not. I'll sleep in here."

"Where? In the parking lot?"

"I guess so. I usually stop in a state park."

"There's enough room in here for all three of us. That would be a waste of money."

"I just think that would be the proper thing to do. I mean, after all, you *are* a married woman."

She knew she would have to tell him. She wondered if now was the time. She turned the map light on again and read the map.

"There's a state park just outside Hot Springs," she said, folding the map. "Let's stay there. It's about an hour ahead."

The park office was closed, but instructions for late arrivals were tacked to the door. As soon as he parked, Marc turned on the lights in the living area, then went to the refrigerator and got himself two beers.

"You and Passion take the back bed. I'll sleep up top." Then, without looking at her, he went outside.

Marc took a chair from the back of the RV and unfolded it next to a tall pine tree. From where he sat facing the RV, he could see her silhouette through the blinds as she moved about. When she appeared in the back window, he knew she was preparing the bed, folding the covers back. The vision he had of her climbing into the bed aroused feelings in him that he knew were dangerous. As he gulped the beer, he saw her walk to the front, then carry Passion back to the bed. After a while he saw her come back to the living area and sit on the couch. Of all the unholy thoughts he'd had about her, he never imagined he would find himself alone with her, in his RV, for the night, in the woods, the moon nearly full—and considering it a predicament, as he did now.

The door opened and she peered into the darkness searching for him.

"Over here," he called.

When she reached him, she handed him another beer.

"You trying to get me drunk?" he asked.

"No. I must be trying to get myself drunk. I don't usually drink like this."

"Here. Sit down." He went and got another chair, and sat beside her.

"Now, isn't this better than an ol' parking lot?" she asked. "You wouldn't even have been able to see that beautiful moon for the security lights."

Seeing the expectant look on her face, he nodded.

"It's a beautiful night. This *is* better. I just hope your husband never gets wind of it. It would be hard to explain."

"You don't have to worry about that."

He looked at her out of the corner of his eye, one eyebrow raised in a question.

She took a long sip of beer. "I'm getting a divorce."

"I see." He thought things were looking up. "How long have

you been married?"

"Nineteen years."

"That's a lot of your life to throw away."

"That part's already gone. Nothing I can do about that. But, I've got a lot of life left. Humph. You sound like my mother."

"So, is that what the big fight with your mama was about?"

"Mostly." She wasn't ready to tell him the rest of it.

"Are you sure you've thought this through?"

"Yep. Ab-so-lutely."

Marc thought, 'better and better,' then tested, "You ought to give it a little time. It may just be the strain of having a new baby."

"Now, you sound like my husband."

"Humph. Doesn't sound like he wants a divorce."

"I really don't give a *damn* what he wants."

Marc was surprised—and pleased—at the strength of her emotion.

"Been to court yet?"

"No. It hasn't been filed. How long does it take—in the real world?" she asked, looking at him.

"What did your lawyer say?"

"I don't have a lawyer. He's supposed to file."

And he hasn't moved either, Marc thought. Back to square one.

"Ya'll will probably make up. You've got the baby to think about now," he said.

"Humph."

For a while, neither of them said anything.

"Is the adoption final?" Marc asked.

A frown creased Vivian's forehead. "Why do you ask?"

"It'll probably be best to wait until it's final before you go thinking about a divorce. The agency may re-consider. May want to give her to another couple."

The frown on her face deepened. Vivian turned the can up. Her resolve hardened.

"*Nobody* can take Passion from me. I'm her mama. I'll do whatever it takes to keep her."

"Including staying with your husband?"

Her eyes narrowed into slits. She exhaled a long sigh.

That was not the response Marc was hoping for. After a while, he stood.

"Come on. Let's go to bed. We need to get up early tomorrow. There's still an hour to Little Rock."

Vivian knew she'd had one beer too many when she missed the second step and stumbled, falling backwards. Marc caught her around her waist from behind. For an instant, she relaxed completely, leaning back against the solid wall of his chest. He pushed her upright, and held her steady. Warm shivers emanated from the place where his hands held her. When she got her bearings, she turned to thank him. From the step, they were eye-to-eye. Their eyes locked. The soft kiss she intended for his cheek, found his lips instead. She felt his lips part against her tongue, and his grip tighten on her waist as he responded, pulling her hard against him. Then she felt his hands loosen and push her away.

"There you go," he said, as though it hadn't happened. But the strain in his voice was evident. "You go to bed. I'll put the chairs away."

After he'd put the chairs on the rack, Marc leaned against the side of the RV and took several deep breaths to calm himself. Could he have imagined the kiss? No, it had been real. It had taken everything he had to push her away. All the women in the world, and he was falling for one that was married. Never! He wouldn't compromise his morals for a one-night stand—rather, a one-week fling. This was crazy! How did he get himself in this situation?! He felt the RV gently rocking as she climbed into bed on the other side of the wall where he was leaning. He jerked away from it like it was on fire, and quickly walked away. He kept walking, oblivious to the other RVs nestled among the pine trees, and the older couples sitting outside as he passed.

"Evening," one of a foursome sitting around a fire said.

Startled, he nodded in return, then began trotting. He broke into a full run. Blind to the reflection of the full moon, he ran alongside the edge of the lake until he was panting from exertion.

When he felt his head clearing, Marc slowed his pace and started back toward the RV. He'd only have to make it until morning. He could do it, he thought, as he opened the RV door.

TEN

Instead of the little foot kicking her, Vivian awoke to a mild pounding in her head. When she realized Passion wasn't there, she became instantly alert and sat bolt upright in the bed. Then she remembered where she was. She peeked through the blinds and saw Marc sitting at the picnic table, Passion in his lap.

In the little lavatory, she splashed cold water on her face, hoping it would help clear the fog. Then she remembered what she'd done the night before—and the feel of his hands on her. What would he think of her now, she wondered, as she slowly pulled on a pair of denim shorts and a cotton sweater.

When she opened the door, Marc called out, "We left a plate in the oven for you."

Vivian got the plate with the omelet and biscuits, found a fork and joined them at the table.

"Morning," she said, in a subdued voice, her eyes downcast. Passion reached for her. After Passion was settled in her lap, Marc handed her the bottle of hot sauce.

"I hear this is good for a hangover," he said, smiling sympathetically.

She was careful to sprinkle it on one side of the omelet, and fed Passion from the other.

"She ought to be full," Marc said. "She ate half of mine."

"This is really good." Vivian picked around the sweet peppers, onions and tomatoes for Passion.

"Aw, you're just hungry."

She sensed his reticence, as it collided with her own.

"Listen, Marc, about last night—"

"Hush. Don't say anything. It was my fault. It won't happen again—until you're free. This isn't fair to either of us." He stood up, and looked off toward the lake. "When we get to Little Rock, I'm putting you on a plane back to…back."

She didn't respond, just kept eating and feeding Passion, as though she hadn't heard him.

"I'm not going back, Marc. Not now," she said quietly.

* * * * *

Out of Hot Springs, they headed east to Pine Bluff on the state highway. The mood in the RV was quiet and subdued. They were both absorbed in their own feelings. Marc felt trapped. He'd been in traps before, but he had always felt more unhappy about it than he did now. He was glad he had chosen not to take the low route, since he wouldn't miss the festival. And she was being so obstinate, they apparently wouldn't need an airport anyway.

Vivian felt the ground crumbling beneath her. She could still step back onto the firmer, safer terrain that she knew, or she could boldly leap forward to embrace the unknown—or forgotten. Instead, she stubbornly stood, with her toes at the edge, feeling it slip away.

When they arrived at Pine Bluff, Marc pulled into the parking lot at Wal-Mart.

"We're going to need some supplies, if you and Passion are in for the long haul," he said, shutting the motor off.

Inside the store, he selected a full size stroller, a body carrier, and a large bag of diapers.

"Think this'll fit her?" he asked, holding up a tiny pink swim-suit against Passion. "The weather is warmer than usual for this time of year. You bring a suit?"

"Yes. Mama wanted me...yes. Now that you mention it, Passion may need some cooler clothes."

Vivian picked out several short sets, in the proper size. She took them and the swimsuit to the basket and added them to the pile, then pushed the basket to the checkout stand. She handed the clerk Walter's credit card. After she'd signed the slip, she turned around, but they were gone.

"Hold these for me," she said to the clerk.

She found them in the novelty department. Both wearing red 'gimme' caps with ARKANSAS-THE NATURAL STATE embroidered on them in gold, Marc and Passion were making monkey-shines in front of the full-length mirror.

"You like?" he asked, when she appeared in the mirror.

"Ya'll look silly," she said laughing.

"Well, you can just look silly with us," he said, placing the cap in his hand on her head. "I'm getting one for Corey too. Did I tell you he made the team?"

When they got back to the checkout stand, she laid Walter's card on the counter. Marc picked it up and handed it back to her. He gave the clerk his own, saying "We'll be wearing the hats."

He looked over the slip the clerk handed him to sign, then

looked up, "We had some other stuff. You didn't send it back, did you?"

"No. She paid for it already. It's right here behind the counter."

Marc looked at Vivian. "I was going to pay for that. You're my guest."

"Thanks anyway. That's a sweet thought. But it's done now."

* * * * *

Vivian was puzzled when he pulled the RV next to the phone booth and stopped.

"Call your mother, and apologize."

"For what? I'm not apologizing to her," she said, pouting. "I haven't done anything. She owes *me* an apology."

"Well, at least let her know you're OK. Call her, Vivian. We're not going any farther until you do."

Vivian crimped her mouth, then opened the door. She knew her mother wasn't finished with the matter and now would surely have a lot more questions. She dreaded making the call, but she knew Marc was right. Relief flooded over her to hear the recorded message on the answering machine. She hurriedly left her message.

"Mama? It's me, Vivian. I'm just calling to let you know I'm OK. Don't worry about me. I know what I'm doing. I'll call you when I get back to Austin. And Mama, I'm…sorry…that you're worried. Talk to ya'."

* * * * *

From Pine Bluff, the roads were tiny and made almost 90-degree turns. They were obviously for the convenience of the farmers whose fields they passed. From time to time, Marc had to slow to a crawl, until he could pass a big tractor or combine.

He named the different crops for Vivian that had emerged only last month. On the outskirts of Helena, Arkansas they crossed into Mississippi and turned south on a road that wasn't much larger, but at least it was fairly straight.

Off to the left, Vivian saw the Lady Luck casino—a little of Las Vegas sitting in the middle of a cotton field. The parking lot was filled with cars, pickups and, to Vivian's surprise, company trucks. A special area was designated for tour busses and RV's, and another was filled with 18-wheelers. She was tempted to ask Marc to stop there just to see what the crowd was like. But he was grumbling about having to wait for the line of cars turning left and how the state should have made the casino pay to widen the road, so she left it alone.

They pulled into Clarksdale late afternoon. Two blocks away the rumble of the bass guitar and the drums filled the air. A big stage, covered with a bright blue canopy, had been set up in the field at the end of the old, red brick train depot. The depot hadn't seen a train in years, and had been converted to a BarBQ restaurant. Marc backed the RV into another field on the side the stage that had been the parking lot before the weeds reclaimed it. He parked next to the big pink and silver bus, its diesel motor droning, that had 'Denise LaSalle' painted on the side in large fancy lettering.

As they exited, sporting their matching caps, one act was ending and a recording of Muddy Waters came through the banks of speakers, while the crew set up for the next act. Marc got down the folding chairs from the back of the RV. Vivian handed him the stroller out the back door, and the cooler with a six-pack of beer.

The crowd was an odd mixture. Former hippies—middle-aged and middle-class now, in their Birkenstocks and khaki shorts—occupied blankets and lawn chairs. A group of aging bikers, sporting long hair and denim jackets with CONNECTICUT CLAN emblazoned on the back congregated on the side of the stage by their gleaming Harley Road Warriors. Sweaty, but too clean to be intimidating. Local Blacks of all ages intermingled. Making their way through the crowd, Vivian pushed the stroller, while Marc carried everything else. They placed the chairs in a spot with a good view of the stage. The backdrop was a large banner—SUNFLOWER RIVER BLUES AND GOSPEL FESTIVAL.

Just as they got settled, Lonnie Pitchford came on stage alone and sat in the chair that had been placed for him in front of the mike. He played acoustic guitar and sang a set of old-style blues. Then, he put the guitar down and picked up a strange looking instrument he called a 'Didly-Bo.' He told the story of how, as a child, he'd made and taught himself to play the one-string guitar. Vivian was absolutely amazed when he played the Star Spangled Banner on it. As a pianist, she couldn't figure how he got that much music out of one string. When he finished his set, she joined the crowd in clapping and yelling. For this crowd he was a young man—in his late thirties, maybe early forties—and she appreciated that he was helping to preserve the music she'd grown up on. When he was in a certain mood, her father had played the old blues singers over and over on their console stereo.

Pitchford was followed by the venerable harmonica-playing Willie Foster, and then several of the old Delta bluesmen, some in their nineties, playing guitars and harmonicas. At nightfall, Eddie Cusic played the music he'd taught Little Milton. Then,

Lonnie Shields brought on the electric guitars, and moved the mood forward two decades. There was a long pause, while the crew frenetically scurried around on the stage, moving instruments and taping wires.

The woman in a distinctive wide-brimmed hat they'd seen working the crowd—serious camera hanging from her shoulder—walked up to them and introduced herself. Panny Mayfield, Features Editor for the Clarksdale Press Register. She asked them where they were from, and did they mind being interviewed? During the interview, a man in hiking boots, shorts and denim shirt with the sleeves cut off and rolled over his biceps, joined them. Panny introduced them to John Ruskey, curator of the museum. Marc told him how much he'd enjoyed the exhibits on a previous trip. Vivian snapped a picture of the two men, capturing the shy smile on Ruskey's face and the broad grin on Marc's. Her little camera looked like a toy compared to Panny's. Someone called Ruskey's name, and he sauntered off to put out another fire. Panny finished the interview by taking their picture. Vivian made a mental note to write for the issue of the paper about the festival, just in case the picture was in it.

Just then, the musicians walked onto the stage and began tuning up. Vivian felt the charge in the air. Sensing the growing anticipation of the crowd, Marc stood and strapped the body carrier around himself. Vivian helped ease Passion into position on his chest. As Marc folded their chairs and hooked them on the handle of the stroller, someone took the mike and yelled "Ya'll take the chillun' home! This ain't Mr. Roger's Neighborhood. It's almost time for the Queen of the Blues—and ya'll know she don't do no chillun' kind of show!" Vivian felt the crowd surging forward.

Marc pulled her in front of him protectively, so they wouldn't get separated as the crowd pushed and jockeyed for a better view.

"Put your hands together for the Imagination Unlimited Band!"

The band opened with a instrumental medley of the Queen's hits, warming the crowd up. By the time they segued into Solo's *Where You Want Me to Put It,* they already had the crowd in their hands. Something Special, the three back-up singers, high-stepped on stage in matching short, black sequined dresses. They took their places behind the mikes that had been set up for them and finished the 90's doo-wop number.

A drum roll sounded. The stage lights began to flash. The announcer's melodious voice called off the hits that spanned more than twenty years. Then, "The Queen of the Blues—Miz—Dee—Neece—La—Salle!"

The crowd went wild. The Queen walked on stage singing *Right Side of the Wrong Bed*, in her deep-throated, sultry voice. Her red and silver beaded dress shimmered under the stage lights. *Don't Jump My Pony If You Can't Ride* was next. The monologue was almost too funny to be sensuous. When she sang *Child of the Ghetto*, a slow ballad about a teenage welfare mother who graduated from college, summa cum laude, with her son some twenty years later, the Queen broke down. One of the crew members tossed her a face towel. Tears came to Vivian's eyes too, as she thought of Ms. Washington and her children, and grand-children, and great-grandchildren growing up in the projects back in Austin. Maybe one of them would 'make it somehow.' Vivian wondered what the song meant to Denise. When it ended, the crowd was quiet.

The Queen composed herself, snapped her finger to set the beat for the band and broke into *Trapped By This Thing Called Love*, then wove into *While You Were Steppin' Out Someone Else Was Steppin' In*. Vivian moved her feet from side to side, and pumped her fists with the beat. *You Can Have That No Good Husband of Mine, But Don't Mess With My Man*, got the women shouting, Vivian right with them. By the time she got to *Drop That Zero, Get Yourself a Hero*, the men were joining in, hands clapping overhead in time with the beat. The breaks between her hits were almost too short for the crowd to show the Queen their appreciation. On *A Woman Needs To Be Loved*, Vivian closed her eyes and swayed with the crowd around her, snapping her fingers in time with the beat. She felt Marc's hands move from her shoulders to her waist as he swayed with her, and the back-up singers chanted 'Love, Love, Love.' When the Queen ended the set on *Down Home Blues*, they were among those shouting thunderously, "More-More-More, More-More-More."

Obviously tired, and a little hoarse, the Queen came back and sang *I Don't Need No Man That Needs Supervision*, then exited the stage, waving to the crowd. "Dee Neece! Dee Neece!" was mixed with "Woo-woo-woo-woo!"

They put Passion in the stroller and sat in the chairs, watching the crowd mill around in the afterglow of the concert. When the crowd thinned, they made their way back to the RV. Vivian put Passion to bed, then changed into her silk nightshirt. She climbed into bed next to Passion, catching snatches of the conversation outside between Marc and Denise's driver about the relative merits of diesel and gasoline engines. The drone of the diesel engine of the nearby bus lulled her to sleep, so she didn't hear the big bus drive away, or Marc quietly latching the door.

Marc leaned back against the counter a long time watching her, as she slept on her side curled around Passion. She'd thrown the light blanket off in the warm Mississippi night, and the full length of her legs was exposed. He had the urge to touch her hand, to gently rouse her, then lead her to the overhead bed with him. He knew that, even if she was willing, it would only complicate things. But, if she refused, it would even the score, in a way, so she could stop looking at him out of lowered lashes.

He took the two steps to the foot of the bed, bent over and reached to touch her, then stopped. Something about her hand, draped protectively across Passion, struck him as odd. He stared at it a moment until it came to him. The wide band around her finger where the ring had been was several shades lighter than the rest of her hand. It was a stark reminder to him that, no matter what *she* thought, she still belonged to another man. He turned and walked to the ladder.

* * * * *

Crane parked his pickup among the scrub cedar trees. George Jones' mournful voice, blaring from obviously cheap speakers, broke the quietness of the night. He felt kind of sorry for Captain Gormann. He was one of very few people who got invited to Gormann's house—if you could call it that. The five-acre tract in Dripping Springs was all he'd gotten in the divorce, so he'd put an old Airstream trailer on it and called it home. The drive over from Garfield had taken Crane an hour. It would be an hour back. Barbara was gonna be even more steamed if he stayed too long. He was determined to make this marriage work—his third.

He'd only stopped in The ShowUp Bar for one drink Thursday after work, before he went home to face the baby's constant crying. Barbara said he would grow out of it. The place had been full of cops—the younger ones that he didn't really know. The place was different now. Not smoky like it used to be. The young ones didn't smoke. The few seasoned ones, like himself, didn't welcome him. They felt he'd broken rank on that community policing thing, just because he'd expressed the opinion in the Association meeting that they should at least give it a try. So when Gormann came in the bar that night, he was so glad to see a friendly face, he had another drink. Then another.

It was his own fault, opening his big mouth about the tape. Promising to show it to him. But the drink always made him talk too much. That was what Barbara said. The other two had said it too, but he hadn't listened to them. Barbara was different. Or maybe *he* was. Maybe he'd gotten old enough to figure out that somebody could care as much about him as his brothers in blue. More, maybe. But what the hell. If he could give his old buddy a little fun, that was little enough to ask. He'd just have to be careful not to mention Gormann's ex. Then he'd be there all night listening to him bitch about her. Barbara wouldn't understand that at all. He climbed down out the truck just as Gormann opened the door to the trailer.

"Hey! Come on in," Gormann said, clapping him on the back. "Wanna shot?"

"Gotta beer? I can't stay too long," Crane said, ducking to go through the door. He wondered how Gormann managed to be such a natty dresser from the shabbiness of the trailer.

Gormann handed him a longneck from the fridge. "You bring that tape?" He took the tape Crane handed him and inserted it.

"Sit down, buddy. Make yourself at home."

Crane sat on the couch, as Gormann sat in the olive green Bar-Co-Lounger, patched with duct tape. When the bride appeared, Gormann shot him a disdainful look. Crane just shrugged and nodded toward the VCR. During the 15-minute segment, Gormann's racist comments made him uncomfortable. But again, he didn't say anything to him about it. He never had. Even when he was a rookie patrolman, assigned to Sergeant Gormann. Now that Gormann was about to retire, what would be the point? When the bride and groom appeared walking back down the aisle, he said, "That's all."

"Gosh darn, buddy. That was pretty good," Gormann said, punching the re-wind button. "Let's play it again."

"I got to be going. Barbara's already pissed about me leaving her on a Saturday night."

"I hate for you to come all this way, then leave so soon. Why don't you leave the tape with me?"

"Aw, Cap'n. You know I can't do that."

"Whaz the matter? Don't trust me? Huh?" he asked with that snaky grin.

Crane didn't, really. He remembered that other time he'd 'loaned' Gormann a piece of evidence. That little 'chain of custody' problem Gormann caused him. Got his ass in a real crack over it, too. Then Sergeant Gormann came along and rescued him—as though he was innocent in the deal. Gormann had thought it was pretty funny, but Crane had failed to see the humor in the threat of a reprimand in his file.

Of course, that was nothing compared to the 'little tricks' he'd seen Gormann play on the street. His favorite was the knee to the stomach of a 'uncooperative' detainee. Then, when the man fell forward from the blow, he'd accuse him of lunging at him. Bingo. Assault on a PO. Off to jail—with his manufactured probable cause. On the other hand, Gormann had put away more than his share of real criminals. Crane had to admire him for that—even if he didn't admire his methods. He also had mixed emotions about Gormann's penchant for dark meat.

"Let's just watch it one more time," Crane offered. "Then I've really got to go."

"Awright, buddy. That's better."

* * * * *

Marc and Passion were up and waiting for her again Sunday morning. They had a light breakfast of fluffy pancakes. Looking out the window at the deserted train station, Vivian found it hard to believe it had been the site of so much excitement only hours before. The paper flyers and plastic cups littering the ground, and an old man picking up cans, were the only evidence.

"Are we leaving now?" Vivian asked, as she dried and put away the last plate.

"I hadn't planned to, but we can, if you want."

"I don't care. We stowaways are on your schedule."

"They're going to do gospel this afternoon. I'd planned to stay. You like gospel music?"

"I like *real* gospel music."

"Well, it doesn't get any more real than they do it here. I thought we'd go down to the Museum and fool around for a while. There was a great exhibit when I was here last time. And they were planning a renovation. The flyer I saw last night said the music would start at 2:00. That would give us a couple of hours."

When they emerged from the RV, they waved at Ruskey, directing the clean-up crew of young boys and teenagers, who were scouring the grounds picking up trash. They strolled the four blocks through the downtown, window-shopping at the stores closed for Sunday, past the modern Clarksdale Public Library, to the Delta Blues Museum next door in the old library building. They managed to get Passion and the stroller up the wide, but steep flight of wooden stairs.

They followed the chronological exhibit that started in Africa with the banza—a stringed instrument made from a gourd. The six-foot pasteboards traced its treacherous journey to America with slaves, then the development of that instrument into the banjo, blending with European folk music, then branching off into modern American country music. Another branch wound its way into the development of the guitar, showcasing musicians born and raised in the area, leading through the old blues masters like Muddy Waters and Howling Wolf. From there it split into three branches: the R&B greats—Jerry Butler, Rufus and Carla Thomas, Roebuck 'Pops' Staples, Ike Turner; the modern blues singers— 'Little Milton' Campbell, Tyrone Davis and Jimmy Reed, and the women—Dorothy Moore, Thelma Houston and of course, Denise LaSalle; and the gospel music giants like the Rev. C. B. Franklin—Aretha's daddy—and Sam Cooke, who originally sang gospel with the Soul Stirrers. All of them, and many more, had been born within a fifty-mile radius of Clarksdale. Vivian wondered what it was about the area that incubated such an abundance of musical talent, that had influenced every aspect of American music—even Elvis. All those folk, in their own venues, had carried the Mississippi Delta music all over the world.

They arrived back at the depot just as the first group started to sing. Teenaged boys in matching, rust-colored suits. Although this was clearly a different crowd, Vivian recognized some of the folk that had swayed with them to the blues the night before.

"You think I should change clothes?" Vivian asked, looking from her spandex shorts and oversized t-shirt to some of the women dressed as though they had come straight from church— hats and all. "I didn't bring a dress, but I do have some long pants."

"You look fine. Those sisters are gonna want to trade places with you before the sun and dust gets through with them. Besides, nobody here knows us. So what, if they talk about us?" he asked, smiling and shrugging his shoulders.

She grabbed the hem of her shirt and stretched it out, showing the pictures of three 'Cleopatras' and the wording 'When God Made The Black Woman, He Was Just Showing Out.'

"You think this is inappropriate?"

"Can't argue with the truth," Marc said, with a crooked smile.

They stopped at the RV and picked up the folding chairs. Then they bought sausage wraps and red sodas from the BarBQ vendor. At first they were among the few braving the sun to get close to the stage. The majority hugged the shade against the building across the way. As the afternoon wore on and the building cast a longer shadow, the others followed it closer to the stage.

Gospel quartets and quintets from throughout Mississippi and Arkansas, sang in sweet harmony, weaving ancient scriptures into their songs, backed up by modern electric guitars and pianos. Each group was better than the one before. The female quintet from Fort Smith, Arkansas nearly turned it out. The Sons of Wonder from Friars Point, Mississippi had the crowd on their feet, waving their right hands. When the young lead singer in the high-collared white shirt and brocade vest leaped the five feet from the stage into the dust, the crowd formed a circle around him, urging him on. As the guitars and drums played the same hypnotic beat over and over, and he sang himself farther in the trance, people all around the circle began doing the Holy Ghost dance in time with the beat.

Vivian felt the spirit and wanted to join in, but she'd been raised in the staid AME Church, so she didn't know how. The woman next to Marc was a little deeper into the spirit and he moved the stroller just in time to catch her as she threw her arms up in the air in complete surrender, then fell backwards. Watching the woman twitching in Marc's arms, mouthing 'Yes, Jesus. Yes, Jesus,' Vivian wondered what it felt like to be overcome with the spirit. Were only special, chosen people touched in that way? Or were they ordinary people who had something happen in their lives that they just couldn't handle? If that was the case, would she be the next one slayed with the spirit? The thought frightened her a little. They didn't notice when night fell.

The Jackson Southernaires, in their midnight blue tuxedos, was the last group—and the best. Years of performing had polished them to a fine sheen. They sang *The Old Ship of Zion*, accompanied only by a quiet, steady cymbal beat and a tinny piano. Then, several of the old favorites, but most of their songs were their own. One voice would soar high, while another reached for the depths of the bass, then both wove back through the harmony of the others. Their choreography included the guitar players, in perfect synchronization. They moved the crowd with ease from the frenetic *Hooked on Jesus* to the soothing *Mighty Long Way*. When they walked off stage more than an hour later, the refrain of *Your Grace and Mercy* trailing them, the crowd's response was the same as the night before. "More, more, more. More, more, more."

* * * * *

After so many hours of church, Marc and Vivian were humbled and quiet. They stopped at the tables set up under a striped canopy and bought several CD's the Southernaires and other groups were hawking. Then they stopped by the BarBQ stand again on the way home. This time they tried the chopped beef sandwiches. While Vivian settled Passion in bed, Marc spread out the sandwiches on the table, cutting them in fourths.

"I've really enjoyed this," she said, flopping in the chair. "Thanks for bringing me."

"There's another one in August. Would you like to come again?"

"I'd love to."

Although neither verbalized it, they both wondered whether she would be free by then. When they finished, Marc rolled up the greasy butcher paper and put it in the trashcan under the sink. He took two beers from the refrigerator, and offered her one.

"Put it in the freezer," she answered. "It ought to be good and cold by the time I get out of the shower."

Vivian closed the folding door, stripped her dusty clothes off and stepped in the shower. She let the water spray into her face—being careful not to wet her hair—and over her body, washing the Delta dust off.

Marc sat on the couch opposite the table, listening to the water pump and envisioning the water running over her naked body. He stretched his long legs and propped his feet in one of the chairs, trying to push the thought out of his mind. He wondered if he was making payments on his ticket to Hell—drinking beer and indulging lecherous thoughts—adulterous even. And so soon after their marathon church session.

Since she'd planned to be at her mother's, Vivian hadn't brought a robe. She was reluctant to let him see her that way, but what choice did she have? She tugged at the hem of her short nightshirt before she pushed the folding door back open. On her way from the shower, Vivian took the beer from the freezer.

"You ready for another?" She handed him one and sat in the other chair opposite him. He looked so comfortable in that position, she stretched her legs toward the couch, then scooted down in the chair until her feet reached it. She took a sip, then leaned her head on the back of the chair, her eyes closed.

"Tired?" he asked.

"Mm-hmm. It's been a long day. Good though."

Marc only intended to rest his hand on her foot, but he began rubbing his thumb across her arch, applying not quite enough pressure to hurt.

"Oh, that feels good," she said dreamily.

He lifted her foot onto his lap and watched her relaxing, as he slowly massaged it. There was a look of pure pleasure on her face as he rubbed both his thumbs under it, while his fingers gripped the top. In a circular motion, he worked his thumbs up to the ball of her foot. Then, he took each toe and rolled it between his thumb and fingers. He squeezed the indentation above her heel between his thumb and forefinger, then rubbed her arch again.

The toes on her other foot were rhythmically curling and squeezing against each other, in anticipation of their turn. When he started on the other foot, she eased farther down in the chair.

Marc closed his eyes against the sight of her knees and thighs slowly and sensuously rubbing against each other. He fought hard against the urge to push them apart, get on his knees between them, then pull her to him. Summoning every ounce of resistance he had in him, he eased her feet off the sofa, and planted them firmly on the floor. Vivian jolted from her dreamy place.

"Go to bed, Vivian," he said in a husky voice.

"But, I'm—"

"Now, Vivian," he said sternly. "Go now."

When she saw the smoldering look in his dark eyes, she stood and walked to the bed.

* * * * *

Monday morning, Marc drove south to Leland, then east to Indianola. He was disappointed there was no statue in the center of town. He stumbled around, asking questions, until he found a small neighborhood street—B.B. King Boulevard. It was the only landmark he could find to mark the legend's birthplace. Vivian took a picture of him and Passion under the street sign. Then, on to Winona where he picked up Interstate 55, south to Jackson. After they toured the hilly campus of Jackson State University, he took Interstate 20 to Atlanta, skirting it, then south on Interstate 75 to Macon. South of Macon he took Highway 49, descending into a valley where the land flattened out. Just before they hit the city limits, he turned on a small road, then a smaller, winding one.

The nondescript house sat way back from the road. As they approached, Vivian saw a couple sitting on the porch. The man stood and walked to the edge, shielding his eyes against the evening sun. The buxom woman joined him, holding a cardboard fan in her hand. Marc drove up the long dirt road to the yard. He killed the motor, then hopped down.

The woman preceded the man down the steps and was the first to reach Marc. She patted him on the back as she hugged him, like she hadn't seen him in a long, long, time. The man was thinner than Marc, but the same height. His skin was taut and leathery-looking—as though he'd been baked by the sun. His woolly hair was nearly white. He stood back, waiting his turn— as though he understood that mothers have dibs. The embrace between father and son was quicker—two smart pats. But when they stood back and looked at each other, the emotion in their eyes was just as strong as the mother's arms around her son's shoulders had been.

Mrs. Kline was appreciatively eyeing the RV, tangible evidence of her son's success, when she saw Vivian. She smiled at Vivian, and Vivian returned it. Noticing his mother's reaction, Marc hurried around to open the door, and helped her down.

"Mama, Pops. This is my friend, Vivian."

ELEVEN

Vivian was shaking Mr. Kline's weathered hand, when the swarm of kids came racing from around the side of the house, shouting, "Uncle Buddy! Uncle Buddy!" They surrounded Marc and he hugged them all in turn.

"Where's Corey?" one of them asked.

"He couldn't come this time," Marc answered. "Maybe this summer."

Vivian noticed one somber-faced boy hung back from the pushing and shoving, as though he was accustomed to being last. He appeared to be about ten years old. Marc waded through the others to give him a hug. The boy's eyes sparkled from the attention, but he didn't say a word. He held out his palm. Marc patted his pants pocket for the keys, and not finding them, pointed to the RV. A grin spread across the boy's face, then he ran and climbed into the driver's seat. Vivian saw him pretending to drive the RV, a serene smile on his face. She wondered if the child was deaf, but was drawn back to the pandemonium around them, as Marc tried to introduce them all to her. Two teen-aged girls came out of the house and got their hugs, all the while eyeing Vivian curiously. The younger ones were still tugging at Marc, all talking at the same time. Mr. Kline shooed them off. It was obvious he was the patriarch of the family by the way they instantly obeyed, taking the chaos with them to the side of the house. He walked back toward the porch. Mrs. Kline took Vivian's hand and led her behind him. Marc followed, a niece hugging him on each side.

Mrs. Kline dispatched the girls to fix plates for Marc and Vivian, as the four of them settled in the chairs on the porch. Marc answered the questions about Texas and how he liked it, his new job, was he eating right, how was the trip, any car trouble? They spoke in one voice, although not at the same time. One would start the question, the other finishing it. Maybe that was how it was after fifty years of living with the same person, Vivian thought, as she fielded their questions about her. Grew up in Fort Worth, worked in political campaigns for several years, now a student in law school, met Marc at an function at the capitol, Georgia is beautiful. Never been here before.

The girls brought them plates of fried chicken, mashed potatoes and green beans, and glasses of tea, then sat on the edge of the porch. Vivian saw them casting admiring glances back at their uncle, while she savored the food. The mound of mashed potatoes was dented with a generous dollop of melted butter. And the succulent chicken was fried to perfection. She was biting into the fleshy part of the second drumstick, when the parade of white-plumed birds wandered into the front yard. She held the leg away from her mouth, looking from it to them, wondering how long ago it was pecking around in the yard with its friends. She gingerly laid it back on the plate, then picked at the beans and potatoes, still eyeing the chickens.

None of them noticed the somber-faced boy approach the porch, holding Passion in the way a ten-year-old would.

"Uncle Bu-bu-bu-buddy. I found this ba-ba-ba-baby in your RV."

Vivian's heart went out to the boy when she realized why he'd been so quiet before.

"Lordy, look a here. Bring me that baby."

The boy walked up the steps and handed Passion to Mrs. Kline.

"Aw, ain't she pretty, " she said.

Vivian knew without looking that Passion was doing her flirting thing. Mr. Kline reached over and poked her in the stomach, just as Marc had done. The teenage girls scooted over to where Mrs. Kline sat, tugging playfully at Passion's feet and waiting their turn to hold her. Vivian felt the subtle attitude shift from curiosity about her, to acceptance.

"She probably needs a dry diaper. Be right back," she said, heading to the RV. The boy fell in step beside her.

"I'm Vivian. What's your name?"

"Lil' Bu-bu-bu-buddy."

"They named your uncle after you?" she asked, smiling at him and ignoring his stutter. He gave her a puzzled look, then grinned at her when he figured out she was fooling him.

"Would you help me bring the baby's things in?"

"Sure."

When they were inside the RV, she pointed toward the bag, "Let's see. You take this bag. I'll get the stroller. It's kind of bulky. It's probably too heavy for you."

"I'm a b-b-b-b-big b-b-b-boy. I can bring the stroller," he insisted.

"Alright, Lil' Buddy," she said. She let him struggle it out the door, knowing it was important to him to do it himself. Outside, she told him how to set it up.

"It'll roll easier that way."

"I like you," he said.

"I like you too, Lil Buddy."

Mrs. Kline took the baby inside, both of Marc's nieces trailing her.

"That's a pretty lil' baby," Mr. Kline said, as soon as they were alone.

"Yes, she is. Sweet too," Marc said.

"Vivian seems like a nice girl. Must be smart, too. Going to law school and all." He puffed on the pipe, thoughtfully.

"Yep."

The quiet of the late evening reminded Marc of many like it that he'd spent on the porch with his father and his brothers, after the men's work was done.

"I noticed that girl ain't wearing no ring," Mr. Kline said.

Marc knew his dad was a man of few words—and keen observation. Marc thought about the light-colored band around her finger. He'd been so worried about her husband, it hadn't occurred to him he might have to answer before he got back to Austin. It was such a long story, he didn't know how to tell it in a way that would make sense to his father.

"Well, Pops—"

"You bringing shame on the family, Buddy," he interrupted, in his matter-of-fact manner.

His father's remark struck Marc to his core. He could see

how it could be viewed that way. There was surely nothing he could say now that would make traveling across the country with another man's wife anything less than shameful.

"We Klines ain't never had much, 'cept our land. And our pride. You the first to graduate college. And we real proud about that. But we always prided ourselves on taking care of our own. There has never been a child born in *this* family that couldn't lay rightful claim to the name. Not in my time, and my father before me, and his father. I don't know what they teaching up there in that college, but I *know* I taught you better. Didn't I tell you, if a girl ain't good enough for you to marry, she ain't good enough for you to lay with?"

Marc opened his mouth to speak, then closed it. He didn't know how to say he had only *wanted* to lay with her.

"She's just a friend, Pops."

"Friend, my ass. I ain't for this new-fangled stuff. I expect you to do the right thing by that girl. *And* that baby. And that's all I got to say about it." Mr. Kline stood and walked in the house.

Marc was dumb-founded. How could he explain that Passion wasn't his baby, without making Vivian look like a tramp in his father's eyes? He certainly couldn't defend her honor by telling the truth—that she was already married.

When Vivian and Lil' Buddy got to the porch, Marc's face looked like it was going to cave in on itself.

"Something wrong?" she asked.

He put on a smile. "Naw. Go on inside. Lil' Buddy's got a lot to tell me about what he's been doing since I was here last summer."

Passion sat in Mrs. Klines's ample lap, while one of the girls fed her mashed potatoes.

"I need to change her, Mrs. Kline," Vivian said.

"Call me Ruthie, hon."

"Let me. Let me," the other girl said.

Vivian looked uncertain as she handed her the bag.

"They can take care of that baby. They're used to having babies around," Mrs. Kline said, to allay her concern. "Take her in the bedroom," she instructed the girls. "Come on, sit down, Vivian."

"How long have you and Buddy been together?"

"Together? Oh, we're not together." Seeing Mrs. Kline's knowing smile, she added "I mean, not in *that* way. We're just friends."

Mrs. Kline's ample bosom heaved with her chuckle. "Honey, you can think what you want. But I know my Buddy. I haven't seen him look at a girl the way he looks at you. Not even that girl…Corey's mama. He gets fixed—just like his daddy. You know what I mean?"

"No, I'm not sure I do." Vivian hoped that Mrs. Kline didn't notice how her cheeks and the top of her ears were burning.

Mrs. Kline chuckled again. "Fixed. You know, he gets fixed on a thing, and won't let go. He's fixed on you. *And* that baby."

Their conversation was interrupted by loud voices on the porch. The screen door creaked when Marc opened it for his sisters.

"Ya'll late," Mrs. Kline said.

"We knew Buddy wouldn't be here til now." Turning to Vivian, she said, "How're you? I'm Doreen. This is my sister Nola Faye."

"Pleased to meet you. I'm Vivian." The way they both stared at her made her uncomfortable.

Even if she'd seen them on the street, she would have known they were Marc's sisters. Although they looked alike, they were a study in contrast. Doreen was tall and thin, Nola Faye a few pounds past a load. Doreen was quiet and reserved, Nola Faye loud and bold, with a twinkle in her eye.

"She don't look nothing like that uppity girl," Nola Faye said under her breath to Doreen.

"Ya'll want some dinner?" Mrs. Kline asked. "And you mind your manners, Nola Faye."

"What?!" Nola Faye asked, an innocent grin on her face. "All I said was she's prettier than that ol' girl. 'Cept for that hair. But I can take care of that. How long you gon' be here?" she asked Marc.

"Well, I don't know. It all depends on how you act," he replied smiling at her.

"Boy, you know I'm always the same—all the time."

"Then we may leave in a few minutes."

"No you ain't," she said plopping on the couch next to Vivian. "That won't be enough time for me to find out all I need to know about your 'friend.' Doreen, bring me a plate," she yelled. "Now Vivian, how long you known Buddy?"

"Don't mind Nola Faye," Marc said. "She's the family detective. Always in everybody's business. At least let her catch her breath, Nola Faye. You know you take a little getting used to."

"A while," Vivian responded politely.

"Uh huh. Not long enough to make him give you a ring," she said taking Vivian's hand in hers. "You come by the shop. I'll tell you how to do that. And I can do something about those nails too while you're there. I got a reputation of doing the fanciest nails in the county. Folk come all the way from Macon to get me to do their nails." She put Vivian's hand down to accept the plate from Doreen. "So what kind of work you do?" she asked, then bit into a piece of chicken.

"I'm in school."

"Ain't you a little old for that?"

"Oh, I don't know. We look to be about the same age. Didn't you have to go back to school to learn nails? I'm pretty sure when you first went, back in the day, they weren't doing those."

Nola Faye let out a whooping belly laugh. "I like this one, Marc. She's got a lot of spunk."

When the girls appeared in the doorway with Passion, Nola Faye almost dropped her fork. She turned to Vivian. "Yeah, girl, you *got* to come by the shop. We got some serious talking to do." Nola Faye rolled her eyes at Marc. Doreen gave him the same look. He turned and walked out the door.

Marc stood on the porch, stinging from the scorn of his father and sisters, staring out at the night. Then, he jumped down and walked to the RV. He found Lil' Buddy in the driver's seat. He took a beer and a soda from the fridge. He put the soda in the console by his nephew and sat on the couch drinking the beer.

"Where're we going this time, Lil' Buddy?"

"Alaska."

"Can we get there from here?"

"Yep. I got it all worked out. Gonna' catch a big ferry out of Vancouver."

"OK," Marc said, turning the question over in his mind. Finally, he had to ask it.

"How's your dad?"

"He's gonna be OK."

Marc saw the boy's face close up. He knew it wouldn't do any good to try to penetrate that wall, so he changed the subject.

"You still writing poems?"

"Yep."

"You show them to anybody else yet?"

"Nope."

"Can I take some back with me?"

After a while, he asked, "You gon' show Vi-vi-vian?"

"Would that be OK with you?"

A long pause. "Yeah. OK."

While they rode in comfortable silence, Marc thought of his father's words. Knowing the women would keep Passion in the house with them, and remembering the close call of the night before, he decided it would be best for Vivian to stay in the house, too.

"Gotta get off here, Lil' Buddy. I'll catch up with you in Vancouver."

He took Vivian's bag and started toward the house. Just as he reached the porch, he stopped and waited for the headlights coming up the road. When he recognized the truck, he called out, "Vivian. Come here."

The screen door slapped close, as she walked to the edge of the porch, just as the men climbed out of the truck. She looked from her bag sitting on the porch, to the men hugging Marc and shaking hands.

"Ya'll meet Vivian. This is my older brother, Lee. And my

baby brother, Junior."

"How you doing?" they said in unison.

"And this is Nola Faye's husband, Gene."

Looking at the short, skinny man holding the '40-ounce', Vivian thought 'Jack Sprat.'

"Nola Faye told me ya'll were putting in a hot tub at her house," Marc said. "Where's Nathan?"

They all looked off, each waiting for the other to answer, then back at Marc.

"Still the same, huh?" he asked

They all nodded.

"Can't ya'll do something to get him off that crack?"

"Can you?" Gene asked, then reached in the cooler in the back of the truck and handed Marc one of the big bottles of beer. "Miz Vivian, would you mind telling my wife that her husband's hongry. Say it just like that too—hon-gry." All the men broke out laughing.

Vivian was surprised at how quickly Nola Faye moved in response to her message.

"Come on Doreen, you know Lee and Junior are hungry, too. You too, Vivian."

They all sat around on the porch, catching up on the news since Marc's last visit. When Mr. Kline announced that it was "time to shut this roadhouse down," they loaded up the truck with kids and left. Mrs. Kline showed Vivian to the bedroom where Passion was curled up, fist at her mouth. Marc headed to the RV.

The next morning, her little alarm clock went off, kicking

her. Vivian changed her, then dressed them both. The aroma of coffee lured her to the kitchen.

"That's yours," Mrs. Kline said, pointing to the steaming cup on the table, and reaching for Passion. "I heard ya'll stirring. This is the sweetest little baby. I wish she was Marc's."

"I do, too." Vivian startled when she realized what she'd said. "I mean…I didn't mean to say that."

"Nuthin' wrong with wishing, chile. Wishing is what starts most things that end up getting done. Buddy'll make a fine daddy. Reach me a bowl out of that cabinet. Put a little of that rice in it for this baby. Get yourself some if you want. Eggs and bacon in the oven. Those kids'll be here any minute, and they'll eat every slappin' bit. I keep all my grandkids when they ain't in school. Except Lil' Buddy. He stays with me. His mama and daddy both— On the weekends, he goes with the others most times."

"How're my ladies doing this morning?" Marc asked from the doorway.

"Come on in here, boy, and get you some breakfast." Mrs. Kline's face beamed. "Vivian here don't seem to eat much, but this baby makes up for her."

"Watch her. She'll eat everything you have," he said, fixing his plate. "Where's Pops?"

"He went with Lee and Junior 'nem. Them boys can take care of all the work since they bought that big ol' tractor. It's air conditioned. Did you know that? Lordy, what's this world coming to? I remember when it took all of us to do it by hand. You remember?"

"Of course, I remember."

"Well, now they plowing up half the land in the county. They just let Early go along. They all playing like he's still the boss, but I 'magine he's mostly in the way. Never mind them. You take Vivian and show her around. Take the old truck," she said, pointing to the keyrack by the back door.

* * * * *

Marc drove the narrow dusty roads. He took her by the building where he'd attended school. It had a fresh coat of paint, and the sign out front now read 'Senior Community Center.' Marc was glad the building was being used. It had sat vacant for years after integration. Then they passed the big school that had been built after he left to accommodate all the students—Black and White. The contrast between the two was striking. The tour of the little town didn't take long, most of it spent on the college campus. When they passed the crack house, he peered hard out the window, searching for Nathan.

Before noon, they were back on Kline land. Marc stopped the truck at the edge of a large stock pond. He took her hand and helped her down, then led her out on the pier.

"I used to spend a lot of time out here. Me and Nathan. He's my twin. If we weren't swimming and messing around, we were avoiding work and reading. Kept a stash of books right under here. Then, it was full of bullfrogs and butterflies. Haven't seen any lately."

"You never told me you were a twin," she said reproachfully.

"We used to be real close. 'Til he came back from Nam," he said, tightening his lips and looking off, with the remembrance. "Then…"

"Where is Nathan?"

"Around. Wanna go for a ride?" he asked, changing the subject and pointing to the flat-bottomed boat tied at the end of the pier.

He helped her get settled in the boat, then pushed away from the pier. "I used to pretend this was the ocean, and I was sailing for the New World. It was a lot bigger then," he said, laughing.

When they got to the middle, Marc laid the oar inside and lay back across the seat. Vivian followed suit. They lazily drifted awhile, neither of them saying anything.

"You want to go swimming?" he sat up and asked. "You said you brought a suit."

"Nah. I don't think so. I'd have to fool with my hair all afternoon. Besides, I need to go back and see about Passion. I hate to leave her on your mother all this time."

"Don't worry about it. Mama's never happier than when she's got a baby to fuss over." Marc pulled the t-shirt over his head and dropped it on the floor of the boat, revealing the broad expanse of his chest, then took off his sneakers and stuffed his socks in them.

"What are you doing?" Vivian asked. "You didn't bring your trunks."

"Don't need 'em," he said, smiling at her mischievously, while he unbuttoned his shorts. "Turn your head and close your eyes. No fair peeking."

"You're not doing what I think you're doing, are you?" she asked, her head turned away, eyes closed. She felt the boat rock and heard the splash, as he dove into the water.

"You can open your eyes now."

She saw him shiver a couple of times.

"Cold?" she asked.

"Yes, indeed. Some people would call this refreshing," he said, as he swam away.

He swam in circles around the boat, the wake gently rocking it. Vivian watched his muscles flex in a perfect breast stroke. She stretched out on the seat and pulled the cap down to shield her face against the sun, enjoying the lazy rocking of the little boat. She could hear the rhythmic swish as he propelled himself through the water, and felt herself being lulled by it.

A sudden quiet intruded on her drowsy state. She sat up and looked around, but didn't see him. She jerked her head from side to side, searching for him. Panic began to rise in her gut. She called his name. Then again, more frantically. The boat rocked when she stood up and looked toward the house. She knew she couldn't scream loud enough to be heard up there. She considered diving in to search for him. The pond that had looked so small before, now looked like a lake. She got on her knees and leaned over the side of the boat, trying to see into the murky water. She scrambled to the other side. Just as she leaned over, Marc sprang straight up out of the water, right in front of her face. She jerked back to keep from getting wet. He lay his forearms on the edge of the boat, laying his head on them, and gasping for breath. Vivian was overcome with relief that he was alive. As she reached over to comfort him, he raised his head and grinned at her. "Gotcha!"

"Fool! You nearly scared me to death! I thought you had drowned!"

"You didn't jump in to save me," he said, still grinning. He shook the glistening drops of water from his hair. "I used to be able to stay under a lot longer."

She pushed his forehead backwards. "I ought to drown you myself."

"I feel like I *am* drowning, Vivian." His face was serious.

"I'm glad you didn't." She laid her arms around his shoulders, and pressed her cheek against his. When he pulled his face back, she touched her lips to his. His fingers circled her forearms. His tongue parted her lips and probed the depths of her mouth. She responded with a hunger that surprised them both. When he felt his arousal, he pulled away and swam hard to the edge of the pond, then back to the other side of the boat.

"Don't look," he said, as he hoisted his body inside, then pulled on his shorts.

On the ride back, she saw wetness seeping through his pants in the outline of his briefs.

"You fooled me. I thought you were swimming naked. What's your mother going to think when she sees you?"

"Nothing different than they already think," he said, staring straight ahead, lost in his own thoughts.

* * * * *

They spent the next day driving dusty roads across the flat land, and visiting his friends. Mrs. Kline had insisted that they leave Passion with her.

"Let's go by your nosy sister's shop. Maybe she'll wash my hair. It's still full of that Clarksdale dust. Besides, I haven't been to a beauty shop since I got Passion."

"You sure? She's gonna put you through the third degree, you know," he said chuckling. He drove into town and parked in the block that contained the Black businesses.

"Girl, I been waiting on you," Nola Faye said. "It took you long enough."

The beauty shop was small and neat. Faded Ultra-Sheen posters adorned the walls. Vivian was surprised to see Doreen pressing her customer's hair. She didn't know anybody got their hair pressed anymore. One of the teenagers was at the shampoo bowl, washing another customer's hair. Nola Faye wore a bright orange pantsuit, the exact shade of her long nails that she was filing. She pushed herself out of the chair, then stood behind it. Patting the back of the chair, she said "Come on over here."

Vivian obeyed, and Nola Faye began removing the pins from the bun. Marc sat in one of the dryer chairs and began thumbing through the latest issue of Jet magazine.

"Honey, you need to let me cut this mess all off," Nola Faye said, massaging Vivian's scalp.

"Cut my hair?"

"Long hair makes a woman your age look old. Ain't that right, Doreen?"

"Old—trying to look young," Doreen said matter-of-factly. "But, that's just my opinion. A woman has a right to wear her hair anyway she wants."

Vivian could tell she was the peacemaker of the family.

"Marc, don't you think she ought to cut this stuff off?" Nola Faye asked.

He put his palms up and rolled his eyes. "I'm not in that," he said, shaking his head and smiling.

"But what do you *think*?" Vivian asked, now slightly intrigued by the idea.

"Well, you were saying the other day that you didn't have

time to fool with it, now that you have the baby. And it *does* keep you from swimming. But I agree with Doreen, it's *your* hair. Don't let Nola Faye talk you into something you'll regret. If you like it long, keep it that way."

Vivian pursed her lips. It wasn't particularly what *she* liked. Walter liked it. Said he didn't want a woman who looked like a man. It didn't matter to him what a hassle it was to her, or how much of her time it took.

"Alright, Nola Faye. Cut it. But don't have me looking stupid now. Are you sure you know how to use those scissors?" Vivian asked, teasing.

Nola Faye put her hands on her full hips. "Is the Pope Catholic?! Is a pig pork?! Marc, you go on down the street to the domino shack. We gon' be busy for a couple of hours. I'm gon' get ahold of them nails, too."

A couple of hours later, when Marc peeked his head in the door, Vivian was admiring her new nails. Nola Faye had persuaded her to the French manicure, rather than a color, "Cause you ain't gon' have time to keep a bright color up proper, with a baby and all."

"I like it," he said, smiling and nodding approvingly at her new haircut. "Looks real sophisticated. Nola Faye just might know what she's doing."

"Shut up, boy," Nola Faye said affectionately.

"I like it too, Nola Faye. I should have done this years ago," she said, reaching in her purse. "How much do I owe you?"

"Family don't owe. You almost family. Next time you come, if you ain't family all the way, you pay me double."

TWELVE

"Gloria! How're you doing, babe?"

"Walter? Fine. Fine. How about you? You still in Washington? How's the weather up there?"

"Everything's fine. Listen, babe, don't have much time. Let me speak to Viv."

"Uh, she's not here right now, Walter."

"This is the third time I've called and she hasn't been there. What's up, Gloria?"

"Well, I guess you're just calling at the wrong times, Walter."

"I *know* she's there. Tell her I said she better come to the phone. Right now."

"Ex-cuse me? Better?"

"Look, Gloria, just get her on the phone. I don't have time for this."

"Seems to me you've had *plenty* of time on your hands."

"That's really not your business, Gloria. Put Vivian on the phone," he demanded.

"Listen, boy. Don't you get on your high horse with *me*. After what you've done, you need to be taking real low. And especially with me. You haven't forgotten all the money I've loaned you so

Vivian doesn't have to suffer your little lapses of judgment?"

"Oh, I guess you're going to wipe my face with *that* now!"

"If you'd kept your face clean, you wouldn't have to worry about it getting wiped for you!"

Gloria slammed the phone down and folded her arms across her breasts. How dare that arrogant SOB use that tone of voice with me, she fumed. She was so agitated she couldn't sit still. Even though she had never regretted giving up the habit, she wanted a cigarette now—bad. More so than any time in the five years since she'd quit. She remembered where there might be one. She marched down the hallway into her bedroom and jerked the dresser drawer open. The unopened packages of neatly stacked pantyhose were evidence that she never intended to wear another run in her life. She rummaged through them, running her hand to the back of the drawer. In the next drawer she pushed aside the beautiful lingerie sets, some with the price tags still on them. Then it came back to her. She got on her knees and opened the cedar chest at the foot of her bed. There it was—that last pack she'd hidden, just in case. The matches were there, too, and she was surprised to get one to light after so long. She lit the cigarette and sat on the floor leaning against the chest, enjoying the sensation—too much. Exhaling the smoke, she decided she'd only have that one.

Laying on top of the quilt her mother had made for her wedding present was the picture of Del and Babysis. With her free hand, she picked it up and stared at it, remembering her husband taking it the day it snowed. It seldom snowed in Ft. Worth—and it was the first snow for the girls. They were three and five, and she had been twenty-seven. Even though the photo was a black and white, she remembered the hideous orange coat she wore. She hated it, but it was all she could afford then. The smile on her face was full of confidence that it wouldn't always be that way. Del was stooping, making a snowball. Even then, she had a way of accepting things as they were, then making what she could out of it. Babysis just stood in the snow, up to her ankles, with a look on her face, not quite horrified, but not knowing exactly what she was supposed to do. They were still that way.

Funny, Gloria thought, how their little personalities formed so early, and didn't change. They were so unlike her. Neither of them had her shrewdness, nor her head for business. No matter how hard she tried to teach them that you had to grab life, and twist it and wring it until you got something much better out of it than it was willing to just give you—it hadn't taken with either of them. So here she was, nearly seventy years old, having gotten what *she* wanted, still twisting and wringing for them, until they figured it out. The cigarette had burned down to the filter. Gloria remembered the chore that Walter's call had interrupted. She put the picture away, and closed the chest.

Walking to the closet, she thought 'That fool just doesn't know who he's dealing with.' He'd been happy to sign those papers.

"Humph, law degree don't mean you smart," Gloria said aloud, as she took down the full length mink coat and the matching cloche hat to take to the furrier for storage. She headed for the pearl gray Lexus in her garage.

* * * * *

Marc was gone with his brothers, when Vivian got up Wednesday morning. After all the kids had eaten, she cleaned up the

kitchen, while Mrs. Kline, content to hold Passion, told her stories about Marc's antics as a little boy. When the dishes were put
away, Vivian walked out on the back porch and stretched in the
warmth of the sunshine. She heard from around the side of the
house, "Sh-sh-sh-shut up! Ju-ju-just shut up!"

Vivian walked to the edge of the porch and peeked around to
where the ruckus was. She saw the fury on Lil' Buddy's face. He
was fighting back tears, surrounded by his cousins, all of them
taunting him.

"Bu-bu-buddy c-c-can't t-t-talk!"

Vivian jumped down off the porch and marched into the
middle of them.

"Yeah, and you've got a knot on your head," she said, glaring
at the one who'd said it. Then she went around the circle, poking
each one in the chest. "And you've got buck teeth—gonna need
braces. And you've got skinny legs, like mine. Can't do nothing
about that." She was merciless, as she called them all out, one by
one, saying something about each one that she intended to hurt
them as much as they'd hurt Lil' Buddy.

"You know, God gives every one of us a challenge. And he
gives us all a special talent. I know what Lil' Buddy's special
talent is. What's yours?" she demanded from the oldest boy. He
looked down at his feet. Then she went around the circle again,
her eyes blazing with anger. She didn't even spare the four-year-
old, who had enjoyed Lil' Buddy's torment as much as the others. "What's yours?" she demanded of each of them, until they
were all looking down, shifting their feet in the dirt. "Come on,
Lil' Buddy." She took his hand and led him to the back porch.
She flopped down on the steps, still angry, and wondering why

children were so cruel to each other.

"It's *my* fi-fi-fi-fight. You can't d-d-d-do it for me." he said, glaring at her, then walked back to where the children were.

Vivian propped her elbows on her knees and buried her face in her hands. The boy was right. She shouldn't have stuck her big nose in it. Then she heard, "I can sing."

She looked up to see a little girl about six, the one she'd accused of having a big nose. She sang *Jesus Loves Me, This I Know* in the sweetest voice Vivian had ever heard. When she finished, Vivian nodded, smiling, not knowing what to say. Then the little girl ran around the side of the house. Vivian put her head back in her hands, so ashamed of herself that she didn't look up when she heard the screen door open. Early Kline sat in the rocker behind her.

"You done right. I heard it through the window. You sho' told them 'bout theyselves." He chuckled through the pipe clenched in his teeth. "I try not to show it, but I have special feelings for Lil' Buddy. They pester that child so. I don't interfere 'cause he's got to take up for his own self. Maybe I should tho'. Buddy used to stutter. Grew out of it. Or maybe was them speech classes he took. He had a hard growin' up—but he don't let nobody push him around."

"Mr. Kline, I don't want you to think I'm mean. I shouldn't have said that to the children, and I'm going to apologize to them."

"Naw. Needed to be said. Means you a good-doing person. I'm just sorry that my son hasn't done right by you and the baby. He's had better teaching than that. But he's gon' make it right. I'll see to that."

"Huh?" Vivian turned to him with a puzzled frown on her

face. Then it dawned on her what he thought.

"Course, you bear some of the blame," he said, matter-of-factly. "Most times, the woman has to *make* a man do right. Didn't yo' mama tell you that if a man can get the milk for free, he don't have to buy the cow?"

Vivian was furious that he would talk to her like she was a child. Even more so, that he would question her morals. But, out of respect for his age, she contained her anger. She looked at the lightened band of skin around her finger, then up at him.

"Yes, my mother did tell me that, Mr. Kline. But, here's the part she *didn't* tell me about. What if the man won't buy the cow because he's already got one? Then turns out, the new cow has a calf—from the man getting the 'free' milk, you know." Her tone was sing-song, as though she was telling a bedtime tale. She leaned back against the porch column, and continued.

"Now, the new cow doesn't want the calf if she can't have the man, so she gives the little calf to him and goes off looking for another man. But, the man doesn't want the little calf either— since all *he* wanted was the 'free' milk. So, he takes the calf to the cow he already has and tells her 'I brought you a present.' Now, *that* cow always wanted a calf herself, but she couldn't have one. She knows this calf comes from the 'free' milk, but she also knows that neither the man, nor the other cow, want the calf. She worries that the little calf won't thrive, not being wanted and all. So, what is the old cow to do? What would *you* tell the old cow to do, Mr. Kline?"

She paused, but not long enough for him to answer.

"*That's* the part my mother didn't tell me about, so I had to figure it out for myself. I'd tell the old cow to get rid of the man and keep the calf. That way, everybody can be fairly happy." She smiled tightly at him. "My mother tells me that 'fairly happy' is about all one can expect from this life."

Vivian stood and stretched, then turned back to him.

"I'm glad we had this little chat, Mr. Kline. Now, I'm going to take a little nap." She paused, then threw her chin up. "And, by the way, I'm keeping the little calf." She walked around the side of the house and didn't stop until she got to the RV.

Inside, Vivian threw herself on the bed. She couldn't decide whether to cry—or spit. When she heard the knock, then the door open, she dreaded having to face Marc. How could she explain that she'd behaved uncivilly to nearly all his family?

"Vivian?"

She sat up on the edge of the bed, when she heard his voice.

"Can I come in?"

"Sure," she said, nervously patting the nape of her neck where the bun used to be.

Early Kline walked in and leaned against the counter, looking ill at ease. He cleared his throat.

"I ain't much good at apologizing."

Vivian nodded, her lips pressed together tightly.

"'Cause I ain't wrong 'bout much, you know," he said matter-of-factly, a faint pout on his bottom lip.

Vivian nodded again. He shifted to the other foot.

"I don't know many women who'd do what you doing. Must take a lot of grit."

Vivian didn't say anything.

"Well, I just wanna say, I think Marc would do good if he can keep you." He folded his arms across his chest and looked off.

Silence pulsated in the RV, as each of them waited for the other to speak.

"Is that it?" Vivian asked, finally.

He nodded.

"You did fine," she said, with a slight smile.

He nodded twice, then walked out.

* * * * *

Thursday, Marc and Lil' Buddy left early. After breakfast, Vivian took Passion on the back porch and sat in Mr. Kline's rocker. The kids refused to acknowledge her presence, offering only a stony silence.

"What are you doing?" she asked, leaning over the oldest boy's shoulder.

"Drawin'," he said, tersely.

"That looks like Passion."

"Course it does. It *is* her," he said, looking at her as if she was too dumb to see the obvious.

"I guess drawing is your special talent."

"Maybe."

"We're bored," the older girl said, now that their pact of silence had been broken by the leader.

They all turned and looked at Vivian, as though it was her responsibility to do something about it.

"What would you like to do?" she asked.

"I don't know."

"And I don't think it's fair that Lil' Buddy gets to go with Uncle Buddy and we don't," another pouted. "Do you think that's fair?"

"Well, maybe—"

"Aw, she just gon' take up for him," the oldest boy said, not looking up from his drawing.

"Tell you what. Why don't we do something they don't get to do? You think it's warm enough to go swimming?" Vivian asked.

"Sure." They all raced into the house and were back in a flash wearing swimsuits and cut-offs, towels slung over their shoulders.

"Here, hold Passion, while I get our suits."

Vivian wiggled into her suit, then pulled her denim shorts back on. She fished Passion's new suit out of the bag.

Passion was in for a bumpy ride from the house to the pond. The kids took turns pushing her stroller. They showed Vivian where the wild berries grow, but it was too early in the season for them to have a treat. The big girl raced the boys to the end of the pier and they all dove in. Vivian and the younger girls walked to the edge of the pond and waded in. Vivian bent over and held Passion so that her feet splashed in the water, while the girls swam away. After a while, the oldest girl swam over to her.

"Want me to hold the baby so you can swim?"

Vivian thought about the sparkling clear pool she had at home and never used. "Be careful with her," she said, handing the baby to her, then waded into the cold, muddy water. She swam to the other side, and back. On her next trip across she noticed that the boys had stopped their raucous play and were staring toward the road.

Lil' Buddy hopped out of the truck before it came to a full stop, ran down the pier, and jumped, arms and legs swinging in the air. Vivian waded to the edge to meet Marc.

"Enjoying your swim?" he asked.

"Yes. You bring your trunks?"

"Don't need 'em," he said smiling mischievously, taking off his shoes and socks. He pulled off his shirt and threw it toward the truck.

"You can't do that in front of these kids!"

Marc took a running leap into the water. "Come on," he yelled back from the middle. Vivian swam out to him. Just as she reached him, he ducked under the water. She tread water, looking around for him. She wouldn't fall for that same trick. When he rose up between her legs raising her in the air, she squealed and grabbed his hair to maintain her balance. He carried her on his shoulders for a couple of steps before dumping her into the water. The boys swam over and pounced on Marc. Their horseplay was too rough for Vivian so she swam back to the edge, took Passion and sat her in her lap in the shallow water. When they were all worn out, the kids piled in the back of the truck for the ride up to the house.

After they'd finished the sandwiches and lemonade Mrs. Kline had ready for them, she ordered all the kids to take naps, despite the half-hearted protests of the older ones. She took Passion with her to her bed. Marc and Vivian sat on the back porch, rocking like old folks, stealing glances at each other like pre-teens.

"You enjoying yourself?" he asked.

"Having a good time. I can see why you would think about moving back. But what would you do?"

"Write."

"Uh hum," she said, nodding and yawning.

"I'd planned to leave tomorrow."

"OK," she said, her eyes closed. "What time?"

"In the morning. Early."

"Uhm," she said, as she drifted off to sleep.

When Vivian woke, the sun was low and she was alone on the porch. She stretched, then opened the screen door. Marc and his mother, Passion in her lap, were at the kitchen table.

"We been waiting on you." Mrs. Kline said. "Everybody's gone over to Nola Faye's. She and Gene are frying fish to christen their new hot tub. You can go like that. I think you're s'posed to wear a bathing suit in them things."

"I've *got* to shower. Won't take but a minute," Vivian assured them.

Vivian showered, washing her hair, and rinsed her swimsuit out. She dressed and slipped her feet in her sandals. She put a little gel on her hair, combed it straight back and smooth on her head, then tied a scarf around it. As she put on the red gimme cap she thought, 'This is *too* easy. Should have done it years ago.'

"I want to ride in that big buggy of yours, Marc," Mrs. Kline announced.

Marc helped his mother climb the steps into the RV. Vivian sat on the couch with Passion, "Sit up front, Mrs. Kline. The view is better."

When they got to Nola Faye's turn-off, they could see the colored plastic lanterns strung all around the yard and a crowd of people.

"This looks like a little more than christening a hot tub,

Mama," Marc said, a hint of reproach in his voice.

She chuckled. "I'm not supposed to tell you, but we wanted to throw a little party for ya'll on your last night here. Invited just about everybody in the county. 'Cept his old girlfriends," she said, turning to Vivian and winking.

Gene manned the big frying kettles, fish in one, potatoes in the other. Card tables covered with butcher paper held dishes of all kinds. Several couples were dancing to Bobby "Blue" Bland growling *Two Steps From the Blues* on the tall speakers. Marc walked around speaking to his old friends and neighbors, introducing Vivian as his friend. They stopped a while by the noisy bid whist table where Junior was holding forth. He stood straddle his chair, slapping cards on the table, making his 'six no low' with ease, and talking much noise. They moved on to the domino table where Mr. Kline and his buddies were 'teaching' a couple of young upstarts who'd had the temerity to take on the old bulls.

"Come on, old man," one of the brash young men in the baggy denim shorts challenged. "What you gonna do 'bout *this*! Ha!" he said, slamming his domino on the table. He looked quite pleased with himself, but the partner he'd dragged into these uncertain waters looked slightly fearful.

Early studied the bones in his hand a long time, as though he'd been bested. The slightest hint of a smile surrounded the pipe firmly clenched in his teeth, as he winked at Vivian. Quick as a striking cobra, he slammed the bone on the table hard enough to make the other dominoes jump and fall back into place.

"Aw-w-right, let's have some *real* players at this table," he announced, looking pointedly at the upstart, rising from his chair. As the young man walked away in disgrace amid the catcalls of the other men, Early called after him, "And don't come back messing around with grown men 'til you get a belt to hold them baggy pants up with. Real men don't show their drawers in public." Chuckles rose from the group of old men, while they readjusted the seating, and got back to the real game.

Vivian and Marc fixed plates, then took one to Mrs. Kline. While Vivian held their plates, Marc dragged two chairs over for them to sit with Mrs. Kline and her friends. Passion was being passed from lap to lap. Marc was the only one to notice Lil' Buddy walking toward the RV with the pretty little girl with the long braids pulled up into a ponytail. Through the big windshield, he could see them sitting in the cab—Lil' Buddy driving—and wondered where they were off to.

The Electric Slide came over the speakers. Marc pulled Vivian out of her chair and they joined the group, bobbing and dipping in unison. The sliders dispersed when Teddy Pendergrass came on crooning *Turn Off the Lights*. Marc took Vivian's hand and held her back. He put his other arm around her waist and pulled her to him. Other couples joined them. As they swayed together, barely moving their feet, Vivian slid her arms around his neck and lay her head against his chest. They didn't notice when the song ended and *You Give Good Love* came on. As the song died away, the sound of clapping rose. They opened their eyes and were embarrassed to see that they were the only ones dancing in the circle formed by friends and kin. Recovering quickly, Marc raised Vivian's hand in the air, laid his other arm across his waist in a mock flourish, and bowed at the waist toward her, then to the crowd. His antics brought on more clapping and laughter as the circle dissipated.

As midnight approached, people began leaving. Marc walked around saying good-bye, promising to see them in August, and inviting them to Texas.

* * * * *

Mrs. Kline had a big breakfast on the table when Vivian and Passion came in the kitchen. Mr. Kline and Marc were already seated. As they ate, Vivian saw tears glistening in Mrs. Kline's eyes.

"You packed?" Marc asked.

"Yes. It's all together."

After breakfast, Mr. Kline helped Marc take their bags and the stroller out to the RV.

Vivian offered to help Mrs. Kline clean up the kitchen.

"Chile, you go on. I've got all day to do this. Ya'll have to get on the road."

"Thank you so much for making me and Passion feel welcome in your home. We've really enjoyed our stay."

Mrs. Kline hugged her. "I'm glad you came. You take care of my Buddy, now."

When the women got to the RV, the motor was running. Marc hugged his father—two smart pats. Vivian got Passion settled on the bed with her clown rattler, then sat in the passenger seat in time to see Mrs. Kline hug her son as though she wouldn't see him for a long, long time. Early walked to Vivian's window.

"You take care of Buddy—and the little calf. See you in August, right?"

Vivian gave him a crooked smile in response.

As they drove off, Vivian saw the Klines through the back window, their arms around each other, waving back at them.

"I wonder what Pops meant, calling Passion a 'little calf'."

"It's our little joke," Vivian answered, then changed the subject.

When they got to Montgomery, Vivian asked, "Are you taking 65 to I-10?"

"That's the shorter route to Austin, but I thought we'd go back through Ft. Worth. We've got time. You've got some unfinished business with your mother."

"I'll take care of that. But not now."

Although it was a long, hard drive, Marc rejected Vivian's offer to take the wheel.

At Biloxi, he pulled off. "See what Mama put in that sack."

They had a quick lunch on the beach, then headed on toward Texas. Late that night, he turned into the parking lot at the casino boat in Lake Charles, Louisiana.

"I was trying to get us to Texas tonight, but it's too far to Beaumont. We'll stay here tonight. They'll charge us $3 to park, but it's a bargain. There's a state park a few miles off the road, but we don't need the amenities. I just need a few hours sleep. You can go on the boat if you want. I'll stay with Passion."

"I'm not much of a gambler. Let's just go to bed."

When Vivian woke, they were just inside the Texas border.

THIRTEEN

Walter was disappointed to find the house empty. He'd flown back a day sooner than he'd planned, certain that Vivian would be home. The conference had been informative, and he was pleased with the contacts he'd made in Washington. As soon as the primary election was over, he would be able to relax a little. The November general election was a long way off.

He understood Vivian not believing him, but he'd been sincere when he told her he would spend more time at home. He intended to start today. And it didn't have anything to do with the little 'problem' he'd had with that girl in DC. That had never happened to him before. It wasn't that he was getting old or anything, he assured himself. She just didn't turn him on. He'd grown bored with the political groupies. Besides, she reminded him too much of that other woman. That bitch. Just thinking about her—and the way she had tricked him—made his blood boil. He was relieved that all those months of blackmail were behind him. Now, he didn't have to worry about that. Besides, he had a good wife. Pretty. Still firm. He was going to be a good husband. Time for him to settle down anyway. And he would even try to get to know the baby.

The effect of the baby on Vivian had been remarkable—once

she got over the shock of it. Lately, he'd noticed a certain glow about her. And she was wearing this new perfume. It smelled even better than the one she always wore. Her talk about divorce made him realize he'd been taking her for granted for too long. She'd talked about it before, but he hadn't taken it seriously. He still didn't believe she meant it now. She was just a little over-wrought. But her refusal to come back to their bedroom had gotten his attention.

He'd stopped on the way from the airport and bought thick T-bones. She had a way of grilling them to perfection. They would have a candlelit dinner by the pool, just like they used to. Maybe go for a little swim. Then he'd persuade her to come back to his bed. They could start where they'd left off—before all the changes that political life had thrust on them. Maybe it was time for him to think about moving on. Tomorrow, they could buy a baby bed, and put it in the room next to theirs. As he closed the empty suitcase, and opened another one, he had the feeling that his life was getting back on track.

The sound of an engine from the circular driveway in front of the house drew his attention from his unpacking. If he'd known their planes were so close together, he would have waited for her and saved her the taxi ride. He walked to the window and turned the wand on the mini-blinds just enough. Since the vehicle in the driveway was a motorhome, he assumed the driver was at the wrong house. He was about to turn away to finish his unpacking when the driver's door opened. He didn't recognize the man who walked around, opened the back door and held his hand out. Then he saw Vivian emerge from the door with the baby sleeping on her shoulder. She took the man's hand to steady herself and stepped down. She looked different somehow. She was smiling at the man, a smile he hadn't seen in a long time. His brow furrowed, as the picture burned into his brain. There was a time Vivian had smiled at him that same way. Then the man reached inside and pulled out two bags and a stroller. Walter's eyes narrowed as he sucked his bottom lip in and bit down on it. The nerve in his eyelid began to twitch. He stood watching them walk toward the front door, until they disappeared from his view under the eave of the house. He listened for her key in the lock, and thought it took too long. Finally, the door opened and he heard muffled laughter. He eased to the bedroom door and listened, but he couldn't make out the words. Maybe the man was a relative of hers. But after all these years, he was sure he knew all of her family. He heard the door close, then the sounds of her dragging the bags to the bedroom.

Passion stirred, but didn't wake, when Vivian lay her on the bed. As she brought the bags to the room, she pondered whether to unpack now, or read her assignments. But it was Saturday. She had plenty of time. Yawning, she realized she'd drunk too much and slept too little on the trip. But she hadn't had so much fun in years, so it didn't matter. The serious stuff could wait until later. She'd have the house to herself all day tomorrow. She stretched out on the bed next to Passion and fell asleep thinking of Marc.

A couple of hours later, Vivian was roused from her nap by a little finger sticking in her nose. She leaned over and planted a kiss on Passion's cheek. "I'll bet you're hungry." She padded to the kitchen and got the food, a spoon, and a clean bottle. When she turned around, she was startled to see Walter standing behind her, his arms folded across his chest.

"How long have you been here?" she asked, struggling to keep her annoyance from showing.

"Not long," he answered.

"Have a good trip?" she asked, in a disinterested voice. She waited for him to move out of her way.

"Yes, I did. You?"

"Yes. Excuse me," she said, walking around him.

Walter turned and stared after her. He couldn't believe she'd cut her hair off.

Vivian fed Passion, decided to leave the unpacking and washing for tomorrow. She could hear Walter at the bar, as she curled up on the bed with Passion and her textbook. She would just pretend he wasn't there. She smiled to herself, thinking there was nothing he could do to ruin her good mood. It wouldn't be long before she wouldn't even have to look at him at all. Later, on her way to the kitchen to get a soft drink, she saw him sitting in his big chair, a hi-ball glass in his hand. She felt his eyes following her. When she came back, he was smiling.

"I brought some steaks. Thought you could grill them. We could eat by the pool. What'd you say?" He looked at her expectantly.

The sound of his voice irritated her even more than his presence.

"I'm not hungry, but you go right ahead," she said, with a forced politeness in her voice, not breaking her stride. She quietly closed her door behind her.

When her bedroom door opened she looked up from her book and fixed him with a blank stare.

"I wish you had gone to Washington with me, Viv," he said, leaning against her dresser.

Her expression didn't change. Walter walked over to the bed and looked as if he wanted to sit down on it. Vivian didn't move her legs.

"I had time to do some thinking while I was gone. About all that's happened the last few years. I really miss you. Why don't you come upstairs with me?"

Vivian continued to stare at him, not responding to his smile or his eyebrows raised in a question.

"Come on, honey," he coaxed, holding his hand out.

She didn't move, but tensed when she saw the frown cross his face, and the muscle working in his jaw.

"You know, I don't take rejection well," Walter said.

"Me neither, Walter," she said dismissively, then went back to reading the book.

Walter didn't know what to say. Now didn't seem like the time to ask her about the man. That had to have an innocent explanation, and he would look foolish and insecure to accuse her. He couldn't fathom Vivian seeing another man. She wasn't that kind of woman. He trusted her. Her free rein of his campaign and legislative offices brought her in close contact with all kinds of men. He'd noticed more than one giving her the once-over, but that only served to boost *his* ego. She'd been oblivious and business-like in her dealings with them. She was unimpressed by power, or money, or flattery. The only time he'd felt even a twinge of jealousy was with that fellow from the Midnight Basketball project. Every time he turned around, it seemed the man was hanging around the office, grinning in her face, seeking help to get a state grant. That was the kind of thing she would get excited over. It *had* bothered him just a little that time she went to the game with him in the middle of the night. He'd come home around 3:00 a.m. and found them sitting in the man's car in the driveway. The next day, he'd made a few calls, and sent a couple of letters that netted the fellow what he wanted, and he went on his way.

Walter knew she was ignoring him, pretending to read that book, and it infuriated him. She was his wife. She couldn't treat him that way.

Suddenly, he snatched the book from her hands and threw it across the room. When she didn't react, he grabbed her by her arms and jerked her up from the bed.

"I'm trying to talk to you, Vivian," he said, shaking her.

She was unresponsive, wouldn't look at him.

"I'm trying to tell you I'm sorry. I'll make it up to you. Are you listening?"

When she didn't respond, he shook her again, harder. He wanted to scoop her off her feet and take her upstairs—drag her if he had to. He thought it ironic that he'd been one of the sponsors of the marital rape legislation. Now he had a glimmer of what the opponents had in mind. It wouldn't *really* be rape. She *was* his wife. But what if she fought him, or called the police. With the primary election right around the corner, the newspapers would have a field day. He slowly released her arms. He started out of the room, then he turned around, walked past Vivian to the bed. Very gently, he picked the baby up and laid her against his shoulder, then walked to the door.

"Whenever you're ready, Vivian." Then he walked out. He stopped by the bar and filled a glass with his one free hand, then climbed the stairs.

Vivian lay on the bed staring at the ceiling. Her brows were nearly touching, she frowned so hard. The blood tasted salty where she'd bit her lip. She didn't hear the baby crying, so she must not have awakened. Surely the movement of the bed would waken her, if she went upstairs and plunged a butcher knife in his chest like she wanted to. This was the last time he was going to get the chance to shove her against a wall. He always did that to her, put her in a position that she had no choice but to do what he wanted. But not this time. She wouldn't go to him, even with the baby as the lure. He wouldn't hurt the baby. But what if he lost his temper? How far would he go to get his way? Would she do it for the baby? Yes, she finally decided. The thought of his hands on her skin, of him inserting himself in her, of his groaning orgasm was so distasteful that her nose twitched, drawing her top lip upward.

She rose from the bed and tip-toed to the living room. She looked up to the door at the top of the stairs. The light was out. The house was quiet. She went back and sat on the edge of her bed. It was 12:30. An hour had passed. She wondered if he was asleep. She stared at the clock, the hand moving in excruciatingly slow ticks. At 1:14, she could stand it no longer.

Vivian slung her purse over her shoulder, then picked up the two bags. Maybe it had been Fate that made her delay the unpacking. She was weighted down, but didn't let either touch the floor, until she reached the back door. She got the bags in the trunk without making a sound except the swish of her silk robe as she walked. She opened the door of her car, then threw her purse inside. What else did she absolutely need? The textbooks. Back in her room, she picked up the one from the floor where Walter had thrown it, then gathered the others into her backpack. Another trip to the car. This time she put the key in the ignition, just enough to keep the buzzer from sounding. Only the overhead light in the car illuminated the garage.

Vivian steeled herself as she walked up the stairs. She stood over the bed, wondering if she could pick Passion up without waking her. From the rhythmic snoring and the glass on the nightstand, she doubted Walter would wake, but she was skittish anyway. She slipped one hand under Passion's face and the other under her body, and carried her out, holding her prone in front of her. When she reached the bottom of the stairs, she lay the baby on her shoulder.

She eased into the driver's seat. Damn the carseat, damn the seatbelt, damn Officer Friendly. She pressed the garage opener on the visor, then immediately turned the key. As soon as it caught, she put the car in reverse.

* * * * *

Vivian parked the car in the curved driveway of the Capitol Ambassador Hotel. As she started out of the car, the valet ran around to meet her. He looked at her strangely, then she realized she was wearing her bathrobe. She smiled at him sheepishly, then drove away, leaving him staring after her puzzled. She remembered an economy motel on the freeway and drove there. The office was closed, but there was a walk-up window. The need for that kind of security made her uncertain. Then she saw there was a line of people at the window. She pulled out of the driveway. None of her plans were working out. She headed for Del's, but halfway there, thought of disturbing her whole household in the middle of the night. She turned around and drove to the only other place she could think of.

* * * * *

It took several rings on the bell before a light came on in the house. Vivian shifted from one bare foot to the other on the porch, adjusting the weight of the baby, wondering if she was doing the right thing. But what else *could* she do? Where else *could* she go?

"My Lord! What . . .? Come on in," Cora said. "Sit down, girl." She took Passion from Vivian and left the room.

"Come on in the kitchen," she said, after she'd put Passion to bed. Vivian followed her. Cora turned the fire on under the tea-kettle and sat at the table. She didn't say anything, just looked at her with all the questions on her face, and waited.

"I need a place to stay for tonight," Vivian said.

"Why?" Cora's face was impassive.

"I don't have anyplace else to go," Vivian said, dejectedly.

"What about your husband?"

Vivian looked up, surprised. "How did you know I was married?"

Cora crimped her mouth, then smiled. "You think I'm blind? That I couldn't see that big diamond you were wearing?"

Vivian looked down at her hands in her lap, feeling stupid. The skin where the ring had been was almost the same color as the rest of her hand now.

"You must think I'm terrible," Vivian said, her eyes downcast.

Cora got up and walked to the stove. She came back with two cups of hot tea. "No. I thought you had trouble. It was all in your face from the first time I saw you. We all have trouble sometime. But sometimes, Vivian, a baby brings a lot of weight on a woman's mind. She starts thinking about herself different. Not young and sexy for her man. And she wants that feeling back. But babies weigh. They take all your time and energy—and you want to give it. But they do weigh."

Vivian looked into Cora's kind eyes. She couldn't hold it any longer.

"Yeah. Especially when it's another woman's baby." She watched the frown crease Cora's face, as her eyes widened.

"So where'd you bury him?" Cora asked very seriously.

When she finished laughing, Vivian told her what had happened and how she ended up on her doorstep. She was certain from the emotion on her face that Cora would have handled the situation differently than she had.

"Well, honey, you can stay here as long as you need to," Cora said, patting her hand. "Does Marc know about this?"

"Not exactly."

"Not *exactly*? What does that mean?"

"He knows I'm getting a divorce, but he thinks we're adopting Passion."

"You've been halfway cross the country with him, and haven't told him the truth?! What kind of relationship is that?!"

"I don't have a relationship with Marc. He's just a friend."

Cora looked at her like she was a dunce, or maybe thought *she* was one. "Girl, I'm going to bed. I've got Sunday School in a couple of hours."

* * * * *

When Vivian woke, well after noon, the house was quiet. She saw Passion's bag in the hallway as she passed. She peeked in the other bedroom, but no one was there. She walked through the living room on her way to the kitchen. There was no sign of Cora or Passion. She poured a cup of coffee and took it with the newspaper to the patio. She hadn't read a paper in more than a week. The bright light from the sun directly overhead dappled through the canopy of huge pecan trees. She dragged Cora's little stool over to the swing and propped her feet up.

The peaceful movement back and forth made her unwilling to read any of the articles whose headlines suggested contentiousness. It was the same old stuff. She didn't care what the latest issue was that the politicians were accusing each other of mishandling—and none of them was doing anything about. Or what the body count was in some far away country where the people hadn't figured out how to get along with each other. Or even the latest controversy raging through the letters to the editor. So she read the advice column and the gardening column, then folded the paper neatly and lay it down beside her. She watched the birds playing for a while, then put her head back and closed her eyes, absorbing the serenity.

The sound of metallic creaking jerked her eyes open. Vivian was surprised to see Marc grinning at her from Cora's chair.

"Good morning," she said sheepishly, sitting up and straightening her kimono that had fallen open to reveal too much of her thigh.

"It may be morning somewhere in the world," he said, with a

crooked smile.

"What are you doing here?"

"I came to visit Cora. I usually have dinner with her on Sunday. No one came when I rang the bell, but I saw your car out front, and figured ya'll were sitting out here. What are *you* doing here?"

"I came to visit Cora, too," she said, looking off.

"In your robe?" his eyebrows raised in a question, his face turned serious.

"You may as well know. I'm staying with Cora for a little while."

He waited for her to explain farther, but she didn't. She folded her arms across her chest, as if to say 'end of that story.'

"So you still running away?"

"I am *not* running away," she said huffily.

Marc sat back in the rocker, watching her. He fought to keep the smile off his face at the thought that she'd left the husband. Things were looking up again. He was glad that he had not allowed either of them to succumb to the ever-present temptation on the trip, glad not to be cast in the role of home-wrecker. Then he considered the possibility that it was just a spat. He remembered the many times Allison had left in the heat of an argument, vowing never to return. He'd lost count by the time *he* left. He only left once. There'd never been an outside person on his part, nor on hers, he believed. He wouldn't have suffered that one minute, not even for the kid's sake. He hadn't been raised with infidelity as acceptable behavior in a relationship, so it was troubling to find himself skittering on the edge of something like that.

"So, has he called?"

"He who?" she asked, knowing full well who he meant.

Marc looked at her like a parent at a lying child.

"No. He doesn't know where to call." When she saw his brow furrow, she added, "Not that he would call anyway. It's over. We've said all that there is to say. Nothing will make me go back."

He liked the way her jaw was set, and hoped she was as sure as she looked.

"What about Passion?" he asked.

"What *about* Passion?" she responded, sitting up a little straighter.

"He has rights, you know." He was surprised by the fury in her eyes when she turned to face him.

"Rights?! What rights?! He has no rights! She's *my* baby."

"Well, now, Vivian, maybe you shouldn't box yourself in a corner. The judge can make you accommodate him. Besides, it's important for a child to know both her parents."

"Humph," was all she said, as she folded her arms tightly across her chest.

He wondered what was hidden beneath the pout of her lips and the squint of her eyes. He hated the thought that she might behave like Allison over the baby. He was more than willing to give women all their due, but, by God, men had some due, too. The good ones got the short end of the stick enough, always getting lumped with the irresponsible ones, and having to be repentant for sins they hadn't committed, but—

"I'm going to get a soda. You want one?" she asked, icily.

Her question broke into his mental froth. When he realized

his mouth was set in the same crimp as hers, he forced a half-hearted smile.

"Sure. Thanks," he said, watching her walk away.

Even the stupid birds are bickering, Marc thought, watching two of them spreading and flapping their wings at each other—as though a damn bird could be intimidating. But he knew this ritual posturing was between the males of the species. He wondered how male and female birds argued. And why? Like why was he arguing with Vivian? It was just stupid. And especially when the whole situation was taking a turn that he liked. And what was taking her so long with the drinks?

Glasses of ice and two cans were on the table. Marc leaned against the counter in the kitchen a while, waiting. Then, he walked through the house. Well, at least she didn't leave, he thought, when he saw her car through the sheer curtains at the living room window. He peeked down the hallway. All three doors were closed. May as well use the john, as long as he was inside. Just as he raised his fist to knock, the door opened and she walked right into his arms.

"Vivian, I'm sorry that…it isn't my business. I just—"

"It's OK. Don't worry about it." She looked down, avoiding his eyes and began nervously rolling the silk of the kimono between her fingers.

Wanting her to understand, he cupped his hand under her chin and raised her face. What words could he use? She still didn't look up. Her lips were full and sensuous in the pout that showed she wasn't over it. He wanted to kiss the anger away. He bent down and touched his lips to hers. He saw her lashes flutter, the only sign that she felt his touch. There was tension in her lips that hadn't been there that time on the pond. He pulled back and looked at her, but he couldn't read the expression on her face. He put his hand on the nape of her neck, feeling the wetness at the edge of her hair, and pulled her lips to his again. She smelled of the plain white soap he'd used as a child. He felt her soften, then parted her lips with his tongue. She melted against him and he put his arms around her waist, pulling her harder into him. He felt the tension drain from her body. Where her nipples pressed against his chest, he felt fire. Did he dare touch them? He'd only sought reconciliation with the kiss. To touch her there would take the quest too far, in a direction he knew he couldn't control. But her arms pulling around his shoulders and her thighs pressing against his made him forget his promise to wait until she was free. She was free enough.

She stepped back when her effect on him became obvious. He wouldn't let her go, stepping into the space she'd created between them, and pressing her against the door. When her eyes fluttered open briefly, her lids were heavy with desire, matching his own. He wrapped his arms around her, then slid his hands down her body until they touched the firm round mounds of her buttocks. He couldn't resist squeezing them, just a little. Then more. He felt, more than heard, her moan. The vortex was stronger than his willingness to resist it. He pulled the silk robe up and touched her bare skin. He buried his face in her neck, as he squeezed and squeezed. He felt her pulling his shirt out of the back of his pants, then caressing his back. It took all the restraint he could muster not to dig his fingernails into her flesh, the way hers were digging in his back. When she raised on her toes, he pulled her against his hardness and slowly ground her hips against his, undulating her with his pelvic thrusts. Through the sweet aching permeating him, he heard a door open. When he pulled away from her, she reached for him. He turned her and nudged her toward her bedroom, then walked to the living room, anxiously smoothing his pants, then his hair.

"You can just forget about dinner," Cora said, breezing into the living room.

She cut a stunning figure in a kelly green suit, trimmed in white, matching pumps, and wide-brimmed hat. She dumped Passion into his arms.

"We ate at the church. Then we took a plate to Mrs. Daniels. She's been feeling under the weather," she said, removing her hat. "I need to change. I thought I was going to suffocate in these clothes. Feels like summer already."

Marc nodded and smiled at the end of every sentence. He was glad she was rambling on, so she wouldn't notice the perspiration on his brow. He felt foolish, like a kid caught with his pants down, but was glad he'd pulled it off. She walked out of the room, still chattering. He relaxed the tight smile, and tweaked Passion on her cheek, then let her hold his forefinger in her fist. He could hear Cora from the other room, but couldn't make out what she was saying. She was still prattling a mile a minute, when she came back. She walked over to him and took Passion from his arms.

"Time for her nap." She started out of the room again and he was about to exhale, when he heard, "And tuck your shirt back in, boy."

FOURTEEN

"Gloria, this is Walter. How're you doing?"

"I'm fine, Walter. Why?" She thought his tone was subdued and humbled, but she was still pissed.

"Gloria, you don't have to talk to me like that. I'm, uh, sorry about the way I spoke with you the last time. I was under a lot of pressure."

"Humph," she responded curtly.

"Well, how's the weather up there?"

"Fine."

The line was silent.

"You go to church this morning?" he asked politely.

"Yes, I did. Why?"

"How was the sermon?"

Gloria held the phone out and looked at it, a frown on her face, her mouth crimped with annoyance. She put the phone back to her ear.

"You're not interested in my church—or my soul. What do you want, Walter?"

There was another long pause.

"I just want to apologize, Gloria."

"OK. You've done it. Let me speak to Vivian."

She heard the pause.

"She's out right now."

"Out? Well, tell her to call me when she gets in. Good-bye, Walter."

Gloria hung up the phone, her brow still knotted. Why had Walter called her, she wondered. She didn't like the feel of it. Something was up. She picked up the phone.

"Hi, Del. This is Mama. How you doing?"

"Great, Mama. And you?"

"How're the boys?"

"They're good. I'm glad Spring Break is over, though. They nearly ran us ragged."

"And Petey?"

"He's fine. They're all out back. Grilling burgers."

"Is Vivian there?"

"No. Is she back?"

Gloria heard the surprise and wariness in Del's voice.

"When was the last time you talked to her?"

"She was by last week. Told me she was spending Spring Break with you. Ya'll have a good time?"

Gloria's lips pursed. "She was here. But she didn't stay long. I'm sure you knew about this baby. Why didn't you call me?"

"Well, Mama, she, uh, wanted to tell you herself. I didn't think it was my place. But isn't she a pretty baby?"

"Yeah, well you always did cover for her. It used to make me mad. But now, I guess it's a good thing. When I'm gone, all you girls will have is each other."

"Mama, don't talk like that. You'll probably outlive us both," she said, with a nervous little laugh.

"Did she tell you she's planning to leave Walter?" Gloria asked.

"Uh, she mentioned it. Do you blame her? I told her she could stay with us. She said when school is over, she's coming back to stay with you for a while. Funny, Walter called a little while ago looking for her. You think she left him?"

"When you talk to her, tell her to call me right away. OK?"

"Sure, Mama."

"Gotta go. Kiss the boys for me. And Petey."

When she'd hung up, Gloria sat at the table picking at her fingernails. Where was her baby? She knew from her voice that Del was being straight with her. And where did that good-looking professor say he was from? Somewhere out South. Alabama? Georgia? She wondered how he figured into this mess. What was his name? All she could remember was Kline. The long-distance operator couldn't give her a number with only a last name. That damned Walter! She walked to her room and knelt in front of the cedar chest.

* * * * *

Early Monday morning, Walter looked around the reception area and smiled appreciatively. Bobby Africa was doing alright for himself. The original paintings of Buffalo Soldiers, the carved ebony figurines, and the woven baskets created an atmosphere quite unusual for a law office. Probably bought it all at Mitchie's Fine Black Art. It was high-dollar stuff and put together real nice. Must have had a decorator too, Walter thought. He accepted the cup of coffee from the tall, brown-skinned beauty, then watched her sashay away, hips moving just right, the long braids swaying across the fullness of her behind. The beads and shells in them made little clicking sounds. He wondered what she did with them in bed. He'd ask Bobby. He was sure he'd know.

He and Bobby went way back—all the way to Philly. Bobby had been a kid from the ghetto who had been given a scholarship to his prep school. Back then, before the turbulent sixties, he'd been plain old Bobby Hardeman. Bobby was more different from him, than Walter was from the White boys from the most prestigious families in that part of the country. Walter knew his mother nearly had a stroke over their friendship at first, but she hid it well. He saw it in her eyes. Bobby was everything that he wasn't— tough, street-smart, a scrappy kid who gave as good as he got. Built like a boxer. He'd taught Bobby the campus mores that the others came there knowing. In exchange, Bobby watched his back. None of the ofay boys would fuck with Bobby. He was smart as any of them, and after the first semester, sailed through all the classwork. At least it appeared that way. Walter knew how hard he studied—when no one was looking. That was part of Bobby's game—never let 'em see you sweat. And would fight at the drop of a hat. It took him a while to learn to fight with words instead of his fists, but when he did learn, he was just as effective. Resigned to their friendship, Walter's mother had pulled the strings that got Bobby a room in the dorm the next semester, so he wouldn't have to make the long train trip from and to the city everyday. Bobby's mom didn't care. For her it was one less mouth to feed.

They'd continued to be roommates at the Ivy League college and at law school. All the way, Walter leading with his winning smile and glad-handing, and Bobby studying and watching his back. When Walter took the job offered by a prestigious Texas law firm, Bobby packed too.

Although Bobby had learned to fit in with that crowd, Walter knew it chafed him. So he wasn't surprised when Bobby opened his own office. Lucky for Walter, too. He'd chafed at being treated like a law clerk at the prestigious law firm. With his Ivy League law degree he'd expected to be assigned the big cases. He'd show those country hicks how the thing was done. The senior partner had tried to counsel him in the slow Southern ways. Two years of toting cases to the courthouse for other lawyers was as close as he'd gotten to any real trial work. He was itching to put his training to work. When he'd approached the senior partner about his concerns, Mr. Mullin had approached him about the White girl. He quit that day in a huff. He met Bobby for drinks to tell him it was time for them to go back North to make their mark. Before the drinks were finished, Bobby had persuaded him to join him in his growing practice.

It hadn't been high-dollar cases, but at least he was in the courtroom—and kicking ass. As usual, Bobby studied and watched his back—smoothing things over with those hick judges, introducing him to people in the Black community that he needed to know. One was Mrs. Willie Burke, a very proper lady, who reminded him of his mother. She sent him the case that made his career.

Mrs. Burke was an old-line Austinite and a precinct chair. Every time he saw her, she told him how grateful she was to him for helping her distant cousin, Iola Washington. She'd shown it by helping him in the political sphere. He hadn't taken the case for the gratitude, and certainly not the money, since there was none. It was more the thought that the woman was powerless and the people with power would trample over her like she was nothing. It wasn't fair. She could have been Bobby's mama, or grama. It had started with his trying to do right, but had ended up with him making his mark.

Looking around the office now, he was reminded that Bobby had made his mark too. Not so much from practicing law. Bobby had 'investments.' A night club here, a chicken shack there. There were always rumors about his extra-legal activities, larger than life rumors. Walter didn't know—or care—whether they were true, and he didn't ask Bobby. Even when Walter had officed with him, Bobby always kept certain aspects of his business to himself. They'd remained thick as thieves, through it all. So who else would he turn to now, but Bobby?

"Back slumming, huh?" Bobby asked, strolling into the lobby. "Come on in. Good to see ya." He clapped him on the back, leading him into his office and showing him to a leather couch. "Oh, Congratulations—Papaw. I meant to send you a card. Didn't get around to it. When's the christening? I know I'm going to be the godfather. Right?" Bobby asked, smiling at his old friend as he sat next to him.

"Sure. Sure." Walter said, distractedly.

"Whazup?"

"Right to the point, huh?" Walter asked, a wry smile breaking through the troubled look on his face.

"Ain't no beating around bushes between us. What for?"

"OK. I want you to find Vivian."

"Vivian?" Bobby asked, trying to hide his surprise.

"She…we had a little spat. She took off."

"When?"

"Saturday night."

"Where?"

"I don't know."

"Stuck you with baby-sitting, huh?"

"Baby-sitting? Oh. No. She took the baby with her."

"Aw, shoot. She's probably with one of her girlfriends. She'll be home when she gets over her little snit. Ya wanna drink?" Bobby asked, pushing aside a walled bookcase to reveal a bar, stocked with top-shelf liquor.

"It's nine in the morning, Bobby, for Chrissake," Walter said, irritably.

"Oh yeah, that's right. So, what's the little spat about? One of your 'friends'? I told you you were going to fuck up if you kept that up. I'm surprised she didn't leave you long time ago. I tell you what, if I find a woman like Vivian, I'm settling all the way down. Guess I'm just looking in all the wrong places. In fact, when I find Vivian, I might make her an interesting proposition. And I can be a Papaw, too." Bobby's eyes sparkled with the tease for his friend.

Walter decided this was not the time to tell him the truth about the baby—and that damned woman. It was embarrassing, having to admit she'd tricked him. Bobby would have a good laugh at his expense over that. But not now.

"Cut the bull, Bobby. This is serious. I've called her girl-friends—and her family. They don't know where she is. I know you have connections. Discreet connections. I need to find her today!"

"OK, OK. Where should I start?"

"The law school. She has classes this morning."

"Why don't you just go over there and wait for her?" Bobby asked, sensing for the first time something was really amiss.

Walter knew then he'd have to face what he'd been thinking in front of his friend.

"I think she's seeing somebody."

"Vivian?! Nah, man! You just tripping. Your sins coming back to haunt you."

"You're probably right, but I just want to make sure. I want to know where she's staying."

"OK. I'll check it out. Where can I find you this evening after work?"

"Meet me at Midtown. Happy hour."

* * * * *

When Crane opened his drawer he saw the tape. Could he steal a little time on the murder case? No, he'd better follow-up on the tape, just to say he had, in case that silly woman called the Chief. He saw the three messages from her on his desk. Didn't she understand the police had more important things to do than harass people about having sex? He grabbed his coat and headed for the pawn shop. Besides, it was close to the murder scene. He'd ease by there too.

He ran the name and DL number of the woman who'd pawned the camera. Her name had come up in several car thefts, but he'd never had enough to charge her. He threatened her with the bond forfeiture warrant in a forgery case and she reluctantly coughed up Danny Blackmon. He couldn't believe his luck. The little shit was in jail—for unauthorized use of a motor vehicle of course. Gang-banger. He was going down this time for sure. He'd pay him a little visit.

* * * * *

"Why are you staring at me that way?" Vivian asked, sitting cross-legged on the quilt.

"I'm wondering how long I can keep my promise."

"What promise?"

"The promise I made us. That was a close call yesterday." He reached for her hand. "For a while we're going to have to be satisfied holding hands."

"What if I don't agree?"

"Agree or not, that's the way it has to be. Oh, let me show you something. I was reading through the newspapers from last week and found this," he said, handing her the editorial page torn from Wednesday's paper. A circle was drawn around one of the letters to the editor.

> What is the price of a Black life? In Austin, it's apparently less than that of a White. A body of a Black woman was found three weeks ago and the police act like it didn't happen. I, for one, wonder if it had been a White woman found, drowned and fully clothed, how long it would be before the murderer would be hunted down and brought to justice?

"One of your students?" she asked.

"Pretty young woman with dreadlocks," he said, nodding. "Hasn't said a word all semester. I was surprised."

"Got published without your help, too," she said with a teasing smile.

"So it seems."

"But 'murderer'? Why did she say that?"

"Bruise marks on the woman's throat. The kid that got in the medical examiner's office found that out. Word got around the class."

"Do they know who she is yet?"

"Apparently not. One of the kids has been hanging around the cop shop. He hasn't found out anything more than was in the autopsy."

"And nobody's reported her missing? That's really strange."

"Even stranger, because apparently she had a baby," he said.

"Wonder who has the baby? Grandmother maybe?"

"Probably. Lot of that going on now. Probably some girl from the country, came to the city to better herself. May not be in close contact with her family."

"Still, it's been three or four weeks since they found the body."

"I know, but…" his voiced trailed off and his eyes squinted. "See that fellow over there? Do you know him?"

Vivian turned to see a young Black man leaning against a nearby tree. Abruptly he started walking toward them. He turned his face away as he passed.

"I don't think so. I didn't really get a good look at his face. Why?"

"I saw him over by the law school while I was waiting for you."

"He's not a law student. There're few enough of us here. I know them all. Maybe he's checking it out for next year," she said, shrugging.

"Yeah, maybe," Marc answered, his eyes narrowed, following the man. Then he began folding up the sandwich wrappers and put them in a bag.

"What's the matter with you? Getting paranoid?"

"No. Of course not," he said, turning on a smile under his wrinkled brow. "You ready?"

She looked at him curiously. "Aren't you going to say it?"

"Huh?" he asked, absent-mindedly.

"You always say 'you'd better hurry'."

"Oh yeah. You better hurry."

"That's better."

* * * * *

As soon as he saw him at the door of the club, Walter signaled the waitress to bring the Vodka tonic he'd ordered for Bobby, and another Scotch on the rocks for himself. He knew they wouldn't have the brand of brandy that he preferred. Walter watched Bobby's face. He knew when Bobby was putting on his good face. He steeled himself and put on his good face too, although he knew he couldn't fool Bobby, either. He watched Bobby shake hands and greet several people on his way to the table. Even after he sat down, he beckoned others to the table for a handshake and a little chat. Walter grew impatient, but didn't show it.

"So? You find her?" Walter asked, when there was a break.

Bobby picked up his drink with one hand and reached into his breast pocket with the other. He handed Walter the envelope and looked off. He didn't want to see his friend's reaction.

Walter's eye twitched as he looked at the pictures of them on the quilt under the big tree. Same man.

"Who is he?"

"Professor."

"I knew I shouldn't have let her go to law school," he said, slamming his fist on the table.

"Not the law school. Journalism. Marc Kline's his name. That's his whole bio, his address, office number. He's better looking than you, too. Looks like you've fucked up bad this time."

"Did you find out where she's staying? Is she—"

"Nah. Not with him," Bobby said, patting his breast pockets with both hands. "My man called while I was driving over here. Here," he said, handing him a scrap of note paper. "Best I could do on short notice. I'll have the name and more information tomorrow. It's somewhere over in East Austin with an old lady." Bobby watched Walter's face for a reaction.

"Want my friend to have a little talk with him?"

"Nah. I can handle it from here. Thanks, man. You always come through for me."

"Always will. Look, I gotta go see a man 'bout a mule," he said with a wink, easing out of the booth.

"My guess is, it's a woman."

"Yeah, you're right. Gotta go see a woman 'bout some wash."

Walter couldn't get over Bobby picking up all these corny Texas sayings. As he watched him work his way back through the club, waving and shaking hands, he remembered how easily Bobby had learned the prep school ways. Damn chameleon, he thought, with amused respect.

FIFTEEN

Tuesday, Vivian sat on the quilt with her legs crossed, a smile beaming on her face. Vivian felt like hugging herself. She'd felt that way since the night before, when all the roses arrived. And all morning in class, she hadn't been able to concentrate at all for thinking about him. The card wasn't signed, but 'I really do love you' said enough. She'd waited all through lunch for Marc to mention it, but obviously he was waiting for her to bring it up.

"The roses were beautiful. Thanks so much."

"What?"

"But so many?! Nearly filled Cora's living room up. She's saying it looks like a funeral parlor. You shouldn't have spent so much money. UT must be paying their professors better than I thought."

"Roses? What roses?" he asked, bewildered.

"That's OK. You don't have to admit it," she said with a crimped smile. "I loved them. Made me feel like a girl again. Of course, back then, my suitors could only afford *one* rose."

"Well, you'd better hurry," he said, gathering up the remnants from lunch, a knot in his brow.

She thought the frown on his face was shyness. Maybe something else. He wasn't really shy. Men just have a hard time expressing themselves, she thought. When they got back to the law school, Vivian smiled at him, then pecked him on the cheek, as she took the heavy bag. She couldn't read the look on his face as he stared after her. After only half an hour in the library, she hurried home to Cora's to enjoy her flowers.

* * * * *

The house was filled with the scent of roses. Vivian hoped Cora wouldn't mind that she had moved her centerpiece of plastic flowers off the dining room table and put the three large vases of roses in its place. The red ones in the middle, between the two yellow ones. She settled at the table with her book and propped her feet in a chair. She looked up when the door bell rang. Must be Marc, she thought, with a smile. She didn't know where Cora and Passion were, but she was glad they were gone. She had a big 'thank you' planned for Marc. When she opened the door, the smile fell from her face.

"What the hell are you doing here?! How'd you find me?!"

"It's a small town. Can I come in? Can we talk?" Walter asked.

She toyed with the idea of slamming the door in his face, but what if he caused a scene on Cora's porch? The old ladies were sitting on theirs across the street, intently watching the only activity on the street. Reluctantly, she pushed the screen door open. She was embarrassed at the showy display the roses made and hoped he didn't ask about them. She pointed him to the couch and sat in the chair on the side. It was awkward facing the man she'd lived with for nearly twenty years. She didn't know what to say, so she didn't say anything, just stared at him. He looked so ill-at-ease, and out of his element, it almost made her smile.

"I'll get straight to the point. I miss you, Vivian."

She didn't say anything, enjoying his discomfort.

"You know I'm a proud man, but I'll do anything you want if you'll just come home. I know I've been a terrible husband lately. And I've done some things that...I want to make it up to you. I don't want to live without you, Vivian. We can make a new start."

Vivian folded her arms across her breasts and crimped her lips.

"I realize I've become the very thing I went into politics to fight. I couldn't beat it. It beat me. If you'll just try to forgive me, I'll be the best husband—and father—there is. I promise, Vivian. Please come home. Give me a chance to show you."

"Well, Walter—"

"You don't have to give me an answer right now," he said hurriedly. "Just say you'll think about it. Remember how it used to be? I want that again. From now on."

She remembered what the last few years had been like. But she also remembered what he had been like before, and how perfect life had been. She wondered if you could love and hate a person at the same time. Or whether you had to hate a person as long as you had loved, for it to all come out even. The love had been longer. Maybe it wasn't too late. Maybe they could salvage it. The front door opened and Cora walked in like a dishpan of cold water.

"Oh, excuse me. I didn't realize you had company," she said, her voice cold and flat, as she looked down her nose at Walter.

He immediately stood, turning on his charm.

"Good afternoon, Mrs. Williams." he said, showing his most

affable smile and offering his hand. "Walter Carlson."

Surprised at Cora's coldness, Vivian stood too, reaching for Passion. "Cora, this is my...this is Walter." She wondered how he knew Cora's name.

Cora looked at his hand, but made no move to accept it, patting Passion protectively on the back, instead, and ignoring Vivian.

"Pleased to meet you, sir," she said stiffly, then walked toward the kitchen. When she reached the door, she stopped.

"Aren't these roses beautiful, Mr. Carlson?" she asked with a smug smile.

"Yes they are. I know roses are Vivian's favorite bloom."

Vivian turned around and stared at the roses. He knew yellow was her favorite rose, too.

When Cora was safely out of the room, she turned to Walter. "Did you send these?"

"I just want to make you happy, Vivian. And the baby. We can give her so much. We can be a family. Maybe we could even look into adopting another one...so Passion won't have to grow up alone, like I did. Think about it. You've made it obvious you care for her. You wouldn't want her to come from a broken home. Come home, Vivian. We can work this out. Tell you what, would you like to go to dinner? Just the two of us...the three of us?"

"Excuse me," Cora said, walking into the room. "Time to put Passion down for her nap. Oh, and Vivian, I grilled a steak, especially for you. It's in the oven with a potato. Salad's in the icebox. Whenever you're ready, just fix your plate." She gave Vivian a hard disapproving glare as she walked to the bedroom.

Vivian turned to Walter and shrugged her shoulders.

"Maybe tomorrow? How about lunch?" he asked "I'll call

you later. Give me the number here."

"Why don't I call you?" she asked, walking him to the door.

"Promise me you'll think about what I said," he said earnestly.

When she realized he was bending down to kiss her, Vivian turned her cheek to him, and felt his lips touch her softly. It reminded her of the constant tenderness he'd once shown her. She stood at the screen door and watched him walk toward his Mercedes. She couldn't put her finger on what was different about him. He still had his air of confidence, but the swagger was gone. Maybe he had come to a realization of what was important. Just maybe—

"Don't even think about it." Cora's voice shattered her thoughts. "I'm not one to eavesdrop, but I couldn't help but overhear. I know you're not going to fall for that bul...line."

Vivian turned to face her. How could she make her understand how it had been before? That he'd been a good husband. That he'd been the first man—the only man—she'd known in *that* way.

"You just don't know him, Cora."

Cora crimped her mouth and rolled her eyes in disgust. "Ain't my business. You're grown. You can do what you want."

Vivian watched as Cora snatched around and walked into the kitchen. She heard the back door open, then jumped when it slammed shut. She didn't understand Cora's anger. Maybe she could make her understand, she thought, following her to the patio.

Vivian settled in the swing and with a push of her foot started it's motion back and forth, trying to think of the right words.

"Cora, I—"

"I guess you think just because I'm old I don't know nothing about men. Humph," she snorted. "I'm just a young girl trapped in this old body. I hate to see you make the biggest mistake of your life. One I already made."

Vivian didn't say anything.

"Don't fall for that ole 'baby needs her daddy' bullshit. If he'd really been a daddy, you wouldn't be here, and he wouldn't be here talking to you about it. I let my boys' daddy get away with that."

"What happened?" Vivian asked.

Cora stared at her a long minute, a look of impatient uncertainty on her face. She began slowly.

"We were planning to get married. Then, when I got pregnant, he said maybe the baby wasn't his. That he wasn't sure. That he'd wait til the baby came before he married me. Girl, that cut me to the quick. *I* was sure. Arthur Lee was the only man I'd ever been with. He knew it. Everybody knew it. I wasn't but nineteen. That was before all these fancy tests and things. Back then, all you had to go on was whether the baby looked like him. Mine looked like he'd spit him out. I nearly died from shame and embarrassment. Nothing hip about being a single mother back then. But I had to go through the whole thing by myself. All the time my belly's swelling and I'm feeling like a cow, he's out at the joints having a good time. I thought when he saw Arthur, Jr., he would make it right. Soon as I'm back to myself, here he comes talking 'bout he still ain't sure. He *knew* that baby was his. I know he had taken up with this painted face woman at the joint. Oh, he'd come around, bringing little presents and what-nots. Playing into my wanting things to be right. Never brought nothing important, like milk and diapers. I had to work for those things.

"And the way people treated me hurt too. Most of the 'good Christians' at the church treated me like dirt. There were a few exceptions, Mrs. Daniels and a couple more. I guess they had studied their Bibles a little harder than the others. The rest were whispering behind my back, not talking to me. But even at that, I kept going 'cause you know it ain't 'bout the people, it's deeper than that. Well, time goes by," she trailed off as if she was unsure whether to go on.

Vivian knew her face was open with curiosity, but she didn't feel she should pry. She could see how painful it was for Cora, peeling back layers of her past. She waited. Finally, Cora continued.

"There was a young man came here to Tillotson College. Lewis. Joined our church. He started keeping company with me. Sweetest man. Always talking to me about going to college. Like I could go to college, with a baby. It didn't bother him at all that I had a baby. He took up more time with Arthur Jr. than his own daddy did. Well, Arthur Lee got wind of that, and here he comes, sweet-talkin' me 'bout baby needs his daddy. Just 'cause he don't want nobody else to have me. But, I'm thinking about what's best for my baby. See, I never knew my daddy. I always felt like there was a big hole in my life. I didn't want my boy to have that hole in his. So, I sent Lewis away and took back up with Arthur Lee. For a while there, he was real steady. Lot of talk about getting married, but no follow through. Then I get pregnant with Jimmy. He started that same ol'...stuff, 'bout he ain't sure. That did it. He wasn't no real man noway. He wouldn't have been a good influence on my boys. He certainly wasn't a good influence on me. That was the last time in this life I'm a twice fool. I told Arthur Lee if he darkened my door again, I was gonna call the sheriff—to come get his body off my property. Meant it, too. By that time, Lewis had left. Went to Howard Law School up in Washington, D.C.

"I put my mind to raising my boys the best way I could, and put away the dream Lewis had given me of going to college. I guess, in the end, it didn't turn out too bad. I own this little house free and clear. My boys turned out good. God-fearing men. Love their mama. I got a little pension. And in a way, I got to go to college for 35 years. Life's OK," Cora mused, then turned and looked at Vivian.

"I never had a daughter. But if I had, she'd be about your age. All I could tell her is, don't be no twice fool." Then she looked off toward the back of the yard, to hide the glassiness in her eyes.

Vivian tried to draw the parallels in her mind, but she couldn't make them fit.

"Where is Arthur Lee?" she asked.

"Cemetery. Drank himself to death."

"And Lewis? What happened to him?" Vivian asked, as she rocked back and forth.

"He lives in Detroit. He's a judge now."

Vivian could see the young girl peeking through Cora's sheepish smile.

"He called me the other day. We talk a lot on the phone. For about a year now. You know, it doesn't seem like forty some years have passed. His wife died a couple of years ago. He's about to retire. You know, he's never been to Jamaica."

"Well? You gonna take him?" Vivian asked, boldly stepping

into Cora's business.

"We've already made the reservations," Cora winked at her. "Told you, I'm just a young girl trapped in this old body."

"Wonder how it would have turned out, if you had done it a different way?"

"Over the years, I thought about that a lot. But it didn't make any difference. I set my own course. There were times when I felt like God was punishing me for my mistakes. Then, I decided God isn't like that. Maybe, He was saving the best for last."

"I hope so, Cora. Speaking of saving the best for last, I believe I'll go have that steak now," Vivian said, standing and stretching.

"What steak?" Cora asked with a grin.

* * * * *

In all his years of questioning suspects, Crane had never gotten used to the stench. Alcohol, body odor and dirt combined to make a smell that was peculiar to jails. And they all smelled alike. He always tried to get out of there before it settled in his clothes.

The punk across the table was staring at the wall, trying to show his disdain. Couldn't have been more than twenty years old. And trying to be a hard-ass. Crane knew from the hand-drawn tattoos on his knuckles, which gang he claimed.

"Where'd you get the camcorder?" Crane asked.

"Don't know nothing 'bout no camcorder."

"If that's the way you want it, you little shit. Pawn shop hit comes back to a Rhonda Pearson at your address. Guess I'll have to charge your girl with burglary then. Second degree, you know. And they got plenty space in the women's unit. You can go back to your cell now." Crane rose to leave.

"Ain't no burglary."

Crane stopped. "Oh, I got plenty burglaries with camcorders taken. Enjoyed our little visit—you little shit." Crane started for the door.

"Wait a minute, man. Rhonda's pregnant. She can't do no time."

"Taxpayers gonna pay for it either way—Brackenridge Hospital or the Women's Unit at Gatesville. Makes me no difference." He opened the door.

"Naw, man. Naw," he said, banging the table. "Can't you just put that on me? I'm going down anyway."

"You wanna tell me about it?" Crane asked, nonchalantly.

"Yeah, man. I'll tell 'bout it—if you promise to leave my woman alone."

"You want to talk to your lawyer?"

"Naw. Court-appointed lawyer ain't worth a shit. Just gimme your word."

"You got it," Crane said, sitting back down.

"OK. See. This dude come around trying to sell this car—a white Corolla. Bout a eighty something. Ain't got no title. So, I know the deal. I jack him up. Tells me some bullshit 'bout he found it out by the lake—keys in it. Sure 'nuff, he got the keys. So I offer him $100. I figure seats, battery, wheels. I can turn a nice little profit. I got a baby on the way, and all. He say he'll throw in the camcorder if I give him $200. We settle on $150. I made a little change on it. I rent the car out to a couple a times to some dudes. Then I figure it's hot. So I take it down to Mason Manor Apartments and clean it out. Set it up on blocks. Give the camcorder to Rhonda. She need the money. Since she got a drivers license, she can pawn things. You ain't gon' hurt my woman, are you?"

"So who's the dude you got the car from?"

"I don't know, man. Just some dude. You gave your word. I thought you was straight up—not like the rest of these laws."

Crane nodded, then walked out the door.

He put the white Corolla in the computer. Bingo. Mason Manor Apartments. Abandoned. He ran the VIN—registered to a Porsche Timmons. He wondered why she hadn't reported it stolen. He called the number listed in the phone book.

"This number is no longer in service."

* * * * *

Vivian had stared at the book for two hours, but she hadn't advanced five pages. She couldn't concentrate. Her mind kept wandering to Cora's story. Being so absorbed in her own problems, she hadn't thought much about Cora's past. She had just assumed Cora was a widow. She couldn't imagine the woman she knew allowing a man to mistreat her. The more she thought about it, she really wasn't in that different a position than Cora had been, except that she had more good memories. And she didn't have youth to blame. She began to see the parallels. The phrase Cora had used—'bringing little presents and what-nots'—kept running through her mind. Vivian eased up from the bed, careful to not wake Passion.

The flagstones that led to the side of the house were cold under her bare feet. The pungent odor of old garbage assaulted her when she opened the top on the big can. It took three trips outside to dispose of the roses. She didn't even keep the vases.

She dialed her number from the kitchen phone. When she heard his voice, she took a deep breath.

"This is Vivian. I'm not coming back. Have your lawyer file the papers. You know where to send them. Good-bye, Walter."

Vivian pressed the hook, then dialed again.

"Mama? It's me."

"Vivian! Where are you? Why haven't you called me? I've been worried to death about you."

"I'm fine. I've moved. I wanted you to have the number where I'm staying."

"With the professor?" Gloria asked hesitantly.

"Of course not. A friend of his. You'd like her, Mama. She's about your age. Retired. She keeps Passion for me, so I can finish school. I was thinking maybe then, we could stay with you until I take the Bar exam. Think about it. We can talk about that later. It'll be a couple of months."

"I don't have to think about that. You know you can stay with me, as long as you want. Are you really going to keep that baby?"

"Passion, Mama. That's her name. And yes, I'm going to keep her."

"Walter's not going to take his baby if you leave him?"

"I've *left* him. And no. He doesn't want her. She's mine, Mama."

Vivian shifted her feet, through the silence on the phone.

"Then, I guess I've finally got a granddaughter."

"I'm glad to hear you say that, Mama."

"But I think you and the baby ought to stay in the house, and make *him* move."

"He can *have* that house. I'm taking my self back."

"That's *your* house," Gloria said firmly.

"Well, take this number down. 555-9815. It's getting late, and I've got class tomorrow."

"Will you see the professor?"

"Yes." Vivian heard the defensiveness in her own voice.

"I want you to be happy, baby. Tell him I said 'Hello'."

* * * * *

Marc was glad when morning came. His night had brought little rest. Intending to work on his book, he'd stared at the computer screen until the image was burned into his eyelids. He hadn't entered one complete sentence. Under ordinary circumstances, he would have staked his claim against all comers. But this was different. He was at a distinct disadvantage.

Roses! He'd have sent her roses if he'd thought she'd have been so happy to get them. He just hadn't thought of it. Not only did the man have a legal claim to her, but he *knew* her. Knew things about her Marc had yet to learn. And Walter clearly wasn't going to roll over and play dead. He was courting her. It infuriated him, but there was nothing Marc could do, but watch and wait.

He felt impotent, hog-tied. He desperately wanted to strengthen his position. All night he wrestled with himself to keep from dialing Cora's number. What if she succumbed and went back to her husband? What would he do? Find somebody else. Yeah, right. He picked the receiver up. He put it down. He didn't want her unless she was sure. Lie. He wanted her, period. But he knew there was nothing he could do—but wait.

* * * * *

Marc stopped at the secretary's desk and picked up his mail.

He thought she looked a little more wide-eyed than usual for that time of morning. Maybe he was just dragged out from lack of sleep. Or maybe *she* was. Although she was a model of efficiency in her job, Marc knew Dorothy had a very active night life for a woman in her fifties. She bragged about being the 'queen' of the Broken Spoke Saloon. Dorothy looked as though she was going to say something, but the phone rang, drawing her attention. She picked it up and began speaking into it, still looking at him with wide eyes. She raised a finger at him. He waved back at her and walked on to his office.

Marc shuffled through the stack of journals and credit-card offers in his hand, as he opened his door. He immediately recognized the man sitting in his guest chair, as though he owned the place. In contrast to the calmness the man displayed—his hands folded in his lap—Marc felt every muscle in his body tense. But he showed no sign, as he calmly shut his door.

"Good morning, Representative Carlson. What can I do for you?" His voice was clear and steady, but his eyes were wary.

Walter let the seconds pass for effect, the wall clock audibly marking them.

"Leave my wife alone."

His voice was just as clear. Their eyes met. Neither blinked. Marc casually dropped the mail on the desk, raised his leg and perched on the edge with his arms folded, and looked down at Walter.

"What makes you think I'm bothering your wife?"

Walter's expression didn't change. He pulled the pictures from his breast pocket and tossed them, face up, on the desk. Marc cast a sidelong glance at the one on top, the one of Vivian feeding him a bite of a sandwich, and fought to keep the shock out of his eyes. The bastard had spied on them! He looked back at Walter, as though the pictures were of people he didn't recognize.

"She doesn't look bothered to me," he said, nonchalantly.

"Well, she is. I think Vivian may be going through the change. She's been acting a little out of character lately. You know, she's gotten to that age where women…well, you know."

Marc seethed at the way the man talked about her, but never broke eye contact with Walter. He hoped that his deep breathing didn't betray the emotion he was feeling.

"I know about your little trip," Walter continued. "Got my credit card bill. I'm not going to ask you—or her—about what happened. Vivian's an attractive woman. You wouldn't be much of a man if you didn't respond to her advances. I've forgiven her. I'm sorry you had to be the pawn in her little game. But it's over now. She's come to her senses. She asked me to speak with your department chair about it."

He waited to see what effect that would have. He saw none.

"But I really don't think that's necessary. I thought you and I could discuss this, one man to another, and come to an understanding. You know what I mean?" Walter asked, standing and tucking the pictures back in his breast pocket, to indicate that the conversation was over.

Marc felt the tension in his jaw, and his fists clenching, folded under his armpits. He felt like decking him. How could he say those things about Vivian?! But, it was more than that. It was a man thing now. He'd never reacted well to being put down, to being pushed around—from way back when the kids teased him about his stuttering. Still, he recognized this was a situation where he couldn't claim the moral high ground, so it was imperative for him to remain calm.

"If I didn't know better, Representative, I'd think you were using your position to threaten my job," Marc said, evenly.

"No, not at all," Walter returned, cool as a cucumber. "I'm threatening *you*."

Before he could stop himself, Marc grabbed Walter by his lapels and shoved him against the wall. He got right in Walter's face, and spoke through clenched teeth.

"Don't threaten me, mother fucker, unless you really mean it. You might be able to take my job, but you can't take the pleasure of me kicking your ass." As he spoke, he jerked Walter off the wall, and shoved him back, to make his point.

Walter was surprised by the unexpected attack, but instinctively threw his arms up to break Marc's hold on him.

Marc stopped his forward rush, his forearm aimed at Walter's throat, when he heard the brief, hesitant knock on the door. Out of the corner of his eye, he saw the door open and Dorothy poke her head in.

"Is everything OK?" she asked, even more wide-eyed. "Should I call security?"

Marc backed away from Walter, never taking his eyes off him.

"No, Dorothy. Everything's OK. My guest was just leaving."

Walter straightened his clothes, hesitated a moment, then walked past her, breathing hard.

Marc fists clenched, as he watched Walter walk out the door.

"It's OK, Dorothy. Really." She didn't move. "I'd appreciate it if you didn't mention anything about this."

"Of course I won't, but I still think we should call security."

"No," Marc said, quickly. "Is that your phone ringing?"

Dorothy looked as though she wasn't sure which matter to attend to, but went to the phone, closing the door behind her.

Marc sat in his chair, propped his elbows on the desk and rubbed the heels of his hands against his eyelids. What to do now? Leave her alone. That was the only sensible thing to do. He'd brought this on himself. She'd never initiated any contact with him. Never. It had always been him. Calling her. Following her. Maybe she *had* told her husband he was bothering her. No, she wouldn't do that. In any case, he didn't need to be stuck in the middle of this kind of mess. Leave her alone. Forget her. That's what he'd do, he decided. He rubbed his hands together, as though he was through with it, then gathered his papers and walked to his class.

SIXTEEN

Vivian was surprised he wasn't standing under the tree, with the quilt over his arm, a sack or a box in his hand. After the crowd of students had gone their way, she sat on the top step and waited. Maybe his class had run over. Then, she remembered his 50-minute class was at 10:00. Maybe one of the students had come up with something else about the murder, and had held him over to talk about it. Yeah, that was it.

She glanced at her watch—12:15—and waited. At 12:30, she started for the library. He'd know where to find her. She did her best to concentrate on her casebook, but she kept looking at her watch, and at the door. She'd sat near the door so he would see her right away. Why didn't he come? Even if just to say they couldn't have lunch. It was just plain inconsiderate, standing her up without a word. She thought about calling his office. But what would she say if he answered? At 1:45, she packed up and walked to her car.

* * * * *

When he wasn't there Thursday, her heart sank. She sat on the step and waited. She'd expected him to call last night, but he hadn't. How could he treat her like that? She felt like a fool, sitting there waiting for him. And she'd thought her single friends had been exaggerating with all their tales about how low-down men were, and the way they acted! Maybe they weren't exaggerating. It had been so long since she dated. Maybe everything had changed. If this was the new scene, she'd have no part of it. She gathered herself, and tried to remember what she did after class before she met him. So much had happened. She used to go home to her study. That was it—seemingly a lifetime ago.

But this was her new life, the one she'd looked forward to. So why was she crying? She wiped her eyes with the back of her thumbs and stuck her chin up. No point in going home. Cora was *his* friend. She couldn't talk to Cora about him. Del and Cynthia were at work. And Karla—oh well. She headed for the library.

* * * * *

Friday, when she saw him under the tree, her initial reaction was to run to him and throw her arms around him. Then she thought about the way he had treated her for two days. Pretending he wasn't there, she turned and followed the knot of students toward the library. Even when she heard him call her name, she kept walking.

"Wait! Stop!" he said, at her side, holding her by her arm. She turned and looked pointedly at his hand on her arm, then rolled her eyes up at him.

"I've got something to tell you," he said.

"No. That's OK, Professor Kline. I already got the message." She pulled her arm away, and started off.

Marc pulled her back and turned her around to face him. He cupped her face in his hands, pulled her to him and kissed her so deeply it left her breathless. The backpack fell from her shoulder and hit the ground with a thud, as she surrendered to him. At the sound of it, she broke from his embrace and looked around self-consciously.

"I tried to stay away from you, Vivian. All the reasons I should are clear to me. I just couldn't do it. The last two days have been torture for me. Wondering if you would go back to your husband, wondering where I fit in. I can't be your secret love. Tell me that you're sure about the divorce, and I'll be by your side. Through whatever comes."

Relief rushed over Vivian. She put her arms around his waist and lay her head on his chest, a big smile on her face, tears of joy clouding her eyes. He kissed the top of her head as he rubbed his fingers through the short hair at the back of her neck.

"Would you have lunch with me? I know a special place you've never been before."

She stepped back. "Marc, I'd be delighted to have lunch with you."

Marc picked up the backpack, slung it over his shoulder, and held his other hand out to her. She slipped her fingers through his and they walked to his car.

As Marc drove north on 'The Drag,' holding her hand all the way, they passed throngs of people. Most were students, some were 'drag worms'—the young and alienated homeless—although sometimes it was hard to tell one from the other. Spiked hair of vibrant reds, blues, greens, and purple was popular. Some were university employees. A few were the chronic alcoholic home-less. Farther north, they passed the courts motel she'd looked at. The bikers were still there. Marc laughed when she told him about that experience. Then he turned into historic Hyde Park—an eclectic neighborhood just north of the campus. Along the streets shaded by huge trees, they passed a mixture of small and large houses, some beautifully restored, a few obviously neglected, student housing.

"There aren't any restaurants in this area," she said, looking at him quizzically.

"I know," he said, smiling at her.

He slowed down and parked the car in the driveway of a small corner house, surrounded by a waist-high white picket fence. The entrance was set diagonal to the street. The door was arched at the top, with large decorative black hinges. Vivian thought the house looked like something from a Black Forest fairy tale—Hansel and Gretel maybe. Marc got out and opened her door, offering his hand to help her out, then led her through the vine-covered arch over the gate.

In the living room, there were Indian throw rugs on gleaming hardwood floors. Bookshelves, crammed with books, lined every wall. No couch, only a desk in one corner, two wing-backed chairs—and a serious stereo system. Marc stopped there and turned it on. The house began to exude the soft sound of a jazz guitar.

"Come on in the kitchen, lunch will be ready in a shake," he said, opening the glass-paned doors in the wide, arched opening into the dining room.

Vivian followed him through it, and the smaller arched doorway into the kitchen. She marveled at the skill of the carpenter who'd made all the doors to fit exactly, probably without the benefit of power tools, judging by the age of the neighborhood. In contrast, the kitchen had all modern appliances. He patted the tall stool in the corner where the counter made an L.

"Sit here," he said, then began setting up. He put water on to boil for rice, took shrimp and a bottle of wine from the refrigerator. He filled two long-stemmed glasses, handed her one, then softly clinked his glass to hers. He deftly peeled and de-veined the shrimp, chopped scallions and peppers.

"I love shrimp. Can I help? I'm pretty handy in the kitchen," she said.

"Nope. Just relax. I invited you to lunch."

Each bottle or packet of spice or herb he took from the cabinet, she took from him and examined. Finally, she went to the cabinet and surveyed the whole collection.

"Where do you get this stuff? I've never heard of some of it."

"Here and there. The Indian market up on north Lamar. The Vietnamese market. Different places."

"You think that's enough butter?" she asked, a look of mock horror on her face when he dropped nearly a whole stick in the skillet.

He gave her a sly smile. "It's no-fat, no-cholesterol butter. Really. No calories either."

Marc handled the skillet like a professional chef, tossing it to stir the ingredients, adding a touch of this, a pinch of that.

"That smells *so* good. Where'd you learn to cook?" she asked.

"Everywhere. Mama taught us all the basics. Then all the places I traveled, I learned a little something. This is about ready. Wanna eat in the dining room or outdoors?"

"I like the music, but you pick."

"Bring your glass," he said, handing her a plate. At the back door, he flipped a switch and music came from speakers outside.

In the shady back yard, Vivian could hear intermittent shouts of children playing at the nearby park over the sweet sounds of the guitar. They sat in the redwood chaise lounges, their feet propped up, balancing their plates in their laps. Marc said the grace. The motorhome parked at the back of the lot, facing the alley, reminded Vivian of how much she'd enjoyed their trip. They playfully argued about what had been the best part of it, but carefully avoided any mention of the stolen kisses, or the two days they'd been without each other.

"Delicious!" she said, scooting the last bits of rice on her fork with her thumb.

"Want some more?"

She smiled and nodded. "I'll get it."

As she was re-filling her plate in the kitchen, the music changed. Johnny Taylor's plaintive voice came through the speakers. She remembered when he'd been 'Little Johnny Taylor.' He was still just as good. Better, now. Still singing of lost love and stolen love. She leaned against the counter, listening to his soulful plea, *Walk Away With Me*. When the song ended and she carried her plate back outside, Marc appeared lost in thought, the expression on his face unreadable.

"Did you play that on purpose?" she asked.

"It's been playing a lot lately."

They finished the meal in silence. He took her plate and she followed him into the kitchen. Vivian thought she'd bust, she'd eaten so much. Thank Heavens for elastic waistbands.

"At least let me do the dishes," she said.

"Forget 'em. I'll do it later. I'd better get you back to school."

She turned and leaned back against the counter.

"It's Friday. This is my free day. I usually cool out on Friday afternoon. I study on Sunday night."

"So what do you do on Fridays?" he asked.

She thought a minute. This was the first Friday of her new life.

"I'd just go to Cora's, but she and Passion aren't home. This is her day to clean up at church. Maybe I'll just take a nap while the house is quiet."

But what if Walter showed up? She didn't want to be alone with him. There was nothing to talk about. She didn't even want to see him reduced to begging—or face his wrath at not getting his way.

"I'm not sleepy," she announced. "Are you free this afternoon?"

He nodded.

"You want to go to the movies?" she asked.

"Not really," he answered, staring at her, a mysterious smile on his face.

"Well, we don't have to go to the movies. What would you like to do?"

"You really want to know?"

"Yes. What do you want to do?"

"I want to take you in my bedroom and make love to you 'til you can't stand it."

Vivian's eyes flickered under his steady gaze. She looked down, remembering the two rash moments when she had thrown herself at him. Now, she wasn't so sure. Maybe they needed a little more time. Maybe a lot more time.

"I thought you said we'd have to just hold hands."

"We could *start* with that," he said, walking to her and lacing his fingers through hers. "Like this."

"Then we could finish our kiss." He pulled her hands to her sides and kissed her, softly at first, then deeper. Where his chest pressed against her, a tingling started in her nipples, then radiated through her body. It had been so long since she'd felt that sensation. She nervously tried to pull her hands up, but he wouldn't let go. He pulled them behind her, making her arch against him. He nibbled at her lips, then her ear.

"Marc—"

He covered her mouth, and let her taste his sweetness. "Then I could kiss you here." He bent down, closed his lips gently on her nipple through her blouse, then a little harder. When she moaned and pressed against him, he took a mouthful and sucked. She freed her hands from his and clasped them around his neck, pulling him against her. His hands were on her bottom, squeezing rhythmically and pressing her against the bulge in his pants. She liked that. Walter never did that. When she felt his knee between her legs, easing them apart, she put her hands against him, to push him away. But the muscles in his chest tantalized her fingertips, so she pulled, then pushed—then pulled, massaging. When he lifted her and sat her on the counter, she grabbed his shoulders to balance herself. He slowly unbuttoned her blouse, and unhooked the clasp in the front of her bra, then caressed her breasts with his hands. They felt unfamiliar, larger. This was going farther than she was ready to go, she thought—and not fast enough—as she felt his thumbs slowly rubbing across her nipples. His hands roamed up her thighs inside her wide-legged walking shorts, leaving a trail of fire in their path. She didn't resist, when he pulled her legs around his hips, then pulled her against him and lifted her from the counter. He carried her to his room and gently lowered her on his tall bed.

The heavy curtains were drawn against the bright afternoon sun. A large armoire, and a nightstand were the only pieces of furniture in the darkened bedroom other than the massive four-poster bed, with its matching footstool. Thick carved posts rose from the headboard and footboard, each topped with a large polished wooden ball. He pulled her shoes off. He laid her back, then climbed in the bed and lay beside her, leaning over her, and lacing the fingers of one hand through hers. He kissed her lips slowly, once, twice, three times. The last time, he touched her tongue with his, then sucked it into his mouth. She squeezed his fingers tightly—fighting surrender. No matter how good it felt, she shouldn't do this. She was a wife—and a mother. She tried to pull her hand from his, but he held it. Sensing her ambivalence, he drew back and looked into her eyes.

"If you're not sure, we should stop now. There's no turning back after this. For either of us."

She pressed her lips together and didn't say anything, thinking. He was more right than he knew. She'd been with only one man. That was the way it was supposed to be. Or was it? She'd kept her promise, but he hadn't kept his. Had his breaking the promise released her? Her breasts rose and fell, as she breathed deeply. She finally closed her eyes and raised her lips to his. He kissed her softly, then rubbed his cheek against hers to seal their agreement.

When he found her lips again, he kissed her with a passion

that she'd never known. She saw him admiring her breasts, and when he suckled each one slowly and lovingly, she was filled with feelings that had been incubating unrequited for way too long. He raised to his knees, slipped his hands inside the waistband of her shorts, then backed off the bed as he pulled them down over her thighs, and off. She watched as he crossed his arms in front and pulled his shirt over his head, dropping it on the floor.

Under his gaze, she felt uncertain, shy, virginal. Her knees were pressed tightly against each other. His eyes savored her body, as though he was memorizing every curve.

Marc leaned over her, and sucked one of her breasts into his mouth, while he cupped the other in his hand, massaging it. He trailed kisses down her stomach, then flicked the tip of his tongue in her navel. She enjoyed the unusual sensation. When he continued down, she clamped her thighs against him. She wasn't sure what he was trying to do. Walter never did anything like that. Marc kissed the inside of her thigh, then backed off. She relaxed when he stood. He pushed his pants and shorts off, leaving them on the floor. He leaned over her and pulled the bikini panties down over her legs. She looked away demurely, then stole a glance back at him as he sat on the bed, and reached in the drawer of the nightstand.

When he laid back on top of her, she felt him at the place where she was consumed by heat. His eyes searched hers. She wasn't sure what he saw, the certainty of how her body felt or the conflict in her mind. He eased on his side, leaning on his elbow, then ran his hand down her thigh. He stroked the outside of it, then the inside of the other one, watching the pleasure building on her face, and planting kisses on her lips and her nipples. His thumb found the place and gently massaged through the curly hair just at the opening. She felt his finger where her lips met. She relaxed to the feel of it, then he slowly drew it back and forth. Vivian thought she would explode with ecstasy. When she felt his finger inside her, exploring, she drew up, then gave in to it. He rolled on top of her, prodding his erection against her again.

"Are you sure, baby?" he whispered, against her lips.

She put her arms around his neck and relaxed her legs. He smiled, and entered just a little. She felt him watching for her reaction. She tensed, her eyes closed, then relaxed. He pressed on just a little more, then stopped, waiting for her response. Each time, when she relaxed, he pressed a little farther. She'd never felt love like this before. Patient. Considerate. Cognizant of her need. She wanted all of it. Planting her feet flat on the bed, she rose to invite him. He accepted the invitation—giving himself to her fully, then withdrew, almost all the way. Her body shuddered all over and she opened her eyes with a look of surprise, but when he plunged again, she closed them and exhaled. Each time he withdrew, she fought to hold on to him, then he'd slowly give himself to her. She felt like she was being pulled in a hundred different directions. She tried to pull it all back together, grasping at him frantically, pulling his hair, scratching his back, trying to hurry him. But he wouldn't allow it. When she opened her eyes, she saw him draw his bottom lip in and bite hard, determined to hold the same rhythmic tempo. She knew he was in control of her body, but neither of them could stop the trembling that was overtaking her. His lips were warm against her ear.

"Now? You say when, baby."

"Yes. Now. Now!"

He covered her mouth and kissed her with an intensity that matched the rhythm of their bodies as it rose in crescendo almost to the breaking point. Vivian put both her hands against his brow and wiped the beads of sweat away. He reached under her, sinking his fingers into the firm, fleshy mounds and pulled her to him so hard she thought he would pull her right into his body—or that he would be consumed into hers. She clamped her arms around him tightly, riding the wave that threatened to roll over her. Finally, he couldn't hold back any more. He climbed on the wave and rode it with her, until it rolled over them both. Tumbling, tumbling, until they collapsed against each other, both breathing deeply and drenched with sweat. Wrapped in each other's arms, they drifted into a sated sleep.

Vivian's shifting under him stirred him awake. Marc kissed her, then rolled onto his back, pulling her on top of him, in one motion. He put his hands against her breasts and pushed her upright, shifting her until she was straddling him. He raised himself to a sitting position enclosing her in his arms, with only the throbbing desire separating them. He scooted back against the headboard, pulling her with him, and at the same time entering her. He felt her relaxing, relaxing, until he filled her up. He felt her contracting around him. When she threw her head back, her breasts were thrust in his face, so he sucked them with a fervor that made her moan with pleasure. He felt the rhythm in her hips as she rolled forward, then back, riding. She reached past him and grabbed the headboard, trying to lift herself. When she began shivering and moaning in his ear, he knew she was getting ahead of him. He didn't want it to be over that soon. He gripped her tighter, trying to hold her.

"Don't move. Don't move. Be still," he slowly whispered in her ear, his voice coarse with desire.

His hold on her left only her upper body free. She rocked back and forth, side to side, shaking her head, straining against his hold. He tightened his grip on her hips, as she breathed his name in his ear, over and over, but he couldn't hold them both. She cried out, convulsed in the throes of passion, and he felt her shuddering all over. He gave in to it—showering her with his love.

SEVENTEEN

Marc stepped through the part in the shower curtain, and dripped water across the floor to the cabinet. He unfolded a big fluffy towel and held it up.

"C'mon out of there. Let me dry you off."

When Vivian stepped out, he enveloped her with the towel and pulled her to him. She put her arms around his neck and rubbed her cheek against his, as he dried her back with the ends of the towel.

"Any regrets?" he asked, his lips against her hair.

She hesitated, then looked up at him.

"I know I'm supposed to feel guilty, but I don't. I feel...wonderful."

He put his hand under her chin and raised it until his lips touched hers. He kissed her so deeply, she felt his passion through the towel. Embarrassed, she pushed away from him.

"I've got to go see about Passion. They ought to be back by now."

"You can call Cora. Tell her you'll be a little late. She won't mind. The traffic will be murder right now, anyway. Just another hour?" he asked, with a mischievous grin. "I'll make it worth your while, I promise."

That was a promise Vivian wanted him to keep, but then there was Passion.

"If I don't leave now, I might stay all night," she said.

"That'll suit me just fine," he said, pulling her back to him, and giving her a kiss he meant to be convincing.

The sound of chimes permeating through the house intruded. Marc drew his head back, frowned, and pursed his lips. He picked up another towel, wrapped it around him and tucked it at his waist. He scooped her off her feet and carried her back to his bed.

"Call Cora. It's probably just some salesman. I'll be right back. Don't go away," he said, giving her a quick kiss.

When Marc opened the door, a flash of white light blinded him. Shocked, he put his hands to his face, rubbing at his eyes with the heels. Blinking to clear his eyes, he strained to see the man with the camera. He looked vaguely familiar.

"What the hell are you doing!" he demanded.

The man thrust an envelope in his hand. Marc looked at it, still blinking. 'Mrs. Vivian Carlson'—no address—was neatly typed on the front. His anger roiled, and he reached for the man. But the man jerked backwards just in time and took off running down the walkway. Marc chased him, grabbing for the camera, but it slipped from his grasp, just as the man ran through the gate, and the towel came loose. Marc stopped to pull it back around himself. By the time he secured it, the man was sprinting down the street. He thought of calling the police, but what would he say? "A man took my picture, then gave me a letter. He went thataway." No crime there.

He unclenched his fist and straightened the envelope, rubbing it back flat with his thumbs. His eyes widened, then narrowed, when he saw the return address—*Taylor, Taylor, and Price, Attorneys at Law*. He frowned, his lips drawn tight. He knew it meant trouble. Big trouble. He could open it, pretending he thought it was for him. But he *knew* it wasn't. He had no choice.

Vivian was sitting on the bed with her back against the headboard. The sheet was drawn around her breasts, her legs crossed Indian-style. She tilted her head and smiled at Marc. Then her expression changed.

"What is it?" she asked anxiously, when she saw the drawn look on his face.

Marc looked at the envelope and wished again that he'd put it away, and opened it later. Reluctantly, he handed it to her.

Vivian eyed it curiously, the frown on her face matching his.

"Where'd you get this?"

"The man at the door. He ran away. I'm almost sure it was that fellow we saw the other day at lunch."

She ripped the envelope open and unfolded the letter. Her eyes rapidly scanned the page. She began shaking her head. Her chest heaved, her eyes widened in disbelief.

"That bastard!"

Marc took the letter from her hand and read it.

> Dear Mrs. Carlson:
>
> Mr. Walter Carlson has retained this firm to represent him in this delicate matter. His strongest desire is for you to return to his home at 12 Cedar Bend, Austin, Texas and resume the marital rela-

tionship. In the event you are agreeable, he has indicated his willingness to participate in counseling.

In the event you are unwilling to accept his proposal, this will serve as a demand that you return his child, Passion Carlson, to him immediately, and in no event, later than Sunday at noon. If you do not, we are authorized to institute civil and criminal action against you for the return of his child on Monday at 8:00 a.m.

Kidnapping and interference with the parent-child relationship are felony actions that carry severe penalties. As a student of the law, surely you are aware that you have no legal relationship to the child. The rights of the biological father will prevail over any claim that you may make.

We look forward to settling this matter amicably, but we stand prepared to take <u>any</u> action necessary to accomplish the goals of our client.

Sincerely,
Velva Taylor

Marc sank on the bed as he read it.

"What does this mean? Biological father?"

Vivian looked up at him, her eyes brimming over with tears. She felt ashamed. She should have told him before. She nodded her head.

Marc saw it all clearly. He put his arms around her and pulled her against him. Vivian's body racked with sobs. If he could have found Walter at that moment, he would have put his hands around his throat and choked him to death. He wished he had known when Walter came to his office. He would have happily beat the shit out of him. Arrogant bastard! Maybe it was best he hadn't known. But why hadn't she told him? Why hadn't she left Walter when she first found out? Then he thought about Passion and the way she and Vivian looked at each other. He caressed her and let her cry.

When the sobs subsided, Vivian pulled away from him, desperately searching around the bed for her clothes, and began snatching them on, her hands shaking.

"I need to go get my baby!"

Marc saw fury, mixed with fear, on her face. He picked her things up off the floor and handed them to her, as he dressed himself.

"He's fucked with me one time too many! I'll kill his ass before I let him have Passion!" Tears of rage flooded her face.

"Calm down, Vivian. It's going to be alright." He spoke softly trying to soothe her.

"I should have known he would pull something like this! Bastard! Every time he can't get his way, he just pushes me in a corner 'til I give in. But not this time! Let's go. Take me to my car," she said, wiping her eyes with the heels of her hands.

Although he felt the urgency in her, when she rose from the bed, he gently pushed her back. He unbuttoned the blouse that, in her haste, she had buttoned askew. He fastened the bra that she'd left unhooked, then re-buttoned the blouse correctly. He didn't know how it was all going to turn out, but he wouldn't allow her to go into battle looking like a madwoman.

* * * * *

The traffic was building, as they left the neighborhood and entered the main thoroughfare. Marc expertly weaved the Volvo in and out of the traffic, not quite recklessly, but almost. He couldn't read her face, her eyes almost slits, her mouth drawn so tight her lips disappeared. So many questions ran through his mind, but none seemed appropriate to ask now.

"You need to talk to a lawyer," he said.

She didn't say anything for a long time.

"The ones I know are his friends."

They both pursed their lips.

At Cora's, Vivian jumped out of the car and ran to the door. She rushed into the house, past Cora, into the bedroom. Passion was sleeping, but Vivian picked her up and held her against her heart, rocking her from side to side. She lowered her arms and looked into Passion's cherubic face, then hugged her back to her, possessively.

"He can't take you away from me," she whispered. "Don't worry, baby. I'll take care of you."

In the living room, Cora looked at Marc puzzled, as he pulled Vivian's keys out of the door. He reached in his pocket and handed her the letter.

As she read it, her frown deepened with each paragraph. At the end, she looked up at Marc.

"Um-um. Po' chile. What's she going to do?" Cora asked with a worried look on her face.

"I don't think she's going to give him the baby," Marc said, shaking his head.

"You know all about this adoption stuff. What *can* she do?"

"I'm not sure she can do anything. If he can prove he's the father, he's got the big stick."

"But he doesn't care anything about that baby. Even that day he came over here, he didn't show the least bit of interest in her," she said, disgustedly.

"He's been *here*? When?"

"The other day. Wednesday, I think it was," Cora answered distractedly.

Marc wondered why Vivian hadn't told him, and what that meant. Then he remembered he hadn't told her Walter had been to his office.

"Slick Willie, sweet talking her. I thought you sent those roses. If I'd known they were from him, I'd have thrown them out myself. But she beat me to it. All that BS about 'baby needs her daddy.' Humph," Cora grunted, folding her arms across her chest.

"So you knew about this? Why is it I'm the only one outside the loop?"

"I can't speak to that. I only found out when she moved here. You think she'll go back to him?"

Marc let out a long sigh. "I don't know. She said she'd do anything to keep Passion. She may have to." He sat on the couch and sighed again.

Cora looked at the man she had come to think of as a son.

"Do you love her?"

Marc clasped his hands together against his mouth, his elbows propped on his knees. He looked up at Cora.

"Yes," he confessed for the first time, even to himself.

She saw the pain in his eyes.

"Then what are you going to do?"

"I don't know," he said, dejectedly.

"You don't know?!"

He tightened his lips, and shook his head.

"I'm not going to force her to choose between me and the baby."

"Scared you'd lose?" Cora asked.

"Maybe."

"There's got to be a way. She shouldn't have to make that kind of choice, to pay that kind of price."

"It may come down to that."

"That's bull! There's a lady belongs to my church who does divorces. I'm going to call her right now. You go see about Vivian."

* * * * *

Saturday morning, Marc was at Cora's thirty minutes before the appointment with the lawyer. He was relieved to see Vivian's Camry was still there. He wasn't sure why he'd come. He wasn't even sure she wanted him to. He'd spent the night at his computer, researching legal databases. Nothing he'd found led to a different conclusion than he'd already come to.

When she stepped on the porch, he opened the car door. Marc met her on the walk and hugged her to him, offering his strength. Vivian sank against his chest, drawing it from him.

"I'll go with you, if you want me to," he said.

"I'm glad you came. I need you."

* * * * *

Marc worried as Vivian directed him along East 12th Street, one of two business thoroughfares through East Austin. He wondered what kind of lawyer would have an office amid such deterioration. He was relieved when he turned on San Bernard and drove past the large houses that had been the showcases of Black Austin—back in the day. They still were. He parked in front of a big two-story house. The small sign in the neatly trimmed yard told him it was the right one.

Vivian knew the lawyer was doing Cora a favor by seeing her on a Saturday. Cora had told her that Mrs. Black lived in the house and kept her office on the ground floor. She wasn't sure of the proper protocol. Should she knock, or go right in? When she turned the knob, the door opened.

"Mrs. Black?" Vivian called out tentatively.

"Back here. Come on in. Lock the door. The neighborhood's not what it used to be," Vivian heard her call back.

They followed the sound of the voice, through the living room that now served as a reception area, into what must have been the dining room in grander times. The room was filled with plants flourishing in the bright light from the tall windows along the wall. Bookcases with law books lined the opposite wall. The diminutive woman who sat behind a desk didn't look happy or unhappy to see them. Her face was completely void of any emotion, and her eyes looked like they could pierce steel. The desk was brimming over with papers, books and folders. Vivian expected that any minute, the delicate balance would be disturbed and it all would tumble off to the floor. Mrs. Black stood up and extended her hand across the desk.

"Geraldine Black. Vivian? Sir," she said, giving each of them a curt handshake.

"Marc Kline."

"Sit down. Cora didn't tell me a lot about this, but she said it was urgent. I assume it's not a divorce," she said, eyeing Marc. "What's the problem?"

Vivian handed her the letter, and was surprised that a woman her age could read it without the aid of glasses. When the lawyer looked up, her gaze riveted to Marc.

"Who are you?"

"He's my friend," Vivian answered.

"Lover?" she asked, her eyes moving back to Vivian.

Vivian blushed and her ears burned violently. "He doesn't have anything to do with this."

"Yes or no?" she demanded.

"I don't see—"

"That's what Walter's lawyer is going to ask you in court. And you're going to have to have a better answer than that. You might want him to step out for the interview. I'll have to ask some questions you might find, shall I say, delicate." She looked at Vivian with raised brows.

Vivian looked at Marc, then slipped her hand into his.

"No. He can stay. I have nothing to hide," she said, throwing her chin up, defensively.

"Good. 'Cause it looks like Walter does. What I get from this letter is that he played around on you 'til he got a baby by another woman. Right?"

"Yes. That's right."

"Who's the mother?"

"I don't know. He won't tell me. And we haven't heard from her since he brought Passion home."

"That the baby's name?"

"Yes."

"How old?"

"I don't know."

"Five or six months, I'd guess," Marc interjected.

"How long have you had her?"

"A couple of months."

"Not long enough. You need at least six months."

"To do what?"

"Claim of abandonment. When did you move?"

"Last week."

The lawyer rolled her eyes. "How long has Mr. Kline been 'your friend'?"

Vivian looked at Marc.

"I met her March 2nd."

The lawyer reached under a stack of papers, pulled out a calendar and looked at it, while he explained how they met.

"I know Walter. He's got balls. But I'm surprised even *he'd* call a press conference to announce this. 'Course I can see his reasoning. You could bring the baby out in public that way," she said, nodding, as though she were talking to herself. "Plus it sounds good, politically. Still, it was mighty risky. Did you start adoption proceedings?" she asked, looking up at Vivian.

"No, not that I know of," Vivian said, looking down.

"You talked to any lawyers? Signed any papers?"

"No," Vivian said, shaking her head.

Mrs. Black fixed her with a stare.

"You really want this baby?"

"I'm her mama."

"How much are you willing to pay for her?"

"Pay for her? What do you mean? How much will it cost?"

"You willing to go back to Walter?"

"No! Never!"

"You willing to terminate your 'friendship'?"

Vivian looked at Marc, then back at the lawyer. "No."

"It would make this a lot easier," Mrs. Black offered.

"No," Vivian said, emphatically.

"Then it's going to cost you a lot. Not just in money, either. And you may lose the baby anyway."

Vivian felt the lawyer's piercing eyes watching for her reaction, her face expressionless.

"How much?" Vivian asked, mentally counting her inheritance.

"Well, first let's see what we're dealing with. Do you have any proof of Walter's adultery?"

"You mean, other than the baby?" Vivian asked quizzically.

Trying to hide the smirk, the lawyer asked, "He have any proof of yours?"

Vivian drew herself up indignantly. "My what? Are you accusing me of adultery?!"

"Some," Marc said quietly.

Both women turned to look at him.

"What exactly is the nature of it?" the lawyer asked.

"At least one picture—maybe more—that could be viewed as incriminating."

"Tell me about the pictures," the lawyer said, her eyes intently focused on Marc.

"The man who delivered the letter took my picture."

"So? Was Vivian in the picture?"

"No. She was in the, uh…other room."

"So what's incriminating?"

"I, uh, was shirtless."

"Pants?"

"Towel," Marc said, drawing his lips back in a tight smile.

"So they got a picture for a beefcake calendar. So what?"

"I believe the man has been following us. We have lunch together."

"So there may be pictures of you together?" A frown crept on her face.

Marc nodded. "And a credit card bill."

"Men's clothing?" the lawyer broke in, crimping her mouth and turning the frown to Vivian.

"No. For the baby," Marc answered.

"So what's incriminating about that?"

"The purchase was made in Arkansas," Marc said.

"Arkansas?"

"Vivian and I took a trip together. It wasn't planned, but..." he threw his hands up helplessly.

"Were you living with Walter when you took this trip?"

"Look," Vivian said, "nothing happened on the trip. In fact, nothing happened between Marc and me until I'd already divorced myself from Walter."

"You're divorced?" the lawyer asked, the frown easing. "Well, that's different."

"I, I mean, I'm divorced from him in my heart," Vivian said, looking down at her hands, realizing how naive she sounded.

"Well, that's the place to start," the lawyer said, the barest hint of sympathy in her voice, "but I'm afraid that's not enough. Judges like to think they have something to say about it."

She drummed her fingers on the desk for a while, lost in thought. "I haven't had a fact situation quite like this. It's intriguing, really. I assume you want a divorce, but what do we do about the child? She's not a child of the marriage so she doesn't fit in the divorce—except, of course, to prove fault. Fault has to be proven to justify the judge awarding you more of the property than half."

"I don't care about the property," Vivian said. "He can have it all. I just want my freedom—and my baby. The election is in two weeks. Walter's no fool. He's not going to file anything in court before then. It would be a public record. He'd be afraid of it getting in the newspaper. And I don't want to do anything to hurt him, I mean, his chances of getting re-elected. Can I get temporary custody, at least? I mean, I've had her all this time. Maybe I can stretch it out to six months."

The lawyer thought a minute. "You might be on to something there." She rummaged in the piles of papers on the desk and handed Vivian a form.

"Here. Fill this out." She turned to Marc. "Are you in this for the long haul? Or just til the going gets tough?"

"As long as she wants me to be," he said, looking at Vivian.

"Then, you fill one out too.

"Now Vivian, you meet me in front of the courthouse at 7:55 a.m.—sharp—Monday."

"What are you going to do?" Marc asked.

"Temporary custody of an abandoned child. The longer she has possession of the child, the stronger her position will be. No divorce, yet. We'd have to serve him if we filed a divorce, and he'd answer that. I'll fax his lawyers a copy of the custody petition as a courtesy, so that he can't say he didn't know about it. I'm betting Vivian's correct, he'll pass on this 'til the election is over. I could be wrong. He might show up."

"And if he does?" Vivian asked.

"I don't know. I'll think of something. My money says he won't."

"But what about the noon deadline tomorrow? If he comes, do I have to give her to him?"

"Do you know for a fact that he's the father?"

"Well, he *said* he was."

"I repeat, do you know for a fact?"

"Well, no," Vivian said, uncertainly.

"See that man out there?" the lawyer asked, pointing out the window. "Would you give the baby to him?"

"No, of course not."

"What if he said he was the baby's father?"

"Never mind all that lawyer stuff," Marc broke in. "I'll handle him."

"It would be better if you didn't have a confrontation with Walter," the lawyer said.

"I know. The next time, I'm gonna hurt him bad."

"What do you mean 'next time'? Have you had a confrontation?"

"He came by my office for a 'man-to-man' talk," Marc said, with a sneer.

"That's pretty bold. And he's having you followed? But he's made no attempt to take the baby? What does he want?" she asked, turning to Vivian.

"He says he wants me back," Vivian said, looking at her hands in her lap.

"Hmmm. Seems to me both of you need to behave as though you're being watched by the Pope. I hate to run, but I've got my Douglas Club meeting at 10:00. Leave the forms on the desk.

Lock the door behind you. See you Monday, Vivian. You and the baby come alone," she said pointedly looking toward Marc.

EIGHTEEN

Marc drove straight from the lawyer's office to his house and parked the car in the driveway. Inside, he stopped at the stereo.

"If you stayed the night, what time do you think we'd go to bed?" he asked with a boyish grin.

"Marc, I couldn't stay the night. You heard what Mrs. Black said. We have—"

"Just pretend. What time do you usually go to bed?"

"I don't know. Around 10:30, I guess."

"I'll put on five CD's and set them to re-play. It's Saturday night. You can stay up a little later," he said with a wink. "The timer will turn it off at 11:00 and back on at 11:30 in the morning." He walked to the lamp, unplugged it and plugged it into the circuit with the timer.

"C'mon," he said, taking her hand and leading her into his bedroom. He hurriedly threw some clothes in a gym bag, while she sat on the bed, watching in puzzlement. He set a timer on the bedroom lamp. "This one will come on at 9:00 and go off at 11:15. On to the kitchen."

"What are you doing?"

He took out a grocery sack and rummaged through the refrigerator, pulling out eggs, bacon, lettuce, milk, and various other items until the sack was full. He led her out the back door, unlocked the door to the RV and tossed the gym bag inside.

"Put this stuff in the fridge, while I unhook," he said, handing her the sack.

Marc unplugged the heavy extension cord from te side of the house, looping it around his arm as he walked toward the RV. He opened an outside compartment and stuffed the cord inside. He climbed in the driver's seat, started the motor, and pulled into the alley.

"We'll pick up Passion and Cora and take a little trip. That way you don't have to worry about any deadline. And I don't have to worry about hurting that dumb-ass husband of yours."

"Are we running away?" she asked, with a impish smile.

"Nope. Just taking a little family outing."

Vivian felt a warmth radiating inside her, thinking of them as a family.

* * * * *

Cora met them at the door, an anxious look on her face.

"Well?"

"Mrs. Black's going to file something Monday. I thought we'd take a little trip. The four of us. You game?" Marc asked. "Pack a couple of things and we'll tell you all about it on the way."

"I can't leave. I've got church tomorrow. It's Woman's Day. I can't miss that."

"Aw, come on, Cora," he pleaded. "We need a chaperone. And I don't want Vivian or the baby to be here—in case he tries to make good on his threat."

"He better not come to *my* house again. Ya'll go on."

Vivian walked in the room, handed a couple of bags to Marc and went back to get Passion.

"Cora, sure you don't want to come? It'll be fun. An adventure," Vivian said, when she came back with the baby.

"No, I'll just hold down the fort. You try to enjoy yourself, honey," she said, giving her a hug. "Just try to relax. I'll take care of everything here."

* * * * *

Marc headed east out of Austin. Thirty minutes later, he turned into Bastrop State Park and pulled over at the headquarters sign. When he came back, he said, "They don't have any spaces. I should have known. This is a real popular park, you need reservations weeks ahead of time. Sometimes they have cancellations. But not today."

"What are we going to do? Go home?" Vivian asked, worry and disappointment showing on her face.

"Naw, I know another place. This road goes through the park and ends up in another state park near Smithville. It doesn't have as many facilities—no swimming pool, no golf course—so there're always spaces available there. It's a beautiful drive."

The narrow road meandered through the park. They passed through the RV parking area, and sure enough, every space was taken. Farther on, the area reserved for tent campers was full of brightly colored tents. Vivian noticed that this park was filled with children, in contrast to the one where they'd stayed in Arkansas.

The outcropping of pine trees gave way to oaks and cedar as they passed the sign that read Buescher State Park. This park was nearly deserted. After Marc stopped at the headquarters, he pulled in the first area set aside for RVs. Theirs was the only vehicle.

"Pick a space. You can have your choice, madam."

"What about that one under those trees?" she asked, pointing.

"Your wish is my command," he said, in mock seriousness, as he backed in the spot and killed the motor.

Marc got the chairs down and sat them out, while Vivian spread Passion's quilt on the picnic table and placed her on it. Marc immediately picked Passion up and carried her to his chair.

"You can't leave her there like that. She'll flip her little self right off. We're gonna have to get one of those portable baby beds," he said, settling into the chair. "This is a good spot. It'll be easy to tell if we were followed."

"I can't believe you're so paranoid."

"I may be, but you know you've been followed ever since you moved to Cora's."

Vivian turned to him in surprise.

"What makes you think that?"

"Did you tell him where you were staying?"

"No."

"How do you think he found you?"

A frown creased Vivian's forehead as the realization sank in. Neither of them said anything for a couple of minutes.

"Why didn't you tell me you'd been seeing him?" Marc asked, a hint of accusation in his voice.

"I wasn't *seeing* him. What do you mean? He just came by. He didn't stay long. I didn't think it was important."

"Oh, I see. I guess you wouldn't think it was important that he came by my office and threatened to have me fired."

"Did he do that?"

He nodded.

"Obviously, *you* didn't think it was important enough to mention it to *me*," she said, defensively crossing her arms over her chest.

"He said you told him I was bothering you." He looked at her out of the corner of his eye, checking.

"And you believed him? Well, thanks for giving me that much credit. For believing that I don't have enough sense to tell you myself, if I felt that way."

"It's not about sense, Vivian. I just didn't know. He *is* your husband."

"You could at least have asked *me*. And he's not my husband."

"Look, Vivian, I don't want to argue with you. Neither of us has been exactly up front with the other. We'll have to do better—if we're going through all this shit together."

"I'm the only one that *has* to go through this 'shit'," she said, rolling her eyes at him.

"How do you figure?! First, you drag me half-way cross the country under false pretenses, put me in a bad light to your mother, then to my own parents. Next thing I know, my job is being threatened. Now, you've got me hiding out in the woods. What the hell do you mean, *you're* the only one that has to go through it! I just don't get that."

"Well, you just get this. Whenever you're ready to go, you just start your motor 'cause I'm ready now!"

Vivian marched to the RV and slammed the door. Marc turned

to Passion in his arms, shaking his head.

"Was it something I said? Naw, yo' mama's just crazy. And if she thinks I'm going to apologize to her, she's really lost her mind. Come on. Let's go for a walk. Maybe she will come to her senses by the time we get back."

* * * * *

The long walk did Marc a lot of good. At the playground, he tried to put Passion in the baby swing, but she was too small, so he sat in the big kids' swing with her in his lap. The back and forth motion soon lulled Passion into drowsiness. She yawned, then looked at him a minute before her lids closed. The peaceful look on her face made him regret the storm that lay ahead, and he wondered how it might affect her. He stood, careful not to wake her, and started to the RV.

By the time he got back, he'd convinced himself Vivian would be ready to apologize to him. He remembered how hard-headed she could be, even with her own mother. But this was different. He was clearly in the right. As he approached the RV, he frowned when he saw that she'd left the screen door open. What was she thinking about? They'd be swatting mosquitoes all night. Careless, that's what she was. Inconsiderate, too. He walked in, closing the screen behind him. Vivian was not there. He lay Passion on the bed, and patted her softly until she was still again.

Marc walked back outside and sat in the chair, waiting. He was even more convinced that she owed him an apology now. What was she trying to prove, going off like this? Didn't she realize she could be putting herself in danger? Or maybe he'd put her in danger by leaving. If that fool was crazy enough to come to his office, no telling what he'd do. Surely he wouldn't hurt her. Or would he? Marc frowned. As he pondered that thought, he heard Passion crying, and sprang from the chair. He found her on her back, kicking her legs and having a screaming fit. When he reached for her, the aroma told him why.

"You could have saved this for your mama," he said, a wry smile on his face. He got the blue box and a diaper from her bag. She quieted as her eyes followed him. It took several towelettes to clean up the mess. "Whew! What have you been eating, little girl?!" he asked, scrunching his nose. He wiped at the dark spot on her buttock with a towelette. Roughly heart-shaped, the size of a nickel. When it didn't come off, he rubbed his thumb over it, thinking. He put a clean diaper on her, then felt in the bag for a jar of food.

"I'll bet you're hungry." He walked to the kitchen for a bowl and spoon. Through the screen door, he saw Vivian walking up the road. Relieved, he stepped outside and waited. She stopped. When he started walking toward her, Vivian started walking, then ran into his arms. They were both talking, neither listening.

"I was so worried about you," he said, caressing her back.

"I shouldn't have picked a fight on you."

"Don't leave like that again."

"After you stood by me."

"I shouldn't have accused you."

"I shouldn't have taken all my worry out on you."

Tears ran down Vivian's face, as they hugged each other. She wondered if there would ever be a time when all the tears would be wrenched from her, and whether there would be a time when there was nothing but joy. She could see the mountain. But she felt the strength welling up from a place deep inside her. They walked to the RV with their arms around each other.

Later that night, Vivian lay on the bed curled around Passion. She felt Marc ease into the bed and curl his body around hers.

* * * * *

Vivian anxiously glanced around, looking for Mrs. Black. She took no comfort from the drawn and fearful faces she saw trudging toward the courthouse. Passion kept pulling at her earring. Mrs. Black appeared behind her.

"Pretty baby," she said, matter-of-factly. "OK. Just follow me."

They lay their purses on the conveyor belt and walked through the metal detector. Nothing in law school about that. It was intimidating to Vivian.

"Listen to my questions. I'll try to phrase them so you'll only have to say 'yes'. If you see Walter, let me know."

Vivian followed Mrs. Black into the clerk's office and watched as she made small talk with the clerks, asking about this one's baby and another's surgery. She was obviously in her element. She handed one the check she'd written, and took a file from her.

"Come on. Fifth floor."

"What are you going to ask me? What should I say?" Vivian asked anxiously, in the elevator.

"Yes. Just say yes—unless the answer is no."

In the courtroom, Mrs. Black pointed Vivian to a seat, then walked to the bailiff's table, handing him the file and making more small talk.

"All rise."

The judge came in and sat at the tall bench, taking the first folder from the clerk and frowning.

"In the Matter of an Unnamed Child," he called out.

Mrs. Black walked in front of the bench and began talking to the judge in tones that Vivian couldn't quite make out. She watched the judge's eyebrows raise slightly, never losing the frown. Then Mrs. Black turned to her and summoned her forward with two flicks of her wrist.

The bailiff instructed her to raise her right hand, and administered the oath, then pointed her to the witness stand. Vivian shifted in the seat and grabbed Passion's hand away from her earring.

"Is your name Vivian Carlson?"

"Yes."

"Do you live at 2274 E. 14th Street, Austin, Texas?"

"Yes."

"Do you have possession of a child, three to five months old?"

"Yes."

"Have you had possession of the child for two to three months?"

"Yes."

"Did the parents of the child leave the child in your care without expressing any intention to return?"

Vivian frowned uncertainly. One of the parents had. Noticing her hesitation, Mrs. Black gave her a stern look.

"Yes."

"Are you willing to continue to care for the child?"

"Yes, of course."

"Are you asking the court to appoint you temporary managing conservator of the child?"

"Yes."

"That's all, Your Honor. I've prepared an order. It's there in the file."

"You're not asking for the appointment of an ad litem?" the judge asked.

"Not at this time, Your Honor. Our primary concern right now is some authority in the event of an emergency. A medical problem or some such. Day care. That kind of thing."

A disgruntled look crossed the judge's face and Vivian nearly panicked.

"We'll come back for further orders at a later time," Mrs. Black said, assuringly.

"I'll set a date now. June 15th. Petitioner is named temporary managing conservator," he said, signing the order, then handed the file to the clerk and accepted another.

Mrs. Black beckoned Vivian off the witness stand as the judge called the next case.

* * * * *

Walter's feet were propped up on the massive desk. He was pissed about it all, especially the way this silly woman was trying to order him around. When he received a copy of Ms. Taylor's letter Friday on his fax, he'd been certain Vivian would come running home. Just in time, too. With only two weeks until the election, he was hot and heavy on the campaign trail. He'd planned that she would do that church stuff with him, like she'd always done. She had a knack for dealing with the preachers. He could handle the old ladies. The baby would be an added touch. Instead, he'd spent Sunday making the rounds of the churches alone, shaking hands and smiling until his face nearly broke. This morning, his day began with a frantic call from the lawyer and a fax of the petition for custody. Nothing he could do about it now. Over her strenuous objection, he'd sent Ms. Taylor to the courthouse to observe and report back to him. Now, she was on the phone, castigating him for his refusal to fight.

"Listen lady. I'm not about to go into a courtroom and reveal details of my private life two weeks before my re-election. You just be ready to file the day after the election if that's necessary. Worst case, this whole thing will blow over by November."

"But Walter, as your lawyer, my best advice…"

"I'm a lawyer too, and I know what I'm doing. I'm paying *you*. You do what *I* say." He dropped the receiver on the hook, then tented his hands against his mouth.

Silly bitch, he thought. He didn't even want her, but he'd followed Bobby's advice in hiring the firm. Price, Sr. had insisted it was best for him to have a woman lawyer under the circumstances. He'd assured him she was good. Maybe so, but she sure didn't know jack about politics. He wanted Bobby, but he'd refused, referring him to Taylor, Taylor & Price. All that crap about 'conflict of interest' and 'not his area of expertise' was just a cover for Bobby's feelings for Vivian. Walter knew it.

Ms. Taylor just didn't understand what his goal was. He knew Vivian still loved him because she hadn't filed for divorce. She cared enough not to name him in this ridiculous petition and spread it all over the newspapers. When she got over her little snit, she'd come home, he thought nodding. The only part he couldn't make fit was Marc Kline. If Mr. Kline thought he could take his woman, he was in for a big surprise. Nobody could take what belonged to him.

* * * * *

Election night. The campaign office was filled with volunteers and supporters. Their spirits were high. Balloons, confetti and banners decorated the otherwise drab office. He'd trounced that fool, just as he'd expected. He gave his victory speech early while the TV cameras were there. Then they were gone—on to the more controversial races.

Walter was tired. He didn't feel the exhilaration of the previous election nights. Even with Sherman there pumping him up, it just wasn't the same without Vivian. He'd explained her absence by saying the baby was sick. And that gave him a good excuse for leaving at 10:30. Shante, the girl who'd been a steadfast volunteer the last couple of months, had made eyes at him all night. She was pretty, bright-eyed and fine. Funny, he thought driving home, normally he'd have gone back to sample new charms after he'd taken Vivian home. But Vivian wasn't home. And that old bat she was staying with wouldn't let him talk to her. Every time he called, she'd either say it was a wrong number or that Vivian wasn't there. He heard the triumph in her voice each time. Bat.

Walter walked through the kitchen, ignoring the pizza and chicken boxes on the counter, into the living room with the newspapers strewn about, to the bar. The house was so empty, hollow. What if she wouldn't come back? He pushed the thought out of his mind. He downed one drink at the bar, then re-filled the glass. He stared at the light on the answering machine. Probably his mother. She always called on election night. He walked over and pressed the button.

"Congratulations, Walter. I'm glad you won."

The sound of her voice made him want to drive over to the

Eastside and get her. He re-wound the tape and played the message again. He walked straight to the phone and dialed the number Bobby had given him.

"Vivian's asleep. I'll tell her you called."

Old bat! He climbed the stairs and lay on the bed, staring at the ceiling until sleep finally came to him.

* * * * *

Despite Marc's assurances, Vivian had spent the two weeks until the election with a wrinkle in her brow. She knew Walter had not given up. She couldn't shake the sense of impending doom. She could tell from Cora's eyes that those 'wrong numbers' were Walter. Whenever the doorbell rang, she jumped, expecting it to be him. She'd hoped that the message she'd left on election night would placate him some, but she'd heard the phone ring around eleven and knew it was him. She wasn't surprised at all to get the call from Mrs. Black the next day. Walter's lawyer had filed an intervention in the lawsuit, and a statement of paternity, asking for an immediate hearing. Mrs. Black finagled the thing somehow to have the hearing put off until the June 15th date the judge had already set. Hell of a graduation present, she thought.

But today was Friday, the 12th, and if she didn't hurry she'd be late. Never mind it had taken nearly twenty years, she'd finally accomplished her dream. The Sunflower ceremony was at noon, and it was already ten. Gloria, Cora and Passion were dressed and waiting impatiently in the living room. From the moment Gloria arrived Wednesday night, they'd been a little trio. It was almost like Vivian was an outsider. Still, she was relieved that Gloria and Cora had hit it off. She'd felt so rotten that morning, she was glad they'd kept the baby with them the night before. Graduation jitters, she'd thought, with her head over the toilet. And Passion was getting spoiled rotten, having *two* grandmothers clucking over her at every waking moment.

Vivian sighed again looking at the navy suit she'd planned to wear. It was her favorite and fit her to a T. Lawyer-looking, too. Perfect. But she'd had to suck in so hard to fasten the hook on the skirt, she could hardly breathe. She knew she couldn't stand it through the long ceremony, plus the dinner at the hotel overlooking Town Lake they'd planned. She just didn't understand it. She wasn't eating any more than usual. Maybe it was the 'middle-age spread' she heard her friends talking about. She fished around in the closet and found the suit with the elastic waistband. Maybe she was just getting to that age, she thought. She didn't know what possessed her to buy that suit, she hated the pale pink color. Strong colors looked better against her skin. But comfort was her goal for this day.

* * * * *

The graduation ceremony was held in the Performing Arts Center on campus. Every seat was taken in the huge auditorium. The dignitaries were sitting in the spotlight on the stage. Pots of bright yellow sunflowers lined the front of the stage. Vivian tried to pay attention to the speakers—the Dean of the Law School, the President of the University, the graduate with the highest GPA. Integrity. Honor. Professionalism. Duty.

Gloria sat on her left in the plush red velvet chair, proud as a peacock. From Gloria's other side, Del kept peeking around and grinning at Vivian. Marc sat on her other side, Cora next to him. Gloria held the sunflower Vivian had given her. The tradition dictated that the graduate's chosen person pin the sunflower on them, in lieu of the tassel-turning. When it was time for the pinning, light flooded the auditorium, and all the graduates stood, Gloria handed the sunflower over to Marc. Vivian kissed her mother on her cheek, then turned to Marc. He smiled down at her as he pinned the sunflower on her lapel. That was the last thing she remembered.

When she came to in the nurse's station, they were all hovering over her. Vivian didn't know where she was. She struggled to rise from the cot, fighting the fog off.

"You just got over-excited, honey. Just lay back, Babysis," she heard Gloria saying through the fog.

When she got her eyes to focus, she recognized them all. Del was leaning over Gloria's shoulders. Marc was standing next to Del. Their faces were pinched with worry. Cora was standing back, holding Passion. The look on her face was different, knowing.

Vivian leaned against Marc for support all the way to the van. Del offered to let Marc drive the van, but he sat in the back with his arm around Vivian. Marc suggested that they take her home and skip the dinner, and they all agreed, but Vivian insisted. This was her special day, and she didn't want to miss a minute of it. Besides, Gloria had come all the way from Fort Worth, and Del had taken off a day at school. By the time they were on the escalator to the restaurant, she was feeling like her old self. Even so, she only picked at her food and Marc ate most of the sizzling fajita order they shared. Her eyes clouded up when Gloria spoke of how proud Vivian's dad would have been, and how much she wished he'd lived to see this day. It was Vivian's wish, too, but she felt his presence, and knew he was smiling.

* * * * *

Vivian stared at Walter sitting next to his lawyer at the other counsel table. She felt a little more at ease this time. She took an immediate dislike to his lawyer, in her 'dressed-for-success suit'— ascot and all.

"Your Honor, it's a travesty! She—they—came in here and purposefully misrepresented the situation to the Court. Their claim of abandonment is ridiculous under these circumstances..."

Under the barrage of accusation, Vivian's eyes darted to Mrs. Black. Her face showed no emotion. Every now and then, she scribbled on the pad in front of her on the table. Vivian wondered what she was writing, and why she was allowing this woman to go on and on, saying these terrible things. Finally, Mrs. Black stood.

"Excuse me, Counselor. Your Honor, we set this hearing back in April for the purpose of determining whether the appointment of an ad litem would be appropriate and for continuing managing conservatorship in Mrs. Carlson. I believe it is proper to hear that issue first, rather than the petition filed—late in the day—by Ms. Taylor. If it would please the Court, I'd like to call my first witness."

As Vivian watched the scowl on the judge's face deepen, she steeled herself, and put her purse in the chair behind her, preparing to walk to the witness stand.

"Counselor, I've already decided to appoint a guardian ad litem. Now, in light of Representative Carlson's acknowledgment of paternity, there's no need for an attorney ad litem to represent the child. We'll proceed on Ms. Taylor's motion."

"Thank you, Your Honor," Ms. Taylor said, with a big smile for the judge, and a catty smirk for Mrs. Black. "I'd call Walter Carlson."

Walter exuded confidence as he walked to the stand. His eyes never left Vivian's face as he took the oath.

"State your name for the record, please."

"Representative Walter Carlson."

"And your address?" Ms. Taylor continued.

"12 Cedar Bend, Austin, Texas."

"Are you married?"

"Yes. Nineteen years."

"What is your wife's name?"

"Vivian. Vivian Johnson Carlson."

"Is the woman sitting at that table Vivian Carlson?" Ms. Taylor pointed at Vivian.

"Yes."

"Do you have any children?"

"Yes, one."

"Does Vivian Carlson have any children?"

"No. We tried for a long time, but Vivian couldn't give me a child."

"Representative Carlson, I'd appreciate it if you would just answer the question that I ask," she said, barely masking the consternation in her voice. "Now, what is your child's name?"

"Passion Carlson."

"And is that child the subject of this lawsuit?"

"Yes."

"Does Passion live with you?"

"Yes. At least she did until my wife left—and took her."

"When was that?"

"The end of March. I don't remember the exact date. It was a Sunday. It was—"

"Did she take the child with your permission?"

"No."

"Did she tell you where she was taking the child?"

"No. I had to hire a private detective to find my child."

"So she has secreted your child from you for nearly three months now? Is that right?"

"Yes."

"What was your reaction when you learned that she had sneaked into court and misrepresented to the judge that you had abandoned the child?"

"Frankly, I was shocked. It's not like Vivian to tell a bald-faced lie like that."

"Did you abandon your child?"

"Of course not. How could I abandon my child in my own house?"

"Did your wife tell you why she left, Representative Carlson?"

Walter looked down at his hands, then up at Vivian. She met his gaze.

"No. She just left in the middle of the night while I was asleep. But I found out. She's having an affair with another man."

Vivian almost choked. She looked wild-eyed at Mrs. Black for her to object or do something. It was just a lie. The expression on Mrs. Black's face didn't change. She didn't even acknowledge Vivian's tugging at her skirt under the table.

"Do you know how long this affair has been going on, Representative Carlson?"

"No."

"Do you think Vivian Carlson is a fit mother for your child?"

"There was a time I would have said 'yes', but in light of her recent behavior…If she continues the course she's on—"

"And you're asking the court to order Vivian Carlson to return the child to you and to declare you to be the father. Is that right?"

"I'd like the court to order Vivian to come home. I love my wife. I love my child. I want us to be a family."

"Pass the witness," Ms. Taylor said, smugly.

Mrs. Black didn't say anything for so long, all eyes turned to her. Vivian watched the judge's face, the scowl deepening.

"You've testified that your name is Representative Walter Carlson? Is your first name really 'Representative'?

"No," Walter said, with his 'you're really stupid' look.

"Then would you state your correct name, for the record of course," she returned with a benign smile.

"Walter Edwin Carlson."

"Thank you. Now, Mr. Carlson, when did you hire Ms. Taylor?"

"I don't see what—"

"Your Honor, would you instruct the witness to answer the question?"

"I don't remember exactly. Around the end of March."

"So, Ms. Taylor was your attorney when the first hearing was held in this case?"

"I don't know."

"You don't know? Is that your testimony under oath? On the record?"

Walter shifted in the seat. "Well, I'm not sure."

"You're not sure," Mrs. Black repeated. "Prior to my filing the petition for custody, I faxed a copy of it to Ms. Taylor's office. Are you telling the Court that your lawyer didn't inform you, thereby abrogating her duty to her client?"

Walter squinted his eyes, but he said nothing.

"Exactly when did your attorney inform you of the hearing?"

"I don't remember exactly."

"OK," she said, patiently. "Well, let's see. Was it the day after the hearing?"

"No."

"The day of?"

"Yes," he sighed.

"Morning or afternoon?"

"I believe it might have been in the morning. I'm a very busy man. I have a very full schedule. I—"

"Well, let's see if I can't jog your memory a little. How did you come to know about it? Was it a phone call?"

"No."

"A letter?"

"No."

"Perhaps a fax?"

"Yes."

"What time did you receive the fax?"

"I don't remember."

"OK. Where were you when you received this fax?"

"I was at my home."

"Was it before eight o'clock?"

"It may have been. I don't remember."

"Well, if I showed you records from the telephone company showing a call from Ms. Taylor's fax line to your home fax line at 6:47, would you dispute that?" she asked, waving a stack of phone bills at him.

"Not without seeing those records."

When Mrs. Black laid the stack of bills down, Vivian was surprised to see the name on it was Geraldine Black, Attorney.

"Now your response was filed more than two weeks later. But you had an attorney the day we came to court. And you knew there was a hearing. Why didn't you come to the hearing?"

"Well, I had some appointments that day. And—"

"And you were too busy with other matters to come see about your child? You're a lawyer. Isn't that correct, Mr. Carlson? A good lawyer at that?"

"Yes."

"And you're surely aware that the likely outcome of your not appearing in court would be that Mrs. Carlson would be awarded continued custody of the child? Isn't that correct?"

"Well—"

"So, in fact, you acquiesced in leaving the child in Vivian's care. Just as you had since the night you brought the baby home. Isn't that correct?"

"No. But, see—"

"But? But you had an election in two weeks. Isn't that right? And *that* was more important to you than this child." Mrs. Black's eyebrow raised in a question mark.

"I object," Ms. Taylor said.

"Withdraw the question. Now, Mr. Carlson, you testified that Vivian left on a Sunday night. When did you learn of her whereabouts?"

"I don't recall."

"Don't recall, huh? Do you know Cora Williams?" Mrs. Black turned and looked pointedly at Cora sitting in the audience holding Passion.

"Yes."

"Isn't it true that you went to the house where Vivian was staying with Cora Williams two days after she left?"

"Well, yes."

"Did you ask Vivian to give you the child while you were at Ms. Williams' house?"

"No, but—"

"But the election was coming, so you left the child with her. Didn't even ask for her." She paused, looking at the judge to make sure he got her point. "Now, you've alleged that your wife is having an affair, and alleged that she's unfit to mother the child. And you've testified that she is not the biological mother of the child. Who is the biological mother?"

"I'm the father. That's all you need to know." Walter crossed his arms over his chest.

"Your Honor, would you instruct the witness to answer the question."

"I object. This proceeding is to determine the relative fitness of the two parties before the court," Ms. Taylor interjected.

"Your Honor, the biological mother is a critical party to these proceedings. Mr. Carlson has refused to reveal her identity and we are prevented from notifying her—as we notified him," she said, looking pointedly at Walter.

"Overruled. Answer the question."

He looked at his lawyer, a question on his face. Ms. Taylor nodded.

"Her name is Porsche Timmons."

Vivian ran through her list of suspects. She couldn't place a Porsche.

"What is her address?" Mrs. Black continued.

"I don't know."

"Where is she?"

"I don't know."

"When did you last have contact with her?"

"I don't remember the exact date."

"What was the nature of that contact?"

"She brought Passion to my office and left. She said she was going to New York to be an actress and that it was better for me to raise Passion. I have made efforts to find her, but haven't located her so far."

"How long had you known Porsche Timmons?"

"About a year and a half."

"When did you tell your wife that you had a baby by another woman?"

"The same day Porsche brought the baby to me."

"So, you had been having an affair for more than a year with this one woman. Who else have you had an affair with during your marriage to Vivian Carlson?"

"I object! Irrelevant."

"Sustained."

"Now we've already established that *you* had previously determined that Vivian Carlson is an appropriate person to have charge of Passion. I'd like to explore the reasons you now believe *you* would be a better parent. Have you ever changed Passion's diaper?"

"Well, Vivian took her—"

"I'll take that as a no. Have you ever taken Passion to the doctor?"

"No. She hasn't been sick."

"Have you ever given her a bottle?"

"I told you, Vivian took her away, and prevented me from caring for her."

"No further questions."

"Ms. Taylor? Further questions?" the judge asked.

"Not of this witness. I call Vivian Carlson."

"You may take your seat Representative Carlson. Mrs. Carlson take the stand."

Vivian felt so many emotions as she walked to the witness stand. Anger, fear, sorrow, outrage. She wouldn't look at Walter as she passed the table where he sat or as she answered the preliminary questions about her identity and address.

"Do you acknowledge that Walter Carlson is the biological father of Passion Carlson?"

"That's what he told me."

"And do you admit that you took Passion Carlson and moved from Representative Carlson's house, and did not tell him where his child was?"

"He never showed any interest in Passion."

"Ms. Carlson, were you in Fort Valley, Georgia on March 27th of this year?"

"Yes."

"What were you doing there?"

"On vacation."

"Were you with a man named Marc Kline?"

"Yes, and Ruthie and Early Kline. And…"

A piercing scream shattered the courtroom. Vivian recognized it and looked in that direction. She saw Passion in Walter's arms, screaming her head off. There was a look of shock on Walter's face as he held Passion in front of him like he would have held a ticking bomb. Vivian jerked her eyes from Passion to the judge, who looked rattled and wide-eyed, then back at Passion, then to Mrs. Black, then desperately to Cora, now sitting directly behind Walter with a benign look on her face—the same look Mrs. Black wore. Passion was still screaming and no one was doing anything about it. She hurriedly walked over and took Passion, putting her on her shoulder. She talked to her and patted her until she settled down, then carried her back to the witness stand.

Ms. Taylor was the first to regain her composure.

"Your Honor, we'd ask for a recess."

Mrs. Black was on her feet.

"Your Honor, you've had an opportunity to observe the child with both parties. Obviously, to abruptly change custody of the child would be disruptive and disturbing to the child. I'd ask that you continue temporary custody with Vivian Carlson until the results of the paternity test." She cast a quick, sidelong glance at Ms. Taylor, the hint of a smirk on her face.

"Paternity test?! You can't be serious!" Ms. Taylor shouted.

"Your Honor, despite the statement filed by Mr. Carlson, we dispute the fact of his paternity and are entitled under the Texas Family Code to have tests ordered. The statute vests no discretion in the court, it reads 'the court *shall* order' the test."

Vivian watched the judge flip through a book reading various passages, then look up at Mrs. Black with a curious expression.

"It seems you are correct, Mrs. Black. The parties shall submit to the test." Then he frowned. "Both sides seem to agree that Mrs. Carlson is not the mother. But she is a party, and the law seems to require it. However, I believe it imperative that the biological mother be found and notified. That burden will be on you, Representative Carlson. Temporary managing conservatorship shall remain with Mrs. Carlson. However, Mr. Carlson shall have visitation. Every third day from 1 to 5 p.m., unsupervised, beginning tomorrow. Next hearing will be in three weeks. That's all. Court's in recess."

"All rise," the bailiff called out.

NINETEEN

Vivian observed a strict schedule while she studied for the July Bar exam. She went to the library every day as if it were her job. She spent her mornings there preparing for that evening's Bar Review class. She resented having to do it. She'd worked her butt off for three years in school only to have to take another course to pass the Bar. It didn't make any sense. What was the three years for then? Why wouldn't they let you just take the course right out of college, then the exam. And if the law school was so top-ranked, why did she need to take the course to pass the exam? Maybe it was fear, or lack of confidence. In the end, she decided she'd put too much of her life in this venture to gamble now. She wrote the big check for the review course and subtracted the amount from her dwindling inheritance.

Not only was preparing for the exam taking a toll on her bank account, but on her body as well. Marc had taken to teasing her about how much she was eating. She was down to two pair of shorts that she could wear comfortably. She chalked her increased appetite up to nervousness about the approaching exam and worry about the custody proceedings. She promised herself that as soon as the exam was over, she'd join a gym and take the weight off.

After their daily lunch, she went home to spend time with Passion. But once she was at Cora's, she could hardly wait for Passion's nap time, so she could take one, too. When she returned from the night class, Cora was always waiting up for her. It started with a glass of milk. Cora said she had read an article about women her age needing calcium. Vivian had indulged her at first, even though she hated the taste of it, but that milk thing got old quick. When she resisted, Cora switched to cocoa. Then yogurt, when Vivian complained that she was already gaining too much weight.

Tonight's class had been particularly draining. Oil and Gas was the one subject on the exam that she had not taken in school, so she had to pay close attention and take good notes. When it was over, what she really wanted was a glass of wine. She thought about Cora and this calcium tirade she was on, then considered going to Marc's. But she remembered it was his night to have Corey and he'd planned to take him for pizza. So she stopped at the grocery store and bought a bottle of wine.

* * * * *

"What do you think you're doing, Missy?" Cora asked, aghast at the sight of the bottle.

"I'm not drinking any milk tonight, Cora. I don't care how you disguise it. Forget it," Vivian said, pouring the wine into a little glass with cartoon characters on it that jelly had come in. "And no yogurt either. Would you like a little glass?"

Vivian offered the glass to Cora and was shocked when Cora took it out of her hand and poured the wine in the sink.

"A pregnant woman shouldn't drink alcohol. It's bad for the baby."

"You're right," Vivian responded, reaching for the glass. "But I'm not pregnant and I kinda' doubt you are."

"You haven't had your monthly since you moved here," Cora said, holding the glass out of Vivian's reach.

"So? I'm going through the change. Not that it's any business of yours," Vivian said, her hackles raised at Cora's prying.

"You ain't old enough to be going through the change. Your mama didn't go through it til fifty," Cora said smugly.

"Oh, so you're in everybody's business, not just mine. I'll have you know that some of the best doctors in the state have declared me to be infertile. So I can't be pregnant." Vivian crimped her mouth and shook her head at Cora like she was a child.

"Just goes to show, doctors don't know everything," Cora answered, her attitude unwavering.

"And you just *have* to have the last word. I'm not going to argue with you. I'm going to bed!"

As she stormed through the living room, she heard Cora say, "Goodnight, Lil' Mama."

Vivian flopped on the bed. It was bad enough that she felt big as a cow and her clothes didn't fit, but to have Cora picking at her, too, was more than she could stand. The nerve of her talking about her period! Just because she lived in her house didn't give her the right to get *that* personal with her. She had to admit, she'd thought about the possibility, back when she had that stomach bug that made her nauseated all the time. But, she knew that if it wasn't menopause, it was just all the upheaval in her life. She couldn't be pregnant. It just wasn't possible. She didn't need to be worried with this. Tomorrow was another full day. Plus, it was the third day and having to turn Passion over to Walter again was enough to make her sick. She hadn't decided whether to have lunch with Marc and let Cora deal with Walter, or to be there and make sure Passion saw her face last.

* * * * *

Sunshine streamed through the windows in the dining room.

"Why are you looking so down?" Marc asked, as he took their lunch plates off the table.

"I had this stupid fight with Cora last night. She got all in my business. I got real mad at her and said some ugly things. Now, I'm sorry, but I don't know how to apologize—or whether I want to."

"What about?"

"Can you believe, she thinks I'm pregnant?!"

Marc snapped the dishwasher door closed, then turned back to her.

"You do have all the signs," he said, quietly. "Maybe you ought to see a doctor."

"You're as crazy as she is. Don't either of you understand? I can't get pregnant. I told you that. Besides, you always use protection."

"Except that once. Remember? And, condoms aren't 100%."

She tightened her lips impatiently and looked off.

Marc sat at the table and took her hand in his to draw her attention back.

"I'd like for you to see a doctor, just in case. Who is—" The phone's ringing interrupted him.

"It's Cora," he said, handing it to her and giving her a kiss on her forehead. "Think about it, OK?"

"Cora?" she asked into the phone.

"I was hoping to find you there. Walter called. Said he needed to talk to you right away."

"What is it now?"

"He didn't say. Just that it was urgent."

"Alright, I'll call him."

She dialed her old number, giving Marc an exasperated look.

"Walter? What can I do for you?" … "Sick? Again? Maybe she's just sick of you, Walter. Why don't you leave Passion and me alone." … "I know you're her father. And I know what the judge said. That's the only reason I let you take her." … "Fever? How high?"… "How long?" … "I'll be right there."

She hung the phone up and started for her purse.

"I'll go with you," Marc said, a dark look on his face.

"No. It'll be better if I go by myself. I'll call you later."

"Vivian, you know he's doing this on purpose, just to get you over there. This is just like the last time. And the time before."

"He *said* she has a fever. What am I supposed to do?"

"Then why doesn't he take her to a doctor? Why do you have to go running…to be at his every beck and call?"

"I gotta go, Marc. I don't have time for this."

Marc stood in the doorway and watched her all the way down the walk to her car. He *knew* he was right. He'd felt the changes in her body—her waistline expanding, her hips a little fuller. He liked the way her breasts had filled out, straining against the bra, and the fullness of her nipples in his mouth. Despite the emotional turmoil he'd been through on his way to the decision, he *knew* how he felt about it now.

When he'd first thought she might be pregnant, he'd had that trapped feeling. But she seemed to have no interest in trapping him. Lately, she was so moody, sometimes he doubted whether she wanted him at all. When he questioned her moodiness, she said he was imagining things, and that she was just wrought up over the pending Bar Exam. Why would she want to trap him, anyway? It had taken a couple of days of brooding over it for him to realize that if there was any trapping going on, he'd trapped himself by not being careful enough. It had been his own fault.

The next question was, whether he wanted to be tied to this woman for the rest of his life. When he and Allison had divorced, he'd thought that would be the end of her. But over time, he'd come to realize that he would be tied to her forever. His ties to her wouldn't even be severed when Corey turned eighteen, as he'd thought at first. They'd have graduations together, a wedding. They'd have grandchildren together, for God's sake. He now understood what 'til death do us part' really meant.

He certainly didn't want with Vivian what he had with Allison. That politeness toward an enemy, born of having a shared border, that flared into open hostility at times, until he, deeming himself the more mature and wiser, cooled it for Corey's sake—usually by acceding to her ridiculous demands. But Vivian was nothing like Allison. Not only were their personalities different, but age was a factor, too. Allison had been in her twenties when they'd married. Vivian was forty. And *he* was nothing like he'd been then, either. He'd given up the traveling he loved so much, and taken the teaching position for Allison, then resented her for his having done it. It had been unfair of her to demand it, and unfair of him to resent it once he'd done it. But that was all water under the bridge.

He'd vowed he'd never marry again until he was sure it was for the rest of his life. Was Vivian that woman, he wondered? He hadn't thought about marrying her before. Her being already married was a big obstacle to that kind of thinking. But when he thought of her carrying his child, the thought came to him straight-away. It was his duty. No. Maybe with some other woman, it would be his duty. With Vivian, it would be his pleasure.

Now that he was sure how he felt about it, what next? Going from one child to three in a matter of months would require some adjustments. They'd need a bigger house for sure. Corey was so much older, he'd have to have his own room. If the baby was a girl, she and Passion could share. Two little princesses. He smiled as he picked up the phone and dialed the pediatrician's number.

"Dr. Carrouthers, Marc Kline here. I need the name of the best OB-GYN in town."

* * * * *

Vivian parked in the circular drive. When she approached the door, she had the same feeling as the last time—it was a stranger's house. Hard to believe she'd ever lived there. Seconds after she rang the bell, the door opened.

"Hi, Vivian," Walter said, with a smile. "I'm glad to see you. Come on in."

She stepped into the foyer and surveyed the room. It all looked the same, except for the newspapers scattered about.

"Want a drink?" he asked.

"Where's Passion?"

"Oh, she went to sleep. Come on, sit down. You're looking healthy, Vivian. Putting on a little weight? It looks good on you."

"I just came to see about Passion. Did her fever go down?"

"Fever? Oh, yeah."

"Why didn't you call me back, then?" she asked exasperated.

"Well, we…there're some things we need to talk about. And since you were coming, anyway—"

"We don't have anything to talk about, Walter. You said it all in court." She fixed him with a stony stare.

"It's about these tests. Do we really have to go through all that? I *told* you Passion was my baby. I signed the papers. What more do you need?"

"Let's let the lawyers handle that. Can I just go ahead and take Passion with me now? It would save you a trip across town."

"You know they'll have to draw her blood, too. Why would you put the child through that? Let's just forget this whole thing."

"They've already taken her blood. And mine, too. You know, Walter, this could have been so simple, if you'd just left things like they were. You don't care anything about Passion."

"OK, I admit it. I didn't at first. But she's growing on me. What I really care about is you, Vivian. I still want you to come home. What can I do to convince you?"

"Can I just have the baby?" she asked dispassionately.

His face hardened. "No. It's only 2:15. The judge said til five."

"Fine, Walter. Fine." She turned to leave.

"When the tests come back, the judge is going to give me custody. I'll fix it so you never see her. You won't even get visitation."

"Fuck you, Walter!"

She turned on her heel and walked to her car.

* * * * *

"I still don't think this is necessary," Vivian half-whispered to Marc so the receptionist wouldn't hear. "It's just a waste of money. Besides, it's a waste of time. I need to be studying."

Marc didn't answer her. He pressed her hand to his lips, and kept the smile. She thought he looked goofy. She felt silly.

They were the only ones in the waiting room, and she was glad. It was small and intimate, like a richly furnished private sitting room. Not like the crowded rooms she'd waited in before, carefully avoiding the eyes of the other waiting patients, intermittently checking their watches, wondering whose turn was next, since they were all past their scheduled times.

She'd liked Dr. Mebane right off. He kept their appointment like he respected her time, too. He was about her age and had an air of quiet confidence. Not arrogant. Almost shy, but not quite. His face had been impassive while she detailed the history of her infertility. The instruments had been thoughtfully warmed and his probing had been gentle, like he understood there were no potatoes down there to be grubbed for. Since Marc had insisted so hard on the test, against her wishes, she would take particular delight in watching his face when the doctor pronounced his verdict. She was practicing her 'I told you so' look, when the nurse called them back to his office.

Marc still held her hand as they took seats across from the doctor's desk.

"Congratulations, Mr. and Mrs. Carlson," Dr. Mebane said, smiling. "I'd say your holidays are going to be especially happy this year. You're definitely pregnant. I'm not certain how far along. Twelve to fourteen weeks. Further tests will pinpoint more precisely. Since this is your first pregnancy, and you're in your forties, we need to discuss amniocentesis. That's a test—"

Vivian didn't hear any more. She stared at the doctor in disbelief, then slowly turned to Marc. His 'I told you so' look made him appear even goofier than before. The doctor called her name and she slowly turned back to face him.

"There must be some mistake. Didn't I tell you—"

"Oh, there's no mistake," the doctor assured her. "Didn't you hear the heart beats when we were in the exam room?"

"It's false. A false pregnancy. I'm under a lot of stress."

"My own exam confirmed the test results. There's nothing false about *this* pregnancy. But you don't have to worry. I'm seeing more and more patients your age having their first child. The improvements—"

"Would you excuse me just a minute."

Vivian stood and walked out on wobbly legs. She didn't stop until she got to the little lavatory where she'd given the urine specimen. She sat on the toilet, her elbows on her knees and put her chin in her hands. Several minutes passed as she stared at the little wildflowers on the wall paper. She supposed that pattern had been chosen for its cheerfulness. She was in the wrong room. Where was the room for women like her? Silent tears ran down her face.

"What else, Lord? Why now? After all those years of praying and wanting and wishing and hoping? Why now? Don't You know I can't handle this? It's just too much. I climbed a mountain, and another mountain. Every time I climb one, you just put another in front of me. I'm still climbing. I'm tired. Didn't I do right, to be satisfied with Passion, to consider her my blessing? Why are You punishing me this way? What did I do wrong? It's Marc, isn't it? But You *know* I was a faithful wife for twenty years. And

You know what I went through with Walter. I know I stood before You and said 'til death do us part', but I *was* dead. And You sent Marc to me. What was that about? Just another mountain?

"I'm tired, Lord. My legs are tired. My back is tired. My arms are tired. What if I just quit? Quit climbing. Quit juggling. Just let all the balls fall. Then what? What else could You do to me?"

A soft knock at the door startled her from her conversation. Vivian hurriedly tried to wipe the tears from her face. Another knock. As she stood and reached for a paper towel, the door opened and Marc peeked in. When he saw her face, he stepped into the little room and pulled her in his arms.

"Don't cry. It's going to be alright, Vivian. Everything's going to be OK. I wish you were as happy about this as I am. Maybe tomorrow. I know this isn't great timing, but…sometimes the time chooses you. You said that. If you don't like this doctor, you pick the one you want." He took a paper towel and gently wiped her face. "Come on, let's go home."

* * * * *

Vivian stared ahead without saying a word all the way to his house. Inside, she stood in the middle of the living room, staring blankly, her arms folded across her middle to contain the trembling. Marc wondered if she was in shock. He led her to the bedroom and eased her down on the side of the bed. He pulled her shoes off and made her lie down. When he checked again, she was asleep. A couple of hours later, he sat on the edge of the bed.

"Vivian? It's time to get up. It's almost time for your class."

She opened her eyes and stared at him, then turned her face away and sighed. "I'm not going."

"Would you like something to eat?"

She didn't say anything. After a while, he gave up and left. He called Cora, who told him to let her be.

At nine, he stood by the bed. "Vivian, let me heat you up a plate."

She turned her body to face the wall. Marc didn't know what to do. He called Cora to tell her Vivian was staying the night with him. Then he went and sat in the wing-backed chair in the living room. At eleven, he climbed into bed beside her and gathered her up in his arms. He held her and talked softly and reassuringly to her about his plans until she stopped crying.

When he awoke the next morning, she was staring at the ceiling. He kissed her on her cheek and rose from the bed.

"We'd better get up. Let's shower, then I'll drop you off at the library on my way. You know I'm meeting with the department chair this morning. I'm going to take the job." He went and turned the shower on. When he came back, she was still staring at the ceiling. He sat on the edge of the bed and brushed her hair back off her forehead.

"Come on, Vivian. You've already missed a class. You'll have to study extra today to make up for it. I'll make you a little breakfast."

"I'm not going."

"Aw, Vivian, you've gotta go. The exam is only two weeks away."

"I don't care. I'm not taking it."

"Girl, don't even say that. Now, come on, get up," he pleaded.

Vivian turned her back to him and curled up in a fetal position.

Marc sighed as he looked at his watch. "I'll come back as soon as I can." He leaned over and kissed her.

Vivian thought she was dreaming, when she felt the little finger poking at her nose. When she opened her eyes, Passion was sitting next to her, staring and making 'ou-u-u' sounds. Slowly, a smile broke through the veil of tears on Vivian's face. She sat up and hugged Passion to her. Then she saw Cora, standing by the bed, her arms folded across her chest.

"This baby needs you. You don't have time to be lying around here feeling sorry for yourself. You need to get out that bed and spend a little time counting your blessings—before you go to class tonight."

"Blessings? What blessings?" Vivian asked, flatly.

"You got your health. You got your good mind—despite how you're acting. You got a good man. You got this sweet baby. You got family that loves you. Now, what else you need?" Cora's hands were on her hips. "You think 'cause you have a little trouble in your life, the world's gonna stop turning? Girl, you don't even know what trouble is. Now, you can lie there wallowing in self-pity 'til you waste away, but I'm telling you, I can't raise this baby. I'm too old," she said, taking Passion from Vivian. "Besides, I'm going to Jamaica. So I guess I'll have to take her to Walter." Cora turned and walked out of the bedroom.

At the front door, a sly smile came to her face when she heard Vivian behind her.

"You wouldn't dare!"

Cora straightened her mouth and turned to face her. "I brought you some clothes and stuff. The prettiest gown I found in your drawer. Make tonight your honeymoon. It may be all you get. Some of us didn't get that—yet. We'll see you tomorrow."

TWENTY

Marc stood on the porch, wondering if he'd done the right thing. He'd been gone longer than he'd planned, but when he called Cora, she said she would go right over and see about Vivian. He'd walked over to the Drag to look for yellow roses, since they were her favorite. He wanted to put the smile back on her face. But once he found the flower vendor, he decided it wasn't enough. And, it was too much like Walter.

He wandered in the jewelry store, thinking maybe a necklace or a tennis bracelet. But the wedding rings were in the first counter, and he stopped to look at them. He even picked out a pair. Simple gold bands with a row of ten diamonds across the top. But they wouldn't be able to wear them for a while. He decided to wait until after she'd seen them—to make sure she liked them as much as he did. So he moved on to the engagement rings. Maybe an engagement ring wouldn't be appropriate under the circumstances. And she already had a big diamond. He didn't want to give her *anything* that asshole had given her. The thought that he'd already given her something Walter hadn't, brought a smile to his face.

Marc settled on the mother's ring, and had two birthstones put in it, with a diamond just a little larger in the middle. They now knew to expect a January birth, and that Passion was born in November. Walking out of the jewelry store, he'd been quite proud of himself, for coming up with the perfect gift.

Now, standing on the porch, turning over the little gift-wrapped box in his hand, he wasn't so sure. Maybe it was too presumptuous. Maybe she'd think it was silly. Maybe Cora had taken her to her house. Cora's car wasn't there. He stuffed the box in his pocket and put his key in the lock.

The first thing he noticed was the tall white candle on the table. Maybe Vivian would have left a candle burning unattended, but surely Cora wouldn't. He walked to the dining room to put it out, and saw that the table was set for two. When he pushed the door open to the kitchen, he caught her sampling from a pot on the stove.

"I owe you a lunch," she said, smiling at his non-plussed look.

"You owe me two," he said, recovering, and glad to see her up and about. "Smells good. You been in my spices?"

"Of course," she said, with a coquettish smile.

He walked over and took the spoon from her hand and sampled it himself.

"That's really good. If I'd known you could cook, I wouldn't have been doing all the work."

She smiled out of one corner of her mouth.

"I'm glad you're feeling better," he said seriously.

She looked off, then nodded her head.

"So hows about a little kiss?" he asked, mischievously.

"Don't have time. My sauce'll burn."

"Sauce can wait," he said, grabbing her and giving her a big smack, then a long, slow kiss, until she pulled away.

"My sauce," she said breathlessly. "Get the plates."

Marc reached for her hands across the table. After he said the grace, he dug into the steaming jambalaya. He made such a big show, licking his lips and smacking, she had to laugh. When he'd finished, he reared back in the chair.

"So, did you get a chance to do any studying between all the cooking?"

"No," she said, with a mysterious smile. "I was too busy."

"Doing what?" he asked, his curiosity piqued.

"Counting my blessings."

"So how many did you come up with?"

"I couldn't count them all," she said quietly.

Marc nodded.

"So, you want to study while I clean up the kitchen? You can use the desk in Corey's room."

"No, I don't want to study now."

"What would you like to do?"

"I'd like to take you in your bedroom and make love to you 'til you can't stand it."

Marc returned her smile, held out his hand, and let her lead him to his bedroom.

* * * * *

Vivian sat in the car, turning the ring around and around on her right hand. Cora had given her the message that Mrs. Black had called and wanted to see her. The message had put a real damper on her happy mood. Finally she got out of the car and walked to the door. The secretary pointed to a seat. Shortly, the heavy wooden doors slid apart and Mrs. Black appeared in the opening.

"Come on in, Vivian. How's the studying going?"

"Slowly, but it's almost over."

Vivian walked through and sat opposite the desk.

"You'll do fine. The exam is the last hurdle. Walter filed an answer to the divorce petition," Mrs. Black informed, taking her seat. "He's asking for all the property, of course, based on his allegation of adultery." Mrs. Black's eyes were expressionless.

"I don't care about the property. He can have it. How soon can we get this over with?"

"Sixty days. That's the absolute soonest, by law."

"I see. Whatever he wants, just give it to him. I don't care," Vivian said, counting the time. She'd be five months—and showing. "Can we do it so I don't have to go to court?"

"Hold on, Vivian. I'm looking at a twenty-year marriage, and a sizable estate. Surely you want your share? Think about it. You don't have to decide now."

"Well, I guess I'd like to keep my car. You know he stopped paying on it."

"Are they talking about repossessing it? I can file for temporary alimony."

"They were, but Marc caught it up. I'd like to have the car."

Mrs. Black gave a long sigh.

"Listen, Vivian, you've got to snap out of this. It's my duty to seek whatever my client wants. But it's also my duty to advise. For many of my clients, there's not much property to argue over. Mostly debts. Still, they scratch and claw for every dime. You, on the other hand, have something worth arguing over. There's quite a bit of equity in the house. And there are other assets. Even if there's a 50-50 split, neither of you would be two steps from the po' house. Yet, you tell me you want to give him everything." Mrs. Black leaned forward, her arms resting on the desk.

"You've got to look at this realistically, Vivian. You're forty-something years old. You have no retirement. You're unemployed. In fact you're damn near unemployable. You needn't even think one of those big law firms is going to hire you at a fabulous salary to reward you for all your hard work. It doesn't matter how smart you are. You're Black, female, and old—by their standards. And—"

"And I'm pregnant," Vivian blurted out.

Vivian saw more emotion on Mrs. Black's face than she'd seen in the four months she'd known her.

"Pregnant?!" she sputtered. "Pregnant! You can't be pregnant! That'll ruin everything! How could you do this?!"

"Well, I sure as hell didn't plan it!" Vivian snapped back.

"Who is the father?" Mrs. Black demanded.

"Marc! Who do you think?!" Vivian answered, indignantly.

"Be better if it was Walter."

"Why?!"

"Well, for one, when you go waddling into court, asking for permanent custody of Passion, it would be better to display your husband's virility than proof of his allegations of your adultery. I know this judge. I can tell you, he is *not* going to be impressed. Your chances of getting custody were already small, now they're slim to none."

Vivian frowned, staring at the ring.

"The only bright spot in all this is that I got the results of the tests yesterday."

"What's bright about that? We all know Passion is Walter's baby. That was just a waste of—"

"They're inconclusive."

"Inconclusive? What exactly does *that* mean?"

"Could mean Passion's not Walter's baby. Not enough of the genetic markers matched to get the 95% probability. The mother has to be found and tested, to be sure, either way. I spoke with Walter's attorney this morning. They haven't found her yet. In any case, it seems this is going to go on a while. When are you due?"

"First of January."

"You're definitely going to need temporary support. Will you authorize me to file for it?"

"Let me think about it. I'll call you."

* * * * *

Even though Passion was confidently sitting up on her own, Vivian propped pillows on each side of her and behind her—just in case. She jiggled the clown rattler at her, then held it just out of her reach, teasing her. Passion grabbed it away from her with both hands and pulled it to her mouth, giggling. Vivian giggled with her. They played the game over and over. She couldn't imagine her life without Passion. But the lawyer's words frightened her. She couldn't believe anyone would actually take this child from her. Did she really have to give up one baby for the other? Did she really have to choose? Which one would she choose? The one she already knew and loved? Or the one that was not yet—only tissue now? Despite what the doctor said, she'd read the literature and knew the odds that the baby wouldn't be right.

Or that she might miscarry. She could actually lose them both—and Marc.

What about Marc? What if his assurances were just empty promises? She stared at the ring, as she turned it around and around on her finger. Thoughtful of him. But when the seriousness of the whole thing settled in on him, then what? And if she lost Passion, what would she do, have one stone removed? She could end up with a ring with a missing stone, a retarded baby and that's all. Or if she lost both babies, remove two stones? Sure, she'd prayed for a baby. And He'd answered her prayers. Maybe the other was just an accident. She'd turned it over and over since that day in the doctor's office. The solution was forming in her mind.

She remembered when it wasn't legal. That scary night when her and Sondra's roommate, Audrey, had done a desperate deed and nearly bled to death in their dorm room. She crimped her mouth, remembering being turned away from the hospital run by God's daughters, as that girl's life seeped out of her right there in Sondra's old Volkswagen. By the time they got to the county hospital, Vivian had learned the transitory value of truth. Sondra told the doctor they'd found Audrey that way. Didn't have a clue what was wrong. When Audrey got out of the hospital, she left school, and although not one letter in twenty years had been returned, Vivian had never heard from her again.

She opened the phone book. There it was, big as day—Abortion Providers—and listings for five. How did one decide? She couldn't just call her friends for a recommendation, as though it was for a dermatologist. She picked the one whose ad said 'caring' and made an appointment for the day after the Bar Exam. After she'd hung up, she went back to fiddling with the ring, trying to think of the words to tell Marc.

* * * * *

The instructor had advised them to quit studying at noon on the day before the exam and do something relaxing, something fun, then turn in early. Over the six-week course, she'd followed all the other instructions to the letter. It would be foolish to spend all that money, then not follow the teaching. So, tonight she sat in the darkened theater, staring at the screen, not seeing, not having fun. Still trying to find the right words to tell Marc.

Walking back to the car, she blurted it out.

"I'm going to have an abortion."

"What?!"

There were no more words for her to say. No pretty way to say it.

"You can't be serious!" he said, the frown on his brow clashing with the smile fading from his face.

"There's no other solution to this problem," she said quietly, continuing to walk briskly against the humid July night, not looking at him.

"What problem?! I told you I'd marry you as soon as I can. As soon as you're free. What's the problem?"

"I don't want it like that. You feeling like you *had* to marry me. Like you had no choice."

"I *want* to marry you, Vivian. I want to spend the rest of my life with you."

"That's what you *say*. But I'd always wonder."

Marc took her hand to stop her. He looked in her eyes, still disbelieving.

"You don't ever have to wonder. Or question. I love you. I

want you to be my wife. I thought this all through before we even knew for sure about the baby."

"This is no way to start a marriage. And you never said a word about marrying me before. Odds are, the baby would be defective anyway." Vivian looked away, refusing to meet his eyes.

"Defective?! How can a *baby* be defective?! Products are defective. Services, maybe. Babies aren't 'defective', Vivian."

"I've decided, Marc. I'm going to do it. It's best for all of us."

"But it's my baby, too! You can't just get rid of my baby." Marc's voice broke as he shook his head.

"It's *my* decision," Vivian said firmly.

"How can you do that?! Don't I have *any* say?!"

She sighed. "No."

"That's not right, Vivian. It's just not right. What if you *wanted* to have the baby, and I didn't want you to. You could force me to support it. That's not fair!"

"Fair?! This obviously ain't about fair. I'm going to have a baby I've wanted for a hundred years torn from my body. Then I'm going to burn in hell for it. I don't think that's fair either! I don't have any choice."

"You *have* a choice, Vivian. *All* the choices, apparently," he said, his anger rising to meet hers.

"You just don't understand."

"You got that right. This is crazy. I'm not going to let you do it."

"Let me?! You can't stop me."

He grabbed her by her shoulders. "Vivian! What are you think-ing about?! I thought you were happy about the baby. I am. I swear. I love you. I promise I'm going to marry you. You've got to trust me. Didn't I buy you the ring?"

"Buy?! Buy?! Well, if it's just about money, maybe you can get your money back."

Jerking away from his grasp, she worked the ring off her finger and slammed it in his hand. She got in her car and drove off, leaving him standing on the sidewalk.

* * * * *

Long rows of tables filled the hotel ballroom. Vivian thought how different it looked from the last time she'd been there. The Legislative Black Caucus week-end, it had been filled with Black faces from all over the state, each smiling with their own agenda. She forced herself to concentrate on the exam, and pushed all her other worries to the back of her mind. No time for them today. She wondered why she'd wasted her money on the review course. The exam wasn't that difficult. On the other hand, maybe the course had prepared her so well it just didn't seem difficult. Whatever. It was done. The money was gone. She *had* to do well. The exam was the last hurdle before the finish line. She didn't have the time, money or energy to do it over.

But the exam was no longer the biggest item on her agenda. What loomed ahead reduced the exam to a mere precursor, no longer the climax. She couldn't think about that now. She couldn't think about the deep well of hurt on Marc's face, or how bare her finger felt without the ring, or the chasm she was facing. Now, she had to differentiate between springing interlocutory interests and—oh shit, what was that other one?

She forced herself to concentrate through the ethics portion of the exam. What the hell is this all about? Wasn't ethics just knowing right from wrong—then doing right? If you got to mid-twenties, the age of most law students, not to mention forties like her, and didn't know right from wrong...well, they probably couldn't teach it to you. But what was in the middle? Was there even a middle? Was what she was planning right? Or wrong? It just wasn't that simple.

The inside of the car was even hotter than the July air outside. Vivian left the exam exhausted, but with no doubt she'd done well. She wouldn't have to think about it again for several months, since it would be that long before the grades were sent. One more mountain behind her, a bigger one just ahead—tomorrow. When Marc had called early that morning to wish her well on the exam, he hadn't mentioned it. The unspoken words hung heavy as a stone between them. She thought about Audrey, and wondered if she should have someone go with her. But who? She couldn't ask Marc. He'd made his feelings clear. And not Cora. She didn't want her to know. She'd just have to manage by herself. Take a taxi there and back—just in case—she thought, as she parked in front of Cora's house.

Vivian had hoped to avoid her, but Cora had dinner waiting. Worry had taken her appetite, but Vivian picked at her plate for a respectable time, then excused herself. She took Passion to her bed and told her about her day. Then, she sang softly to her, lullabies from her childhood, until Passion's eyes were heavy with sleep. With Passion cradled in her arms, Vivian wondered if the price was too high, the sacrifice too great. Was she being ridiculous? Passion wasn't even her baby. Yes, she is, she thought resolutely, as she lay her in the crib she and Marc had picked out. At ten, Vivian was in her bed, lights out. Her door was closed for the first time since she'd lived there. She tossed and turned amid snatches of fitful sleep. Over in the night, she heard the door open.

"Where are you going to do this thing?" Cora asked in a quiet voice.

So much for her not knowing, Vivian thought, wryly. She lay on her back, her arm across her forehead, staring at the ceiling.

"The Women's Care Center," she answered flatly.

"Tomorrow? Is that why you can't sleep?"

"Tomorrow. At nine."

"Is it a real doctor? Or just some quack?" Cora asked, disapproval heavy in her voice.

"A real doctor."

"Will you be sick—like it used to be?" Concern edged the disapproval aside.

"I don't know," Vivian answered truthfully, realizing for the first time that she really didn't. Maybe she should have asked more questions. But being sick was minor compared to the other worries she had about it. Her body would get over being sick.

"Vivian, you shouldn't—"

"I don't want to hear all that, Cora," she said impatiently "I've made up my mind. It's my choice."

"I know you have a choice. Women have always had a choice. I had a choice. I could choose to have my baby and bear all the shame and everything, or I could choose to risk dying. Or being butchered. I'm glad you have better choices than I had. But choice ain't everything, Vivian. What about a reason?"

Vivian had no answer. She turned her face to the wall. After a while, she heard Cora close the door behind her.

* * * * *

Two women were in the waiting room when Vivian arrived, their faces hidden behind magazines. Both of them alone, just like her. She picked up one of the magazines from the coffee table and pretended to be absorbed in it. The nurse appeared in the doorway and called out a name. As Vivian watched the woman walk through the door, she felt her heart flutter. Just nervousness, she thought. No, that wasn't it. She was down-right scared. She took several long, deep breaths to steady her nerves. She felt the fluttering again. She put her hand over her heart—as though that would help. But the fluttering wasn't in her heart. Maybe it was just her stomach grumbling from hunger. Maybe she should have eaten a little breakfast, she thought as she lowered her hand to her stomach, but she couldn't have stood the look of censure on Cora's face. There was the fluttering again—right under her hand. She pressed her hand against it, and waited, holding her breath. Could it be her baby? No. She was just imagining things. She exhaled, then breathed long and steady. She felt it again. More like a tremor. Her baby waking up, saying 'hello'? There it was again. It *was* the baby. Her smile was bittersweet. Was it a boy or a girl? She wondered if the doctor would be able to tell? The nurse appeared in the doorway, again.

Relief flooded over her when the nurse summoned the other woman. She wanted just a little more time. She'd never witnessed a miracle. Didn't believe in them, really. But what she was experiencing felt a little miraculous. Another whole person, living inside her. She looked at her watch, then put that hand just below the other one. She eased her hands under her blouse, then inside the elastic waistband of her shorts. Watching the doorway fearfully, she massaged her hands over her bare skin. That was as close as she could get—to say goodbye. She startled when she heard her name, and blinked back tears. The nurse was in the doorway, holding a folder in her hand, smiling at her.

* * * * *

Vivian stepped out into the bright morning sunlight. It was behind her. She'd made her choice. Now, she'd have to live with it. She felt a little trembly in her legs, but she was OK. She wished she had driven her car. Looking around for a place to sit to wait for the cab, she spotted a park bench and started toward it. She stopped when she recognized Marc sitting there. What words to say now? She slowly walked over and sat next to him, her lips tight, still not knowing what to say. He enclosed her hand in his, and looked directly in her eyes.

"Vivian, I have to tell the truth. I'm mad as hell with you. I still don't believe what you did was right. But, I'll have to live with that. I love you. I told you I would stand by you—through whatever comes. So here I am."

Right there in public, in broad open daylight, she pulled his hand under her blouse, under the waistband and pressed his palm against her abdomen. From the look on his face, she knew that he felt the fluttering too.

TWENTY-ONE

Marc grinned all the way to his car, his arm around her. All the agitation that had consumed him for two days had dissipated. He kept slipping his other hand against her stomach, but she modestly pushed it away. At the car, he tried a little too hard to help her into the Volvo.

"I'm pregnant—not an invalid," she protested.

On the ride to Cora's, he outlined his plan.

"I can move your clothes and Passion's bed now. Then we can go shopping for a dresser."

"Wait a minute, Marc. I don't know—"

"Well, if you don't feel up to shopping, we can get the dresser tomorrow."

"I feel fine. That's not it. I just don't think we ought to rush into anything."

"Oh," he said, hurt and confusion crossing his face. "Well, I just assumed that you would want to be with me."

"Of course, I want to be with you. But, you know this thing isn't settled about Passion. Mrs. Black said that the judge is going to hold it against me that I'm pregnant."

"You won't be able to hide the pregnancy in any case, so you may as well do the right thing. It's not like you're some irresponsible…the judge has to consider what's in the best interest of the child. We've been taking care of her all this time. It'll be better for her to be with us, than…him. If I can finally convince you and Mrs. Black to let me go to court with you, I can persuade the judge. It's going to work out, baby. Don't worry." He held out his hand to her.

Vivian slipped her fingers through his, but her brow was knitted with indecision.

When Marc pulled up in front of the house, Cora was bent over tending the bed where daylillies were in profuse bloom. When she stood, consternation and sympathy were mixed in the look she gave Vivian.

"We came to get the baby's bed," Marc said, a crooked grin on his face. "We're actually going to need two."

"Lord, Lord. My prayers were answered," she said, hugging Vivian to her.

* * * * *

Marc felt the blast of cold air across the back of his neck as the air conditioner fought a valiant battle against the mid-August heat. Earlier that night, he and Vivian had sat out back in the chaise lounges, watching Corey and Passion playing, until the heat and mosquitoes drove them in. Now, close to midnight, he sat at his desk trying to work on the book and listening to Kyle Turner's newest CD. He'd put the headphones on, so the music wouldn't wake Vivian or the kids. He couldn't maintain his focus on the book, so he put in the disk with his syllabus for next semester's class.

He'd been surprised that the students had stayed on the Jamicka Doe project—even after he'd given them the extra points on their grades at the end of the semester. Maybe his disdain for these Generation X students wasn't entirely warranted. Twanna Dailey had been relentless in her letter-writing campaign, and it seemed that at least once a week one was published in the letters-to-the-editor section of the *Austin Statesman*. The police department had even responded, through the official spokeswoman, denying her charges of racism, assuring that they were following any leads, and asking for the public's help. Jason Fitzpatrick and Joaquin Lopez had gone home for the summer, but kept in touch with him through email. Jason e-mailed him a copy of the notice he'd posted on the internet's Lost Friends Center, a free missing persons service, with a note that he'd had no response—and what class are you teaching next semester? Joaquin had used the credit card his father supplied him to enter information about Jamicka on several of the commercial sites on the internet that were probably fronts for private investigators. He'd had no better luck— but what class are you teaching next semester?

Every time Marc heard from one of them, the gnawing would start again. He had that gut feeling, but he just couldn't put his finger on it. He'd assigned the project to them, but he hadn't done anything except give Jason the money to get a copy of the medical examiner's report. Jason was a poor kid, living on scholarships, loans, and a part-time job as a waiter. Marc couldn't turn down his sheepish request, since he'd lured him into the project. He wished he'd made a copy when he first read it, back in the spring. Finally, he'd asked Jason to fax a copy to him.

Marc pulled the file from the bottom drawer. He read through all nineteen pages. The pictures hadn't reproduced well, and he was glad. He'd seen autopsy pictures before. Never a pretty sight. The cause of death was entered as 'unknown.' Toxicology tests revealed no illegal drugs, so it seemed especially strange that no one had come forward to claim Jamicka's body. She'd been found in March. Now it was August. Diamond studs in her ears told him it wasn't a robbery gone bad. Bruise marks on the throat would lead to strangulation, but there was no mention of crushing of the esophagus. Drowning seemed the most obvious cause, but there was no water in her lungs. Must have been put in the water after her death.

Reading the description in the report, he was certain that his initial impression about the pendant had been correct—it was an Alpha symbol. None of that satisfied the gnawing. He started again at the top.

Black female, 65 inches long, 132 lbs., brown hair, brown eyes, one mark, right buttock—2 centimeters by 2.5 centimeters, slightly raised and roughly heart shaped; one surgical scar, 12 centimeters beginning at the navel traversing the abdomen. Brain, lungs, kidneys, heart, liver—all normal. Marc put the paper down, wrestling with the idea that kept fighting it's way forward. It was so abhorrent, he tried to bury it. But his training made him take the personal out of it. He stood and walked into Corey's room where they'd put Passion's bed.

Standing over the crib, he wondered how he could think such a thing, and how Vivian would react if he told her that he'd thought it. Passion was asleep in her usual position—on her knees, her fist at her mouth. Corey was sprawled across his bed. Could he do it without waking either of them? As gently as he could, he slipped two fingers under the diaper and slowly folded it back as far as it would go without pulling. It was there. In the dim light coming from the door behind him, he couldn't tell whether it was raised or flat. He fought the urge to touch it for fear of waking her, then gave in and lightly passed his forefinger over it.

Back at his desk, his brow furrowed, he pieced together a scenario. The affair, the pregnancy, the refusal to leave his wife, the threat of exposure. The argument, him choking her, her nails frantically clawing at his face and neck, her fingers catching in the necklace, jerking it from around his neck. Him desperately dumping the body in the lake, then bringing the baby home. Nah. He was just being overly dramatic. He despised the man, thought he was scum, but he couldn't get to murderer. Couldn't imagine Walter getting his hands that dirty. But he had something now— a name. Porsche Timmons. He turned to his computer and sent an email to Jason and Joaquin.

* * * * *

Captain Gormann watched the man walk out of his office. He didn't believe a word of his story. Just a professor doing some research. Bull. The man didn't even look like a professor. Too muscular, no glasses. And Black. But what did he know about professors except what he'd seen on TV? He'd been born a cop. Trained a cop. He had thirty years experience as a cop to hone his instincts. The driver's license checked out. He picked up the phone again and dialed the university. That checked out, too. There *was* a Black professor by that name and description in the journalism department. The niggers were just taking over everything, he thought, as he rubbed his thumb and forefinger over the stubble on his chin that always appeared that time of day. They'd probably get a nigger chief—when they got rid of that woman.

Why would a journalism professor be interested in how long blood from an autopsy would be good? What was the term he'd used? Viable. Gormann made a note to look that up, just to be sure. And why would he be interested in the procedure for getting a sample released? What would he need a sample for? He buzzed Trudy.

"Run me a list of all the autopsies done this year." … "I know I can look it up myself, but you know you can do it so much faster. Come on sweetie, give me a break. You know, me and this computer…"

* * * * *

Walking through the Capitol rotunda, listening to the echoes of his heels clicking on the worn marble, Marc's brow was furrowed the way it had been for several days. Only the baby's moving under his hand on Vivian's rounded abdomen, or the sight of Passion struggling to perfect her crawl, eased it. He didn't like what he was about to do, but it was the best solution he could think of.

Would his plan compromise his morals, his integrity? He didn't even know the girl. Besides, hadn't she compromised hers—having a baby by a married man? But did that justify his playing a part in preventing the dead from receiving a proper burial? Men had conquered nations—some had given up thrones—to protect their women. What he was going to do to protect his, paled in comparison.

"Is Representative Carlson in?" Marc asked.

The man eyed him curiously, but picked up the receiver and announced into the phone, "Professor Kline is here to see you."

Marc thought it odd that the man didn't ask if he had an appointment—and knew his name. Marc didn't recognize him, but he looked enough like Walter to be his brother. The man hung up the phone and pointed toward the door.

Marc took a deep breath to steady himself as he turned the ornate bronze doorknob. Walter didn't rise to acknowledge him. Marc sat in one of the leather chairs with the seal of the State of Texas stamped in gold on its tall back, trying to display the same air of confidence that Walter had worn in his office.

"To what do I owe the honor of this visit, Professor Kline?" Walter asked in a pleasant, but disinterested tone of voice.

"I came to offer you an out," Marc said, evenly.

"Out? Out of what?"

"Prison, probably." Marc's eyes didn't waver.

"Prison? What are you talking about?" Walter asked, with a sneer.

"I don't want to believe you killed the girl, but it certainly appears that way."

Walter sat up a little straighter.

"Killed? What girl?" he asked, his face guarded.

"Porsche Timmons."

"Porsche is dead? How do you know that? If this is your idea of a joke—"

"I read the autopsy report. Saw the pictures."

"Where?" Walter asked, looking at him skeptically.

"ME's office."

A frown latched on to Walter's face. "Are you sure? She's dead? How did she die?"

"I thought *you* might know."

"Are you trying to suggest that I killed her? Why would I kill Porsche?"

"Only you know the answer to that. What I *do* know is that there were bruise marks on her throat. And she was clutching an Alpha pendant in her hand." Marc's face was expressionless, as he watched Walter's hand find his neck and finger inside his shirt.

"I also know Porsche Timmons was Passion's mother. You're an Alpha, aren't you?"

"That doesn't prove I killed her."

"No, it doesn't. It's up to the police to prove it." The threat hung heavy in the air.

"Extortion? Blackmail? What's your game?" Walter asked, with a smirk in his voice.

"You know I don't suffer threats—and I don't play games," Marc said, dead serious. "Right now, the girl is a Jane Doe. Six months and nobody's claimed her. Maybe nobody cares. It could stay that way. You let Vivian have Passion. Sign over your rights. Let us adopt her. I'll forget I ever had a thought about it."

"You must be crazy!"

"Not at all, Representative. I just wanted to put a little bug in your ear—before we ask the judge to order that a sample of the autopsy blood be tested."

"I've already told the judge Porsche is Passion's mother. Even if what you say is true, there's no need to disturb an autopsy. I can't believe you would stoop this low. Don't you have any respect? I would have thought Vivian, at least, had better taste."

"Have it your way, Representative," Marc said, as calmly as he could manage, rising from his seat. "I guess we'll see you in court." His hand was on the knob when Walter spoke.

"Professor? Let me put a little bug in *your* ear. Vivian is my wife. She *is* coming home. You know the baby Vivian's carrying now? It's mine, too. I'll bet she didn't tell you about *that*, did she? Well, ask her."

Marc's hand clenched on the metal knob. He resisted the urge to lunge for Walter's throat, to choke the smirk off his face, to pound his fist into it until there was nothing but bloody pulp.

"You wish," Marc said, and turned and walked through the door.

* * * * *

Gormann looked over the list of autopsies again. What would the man need blood for? He ruled out everything that would be police business. Paternity was all that was left. He penciled through all the male names on the list. In another pass, he penciled through the three women over age 45. That left two. Karen Sellers, White female, age 29, suicide; Jane Doe, Black female, age unknown—approximate age mid-twenties, cause of death unknown. He wanted copies of both autopsies asap.

Where *was* that kid? The one who was always hanging around volunteering to run errands, sticking his nose in everything, asking a thousand questions. He hadn't seen him in a while. Guess he got bored, running for coffee. What was his name? Jose or something. Juan? No, Joaquin, that was it. The wetbacks were taking over too. He had to give it to the boy, though. He sure knew a lot about computers. Well, at least more than he did. And it *had* been nice, not having to deal with Trudy's difficult ass for a while. The women were getting uppity, too. Old White men like him were being robbed of everything they'd worked to build. He was glad he was about to retire. Maybe the young White guys understood all this, since they'd had to grow up with it. The ones he really felt sorry for were guys like Crane and Garrison. Worked their asses off for 18 or 19 years, but still didn't have enough time in. And with young wives and kids, boy were they in for it. Pushed off into little cubicles. Given shit work. They'd have to get with this 'community policing' bullshit.

Never work, he thought in disgust. You have to deal with criminals in a way they understand. A little head-butting here, a little nut-squeezing there. Works every time, Gormann thought, as he surveyed the plaques and framed letters of commendation on his wall. Those were the days. Gone forever. Too many changes. Whole damned department gone soft. And a woman for Chief! Fuck her! No woman could boss him. Forty three days. That's all he had left. Fuck her! Before he left, he wanted to solve just one more. One more notch in his belt. Go out with a bang, instead of a whimper and a gold watch. He wasn't a whimper kind of guy—and he already had a nice watch.

Gormann got the reports on the two women. Nothing unusual in the Sellers autopsy. Pills. The way most women did it. Over some man, too, according to the note she left. The Jane Doe had a recent C-section. Paternity. He knew his instincts were right. He methodically called every hospital in town and got the names of all the Black women who had babies for six months preceding the discovery of the body. Why were they having so many babies? Prison fodder, that's all. He should be happy, he thought. Would keep his country cousins employed, now that the family farm was becoming extinct, and computers and machinery were doing the farm work.

He methodically crossed off the ones 13 and under. He spoke

with all but three, then set off to find them. Shaniqua Rhoades had moved back to her mother's in Elgin. He found Toya Grimes in the Del Valle Correctional Facility, serving time for hot checks. Grama's got the baby. Porsche Allison Timmons was the only one left. Surrendered a Pennsylvania license to obtain the Texas one. He went over to the address and flashed his badge.

The nervous landlord agreed to let him go through her things that he'd put in storage. Gormann knew from his demeanor the man had done something wrong, but he also knew it wasn't wrong enough to be police business. As he opened one box after another, he listened to the landlord's babble about how she'd been a good tenant, always paid her rent on time. Assured him that he was the kind of landlord that didn't bother tenants who didn't bother him. But when she didn't pay the rent in March, he'd gone by. The whole month, there was no sign of her or the baby. So he'd moved her things to the storage shed and re-let the apartment. He needed the money and didn't have time or money for the eviction process.

From the box filled with video tapes, and business cards, it was apparent to Gormann that she was free-lancing as a videographer. The tapes were labeled—mostly weddings, birthday parties and the like. The diary was the most interesting thing he found. He thumbed through it looking for Kline's name, but only found 'W'. No matter which way he turned it, he couldn't get W out of Marc Anthony Kline. Bluffing the landlord into letting him take the diary and the picture of the girl with him had been easy. Sitting in his car, he stared at the framed picture a long time. He'd seen that face before. If only he could place it...

* * * * *

Gloria's brow knitted as she listened to Cora's account of the latest court proceeding. She had liked Cora from the get go, and was sorry Babysis had moved away from her, but under the circumstances agreed it was the best thing for her to do. She and Cora had been planning a small, private wedding for late September, even though they hadn't persuaded Babysis—yet. The professor even agreed with them. But this mess Walter had pulled—claiming the new baby was his, stalling the divorce—would put the quietus on that. The judge had been impressed with Marc's testimony, but still granted Walter's postponement until the baby was born.

When Gloria hung up the phone, that evil look was on her face. Then, she smiled. Walter could dish it out, but could he take it? You give my little girl trouble, Brother, you 'bout to get some, she thought, as she dug in her jewelry chest for the key to her safe deposit box.

* * * * *

Gormann parked the unmarked car two houses down the street, pulled his hat down to shield his face, and scooted down in the seat. Indian Summer had finally passed, and he was grateful for the cool breeze that wafted through the open window. He'd bet a day's pay, the professor was the only one of *them* that lived in Hyde Park. He sat up a little when the professor walked out of the house, carrying a stroller in one hand and baby in his other arm. A pregnant woman followed. They got in the Volvo and drove away. Odd, his bio said divorced. Why would he hide a wife and child from his employer?

Gormann ran the plates on the Camry still in the driveway. Even though he resisted most of the changes in the department, he *did* like this new gizmo in the car, where he could just put the number in himself, instead of going through some dispatcher down at the station. Where did he know that name from—Carlson? Oh, yeah. Him. Why would Carlson's car be parked so far down the driveway? What was the connection?

* * * * *

Cora was expecting them for dinner. As he drove, Marc stole glances at Vivian out the side of his eye. He'd been putting it off. Asking her. There never seemed to be a good time. Why did he even need to ask her? He knew the answer. But Walter's words haunted him. She *had* gone over there every single time Walter called. And she always insisted that he not go with her.

"I've got to hear it from you. Is the baby mine?"

Vivian turned and looked at him, the frown narrowing her eyes.

"I'm not even going to dignify that with an answer," she said, folding her arms across her stomach. She fumed a few blocks, glaring at him.

"I just want to be sure, baby. I didn't mean anything. It's just that with Walter saying—"

"Walter! Why would you fall for that?! You want to be sure? You want to take a test?! Everybody's had one but you. Let's just test the whole goddam world!"

"Don't shout like that, Vivian. You'll scare Passion"

"Don't you talk to me like I'm a child. In fact, don't you talk to me at all."

* * * * *

Gormann was surprised to be able to see Carlson without an appointment, so close to the election. But not really. He'd said he was the representative of the Texas Law Enforcement Officials. You could count on a politician to be a sucker for a group of voters—and law enforcers voted.

The picture on Walter's desk didn't escape his notice. Her face was fuller now and her hair was cut like a butch. But it was definitely her. He just couldn't figure it out. Maybe they were kin.

"Good of you to see me, Representative Carlson. This is just a courtesy visit. Our organization is pleased with your record on issues that are important to us. We know that you only have token opposition, but we intend to help you make a good showing."

"I appreciate your taking the time to come by, Captain Gormann," Walter said, glancing at the business card. "I'm never too busy to see a constituent."

Gormann made small talk about the rising tide of crime, how drugs were ruining the country, how lawmakers were the last line of defense. Carlson nodded his agreement. He had to give it to the jungle bunny, he knew the right things to say. When he thought Carlson was comfortable, he nonchalantly asked his first real question.

"You know a fella named Marc Kline?"

"I've met him."

Gormann noticed the instant wariness in Walter's eyes, so he changed back to the drug issue, prattling on until he thought Walter was comfortable again.

"Thanks for seeing me," he said, rising. "I can't tell you how much your support will mean to our organization. By the way, do you know a girl named Porsche Timmons?"

"Why?" Walter's shoulders tensed.

"When was the last time you saw her?"

"Excuse me. I have an appointment," Walter said, standing and offering his hand.

"Just one more question—"

"Talk to my lawyer—Bobby Africa. Good day, Captain Gormann."

* * * * *

That was enough for him. He'd read that autopsy report. Bastard killed her. Choked her to death. Threw her body in the lake. Pretty girl. Fine, too. Although the fear lurking in Carlson's eyes proved it for him, he knew he didn't have enough to prove it in court—yet. But now would be a good time, with the election only two weeks away. When this thing hit the newspapers, the White guy would win. He would be doing the whole state a favor. What did he have? A body with bruise marks on the throat. A diary with 'W' all over it. The tape. That's where he'd seen the girl. And Carlson was the man on it. That was enough. He'd get the rest later—probably in a confession, he thought, smiling to himself. He could tell Walter would crack under pressure. But he had enough for now, to get a warrant—if he found the right judge. And he knew just the right one. The one who was always talking that 'law and order' crap, trying to ingratiate himself to the cops. He just didn't know—cops' loyalty only lasted until the next case. First time he turned them down for a warrant, he'd be on their shit list, too. Behind his back, they were saying he'd sign anything they put in front of him—even a napkin. Funny thing about respect. Had to be earned. Couldn't just talk up on it.

Gormann wrote up the affidavit accusing Walter of murder,

then set off to find the judge.

* * * * *

"Who the fuck could this be, this early in the morning?" Walter muttered under his breath as he tied the belt on his robe around him. When he opened the door, he recognized the snaky grin.

"Walter Carlson?" the man said, more than asked.

Walter searched his memory for the name.

"I have a warrant for your arrest—for murder."

"What?! You gotta be kidding!"

"You heard me. Are you going to make this difficult?"

Walter saw the man's eyes, squinting with delight at the possibility above the snaky grin.

"No, no trouble. Let me see the warrant."

"Sure, buddy." Gormann handed it to him, then glanced around the expensively furnished room.

Walter read it over twice. He couldn't read the judge's signature.

"Come on in. I need to call my lawyer," he said, walking toward the kitchen.

"I'll give you three minutes. You can call your lawyer and go to jail in your robe. Or you can change clothes now and call your lawyer from the station."

* * * * *

Leaning against the solid metal door with the rectangle cut in it, Walter eyed the three other men with him, in the cell built for two. He tried to maintain a disinterested demeanor. The Mexican national was snoring on the top bunk—as though somebody was going to wake him in time to hit another roof in the morning. The Black kid standing against the wall at the other end of the cell looked scared to death, despite his hostile posturing. The 30-ish White boy on the bottom bunk hadn't shaved or bathed in way too long. The guards were so familiar with him, Walter figured this must have been his home. And they called them 'homeless'. Humph. The stench of alcohol emanating from him filled the small cell. Austin's little 'United Nations' all wore identical two-piece gray uniforms, except the White boy had puked all over his. Walter crimped his toes in the brown plastic slides. That was the worst part. As soon as he got home, he intended to soak his feet in a tub of bleach water. He wondered what the fuck was taking Bobby so long. He heard the deputy bark, "Carlson! Attorney visit!"

TWENTY-TWO

From the familiar comfort of his big chair, Walter's eyes went over the copy Bobby had brought of the affidavit for arrest, again. He didn't practice criminal law, but any first-year law student would know there wasn't probable cause for a murder charge. A body, a diary with references to 'W', a videotape of them having sex. He wondered about the tape. When did she make it? The bitch was even sneakier than he'd thought. He couldn't believe the part about 'when I asked Carlson did he know Ms. Timmons, he asked to talk to his lawyer.' Well, that sure as hell meant he was guilty! Who *was* this judge?! As soon as this was behind him, the first thing he was going to do was introduce legislation to require a test of minimum competency for judges.

"Where the hell did you get $50,000 for the bond?" he asked, looking up.

"Now, that's my business," Bobby said, laughing. "Just don't you leave the county—else I'll have to sic some bad dudes on your ass."

"Did you talk to Barbara Leah?"

"I haven't talked to yo' mama. But *you* ought to. You'll make the front page tomorrow. The wire services will probably pick it up. You don't want her to hear this from some reporter on her doorstep—with a mike and a camera stuck in her face."

While Walter placed the call to his mother and calmed her down, he watched Bobby sitting on the couch, sipping his drink. Bobby's face was impassive as he surveyed the room, but Walter knew him well enough to know what he thought. It was the first time he'd noticed the disorder himself. It had never been that way when Vivian lived here. He hung up the phone, thinking how things were going to be different when she came home. She'd have to come home now. He needed her to support him. Otherwise, people would think he was guilty.

"So what do we do next?" Walter asked.

"We? *We* don't do anything. You stay in this house. Not one word to the press. Don't answer the phone. Don't answer the door. I've already talked with Sherman. He'll send you a fax first if he needs to talk to you. Anything you need, you call him."

"I could have just stayed in jail, if I'm going to be a fucking prisoner," Walter protested.

Bobby cocked his head to the side. "You *could* have. But when you called me, you sure sounded like you wanted to be out. I guess I could surrender you back to the Sheriff—and get my fifty grand back."

He waited until he knew that had sunk in. "And if you pull any more shenanigans like that shit on the courthouse steps with those reporters—I'm outta here. Understand?" His voice was harsh.

The sight of his old friend slumped in his big chair, staring at the floor, softened Bobby.

"See, Walter, you just don't get it. A whole lot of this is about image. Not about guilt or innocence. Or truth and justice. Image. Just think if you were to get in your Mercedes, drive up and down the freeway with a gun, talking about killing yourself. It's image, see? Don't say nothing—to nobody."

Walter nodded his head, that he understood, then looked up at him.

"So, you haven't asked me did I do it," Walter said.

"Aw, man, I *know* you didn't do it—did you?" Bobby broke out laughing at the shocked look on Walter's face. Sobering, he said, "OK, this is the lawyer-client stuff now. Tell me what happened. Just the bare truth. All of it. Let me figure out how to put the spin on it. When was the last time you saw her?"

"In March. In my office. She came by one night. Sherman and I were working late. She brought the baby. She started in on me again about leaving Vivian. We had a fight. Bitch scratched my face up," he said, rubbing his cheek at the memory.

"Did you choke her?"

"Maybe." Then seeing Bobby's stern lawyer expression, "Yes. Yes, I choked her. But I didn't kill her. I swear, man."

"She pass out?"

"No. Sherman heard the ruckus, I guess. He came in and broke it up. She left. I never saw her again."

"So how'd you get the baby?"

"After Sherman left for the night, I stayed in the office, trying to figure out how to keep her from causing problems with Vivian. Sherman came back with the baby. He said that on his way out, he saw the baby carrier in the rotunda and brought it to me to keep security from finding it. I called her over and over, but she never answered the phone. Finally…well, I had no choice."

"You took the baby home."

Walter nodded.

"So Sherman saw her after you did? You reckon he killed her?"

"Sherman wouldn't do anything like that. He's a little flaky. Up 'til now, couldn't hold a job. Had a little nose problem. I'm pretty sure he's clean now. But he's not a killer. Besides, what would be his motive?"

"To protect you?"

"That doesn't make any sense. What he would be protecting me from, happened anyway—since he brought me the baby."

"Hm. I dunno. What's on the tape?"

"I don't know," Walter said, shaking his head. "I didn't even know she made a tape of me. Sneaky bitch!"

"The first thing I need to do is get a copy of that tape. I'll file a discovery motion first thing in the morning. Is there anything else I need to know?"

"Naw, man. That's it. Straight up."

* * * * *

Sherman's face was guarded as he sat across the desk.

"Thanks for coming," Bobby said. "I guess I don't have to tell you that my friend's got his ass in a *real* ringer this time."

Sherman acknowledged the truth with a nervous nod. He felt Bobby watching for his reaction. He squeezed one hand with the other in his lap, then gripped the end of the chair arms to still them.

"We're gonna get him off this thing. I'm certain about that. We both know Walter's not a murderer. I just need to know all the facts. I need your help."

Sherman nodded. He fought to keep from squirming in the chair. He couldn't keep his hands still. "You mind if I smoke?" he asked, taking a silver cigarette case from his breast pocket.

"No, go ahead. In fact, I'll have one with you." Bobby accepted the case Sherman handed him, hoping he didn't cough. He'd quit smoking everything, years ago. "In fact, why don't you have a drink with me," he said, going to the bookcase that held the bar. "Did you know this girl? Porsche?" he called over his shoulder.

"Ah, yeah, I knew her," Sherman said, hesitantly. "She used to come around."

"Did you know about the baby?"

"Well, listen man, I don't know…Walter ought to be here. I mean, I don't know if I should be…What did Walter say?"

"Just relax," Bobby said, handing him the hi-ball glass. "Here, look at this." He handed Sherman a piece of paper. "You recognize Walter's signature, don't you? It's a blanket release. For you—and anybody else—to talk to me. I'll give you a copy if you want. Besides, didn't he tell you to come over here?"

"Well, uh, yes." Sherman sipped from the glass to cover his uncertainty.

"They don't have a case against Walter. What little they have is all circumstantial. Walter told me they had a fight. That would explain his skin under her fingernails. You knew about the fight, didn't you?"

Sherman tightened his lips in that 'my lips are sealed forever' way.

"You know I'm Walter's ace-boon—from way back. I been

watching his back since forever. You know that. You been watching his back too, haven't you?"

Sherman nodded, then took another sip.

"We've never let nothing happen to him before. We're not gonna let anything happen to him now. Right?"

Sherman nodded, staring into the glass as he moved it around making the ice cubes rattle.

"Walter said you broke the fight up. Then she left."

Sherman nodded again.

"What'd she say when she gave you the baby?"

Sherman looked up, his eyes tight.

"She told me to give her to Walter. That Maya would have a better life with Walter than with...her."

"Then what?"

"Then nothing. She left."

"Did Walter see Porsche after that?"

"No. He didn't." He saw the calculating look on Bobby's face. "I mean, I don't think so."

"Did you?"

"No. Not 'til..." He faltered.

"Til what, Sherman?"

"Until I went to the morgue."

"When did you go to the morgue?"

"After they arrested Walter. I went to make sure it was her." He took a gulp from the glass. "I'd never seen anyone dead before...except Uncle Walter. He was like a daddy to me. The only daddy I knew. Remember, he had a heart attack? He looked just like he was sleeping. But Porsh...She didn't look like herself. I mean, I could tell it was her. But, she was all swollen up.

And gray-looking. And her skin…" He squeezed his eyes shut, leaned his face against his hand and rubbed the flesh between his eyes with his forefinger and thumb. "They said maybe the fish had been…" His voice broke.

Sherman took a deep breath to compose himself, gave a long exhale, then opened his eyes. "They said that sometimes when a body has been in the water for a while, the fish…nibble on it."

He took another gulp, then set the glass down. "I need to go, man. You call me if you need anything else."

Bobby watched him walk through the door, and thought, "Maya?"

* * * * *

Sitting in his car outside the office, Sherman knew he was doing the right thing. His bags were in the back seat. He'd shipped everything else to his mother in Philadelphia. He'd left the title to the car and directions where to find it, in an envelope with the letter on Walter's chair. Despite it all, he loved Walter like a brother. Still, it didn't seem fair. He knew he was smarter than Walter. Always made better grades. But Walter always seemed to have something he didn't. Maybe because Walter had a daddy. And he didn't have one…really. Maybe something about having a daddy gave a boy a certain confidence about who he is. Walter could always rise to the top, and he was always left playing second fiddle. It had always been that way. Even with girls. No matter how much they liked him, when they met Walter, it was all over for him. It wasn't that Walter took girls from him. They went willingly. He'd thought it would be different with her.

When he'd met her at a Cocaine Anonymous meeting, he was impressed that she was as determined to get her life together as he'd been. Even though she'd come from the other side of the tracks, he'd admired her spunk. Still, he knew she wouldn't meet his mother's standards—nor Aunt Leah's. So he kept her away from them. Good thing, too. She'd had a fit when they shipped him, and his new-found sobriety, off to Texas. As soon as he'd saved enough money, he sent for her. They'd had a couple of months of bliss. Then, just like the others, when she met Walter, she showed a side he hadn't seen before.

He put up a fight at first, but when he saw how determined she was—well, he'd always lost that one before. He pulled back, played like it didn't mean a whole lot—and nursed the big hole in his heart. He could only watch, and wait until Walter tired of her, then threw her aside like all the others. Seems like he was always cleaning up the messes Walter left. This was no different. That night he'd taken her home from the Buppie Party cinched it for him. Walter and the girl be damned. He wouldn't allow her to hurt Vivian that way. Vivian was the only one that treated him with respect. The little stunt the girl pulled that night, using him that way, opened his eyes real wide. He supposed he should be grateful that it happened. It closed the hole in his heart. Then, the baby came.

The first time he laid eyes on her, he knew. The girl knew too. She didn't care anything about Maya. He hadn't understood at first why she wouldn't just give her to him. That would have been the one thing in his life he wouldn't have messed up. She was so helpless. He would have taken good care of her. Then when he heard the fight, he knew the depths of the girl's evil. He shouldn't have been surprised that she would stoop to blackmail. She was too bold for her own good. He'd admired that about her—in the beginning. He'd seen the wild look in her eyes when she left Walter's office that night, and worried that she might hurt the baby. He'd kill her before he let her hurt Maya. He'd followed her across the Capitol grounds to her car. She didn't even fight him when he took his baby.

At first, it looked like another real mess—until he figured it all out. Vivian wanted a baby. Always had. She'd be a good mother. He knew his plan would work if Vivian didn't leave that night. And she hadn't. If he could just keep her and the baby together long enough, Vivian would stay with Walter just to keep her. Maya would have so many more material advantages with Walter for her daddy. Hoping to give Vivian time to bond with the baby, he'd made it damn near impossible for her to find a sitter. As the doting uncle, he could always be close by to watch over her. It was all working out. He'd even started going to the CA meetings again, like he'd promised his mother.

In his grand scheme, he hadn't anticipated Vivian would leave Walter. And behind some man. But the dude must be OK. He seemed to really care for her. And Vivian deserved that. He'd seen the man with Maya that day in the park, and how tenderly he'd handled her. It could have still worked out. Walter would have to pay child support, but Maya could still have all the advantages. And he could still be the doting uncle. It was all going to be OK. Then the girl's body turned up.

He'd taken a lot of shit for Walter, but he wasn't about to take a murder rap. He'd seen the look on Bobby's face, calculating that he'd seen Porsche alive after she left Walter. No question Bobby's loyalty was to Walter. Bobby would throw him to the dogs in a minute to save Walter. He didn't intend to go out like that.

Sherman patted his breast pocket for assurance. The bulky envelope with the passport and airline ticket to Trinidad was there. He had to get his nerve together to face this one last thing. He'd followed up on the information the lawyer had given him on the phone yesterday. All that was left was to give his sworn statement. He got out of the car, took his jacket off and laid it over the seat. As he walked up the steps to the big two-story house, he picked at the edge of the little round bandage inside the crook of his elbow. Just as he pulled it off, a little old lady with steely eyes, opened the door—a smile on her face.

* * * * *

"She can't do this, can she?" Walter asked.

With his feet propped up on his desk, Bobby's eyes scanned the letter demanding that Walter vacate the house within three days or face eviction proceedings.

"What is this about?" Bobby demanded, a perplexed look on his face. "Who the hell is Gloria Johnson? What has she got to do with your house?"

Walter knew it was time to come clean.

"Gloria is Vivian's mama. I borrowed some money from her. That bitch...I mean, Porsche, was blackmailing me. I paid her, 'til I was tapped out. Gloria was the only person I could get money from that wouldn't be on record. She had me sign some papers. I didn't care, 'cause as soon as the election was over, I knew I could pay her back. Turns out those papers transferred my interest in the house to her."

"Blackmail?! What else haven't you told me? How the hell do you expect me to give you the best defense if you're keeping secrets?!" Bobby fumed. "If you were any other client, I'd quit your damn case right now!"

"I'm sorry. I didn't think it was important."

"You didn't think it was important! Blackmail is a powerful motive for murder. Shit, Walt. I can't believe you've been so stupid. Who else knows about this?"

"Nobody. I mean, just me and Gloria know about the loan. I wasn't stupid enough to tell her about the blackmail."

"Will she tell?"

"She hasn't so far."

"Can you pay her back now?"

"She won't take the money. I already offered."

"Well, you've got to move. That's all. You don't want to stir her up right now. You've got trouble enough with the election only next week. It would have been a cinch. You only had an unknown running against you. Now, he's getting front page coverage—with you. You're the only fool I know that can take lemonade, and make lemons. Damn, Walter! Why the hell—"

A knock at the door interrupted him.

"Yeah?" Bobby called out.

The pretty woman with the beaded braids appeared in the doorway. "Mr. Africa, the runner just brought this tape. I knew you were expecting it."

"Thanks, Tomika," Bobby said, "Put it in the player for me, would ya."

Bobby watched her sashay back out the door, then pushed the button on the remote.

When the bride appeared on the screen, walking alone, Walter was confused. Then the picture changed. He recognized the bedroom. As he watched himself being pulled onto the bed, Walter remembered that day.

Porsche had tricked him over to her apartment. He'd tried to break it off with her, but she'd kept after him. In hindsight, it amazed him how he'd been sucked deeper and deeper, a little at a time. First, the rent. Then, the rent and the doctor bills. Then the rent and living expenses. Then the hospital bill. Then the rent, a bed, diapers and medicine for the baby. She kept upping the ante. He'd given her the money he got from Gloria on her promise that would be the end of it. But it wasn't. That day, she'd threatened to file a paternity suit. As it had turned out, he should have told her to go ahead and do it. Instead, he'd gone over to talk some sense into her. But, she had another plan. Now he could see what it was. He was ashamed that his only real friend—not to mention those cops—got to see him in that position. Going out the door, he'd told her he'd kill her ass. He hadn't really meant that. Abruptly, the bride and groom appeared on the screen, holding hands, walking back down the aisle. Then the screen turned to scribble-scrabble. Bobby walked behind his desk and sat down.

"You know, Walt, you're my friend. And I love you like a brother, man. But I don't know what's happened to you. All that power gone to your head? You've caused so much pain to so many people. People who love you. It's like you don't care about anybody but yourself. You lie to me. You fuck around on your wife. Then you won't give her a divorce—not even when she takes your baby by another woman. Velva told me what's up with that. And that girl. She was just young and stupid. You treated her like shit, too. I just can't figure all this. What's with you? Is this some kind of middle-aged crazy thing, or what? You think you're the big stud or something?"

Walter kept his eyes on the screen, refusing to look at his friend as he accepted the brow-beating. When the scribble-scrabble ended, the picture was grainy and dark, eerie. At first, there was only a part of a picnic table at the side of the frame, right at the edge of water. The scene was vaguely familiar. The picture jiggled as a finger came across the frame. Then it was still again, and the table was centered. In a minute, Porsche walked into the frame and sat on the table, crossing her legs and resting one foot on the seat. She pulled at her close-fitting dress, smoothing it as she sat up straight, her back erect. She looked directly into his face. Walter sat up.

"I told you I had something to say to you. But, you wouldn't listen. I'll bet you'll listen now. You should know by now that you can't stop me from getting what I want. And I'm gonna say it all. You can't stop me now. You recognize this place?" she laughed. "Remember? This is where it all started. You remember the night you brought me here? You can't see the full moon 'cause it's behind the camera, but it's just like that night. Remember how you sped around those curves getting here? I did that too. To-night." She paused, then threw her head to the side. "Course, it wasn't as smooth in my old Toyota. You know how it shimmies at 45? Well, I made it, anyway. When I left your office, I drove around, up and down Mopac freeway, thinking about how you treated me. That was wrong, what you did. You think it's over, don't you? Well, maybe part of it. You think because you have money, and people jump to your tune, you can just send me away. But you can't get rid of me that easy, you slimy bastard.

"Anyway, I was driving around, thinking about it, then I got this idea. I'd go back to the beginning. So here I am. We made love right here on this very table," she said, patting its surface. "Remember all the sweet things you said? 'I love you, Porsche. I never met a woman like you, Porsche. We were made for each other, Porsche. I want to marry you, Porsh.' Well, I remember, even if you don't. I thought you meant it. I thought my life was taking a turn for the better. It's about time. Speaking of time—" She looked at her watch, then half-smiled into the camera. "Excuse me a minute, time to take my pill."

She walked out of the frame. The picture jiggled a little at the sound of a car door opening. The woman's voice and the look on Walter's face, had drawn Bobby back around the desk and he stood behind Walter. They both watched intently, waiting for the door to close. In a minute, she returned to the table. She sat a fifth bottle on the table, then began rummaging through her purse. She held up a medicine vial and shook it, making a rattling sound.

"See these? Doctor said I should take one of these every four hours." She popped two of the pills in her mouth, then held up the liquor bottle toward the camera. "See this? It's your favorite. I was bringing this to you. To celebrate. Your divorce, you know. I spent my last $40 on it."

She struggled the top off the slim-necked bottle, put it to her mouth and turned it up. When she took the bottle down, she grimaced, then wiped her mouth with the back of her other hand, coughing a couple of times.

"I don't know why you like this stuff. It's awful. But it did help the pills go down." She looked as though she was thinking for a minute, then put another pill in her mouth, and took another gulp from the bottle. "I missed the one I was supposed to take at

6. Maybe I did take it. I don't remember. Anyway, doctor says I'm depressed. That brings me back to you. I suppose I *should* be depressed. Well, I am. Double-depressed after the way you treated me tonight. For months. And mad, too, you mother fucker." She put her hand around her neck and turned her head from side to side. "I guess you would have just choked me to damned death, if Sherman hadn't stopped you."

She put another pill in her mouth, then turned the bottle up and took a long drag. Then another.

"Back to you. I would have made you a good wife. I know I don't come from the kind of background you do, but I learn quick. All this time, you been telling me you gonna leave your wife and marry me. Over a year, you been saying that. *Now*, you say I must be crazy to think you'd marry me. A woman like me! What the hell does that mean?! I've been surviving on the little money you gave me. But it's not enough. Not to live the way I intend to."

Her words were slurring, and her head lolled backwards, but she caught herself and looked directly into the camera. Her eyes blinked slowly a couple of times, unfocused.

"I don't even want to marry your ol' tired ass now. You can't even fuck."

Bobby snickered under his breath. Walter looked at him over his shoulder, and Bobby straightened his face.

"Tell you what I *am* gonna do, tho'. I'm gonna go to Sherman's apartment and get the baby. Then, I'm gonna go to your big, pretty house. I'm gonna bring this tape for you. And I'm gonna bring the baby for your wife. So she can see, she looks just like you."

She took another drag off the bottle. "I don't know why you

drink this stuff. It makes you feel stupid. I keep telling you the blow is better. Wish I had some now." She shook her head, as if to clear it. "But first, I gotta be able to drive. Those curves are a bitch. Gonna drive right up to your big ol' house. You may not marry me, you sonofabitch, but betcha by golly wow, you ain't gon' be married to her either when I get through with yo' ass. Hold on. I'll be right back. I've got something else to tell you, Walter. Don't go 'way," she said, slowly shaking her index finger at the camera.

She bent over and took off her shoes, then stumbled down off the table and out of the frame. She lurched back into the frame behind the table, her steps uncertain, hands out as if to balance herself. She turned and looked toward the camera, a wicked smile on her face, then mouthed, 'Watch.' She turned and put one foot in the water, then shivered. She turned back to the camera as she put the other foot in the water. She took one step, then another. She waded out until she had to raise her dress to keep it from getting wet, as the water reached her thighs. When she turned back to the camera, her mean smile turned to a grimace, then she stumbled. Both hands splayed against her chest. As she fell, her arms flew up fluidly. Walter jerked forward, as though he could catch her. Then her arms disappeared below the water. Five minutes later, there was still only the picnic table in the frame. For a moment, the picture went to scribble-scrabble, then the picture changed to the bride and groom feeding each other wedding cake.

Bobby walked to his desk and sank in his chair. He put his elbows on his desk and his face in his hands. Watching the girl die, brought back the worst memories from his childhood in the Philadelphia ghetto. He raised his head and looked at his old friend. Walter had killed her. Not like the carnage he'd witnessed—over a quarter, a loaded die or some other insignificant affront to manhood. But he'd killed her just the same. Bobby put his face back in his hands, trying to blot out the thought—and the sight of Walter, stone-like, with tears on his face.

After he'd indulged himself in the sentimental stuff, the lawyer in him took over. Bobby wiped his hands over his face and sat up straight. It clearly wasn't murder—in the legal sense. Walter would get off. But should he? Bobby knew he could put the right spin on it to save the election. A strong statement about rogue cops, trying to destroy another high-ranking Black official.

"Walter, I can keep you from going to prison, but you won't ever be able to get this off your conscience—if you still have one. There's nothing you can do to right all the wrong you've done. But you can try. At least let Vivian have some happiness. Let her go. You don't deserve her. I'm going to have Velva draw up the papers. And dammit Walter, you're gonna sign 'em!"

TWENTY-THREE

Driving down Avenue F, Marc was surprised to see the old man on the corner putting up Christmas lights, from his perch on a ladder. It was only the first of December. Then he thought, he'd buy some Saturday and put them up. Passion would like that. He could see her little face beaming with wonder. Since it was his weekend to have Corey, it would be a good project for them to do together.

Marc had been pleasantly surprised that Corey hadn't exhibited jealousy when Vivian and Passion moved in. Instead, Corey reveled in his role as 'big brother'—as long as Passion stayed out of his action figures and his baseball card collection.

As he pulled the Volvo all the way down the drive, Marc thought it was strange for Vivian to be gone that time of day. She knew he always came home for lunch. Maybe she just ran to the grocery store. He frowned at finding the back door ajar. He'd have to talk with her—again—about that. Always leaving the doors open, the lights on.

"Vivian?" he called out, walking through the kitchen. Cold cuts for lunch, he thought, looking at the bare stovetop. He picked up the mail from the table and sorted through it as he walked to the answering machine. The light was not blinking, and there was no note, but he punched the button on the machine anyway. Sometimes, Vivian didn't write the messages down.

What was the word for her? Distracted? Yeah—and she was getting worse as the pregnancy progressed. He reminded himself to be patient. Only a month left now. The computer-generated voice came on—"I will re-play messages." Then, the woman's voice—emotionless as usual.

"Vivian. Mrs. Black. Call me the minute you get this message. No matter what time."

When Marc heard Walter's voice, he stared at the machine, an angry squint in his eyes, his lips tight.

"Vivian, I need to talk to you. I'm *so* sorry. About everything. I've thought it all through. You know, that baby…is…kind of sweet. I kinda miss her. I thought, maybe…When this term is over, I'm gonna give it up. I thought, maybe we could…I'll give you what you want. Can you come over?"

Marc banged his fist on the button. He wanted to punch something, kick something. Instead, he walked to the bedroom and threw his keys on the dresser they'd bought for Vivian, that matched his armoire. He closed the two drawers she'd left open. In the mirror, he saw the reflection of her overnight bag on the bed behind him, and the matching suitcases on the floor. He leaned back against the dresser, his arms folded across his chest, staring at them and brooding.

So, she was just going to leave him? What kind of hold did the man have on her? Now that Walter had his House seat back, did he think he was going to take Vivian, too? What kind of fool did they take him for? He wasn't going to take this lying down. Not after all he'd been through for her. He loved her, but she couldn't just play him this way! Marc snatched the keys off the dresser and strode to the car.

* * * * *

The Volvo moved through the noon-time freeway traffic, not quite recklessly. All the way to Walter's house, Marc was oblivious to the honking horns and the other drivers' dirty looks, as he went over what he would say to him. To her. Would he drag her out and make her come home? Would he just punch Walter in the face? He'd been itching to. It would be the next best thing to an orgasm.

Her Camry was parked in the circular driveway, the passenger door standing open. He rang the bell—still not sure what he was going to say—or do. No one came to the door. That infuriated him. Yelling out their names, he banged his fist against it so hard, so many times, his hand hurt. They still wouldn't come to the door. Coward! Why didn't Walter come out and face him like a real man?! He was reared back to kick it in when he came to himself. Breathing hard, he put his foot down and looked around to see if a neighbor was watching. He turned around and hurried to his car.

* * * * *

When Marc turned the corner he saw Cora getting in her car. He sped up, then stomped the brakes, blocking the driveway. He needed to talk to her real bad. Needed for her to talk to *him*, before he did something he'd regret. And that was more important than wherever she was going. He was surprised when she rushed over to his car and got in.

"You're just in time. Drive! St. David's Hospital. Go, Marc!"

He pulled away from the curb asking, "What is it?! What is it?!"

"It's Vivian. Walter called. They're at the hospital. I couldn't make much sense of what he said, other than it's an emergency. What's she doing with him anyway? She doesn't have to let him see Passion any more. What's going on, Marc?"

Marc had no answers, as he raced to the hospital.

* * * * *

At the emergency room, they were directed to Labor and Delivery. In the elevator, Marc pressed the button over and over until they reached the floor. When the door opened, he saw Walter in the wide corridor, holding Passion. She was whimpering and fretting. Marc strode up to Walter.

"What happened?!" Marc demanded. "What did you do to her?!"

Passion reached for Marc, and Walter relinquished her.

Cora stepped close to the men. She'd seen the murderous look on Marc's face. Now wasn't the time.

"Nothing. Nothing," Walter answered. "We were just talking, then she grabbed her stomach and doubled over on the couch. All this bloody stuff came out of her. She was too weak to stand up. I brought her here. I called you. Left a message on your machine. Then I called Mrs. Williams."

"Why the hell didn't you just leave her alone!" Marc shouted.

Cora patted Marc's arm to calm him.

The muscle in Walter's jaw worked, and his lips tightened. "I was going to give her this." Walter reached in his breast pocket.

"Marc!"

He turned at the sound of his name and saw Dr. Mebane walking through the double doors. Instead of the white lab coat he usually wore, he was suited up in surgical blues. Marc met him.

"What is it?! What's going on?" he asked, all the worry and confusion on his face.

"Have you been to the childbirth class?" the doctor asked.

"Not yet. We're scheduled next week. What is it?!"

"Placental separation."

"What does that mean?"

"The placenta is separating from the…the baby's heart tones are down." The doctor saw Marc shaking his head, his eyes squinting, grasping for understanding. He told Marc the plain words. "The baby's coming."

"Oh, my Lord," Cora said, taking Passion from Marc.

"But it's not due 'til next month," Marc protested.

A half-smile crossed the doctor's face. "Babies come on their own time. I'm not supposed to do this, but…I think it'll calm her for you to be there. She's asking for you."

"Is the baby OK?" Marc asked, worrying one fist in the other hand.

"The baby's heart rate is dropping after each contraction. That indicates fetal distress. Not getting enough oxygen. We can't wait. If Vivian can't deliver soon, I'll have to do a C-section. There's the possibility…Well, we've got to get the baby out of there, that's all. Come on. Now. Just do what I tell you."

* * * * *

Sitting across from her in the wide corridor, Walter squirmed under Cora's stare. Disgust was chiseled on her face. His hands were tented against his mouth, his head hanging in shame. How did it come to this? It had all started out so different, so good. Unable to meet Cora's eyes, he looked off toward the door that Marc had followed the doctor through. The look on Marc's face would never leave him. His concern and love for Vivian. The image burned into his brain next to the one of her smiling at Marc that time in the driveway. He could have been the one. He could have felt that. He felt it now. But it was too late.

He remembered the look on her face a couple of hours ago, too. That storm had been brewing for longer than the time it took her to drive to his house. He should have just handed her the envelope while she was standing on the doorstep. Instead, he'd tried to tell her that he wanted her to come home, that he wouldn't hold the baby against her, that he'd raise it as his own. Before he could get to 'I love you,' the torrent unleashed.

Slinging accusations at him with hurricane force, she started with the first affair. It wasn't an 'affair' really, just a thang. Funny how she remembered it so vividly—even naming the other woman's perfume. He couldn't remember her face or name, much less her perfume. *How did you not notice that I didn't wear perfume for nearly ten years? How could you have thought I changed to a new perfume when I'd actually just gone back to wearing my old one? How stupid did you think I was, your coming home in the middle of the night smelling of soap, and thinking that was a great disguise?* When she jabbed her finger in his chest to make her point, he'd tried to cajole her, but that only incited her fury to greater heights.

And that little bitch that worked in your office. How the hell did you think I felt to suffer the bold sneer on that hussy's face? The embarrassed looks, the pitying looks on the other employ-

ees' faces? Didn't you see how out of character it was, for me to cause such a scene that day I threw the girl out? He backed up to the couch and sat down helplessly as she continued to read his cards for him.

What have you ever done to show any appreciation? I gave up so many things that I wanted, so that you could have what you wanted. Why <u>couldn't</u> *I have a kitten? You weren't home enough for your allergies to bother you anyway. Why didn't you ever say 'Thank You' for me watching your back? I stayed up nights filling out those damned reports, while you slept. I put aside my dream of law school for you. Why didn't you show any appreciation—for anything?!* Her hands were on her hips, and her eyes flashing with anger.

Why didn't you ever once say, 'I'm proud of you—of what you're doing—of how you manage the rigors of law school, and still do all the things I need'? Why didn't you ever say, 'I've been there—law school is hell—I know what you're going through'?

When she stopped and walked away from him, he thought it had spent itself. But it was only the eye of the storm—gathering force for the next onslaught. When she walked back in front of him, she started with "You son of a bitch." She took him to the night he brought the baby home, and carried him through each excruciating hour and day of his hiding from her, ignoring her, and worse, ignoring the baby. *You didn't care how I felt! How could you have set me up—with that press conference! You ambushed me!*

When he tried to tell her that it seemed to be the only way out, she snapped, "Shut Up!" Then, she took him to court. The pain she described at hearing his accusation of infidelity was etched on her face. He hung his head. *That hurt me to the core, Walter. After all I've put up with from you, how could you say I was 'unfit,' when I loved and nurtured a baby that any other woman would have thrown out in the street—with you!* When he looked up, the pain had turned to rage.

You're the guilty one! YOU, Walter! Then, you tell Marc— who's given me all the things that you didn't—that this baby is yours!

She jabbed her finger at her own stomach to make her point. Then, her eyes shot wide open, and a jolt went through her. That was when the blood—He shook his head to keep from seeing it. Walter exhaled a long sigh and wiped his eyes. He stood, walked to Cora and handed her the envelope addressed to Vivian. *Taylor, Taylor and Price* was imprinted as the return address. He couldn't look at Cora, but he still felt her eyes on him when he got on the elevator.

* * * * *

The nurse showed Marc how to scrub up and helped him into the paper gown, shoes, and cap. When she hit a big square button with her elbow, the door swung open, and Marc followed her into the brightly lit surgical room. Blue-suited, capped and masked folk bent over Vivian. He couldn't tell if they were men or women, doctors or nurses. One pulled a stool near the head of the table for him. Panic was on Vivian's face and she frantically pulled at the restraints on her wrists. He slipped his fingers through hers, and rubbed her forehead with his other hand. He whispered close to her ear.

"I'm here, Vivian. I just found out. Calm down, baby. Relax. Just relax. Do what the doctor says."

"Oh, Marc—"

"It's going to be OK. Everything's gonna be OK."

"The baby, Marc—" He saw the terror in her eyes.

"It's OK. Dr. Mebane's here. The baby's fine," he said, sooth-ingly—hoping against hope that his words were true. But he heard the heart rate monitor continue to record, slower and slower after each contraction. Mebane's voice broke into his fear.

"OK, Marc. Get ready. Come on down here. Stand over my shoulder."

Marc got there just in time to see the baby's head present.

"Vivian, I want you to push. That's the way. A little harder." The doctor's tone was rhythmic, coaxing her through it. "Come on, Vivian. A little more. We're almost there. Grunt. OK. Take a deep breath. Another. OK. When I say 'now' I want you to push hard—and don't stop 'til I say. Get ready...NOW! PU-U-USSSH!"

The head came through. The doctor pulled the baby's head down, and the top shoulder came through. Then the rest of the baby slipped out, bloody and wet. It was blue, like a big bruise, and hairy—and still. It was the strangest-looking creature Marc had ever seen. He was utterly overwhelmed. He didn't realize he was holding his breath, until the baby started gasping. He couldn't describe the sound it made. Not crying really, more like mewing. As the oxygen coursed through it, it changed colors right before his very eyes. He watched as the doctor toweled it off, cut and clamped the cord.

When Mebane turned and handed the baby to him, Marc's whole face turned into a grin. She was the most beautiful crea-ture he'd ever seen. How could two people make this miracle?

"Let Vivian see," Mebane urged, a triumphant smile on his face.

Marc carried the baby to the head of the table like she was the crown jewel, then held her where Vivian could see her.

"Another little princess, Vivian."

Vivian reached out and touched her hand, then tears streamed down her face. He knew exactly why she was crying—and laughing at the same time. He felt that same way.

As the pediatric nurse hustled Marc and the baby away, he heard Vivian ask, "Marc, did you bring my suitcase? The one on the bed?"

EPILOGUE

The house sat on a hill in the middle of 20 acres, just east of Austin, toward Manor. From Cora's glider rocker on the covered front porch, Marc faced the road, and the morning sun. Gloria's hi-back rocker was on the other side of the little table, where he imagined them setting their coffee cups in the mornings. He still couldn't get over Cora and Gloria selling their houses and buying this one together. The first time he'd seen them together—the weekend of the graduation—they'd acted like they'd known each other forever. Maybe even in another life. He knew that women in their forties were kicking back, feeling confident, but by their sixties, they were kicking up and feeling free. His own mother— nearing eighty—was getting so free, it was scary. He chuckled at the thought of the three of them together—Katie bar the door.

He'd been expecting her, and his dad, all morning. They'd insisted on taking a cab from the airport. Their coming was only one of the surprises for Vivian. The whole wedding was going to be a surprise. They'd tried to persuade her to put aside her concerns about 'appropriateness' and 'under the circumstances.' But she'd remained adamant about a small ceremony. She'd reluctantly agreed to having it at the house, instead of the JP's office. He smiled to himself, thinking about how Cora and Gloria had pulled it all together—and in such a short time.

Not many cars were on the ranch road that early, so when the RV came into view, rounding the bend, he watched it, disappointed—but comparing it to his own. A van followed. When both vehicles slowed and turned into the drive, then stopped, he started off the porch. Must be lost.

By the time he reached them, the vehicles had pulled off the long drive and parked next to his RV. The man in the RV driver's seat looked like Lee. When the back door opened, and Ruthie Kline stepped down, holding on to the handgrip to assure her step, Marc was speechless.

"If they can have an air-conditioned tractor, I can have one of these big buggies," Mrs. Kline said, hugging her son, patting him on the back as though she hadn't seen him in a long, long, time. "It's time for me and Early to do some things, to get some things we want."

Early stood back, waiting his turn.

As Marc shook his father's hand, he heard her, and saw the RV sway. Nola Faye hoisted her weight down and grabbed him in a bear hug.

"Where is that girl? I know she need me to do her hair. Can't have her looking like a chicken on her wedding day. I brought all my stuff," holding up her briefcase. "Come on, Doreen. We got work to do."

They marched toward the house like women with serious business to take care of. The rest of the Kline clan noisily fell out of every door of both vehicles.

Nathan got out of the driver's door of the van. He and Marc looked at each other uncertainly. Nathan walked up to him and clasped his brother's hand, then embraced him.

"I'm glad you came. You looking good," Marc said.

"I'm clean, man. 92 days. But who's counting?" he said, smiling and shrugging his shoulders. "I'm gonna make it this time—for my boy."

"That's good, man. I'm glad. Where *is* Lil' Buddy?"

"Here I am, Uncle Bu-bu-buddy," he said, bouncing around from the other side of the van. He put his hand in Nathan's and beamed at Marc.

Marc put his hand on Lil' Buddy head and shook it, smiling down at him. He didn't dare speak, for fear his voice would betray him. Marc turned toward the house to keep them from seeing the emotion on his face.   "Come on up to the house."

After they'd all had a late breakfast, the women took their giggling and chattering upstairs. Marc lured his dad to the porch. He knew neither Gloria, nor Cora, would appreciate the pipe. They settled in the rockers and watched the road.

"You done good, boy. You make me proud," Early said. "Did I tell you that already?"

"Yeah, Pops. You told me."

"Humph. Sometimes, I forget. Not much, though," he said, jutting up his chin. "Just sometimes."

Both of them peered down the driveway as another RV drove in, pulling a horse trailer. A tall, dark man in a cowboy hat got down and waved at them. A woman got out the other door. Then a 'mutt and jeff' couple—the man as tall as the woman was short.

Then a White couple. They heard a long, gleeful shriek from inside the house, then watched Vivian dash past them, jump off the porch and run down the gravel drive, arms outstretched. As the two women collided, they swung each other 'round and 'round like little girls, amid peals of laughter. Gloria walked out on the porch and handed the men each an ice tea.

"I see Sondra made it. I really pulled one on Vivian," she said, chuckling. "She didn't know Sondra was coming. Her roommate from college. She's a judge in Houston."

"Yeah, Vivian told me about her," Marc said.

"Guess that's her new husband. Good-looking man. Her first husband was good-looking, too. He died. This one's a farmer. Can ya' get over that?! A farmer and a judge. I swear." She laughed, then squinted her eyes. "I don't know who those other people are. I guess, some of their friends. Early, can I put you in charge of making the farmer welcome? You don't suppose there's really horses in that trailer?"

* * * * *

The big 'Noel's Catering' truck had parked in the driveway that afternoon. The crew set up three big red tents on the flatter land near the house. By evening, the long tables under one were laden with bar-b-q and fixings. A bar had been set up in one corner.

Adelma's boys had set up the stereo system they'd brought, on the front porch. Aside from periodically making them change the music to something more 'civil,' the adults had abandoned the porch to the kids, preferring the tents where fans were blowing against the June heat. When Early tired of helping Ike ride the kids on the horses, he'd ambled over to the tent and asked if anybody had 'some bones.' Gloria happily obliged him. He intently studied his hand now, as Gloria sat across from him, holding hers very primly.

"I don't usually play with women, but since they yo' bones, guess I have to. That's not even how you s'posed to hold bones," he muttered.

"Don't count how you hold 'em, just how you play 'em," she returned with a game smile. "What you gonna do, Mississippi?"

"Georgia. Georgia," he grumbled.

At another table, Junior and Angela slapped 'hi-fives' as they routed Donnell and Lee from the bid whist table.

"Rise and fly, Chumps!" Junior shouted above her laughter. "Need some new chumps over here!"

"Chumps, my ass," Gene said, as he and Nola Faye took their seats. "Doreen, you can be fixing these chillun' a plate, 'cause me and my baby gon' whup 'em 'til they hon-gry!"

"Yeah, they think they grown now," Nola Faye chimed in. "Deal 'em up!"

Marc had dragged Cora's glider swing from the back yard to the other tent. The ladies had taken that one over. Cora and Ruthie entertained Mrs. Black and some of the women from Cora's Church group.

Vivian surveyed it all from the RV, where she and Sondra had escaped for a little privacy.

"And then, girl, Mama kicked him out of the house," she continued telling the saga to Sondra. "She understood that I could never live there again. And Marc wouldn't hear of it, anyway. So Del and Petey sold their house and bought it. The boys love the pool. Now, maybe that house can know some happiness." A twinge of sadness crossed her face.

"Sounds like ya'll are playing musical houses. How did you convince your mama to move to Austin?"

"I didn't. Cora did. They hit it off when she came for my graduation. Then when the baby came, she stayed a couple of weeks, a lot of it with Cora. Corey was with us for Christmas, so she stayed with Cora then for a week. But the worm really turned in March, when Mrs. Black gave a little reception to celebrate me joining her law practice. Mama came down. Cora took her sightseeing. That's bluebonnet time, you know. They were scouring the countryside, when they saw the house. I guess they must have been talking about it all along—them both being alone, and all. Next thing we knew, they'd sold their houses and bought that one," she said, nodding toward the house on the hill.

"What if something happens to one of them? At their age, you know?"

"Oh, we took care of that. When they bought the house, they sat us all down—me, Del, and Cora's sons, Arthur, Jr. and Jimmy—and told us what they wanted done. I drew up an agreement for them. And they bought insurance policies on each other. So far, it's working out great. They're good company for each other. They're talking about taking a cruise in August. I had no idea either of them were that well off. Both of them always pomouthing. Pinching pennies. Getting those senior citizen discounts. Hell, I'm the one who needs a discount—going from no children to three in a year," she said laughing softly. "You have any idea what those diapers cost?"

"Nope. And don't want to know. I've got kids in college," Sondra said, laughing with her. She took a sip of wine. "So how do you like practicing law?"

"I love it. Mrs. Black...Gerry. I can't get used to calling her that. She let's me handle all the custody cases. She says I have a certain fire about it. Says she used all hers up on my case," she said, with a wry smile, then brightened. "But what I want to know is, what's this farmer got? You look happier than I've seen you in years. How did you meet? When? Tell me everything."

"OK, here's what happened," Sondra said, crossing her legs under her on the couch. "Last fall, me and Eleanor and Angela took a trip up in East Texas. We were at this beautiful lake—"

"What?" Vivian asked, when Sondra abruptly stopped.

"Girl, is that Walter? Isn't that his car?"

Vivian peered out the window, then set her glass down and started for the door.

Vivian walked up to him and hugged him.

"When did you get back?" she asked.

"Just got in last night. I wasn't sure I should come..."

"Sure, you should have. I'm glad you came. You want to see her? Come on, we'll go find her."

"Well...first I want to talk to Marc."

Vivian looked up to see Marc angrily marching toward them. His stride broke when he recognized Sherman, and he sauntered the rest of the way.

"Welcome home." He offered his hand to Sherman as he put his arm around Vivian, but the look on his face was uncertain.

"I won't stay, I just wanted to get something straight right off. I had a lot of time to think about this down in Trinidad. If you'd be willing...I'd like for you to adopt Maya. I mean, Passion."

Marc looked at him curiously.

"Every child needs a daddy," Sherman continued. "I can't be that for her. I'm not sure I even know how to do it. I trust Vivian's judgment. And you've been her daddy all her life. I'll have my lawyer draw up the papers Monday morning. But there's one condition…"

When Vivian came back from fetching her, Passion scrambled down from her hip and toddled to Marc. He picked her up.

"Passion, this is your uncle. Uncle Sherman."

Passion looked at Sherman, then back to Marc.

"Orsey, Dada."

* * * * *

Cora paced the length of Gloria's bedroom, while Gloria fussed with fitting the dress on Vivian. She checked her watch—1:30. They were running out of time. She walked over and stood at the tall window looking down over the back yard. She nodded her head as a smile came to her face. It was perfect, just like she'd planned.

They'd only been in the house three months, but her sons had transformed the surrounding property into a paradise. Day after day, big trucks bearing 'Williams Brothers Landscaping' signs had come up the long driveway, hauling dirt, hauling rocks, hauling gravel. First, they'd widened the driveway. Then they terraced the long slope down to the road, pulling out the scrub cedar, and putting in Cora's pecan 'orchard.' On the south side of the house, raised beds were built for vegetables. Around back, a large oak shaded the porch against the west sun. On that side, Gloria's rose garden hugged the length of the house. Cora had crimped her mouth and expressed her disapproval at all those 'thorn bushes.' Gloria just smiled. "Cora, it's just like life. You can't get the beauty of the rose, without a few thorns."

Cora remembered standing guard over the two large oaks, while the bricked walk was built out to them that ended in a large patio. A riot of pink, purple, and white impatiens surrounded them now. The folding chairs from her church had been set up in rows on either side of the walkway. She made a mental note to remind Arthur Jr. to get them back before Sunday School in the morning. A white ornate arch, wrapped in green ivy and white roses, was in place on the patio. Large urns with blooming lilies-of-the-valley flanked it. It was all so pretty. Just like she wanted it. Even though she wasn't the bride, it was her wedding—the one she'd never had.

From across the hall where the teenage girls had Passion, she could hear giggling, and occasionally peals of laughter. Mrs. Kline had given them strict instructions not to let Passion get her dress dirty. Dressed in pale lavender, Mrs. Kline sat on the settee, cooing to Baby Joy in her lap. Cora heard the shouts of the younger children in the yard. Intermittent laughter of male voices rose from below. She could hear their heavy footfalls on the hardwood floors, and the rhythmic creaking of the hinges of the screen door opening and closing. The house was so alive. Cora remembered the years she'd been alone. No mama, nor daddy. Her boys grown and gone. No one to mother. No man to love. Now, her life was full, she thought, as she turned from the window. And her wedding *would* start on time.

* * * * *

As the guests gathered and found seats, the sweet sounds from the tape Gene had made played from big speakers on the porch— *I Can't Believe It's True,* by Baby Face, Stevie's *Ribbon in the Sky,* Striesand's perennial *Evergreen.*

At exactly 2 o'clock, the music changed to Luther's *So Amazing.* Del's sons escorted Gloria and Cora down the walkway and seated them together in the first row, then went back for Mrs. Kline and Baby Joy. Gloria noticed Marc's nieces checking Lil' Pete out, and decided she'd better keep an eye on that.

Sondra's black, silk robe blew in the gentle breeze, as she walked through the arch and stood just behind it. Marc followed her in from the side and took his place.

Adelma walked with Nathan. They parted in front of Sondra and stood on either side of the arch, Nathan beside Marc.

Corey had a hard time balancing the pillow with the ring pinned to it with one hand, and trying to hold Passion's hand with the other. She kept jerking it away from him. They'd all told him how important it was for him to make sure she walked down the aisle, like they'd rehearsed. Holding the little basket of flower petals in her other hand, Passion balked when she saw all the people turned around, smiling at her. Gloria and Cora held their breath. When she saw Marc, she grinned and toddled toward him determinedly, pulling Corey by the hand, "C'mon, Brubba."

When she got to Marc, she handed him her basket, then reached for him to pick her up. Cora, Gloria and Ruthie were all calling to her under their breath. The audience was laughing. When he saw she wouldn't give up, Marc bent down and hoisted her up in the crook of his arm, her full pink skirt flowing over his arm.

The music changing to Luther's *Here and Now,* made Marc look up. Vivian was standing at the head of the walk, her arm crooked through Petey's, a bouquet of white roses in her hand. She looked divine in the plain satin sheath. More than forty years had aged Gloria's dress to a soft ivory. Cora and Gloria had worked feverishly to add the pearls and iridescent sequins that sparkled in the sunlight on the scooped neckline, the little sleeves and the matching satin band around her head. The headpiece dipped to a point on her forehead and a teardrop pearl dangled from it. As she smiled back at him, Marc fought hard to suppress a grin, but he lost the battle.

Gloria couldn't stop dabbing at her eyes, so Cora retrieved Passion from him.

When they reached Marc, Petey stepped back. Marc stepped to Vivian's side, offered his arm and she slipped hers through it. Together they took two steps to stand in front of Sondra.

Sondra began, "Dearly Beloved, we are gathered here on this glorious June day to witness, and to celebrate, the union of Marc Anthony Kline and Vivian Rene Johnson. Marriage is a solemn commitment. A commitment to be entered into soberly and seriously. Each party should be prepared to pledge to each other—without reservation—their love, trust, and fidelity."

Marc bent over and whispered in Vivian's ear, "I told you I'd stay with you—through it all. You got to learn to trust me."

She whispered back, "How can I trust you? You said just a *little* wedding." She smiled reproachfully.

In a stern voice, Sondra broke in, "If you all don't mind…"

Snickers rippled through the audience.

"A wedding is a joyous occasion. It not only joins two people into one, but it blends families…"

"Speaking of trust," Vivian whispered, "you're the one who

thought I was going back to Walter. And you're always checking behind me. Checking the door—after I've already locked it. Turning off lights."

"Well, you always leave the lights on, and the doors open."

Sondra cleared her throat loudly. "Excuse us. We're trying to have a wedding here. Never mind that I have worked for weeks on a beautiful speech for this occasion. Let's just cut to the chase—before we lose you two altogether. Pay attention," she ordered.

"Do you Marc, take Vivian to be your lawful wedded wife? Do you promise to love, honor, and comfort her in sickness and in health, until death do you part?"

"I do," he said, with a crooked smile, his eyes on Vivian.

"Do you Vivian, take Marc to be your lawful wedded husband? Do you promise to love, honor, and comfort him in sickness and in health, until death do you part?"

Vivian looked up into Marc's eyes. "Yes. I promise."

"The rings, please," Sondra said, closing her book.

Nathan and Del handed them the matching bands. Twenty little diamonds sparkled in the sunlight, as Marc and Vivian slipped the rings on each other's finger.

"By the authority vested in me by the State of Texas, I now pronounce you husband and wife. You may salute your bride."

Marc smiled down at Vivian, pulled her into his arms, and did just that.

If you enjoyed *THE PRICE OF PASSION*, you'll love

THREE PERFECT MEN

An engaging romantic suspense story of the lives and loves of three Houston women and their entanglement with the rugged men they encounter at a remote lake in the beautiful piney woods of East Texas.

The story abruptly veers from quiet contentment to the horrifying, with the macabre discovery of a teenager's body. The plot races through hairpin twists and turns, revealing the vibrant, complex personalities of the women—and their men—as the reader is compelled forward through this rich and sensuous tale.

And Coming in December, 1998

Audrey is reeling from the ultimate betrayal, facing divorce after 25 years and secretly wondering whether her child could actually be a killer. Should she allow a mother's love keep her from finding happiness?

MaryBeth has survived a bitter divorce and is alone in an empty nest, with only her career for comfort. Can she face the disapproval of society—and her children— for the love of a younger man?

Lt. Kirk Maxwell is the straightest of cops. Can he forsake his duty, for the sassy, full-figured woman who ignites a fire in him that he thought was dead?

Dangerous Dilemmas

Wanna put a smile on a friend's face?
Send 'em ***THREE PERFECT MEN***
$10.95   (314 pages)

Or show them ***THE PRICE OF PASSION***
$14.95   (383 pages)

Circle the title you want and send check or money order to:

Moon Child Books
P O Box 142495
Austin, Tx. 78714-2495
(512)-452-0042; fax (512) 452-5130
http://www.flash.net/~moonchld

Every copy autographed.

TO:

_____

Name

_____

Address

_____

City and State   Zip

From:
(If this area is filled out, the book will be autographed as a gift from you.)

_____

Name

_____

Address

_____

City and State   Zip

Expect delivery within one week, but please allow for two

READER SURVEY

The main characters were not described in this book. Did you notice? I believed that you, the reader, would form your own picture, and that you could get deeper into the story that way. I would love to know how *you* see these characters. If you participate in this survey, it would help me for my next book. What's in it for you? The satisfaction of having your say—or if you tear out this page, fill it out and return to Moon Child Books, you can subtract $2.00 off the price of any book that you order. You game?

Did you notice the lack of physical description? _____
If so, did it bother you? _____
What do they look like to you? (Height, weight, coloring, etc.)

Walter: _____
_____

Marc: _____
_____

Vivian: _____
_____

Do you, or someone you know, look like any of them?
_____

Delma wants to know if you felt any sympathy for Walter by the end of the book: _____

Feel free to make additional comments on another sheet.

Thanks for your help.

Evelyn